THE UNDEAD

DAY SIXTEEN

SEASON THREE

RR HAYWOOD

THE UNDEAD
Day Sixteen

Season Three

The story so far

A new landscape was formed after the storm, and with it, the promise of a new beginning.
One race to dominate this land. One race to survive.
Words were uttered beneath the Saxon while Howie fought the infected.
Words that brought a whole new pressure: To be relentless and unceasing. To charge forward and never give up. To do what it takes to survive.
That pressure was building, and it became too much. Howie faltered, losing his mind as they ran through the fog and sought the doctors so desperately needed at the fort.

The final act was a simple one. A stubborn man spoke through an intercom at the munitions factory, and his words sparked such a reaction in Howie that he fell apart in front of those who love him the most.
The Undead continues ...

CHAPTER ONE

Day Fifteen

It has been a wholly mixed day, and my emotions are spent to almost nervous exhaustion. I must reflect and learn, for it is only by true self-reflection that we advance as a species. I went to the house seeking the first person on the list. He and his family were infected and seemingly trapped in an upstairs room. They surprised me, and after a desperate fumble, I killed them with the assault rifle.

For quite some time after the massacre, I was downright terrified, and waves of adrenaline pulsed through me. I sat in the darkness, waiting for them to subside as I dwelled upon how close to death I had been. However, I had survived, and I had walked away. Just.

The morning after (this morning), we set off again. Jess, my trustworthy steed, and I used country lanes for the first few miles, but the incessant clip-clop of her hooves on the solid ground soon started to niggle. Thereafter we used footpaths, verges, and fields which, although slower and harder-going, were far more pleasurable. The storm had brought down many a tree, which also had to be negotiated.

The day passed slowly. Only when we made camp for the evening, with final rays of the sun dropping below the horizon, did the realities of my interaction with the infected set in.

The first one on the list was infected. He shouldn't have been infected.

He was supposed to be immune.

Something has gone wrong.

NB

CHAPTER TWO

I'm in a dark room, and I'm alone. I know I'm alone, but something is coming after me, so I have to run, except I don't know which way to go. Panic builds instantly as fear pulses and grips my body. I try crying out, but no words will sound from my mouth. It's light now but grimy and grey. I'm in a street so ruined and destroyed it looks like something from the Second World War. An old play park lies in a square, behind rusted railings. The slide has fallen down into a pile of rubble. Rusted swing chains nestle amongst the yellowing grass. The sky is streaked blood red, and the clouds look heavy and threatening. I don't know where I am or why I'm here. I don't like this place. I'm scared, more scared than ever before.

I can't find my axe–it isn't here. Dave isn't here. Nobody is here, but something is coming after me. I can't see it, but I know it is there. I start to walk away, but it's not fast enough, so I start jogging, then running, then sprinting as fast as I can, but I don't really get anywhere. I feel like I'm running on ice–there's no traction underfoot, and that panic builds stronger with every passing second. I'm going to die here, alone and forgotten in this filthy, ruined place.

Tears prick my eyes, blurring my vision, and my throat burns from the silent screams. Trying to look behind, I can see dark shadows flitting between the ruined walls and collapsed roofs of the buildings all around me. Dark shapes, shadows that are evil with intent. A dry laugh echoes round. It mocks but turns into a phlegmy cough that hacks up putrid bile from the throat. Still I run, and still I don't make any progress. Still the fear builds, and still they are coming closer, and still I know I will die here. A certainty. Fact. Stop running then, stop running and face your death with bravery and courage. Stand still, tall, and proud and look them in the eye as they come for you.

I try. Oh god, I try, but I don't feel tall and proud, and I can't find their eyes. I need to be brave like Dave. I need to be strong like Clarence. I need to laugh at them like Cookey. I need Lani's temper and fierce stubbornness. I need Meredith's speed and agility. I need all of them to survive. I can't do this on my own.

They're coming now, closer and closer. Just dark shapes which loom bigger and higher as they encroach towards me. On all sides, they surround me and make me feel small, insignificant, unworthy of life. I close my eyes and whimper in prayer.

Something solid slams into me, ripping me off my feet as they close in for the kill. Being carried roughly along, I open my eyes to see that the dark shadows are now infected, but far worse than the infected I have come to know. These are barely human, with flesh that drips like acid burns from their bones. Blood seeps to weep from a thousand cuts, eyes deep and hollow, but with yellow razor-teeth filed into points, and hands clawed the same. They give chase, but whoever carries me is faster than they, for soon they give up and melt back into the ruins of the houses from whence they came.

I can't see who it is, but they run, vaulting rubble and obstacles with ease until we're far from where I was trapped. I'm carried into a doorway of a church, and inside is lit with infinite candles that burn and flicker to fill the space with golden light.

The floor is swept clean: it's completely free from dust, and the air smells sweet now–gone is the musty dampness of decay. This church represents the warmth of life and living.

I'm put down onto my feet and stagger back to face the man who carried me. As Paco stands back, he grins, showing those perfect, white teeth framed in the tanned face of the movie idol. He looks good, far better than when I watched him die. Grinning sheepishly, he rolls his shoulders as though easing the strain of the burden from carrying me. He's breathing hard, and a light film of sweat coats his face. One muscled arm flexes in front of his face as he uses his forearm to wipe the sweat away.

'Is he okay?' I spin at the sound of the voice and feel a surge of disappointment when I realise it isn't Sarah but a young woman, blonde-haired and slim. She looks radiant, beautiful, and happy despite the look of concern on her face at the peril I was in.

'Say, you got away just in time,' Paco says to me, his deep American drawl so distinctive and clear.

'You shaved your beard off,' I mutter and feel instantly stupid at the first comment from my mouth.

'He wanted to keep it,' the young woman says with a wry smile. 'He thought it made him look enigmatic and mysterious. I thought he just looked old and dirty,' she rolls her eyes but casts a look of warmth at Paco.

'Nice place,' I nod at the pleasant surroundings. It's more than nice; I can feel the safety of this place. The high, vaulted beams sweep majestically up into the apex of the roof. Stained glass windows reflect the candlelight. It feels entirely normal to be here. Nothing strange about it at all.

'Here,' I turn again to see the young woman holding a drink out which I take with grateful hands. Cool, clear water gushes into my parched mouth, easing the soreness of my throat.

'Drink up,' she smiles softly, 'Paco, can you get some more water, please?'

'Sure thing, Boss,' he mock-salutes and walks fluidly through a door at the rear of the pulpit. 'How's my dog?' he calls out.

'Meredith?' I ask as he reappears holding another cup of water for me.

'Meredith?' he asks with a puzzled glance at the woman as he passes me the second cup.

'The dog,' I nod before draining the cup, 'Meredith.'

'Say, I think we're all a bit mixed up here,' he scratches his chin thoughtfully. 'You called the dog Meredith?'

'Er, yeah ... Isn't that her name? You were calling it out during the fight when, er ... like ...' Does he know he's dead? It feels rude to mention it.

'You were what?' the girl laughs. 'That's so sweet.' She rests her hand on his muscled forearm.

'Oh, Paco,' she smiles sweetly, but I can tell there is more to their story than I know. They share a look so filled with emotion and pain that I have to turn my head away.

'I never knew the dog's name,' he says to me quietly after a long pause.

'Um ...' nodding, I try and look like I know what he's talking about. 'So, er ... who is Meredith, then?' I ask lightly over the rim of the cup and watch confused as the girl bursts out laughing. The charged atmosphere is broken, and Paco shakes his head while rolling his eyes in a wholly amiable gesture.

'See this broad?' he thumbs in the direction of the girl next to him. 'This is Meredith.'

'Very pleased to meet you, Mr Howie,' she says with exceptional politeness and even drops me a little curtsy. 'Heard lots about you.'

'Indeed,' I keep nodding as it seems the only thing to do. 'So what's the dog's name then?'

'Who knows?' he shrugs. 'But ... well,' he drops his gaze for a second to look sideways at Meredith, 'maybe Meredith is a good name to keep for her?'

'She likes it,' I add with my own shrug. I look about at the surroundings, suddenly aware that I have no idea where I am.

'Where am I?' I ask, somewhat bluntly.

'You're in a chapel.'

'Church,' Meredith corrects Paco. 'It's not a chapel, and it's not ass. It's arse ... We keep going through this.'

'Whatever! Talk to the hand,' he holds one up to wave in her direction, which she promptly bats away with a laugh.

'How do you know each other?' The connection between them is strong, pouring from them in buckets.

'Paco saved me,' she replies, the laughter easing off as she drops into a serious voice. 'Some men took me from my family. One raped me while the other one laughed. Paco killed them both ...'

'No,' he interrupts gently, 'I killed one. The dog killed the other.'

'Either way ...' she tilts her head back. 'I took my own life,' she adds sadly, and I watch as Paco moves closer to take hold of her hand gently within his. 'Paco stayed with me all night but ...' she pauses. 'But I was in shock and ... Well, I just couldn't handle what had happened, but ...' she smiles gently. 'Mister hero here decided to take all of my sins for his own. He gave me a proper burial and' she adds, 'it appears he may have just redeemed himself from the truly awful, hedonistic lifestyle he led.'

'You can say *that* again,' Paco mutters.

'Question,' I ask them both in a tone that snaps their attention onto me. 'Is this my mind making all this up? Because I know I'm dreaming right now so ...so I can't possibly know this ... What you just told me ...' I motion between them with the now empty cup. 'Hang on. Wait, is Sarah here?' I ask suddenly.

'No, my friend, she is not,' a deep voice snaps from behind me. I freeze in position and hold still.

'Chris,' I say without looking, 'you're here?'

'I am.'

'You shaved your beard off too?'

'Not in a month of Sundays,' he laughs as I turn, and even though I know I'm dreaming, I can't help but feel a sense of elation at seeing him again. He looks the same as ever: big, broad and with that dark beard and bright, intelligent eyes.

'Mate,' I grin without shame, and we clasp each other in a tight hug as the tears prick the backs of my eyes.

'She's not here,' he says once we've separated, 'but we don't have time for that now. There are things you need to know. We're all connected, remember that.'

'Connected? Do what? I want to see Sarah.'

'Connected,' Paco says, 'all of us ... We're all connected ...'

'By what?' I ask belligerently.

'By you,' Meredith says, 'you are the key stone in the bridge.'

'I'm not anything in anyone's bridge. In fact,' I look between them 'the bridge can fucking do one as far as I care.'

'In here is with you,' Chris continues. 'Out there is without you.'

'Fucking what? That doesn't make any sense.'

'Don't let them win,' Paco drawls, forcing me to turn.

'They will achieve one race if you stop now,' Meredith says.

'One race,' I roll my eyes. 'I keep on hearing that now.'

'It's what they want, and it's what they will achieve,' Chris takes his turn.

'You three are like a fucking choir.'

'Grow up and listen!' Chris snaps. '*This* isn't about you. We're dead ... We lost our lives ... This is about *what* you can do ...'

I stare back, shocked and feeling ashamed at my own flippancy.

'You,' he points, 'will see this through.'

'But ...' I stammer.

'No buts,' a fourth voice cuts through, causing me to groan inwardly. Not her. Anyone but her. 'No buts, Mr Howie ... You wanted to lead, so you lead.'

'Debbie,' I turn to stare at the police sergeant dressed so immaculately in her uniform, 'here as well then, and no ... I did not want to lead.'

'Well, you are leading now,' she offers me a smug smile,

'so lead and do a proper bloody job of it. Stop this pissing about and get on ...'

'Whoa,' I cut her off with a wave of my hand, 'no offence. It's great seeing you all again and all that, but ... um ... where is my sister?'

'In time,' Paco says.

'Ah, sod this,' shaking my head, I take a step away, then stop, turn back, and tap the side of my own head. 'I'm dreaming,' I say to all of them 'none of you are real ... so ... yeah ... Bugger the lot of you.'

'He needs something,' Meredith says.

'Too bloody right I do,' I retort. 'I need to see my sister.'

'It'll mess him up,' Paco shakes his head.

'We should do it,' Debbie says firmly.

'Do what?' I ask, completely lost now at the private conversation going on between them.

'I vote no,' Paco says equally as firmly. 'Think what it could do.'

'He needs to believe in himself. He needs to see it through,' Chris snaps, 'and desperate times call for desperate measures.' All eyes are on Paco, even mine, as we wait to see his reaction. He thinks for a second and finally looks to Meredith who nods at him.

'Okay, okay,' he holds both hands up, 'what then?'

'What what?' I ask the group at large.

'Dave,' Chris says.

'I agree,' Debbie replies.

'Dave what?' I say exasperated that this is my dream, but they're carrying on with idle chit-chat and ignoring me.

'Agreed,' Paco nods. 'Listen up, buddy,' he turns to face me, 'what do you know about Dave?'

'Dave? Little bloke? Kills everything? That Dave?'

'He's a regular smart ass,' Paco shakes his head.

'Arse,' Meredith replies.

'Whatever!' the American says. 'Dave was an orphan ... Do you have that word here? Is it orphan here too?' he quickly asks the others.

'Yes, it is,' Debbie says.

'I wasn't sure,' Paco says. 'Lot of different words, seeing as we share the same goddam language.'

'The language we invented, you mean,' Chris replies with a long look.

'Oi!' I interrupt them. 'Dave was an orphan?'

'He was,' Paco nods. 'He was eight when his parents gave him up.'

'Eight? Fucking hell, that's old for adoption, isn't it?'

'They couldn't deal with him,' Debbie says softly.

'Fuck,' I look down at the ground, 'poor sod ... Do you think he remembers?'

'Would you?' Meredith asks in a tone that does not require an answer. 'The point is we are giving you that so you believe us.'

'Huh?' I blanch at her words, but they're gone. All of them, and I'm not in the church anymore but back in the street, surrounded by the grimy, ruined buildings and the dark things mooching about.

'Howie.'

'Lani? Where are you?' Her voice is muffled, yet distinct, and I feel the invisible touch of a cobweb brushing against my cheek.

'Howie!'

'Lani ... Lani, I'm here ...'

'Mr Howie!'

'Lani! I can hear you ... Where are you?'

'Mr Howie!'

'Leave him alone ...'

'Dave? Is that you?' I spin round and round, unable to pinpoint the voices. 'Leave who alone?' A drip lands on my cheek, something wet that I wipe away.

'He needs to wake up,' Lani pleads.

'He needs to rest,' Dave's deadpan voice looms eerily all around me.

'Stop doing that,' I shout at the walls around me. 'I can fucking hear you ... Paco? Chris? Where are you? Where's Sarah?' My voice trails off into a whimper as all the voices suddenly cease, plunging me back into the silence of the ruined landscape that surrounds me and the shadows that threaten to spill out.

CHAPTER THREE

'Howie,' Lani leans over his prone form. Gently calling his name, she strokes the side of his face. He doesn't respond but whimpers quietly, his body flinching and tensing as though trapped in a nightmare.

'Howie!' she calls out louder with a tone desperate to wake him from whatever demons plague his rest. She needs to know he is okay, that he *can* be woken.

'Mr Howie!' she says louder still, using the *mister* to try and penetrate his unconscious form. She can feel how high his temperature is and the currents of tension pulsing through his body.

'Mr Howie!' she tries again, shaking him by the shoulders as fat tears fall from her eyes to land on his cheeks. They quickly get absorbed and dried by the heat from his skin.

'Leave him alone,' Dave drops to her side, his tone dull, yet firm.

'He needs to wake up,' Lani sobs.

'He needs to rest,' Dave replies, shuffling closer to shield Howie with his own body.

'Lani, come away for a minute, love,' Paula gently touches Lani on the shoulder with the merest of pressure applied. 'Come on, let him rest.'

'He needs to wake up,' Lani whispers. 'He won't wake up.'

'He will,' Paula counters. 'In his own time, he will. Let him rest ... come on ...' she increases the pressure on her shoulder, guiding her away.

'This is your fault,' Lani glances up to the shadowy form of Dave, staring hard into his eyes. 'This is your fault,' she snaps in a low, growling voice. 'You should have stopped him ... He only listens to you ...'

'Lani,' Paula steps closer, ready to intervene as Lani leans across Howie to snarl at Dave.

'No, Paula,' Lani retorts without looking round. 'You should have stopped him ...' she repeats. 'Why didn't you see he was going crazy? Why, Dave? Why couldn't you see it?'

'Lani,' Paula's tone is more urgent 'it's done. Come away.'

'I will not,' Lani shrugs Paula's hand from her shoulder. 'You did this ... You fucking did this, Dave ... Howie only listens to you ... Oh, the great Dave who can kill everyone and always at Howie's side. Dave who does everything Howie tells him ... Dave who can't think for himself ...'

'Lani! Enough!' Paula snaps. 'What's done is done. Dave couldn't know what to do.'

'Why?' Lani twists to shout at Paula. 'Why didn't he? We all did ... Why is he so special?'

'Lani, stop it,' Blowers steps closer to the huddled group.

'I won't stop it,' Lani shouts. 'Dave could have stopped him. Dave could have got Howie calm and ... and ... Howie wouldn't be like this now if it wasn't for Dave. We could have ...'

'Clarence,' Blowers calls out, 'we need to get Lani away for a minute.'

'No, you don't,' Lani glares up at the silhouetted forms standing nearby. 'None of us could stop him. None of us are special enough ... Only Dave, but he didn't, did you, Dave?'

'Lani,' Clarence moves into the inner circle, his deep voice soft, yet firm.

'Did you, Dave?' Lani presses. 'Why? Why didn't you?'

'That's enough,' Clarence stops close to Lani's shoulder. 'Move away now.' The command is still gentle as the big man realises how frail Lani is right now.

'Why is Dave so special?' she snaps. 'Why does Howie only listen to Dave? Why him? Why didn't you stop him, Dave? You saw he was going mad ... You saw it ... You pulled your gun on us ... For the love of God, you took a weapon against the rest of us, Dave!'

'He's autistic,' Clarence bends over to press his hands either side of Lani's shoulders, 'and he has Asperger's ...'

'No excuse. He knows enough ... You know enough to have stopped him ...' she shouts at Dave. 'If Howie is hurt then, it's your fault ... your fault, Dave ... YOUR FAULT.'

'Dave cannot read people,' Clarence lifts the girl easily from the ground. 'He cannot read social situations or ...'

'GET OFF ME!' Lani yells. 'This isn't about Dave or what Dave can do or what Dave can't bloody do ...'

Cookey steps in to face Lani, his voice low and trembling with emotion. 'That's not fair,' he says to Lani. 'Don't say that to Dave.'

'Grow up,' Lani hisses.

'No, it ain't fair,' Cookey presses. 'Dave did stop Mr Howie.'

'After he went mad!' Lani shouts. 'He bust through a bloody wall with the Saxon and attacked innocent people ...'

'Stop it,' Cookey pleads in a half shout.

'Dave is unstoppable. Howie could have killed people ... He could have got himself killed ... What if Howie turns? What then? Dave turns with him? Dave would give himself over to be with Howie ... We all know it. Not one of us can get through Dave.'

'Lani, please' Nick joins in, 'this is shit enough ... Just stop it, for fuck's sake.'

'I won't fucking stop it!' Lani's voice rises in pitch and volume, her body shaking with pure fury. 'DAVE SHOULD HAVE STOPPED HIM. I HATE YOU, DAVE ... YOU HEAR ME? I HATE YOU FOR WHAT YOU'VE DONE ...' A slap rings out clear and distinct in the darkened factory floor of the munitions buildings. Instant silence follows the unmistakable noise of skin on skin, an open-handed strike delivered clean across Lani's face.

'None of the others would do that,' Paula hisses, 'but I bloody will ... Now, stop ranting and get a grip of yourself ...'

Lani reels from the contact, with her cheek burning from the slap. Humiliated, tears of rage turn into tears of despair, and her mind closes off to reason with a conflicting spread of numbness. She swallows audibly and blinks hard in the electric, charged atmosphere. All eyes are on her, staring and waiting to see if she'll erupt.

'Sorry,' Lani whispers as she finally reaches up to rub at the tender spot on her cheek. 'I ... I'm ...' she exhales long and slow, pushing the air out as she struggles to master her own thoughts. 'Dave ...' she turns as Clarence eases his grip from her shoulders, 'I ... that was unforgivable ...'

'No,' Paula speaks firmly, 'you had a point but ...'

'What point?' Cookey asks in shock.

'Dave should have stopped him,' Paula says carefully. 'Lani is right. Howie listens to Dave, and she was also right that no one else could get close *because* of Dave ... but,' she sounds out as she turns round slowly to address the whole group, 'Dave *is* autistic, and that's something we have to deal with.'

'How?' Roy speaks up for the first time. 'He can't assess situations like we can.'

'Dave,' Paula asks the small man still kneeling protectively at Howie's side, 'we're talking about you like you're not here ... Do you understand what Lani is saying?'

'Yes,' the flat, monotone voice is impossible to read.

'I don't like this,' Blowers speaks out. 'You're patronising him.'

'I'm not,' Paula retorts, 'and forgive me, but we're in a bloody mess right now, so we need to get this sorted.'

'Yeah, but don't speak to Dave like that,' Blowers replies.

'Blowers, calm down,' Clarence orders, happy to use some strength in his voice addressing a younger male. 'Everyone, take five and relax. Dave will stay with Mr Howie ... We're in a mess, and we're here to do a job, which is to get ammunition. Blowers, organise a watch on that hole in the wall and get someone on the other side too.'

'But ...' Blowers starts to reply.

'No buts,' Clarence keeps his voice steady but let's no mistake as to the intent, 'we sort our own shit out in private ... which means not here. We present a unified and switched-on front to these people ...'

'Got it,' Blowers nods with discipline, forcing his own voice to show respect.

'Paula, I'll need you to communicate with the people here. We need ammunition, and seeing as we've breached their factory, we'll also offer them an escort back to the fort.'

'Okay,' Paula follows Blowers' lead, nodding quickly as the big man steps in to take control.

'Good,' Clarence steps back and rubs his own neck to ease the tension in his tight muscles. 'Good,' he repeats but glances down in worry at the prone form of Howie and feels anything but good.

CHAPTER FOUR

Day Two

He looks up at the sky. It's a deep blue with hues of purple that darken steadily as the day gives way to the relentless and unceasing chase of dark after light.

The *ugly man* has an affinity to this endless cycle. It strikes a chord that resonates with his own relentless nature. His unceasing drive to do what must be done. With an inward snort of dark humour, he realises that he isn't the only one with a relentless and unceasing nature. The small boy, holding his hand and skipping along while staring down at his new shoes, never stops talking. It's just a torrent of questions, of questions that don't have answers, answers that have no questions. Comments, remarks, observations, and an appetite to know everything, coupled with a factual certainty that Gregori obviously has the answers to everything.

The *ugly man* still cannot fully understand why he

stays with the boy. The self-justification that by having a small child will make him less threatening to groups of survivors just isn't true. Gregori doesn't need other survivors. Gregori doesn't need anybody. If he is hungry, he will find food. If he is tired, he will find a secure place to sleep. If he is threatened, he will kill and kill until the threat is negated.

The boy irritates him. The boy annoys him. He speaks too much and moves too slow, but there is something, something Gregori cannot quite grasp or understand. The boy shows no fear of the infected. He seems to know where they will be or not be. How? How can he know such things?

'Gregoreeee,' the boy announces as the prelude to yet another question, snapping the *ugly man* from his silent reverie, 'why didn't you get new shoes?'

'I have shoes,' Gregori's deep voice grunts in his thick, Albanian accent.

'But you could get red shoes like my new red shoes, and then you would have red shoes, and I would have red shoes.'

'I have shoes.'

'Are we there yet?' the boy asks for the hundredth time .

'No.'

'Will my new family be there?'

'No.'

'Who will be there?'

'No ... I ... nobody.'

'Where are we going?'

'You ask this. I answer.'

'Can I have Rice Krispies for breakfast?'

'I not know this.'

'Or Cocoa Pops.'

'...'

'Or Frosties? Is it nighttime now?'

'Soon.'

'Do you have pyjamas?'

'I not know this word.'

'Pyjamas?' the boy giggles. 'Everyone has pyjamas ... but girls have nighties ...'

'Nighties? What is nighties?'

'Girls wear nighties when they go to bed ... Mummy has a nighty and...'

'I understand. No, I not have these. You not have these.'

'Mummy said I have to wear my pyjamas.'

'No.'

'But, Gregoreee ... Mummy said I have to wear them.'

'No. We don't have these.'

'I want my pyjamas.'

'No.'

'Fine,' the boy stops dead in his tracks with a sullen look on his face.

'What you do? We go now ... Come, we go,' Gregori pulls the boy along who simply gets dragged a few feet but stubbornly refuses to walk.

'I want my pyjamas.'

'No have these ... Come now.'

'No!'

'Boy, you come now.'

'NO!' the boy shouts with his bottom lip poking out and his eyebrows dropped to a look of petulant anger.

'No shout,' Gregori glances round the deserted street, at the broken houses, and at the cars left abandoned in the middle of the road. Corpses lie still, with flies buzzing amongst them. They're hot and sticky, and signs are everywhere that the infected have been here. Blood stains, smears, and death surround them, but the boy refuses to move.

'Come now,' Gregori tugs at the boy's hand, urging him to walk.

'NO!' The boy shouts louder. 'I WANT MY PYJAMAS.'

'Boy, no shout,' Gregori hisses in alarm.

'PYJAMAS,' the boy's face flushes red with anger while he stamps his foot on the ground. Tugging his hand free from Gregori, he draws breath ready to shout but finds a big, gnarled hand clamping down to cut the shout off. He struggles and thrashes his head side to side while trying hard to pull away.

'Shush, you quiet,' Gregori fights with the boy while glaring round, constantly scanning the streets, the houses, the windows, and doors. Too many points of access here, too many entry ways to monitor.

'GET OFF,' the boy breaks free and screams the words out louder still, 'GETOFFGETOFF.'

Gregori tries picking the boy up, but as small as he is, the child thrashes with unbelievable energy and violence. His golden face flushes a deeper red as his tantrum builds up higher. With a hard kick to the shin, Gregori swallows in pain and lowers the struggling boy to the ground. Small, tight fists get balled up into small hammers that bounce and strike off Gregori's chest and arms. The Albanian holds his head back, ducking and weaving to avoid the blows while all the time staring round and glancing up at the ever-darkening sky.

'PYJAMAS,' the boy screams with murder in his eyes. Gregori flounders and hesitates. What do you do with a screaming child? The noise is terrible, and with the boy's arms flailing so hard, he can't get close to clamp the mouth. He knows the boy has no fear of his pistol; otherwise, he would draw it and threaten to shoot him. A knife is no good–the boy is too young to have a full concept of having his throat cut or an ear sliced off, and Gregori recognises pure temper when he sees it. The boy was like this last night when he rushed forward to defend his mother by stabbing the infected with a kitchen knife.

A blow catches him to the side of the head, a solid little punch that Gregori absorbs with ease but feels the first prickle of reaction. The sky is darker now, the sun sinking down past the horizon. Shadows lengthen and become deeper. This is not the place to be. They need to move.

Another fist whacks him on the chin as he peers over his shoulder to the many doorways and windows of the street surrounding them. He reacts with lightning speed. One hand shoots out to grip the boy's face, Gregori's hard fingers clamping onto his jaw. Harder pressure is applied until the soft skin of the boy's jaw turns white. He lifts the arm, easing the boy off his feet. Still the boy pays no heed and lashes out with determination. Gregori's gaze darkens, anger building, but the boy equals him and hammers to try and hit Gregori's face. He can't reach, so he goes for the arm holding him, raining blows down on Gregori's forearm until he realises he is having no effect so changes tactic and goes for digging his sharp little nails into Gregori's skin instead.

As focussed on the boy as Gregori is, his peripheral vision still takes in the sides and behind the boy. Dark now. Night is here. This has to end. A much firmer grip is taken, his left hand squeezing at the boy's face while his right lifts up ready to deliver an open-handed slap across the boy's face. He sees it coming and stops attacking Gregori's arm. The boy stares at the open hand with defiance, then glares back at Gregori as though goading him to strike. No fear there, no fear whatsoever, just defiance and rage.

'I not hit you,' Gregori mutters. 'You not hit me.' He

lowers the hand and pushes him with enough force to cause the boy to fall down on his backside. Gregori waits for the reaction, ready to push the boy away if he charges in for another attack, but the boy snaps his head to one side, staring over to the left, then over to the right before looking up at the sky.

'They're coming,' the boy says back in his usual tone.

On his feet, Gregori spins round, ready to face whatever foe comes their way, but there is nothing to be seen, nothing to be heard either.

'Listen,' the boy rises quickly to his feet while whispering across to Gregori, who cranes his head, straining to hear anything. He glances across at the boy with a hard yet quizzical expression.

'Now,' the boy whispers; then, it hits. A wall of sound. Voices primeval and sinister that howl into the night sky. Unseen, yet close, and coming from every direction. Hundreds, thousands, and more that scream with utter venomous energy it prickles the hairs on the back of Gregori's neck. In all his years, after hundreds of murders and mass killings, of all the countries and all the cultures he has visited, never before has a sound such as this reached his ears. There is no doubt as to the source. This country doesn't have big wild animals. Dogs wouldn't sound like that either. It's human voices but collective and together. They howl like wolves but far worse. Scratchy smokers' voices, children's screeches. Females, higher in pitch, and males, lower in semi-baritone–yet all of them screeching with such volume it creates a never-ending and multi-directional sense of threat.

'Come,' Gregori takes two quick steps and grabs the boy's hand, roughly pulling him along as he starts charging down the street. The boy complies, running along in his new shoes while staring around with a strange look at the unseen howls permeating the night sky.

The boy says something–too low and drowned out by the noise. Gregori keeps running but barks out 'What?' at the boy. The sound ceases. Ends with a suddenness that is foreboding and almost deafening in its arrival.

'I said they stop now,' the boy repeats. 'They're coming now.'

'Where?' Gregori spins as he runs, his highly trained senses picking out possible points of access to the street. An open door there, a smashed-out window, a side gate leading to a rear garden, alleys, walkways–there's too many, and this place is too enclosed.

'Everywhere,' the boy says as though talking about something innocuous.

Gregori stops dead and pulls the boy up to do the same. Eyes closed, head bowed, and the Albanian lets his sense of hearing come into play. He relaxes with easy breaths and takes stock of the natural noises around them. No wind and no breeze. The air is heavy and hot. There. A noise. A pattering sound. Running feet. Many running feet. Shoes and bare soles slapping on the tarmac. He slowly turns to make use of directional hearing. From behind. Many from behind. Sides too. Noises of doors being opened, furniture being overturned and slammed aside. Ahead, more noises but less than the others.

'Come,' he tugs the boy and starts walking faster, then jogging while checking to make sure the boy can keep up. He jogs faster, monitoring the boy and sensing the child can go faster still.

At the speed he judges the boy can run at without tiring too quickly, he keeps going while all the time scanning and checking, picking out obstacles in the darkened path ahead as he charges down the centre of the road. The streetlights blink on, slowly in ones and twos, but the solar-powered sodium lights soon illuminate the street. They are visible now, and Gregori knows that their profile will be easy to spot from the predator eyes of the infected.

They are faster than the boy can run. The sounds of the feet drumming get closer, and soon the solid mass of charging human-shaped monsters fill the road behind them. Figures crash from the doorways of houses, spilling out into the street, windows crack and smash as bodies fling themselves to get through at the fresh prey outside. With a quick glance round, Gregori judges the infected will reach them within a few seconds. He stops, yanks the boy back, and quickly swings him up onto his back.

'Hold,' Gregori forces the boy's arms round his chin, placing the small hands on his jaw. 'Tight, tighter,' he barks, 'use legs.' He feels the pressure as the boy's legs squeeze at his sides.

He has two pistols and two knives. The pistols are drawn quickly, one in each hand. He spins to face the charging mass and picks out those closest. Shots boom out as he fires the right, then the left, then the right. Those in front are slammed back as the 9mm bullets ram through their skulls to scramble the brains within. Despite the moving targets, the shots are true, and the hands holding the pistols are as steady as a surgeon.

Those in front are taken down, but there are not enough bullets to shoot the mass. Deftly and with a blur of speed, he ejects the spent magazines and slams fresh ones in while turning to start running again. The pistols are tucked away securely, and he draws the knives. One in each hand, the blades turned up against the forearms.

'Tight,' he commands the boy and feels the pressure of

the hands on his jaw and the legs at his sides increase. He jogs, gets faster, adjusts his rhythm and gait to the weight on his back, and builds his speed up. Breathing easily, he moves with grace and power. His heart increases the flow of blood, his lungs expand to deal with the increased demand for oxygen. His pupils dilate to adjust to the dark shadows and gloomy air around them. He is a machine, relentless and unceasing. As night chases day, so Gregori runs and matches his speed to those chasing him while carrying a child on his back.

From the side, a figure bursts from an open door. Slipping, it goes down on an unseen obstacle, but its forward momentum has it crashing through the thin fence of the front garden. It charges. Direct. Red, bloodshot eyes fix intently on Gregori, the mouth already open to make ready for the bite, fingers clawed at the end of sinewy arms. Gregori doesn't deviate. He doesn't flinch but calculates the point of impact and makes the tiniest of adjustments to speed and direction. At the last second, he simply raises one hand and brushes the sharp steel across the throat of the infected that spins off, spraying a hot arc of blood into the air.

More stagger into view ahead. The drumming feet behind are still as close as before. Gregori counts the foes ahead and stops when he reaches thirty. With a clear mind, he calculates the options, weighing up the risks, threats, and chances of survival with each possible path. He judges the prospect of running into one of the houses, but without knowing if there is an escape route at the rear, the risk of being trapped in a high-walled garden is too high.

'Tight!' He reaches up, taking care not to cut the boy with the knives, and pushes the small hands into his own chin, urging the boy to hold as tight as possible. 'Keep eyes closed,' he mutters.

'I want to watch,' the boy whispers in his ear.

Gregori doesn't have time to answer but plots the kills ahead of time. A solitary infected charges out ahead of the others. He stabs it quickly through the jugular without breaking stride. His eyes search for a gap. Spotting a slight distance in the front ranks, he selects his targets and gets ready for the impact, hoping the boy will remain clamped on.

He veers off to intercept the one coming in from the left, a big, beefy man with a shaved head and covered in tattoos. With a graceful flick, he sends the knife in his right hand spinning away to embed into the throat of the one charging at him from the front. As he cuts the throat of the tattooed man, the one in front staggers into reach with the hilt of the knife sticking out from its neck. Gregori spins, yanking the knife free and lunging sideways to hack again at its neck. Two down, and now the two from the right coming in for the final charge. He simply extends both arms and lets the momentum of the charging infected drive into the points. With a wrench of the wrists, two jagged holes are formed in the throats before he pulls the blades free and steps through them to let them stagger and fall behind.

He starts running again, and his mind has already moved on from the kills behind him to the solid ranks coming from the front. He powers on, driving his legs faster as he aims for the slight gap between two women, one of them naked, with fat breasts slamming up and down with the gait of her own staggered running.

'Boobies,' the boy whispers again, staring at the pendulous things that seem alive and moving of their own volition.

Gregori runs into the gap, arms held slightly out, and

the two women are cut down. The press of infected turn and start pushing in but find their own kind impede their movements. Gregori ducks, weaves, bobs, and presses forward. His fast eyes seek each kill and lock onto the next target while his hands do the work. Sliding into gaps, he weaves and threads a path through the infected, killing anything that stands in his way. Like water through a rockery, he takes the path of least resistance, fluid and graceful despite the weight of the boy clamped onto his back. The boy doesn't scream or cry out but remains silent as the gritty work of killing is done again and again.

With a new factor to consider, the safety of the boy on his back, Gregori works to a different rhythm and cadence than normal, never allowing a hand or arm to reach in from the sides or rear. The heat builds in the muggy air and from the press of bodies exhaling sickly, fetid breath. The boy generates heat too, which traps the air between them. Gregori starts to sweat, his own body reacting to that of the environment as it serves to reduce the external temperature. The boy also sweats with a light perspiration that glistens on his forehead but slowly increases as the beads form and slide down his face. His arms exude sweat; his stomach and back too. The sweat seeps from his pores to lubricate his hands which grip Gregori's chin. They start to slip and slide so the boy digs in, scrabbling to gain purchase on Gregori's stubbly jaw. His legs also start to slide over the sodden material of Gregori's shirt.

While flowing through the gaps created and feeling the pressure from the horde as those chasing up the street join the fray, Gregori feels the boy losing purchase. In response, he drops his head and pushes his chin out, hoping it will give the child something more solid to hold. It works for a few minutes, but the sweat works between the fingers and onto the palms, dripping down Gregori's chin and sliding in thick rivulets down his cheeks.

Desperation sets in. They're surrounded on all sides by a pressing horde of snarling beasts that lunge in ever-increasing, frenetic movements as they go for the bite. He snarls back, his upper lip curling while his body ramps up a gear. His arms blurring with stabs and slices while he works to keep his central core as stable as possible so as not to shift the boy. But he has to move forward–to stay still invites death, so forward he goes, ever forward, with one foot after the other.

A swerve or a sudden veer to the side will see the boy sliding off, but the infected press from behind, and he knows his blind spot is now the weakest point. His left hand tucks the blade into his waistband as he spins on the spot. He moves with such sudden power that the boy slides round on the spot to end up facing Gregori, who wraps that left arm round the boy's back.

'Hold,' he grunts into the boy's ear and feels the small arms loop round his neck.

Now with the boy held to the front, he only has one arm to use, but with the burden held stable, he makes progress, his left hand pressing into the back of the boy's head, pushing it hard into the cavity between his neck and shoulder.

A glimmer of light ahead between the dense ranks tells Gregori there is an end point, a destination to aim for. He moves on, with his right hand doing the work of two. Slicing, thrusting, killing, and slaying. He's almost there, but they press in, blocking his route in a desperate surge. He plunges the knife into a chest, puncturing the heart, which causes an immediate, severe internal bleeding as the muscle haemorrhages blood into the lungs.

Trying to wrench the knife free, the blade snaps, leaving inches of steel stuck in the infected beast's chest. Without a flicker of reaction, Gregori drops the broken knife and draws a pistol. Eight shots ring out as he fires each of the rounds in the magazine. Eight are killed instantly. The pistol is pushed back, a twist of the torso, and he draws the second pistol. Another eight shots and another eight instant kills. Sixteen are killed within a few seconds, and enough of a gap is created that he can push through. The last two block his path. The first gets pistol-whipped straight to the nose, fracturing the bone so hard it splinters and send shards deep into the brain. Gregori shoves the pistol away before bringing his hand back up to reach out and grip the last infected blocking his escape by the throat.

He spins round, holding the writhing beast one-handed by the neck and presents the back of the infected to the still lumbering zombies behind. Fingers, strong and trained, crush the small bones of the voice box, driving them inward to pierce and rupture the airways and cause blood to rush down into the lungs. Still the infected lashes out with clawed hands that reach towards Gregori's face. With a vicious kick, he boots the infected away, and it falls to the floor and trips several more infected as they drive on.

Gregori is away. One-handed, he holds the boy in place while he builds to a sprint. His breathing is hard but regular. His right arm swings to maintain balance and coordination.

Sprinting at maximum speed, he outstrips those still chasing, creating distance as his dark eyes flick side to side, ever-searching for an escape. House after house flash by. Long streets with semi-detached and terraces. The plans race through his mind. Use a vehicle, but that means entering a house to find keys, which takes time, time for the infected to catch up.

He spots an alley to the right, the entrance illuminated by the glow of a solar sodium streetlight. He veers off, turning tight on the spot, and charges down the narrow path bordered on both sides by high brick walls. At the end, he bursts out into a darkened place of an expanse of concrete. His eyes adjust quickly, picking out the rows of garages and a possible escape route, which he takes with barely a pause for thought.

'Can we go home for my pyjamas please, Gregoreee?' the boy asks in a tone so light and innocent that Gregori snorts with despair. A tone that assumes this can be done. He's been running, fighting, killing, and sprinting to escape, but of course, they should go back for his nightclothes, why wouldn't they?

A small hand reaches up to rub at his face, the soft skin of the palm pushing against the stubble on his jaw.

'It hurts me,' the boy rubs at the stubble as though to brush it away.

'Sorry,' Gregori huffs but keeps running.

'Gregoree,' the boy precludes to another question forming in his mind, 'do you do shaving?'

'Yes,' Gregori hisses the word while picking out the lie of the land ahead, noting the undulating terrain, spotting the raised kerbs, the old tyres stacked up, and the debris littering the ground.

'My mummy does shaving on her legs. Do you do shaving on your legs?'

'No,' he takes a hard left into the mouth of another alley, driving his legs to push them further into the near pitch dark.

'Mummy says mummies shave legs and daddies shave faces ... Do the monsters do shaving?'

'No,' he grunts. *Why isn't this boy terrified? He should be too terrified to speak, let alone ask questions about shaving.*

'Where are we going?'

'Find ... find ...' Gregori gives up trying to answer, instead focussing on keeping his breathing regulated as his lungs work harder to oxygenate the blood flow to his muscles.

'Find pyjamas?' the boy asks with hope.

'No!'

At the end of the alley, he takes a left, heading away from the general direction of the horde. He runs down the street, this one appearing less damaged than the previous. Reaching a T-junction, he doesn't hesitate but heads right and keeps his legs pumping to drive on. Smarter houses, bigger, with nice windows and front gardens. Gregori takes it in, constantly scanning the doors and windows. Some damaged with dark smears of blood, but others looking intact and solid.

Still too close to the horde and too close to this area so swamped with them. They keep going, feet pounding the ground as the heat between them builds to uncomfortable levels. The boy shifts position, his arms tired from holding on.

Gregori spots the entrance set back from the road. A high, wooden fence hidden amongst low-hanging trees and thick hedges run wild from years of neglect. A driveway that winds up and away from the road. He takes it quickly, rushing to the side and away from the sparse gravel on the surface of the rutted roadway.

He gets the feeling of space to one side, large grounds

beyond the tree line. There's a gap in the hedge, and he pushes through to the other side but keeps going. Moonlight shines bright overhead and down on the tiled roof of the big building ahead. It's an old manor house, large and detached from anything else. Perfect. Old houses have solid walls, deep windows, and strong doors, and with any luck, enough gap has been created that the chasing horde won't know the direction they took.

But there's light in the ground floor window. Soft and orange, flickering with shadows that speak of candles lit within. No tactics this time, but he heads for the front door, slowing at the last few metres but still holding the boy tight. Breathing hard, he raps his knuckles on the door, turning to glance down at the route they took. Movement inside, voices low and murmuring, a door opens, and soft footsteps reach his ears. He knocks again, softer this time but urgent and fast, and again checks behind to see if they've caught up yet.

'Go away,' a voice hisses through, deep and distinctly male.

'I have child,' Gregori forces his tone to be lighter than normal, quavering his tone to imply a sense of fear.

'Piss off,' the voice responds instantly, 'we've already got enough kids here ... We're full up ...'

'They chase us ... please ...' Gregori pleads at the door before checking behind.

'No!'

Gregori frowns once as he tilts his head at the door. Lowering the boy down, he crouches to press his mouth close to the boy's ear, whispering softly, 'Stay here. I open door from other side ... You stay ...'

'I want to come with you,' the boy whispers back in a pleading tone.

'No, boy,' Gregori speaks softly, with no hint of anger in his voice, 'please do this ... stay here ... I quick ... I Gregori ...'

'Promise?' the boy whispers.

'I promise this,' Gregori whispers, then stands up before moving silently out of the recessed doorway. Staying low, he circumvents the front of the house, heading round the perimeter, checking doors and windows, pausing to listen and absorb the natural sounds and noises. He gains the rear, climbing deftly over an old stone wall to drop into the soft earth of a flower bed. Crossing the raised patio, he makes his way to the wooden back door, and his mind slips into work mode. A house full of targets. Subjects that need to be negated, an objective to achieve.

The remaining knife is drawn, the long, thin blade slides easily between the gaps of the sash window. With the slightest of creaks, he works the interior lock over and pushes the bottom sash up. It creaks on old hinges, squeaking into the night with a noise that would send a burglar packing. Gregori shoves harder, forcing the gap big enough to get through.

Heavy feet running towards him from inside the house. His upper body through, and he pauses with the knife held ready. A dark room, a dining table to one side.

'He's coming in the back,' a voice shouts.

'Get the shotgun up here,' another yells. Gregori's eyes stare hard at the door as his brain processes the incoming information. Shotgun. England only allows double-barrelled shotguns, not large capacity pump actions. Two shots to deal with.

'In the kitchen,' the first voice yells out. An interior door is kicked open with a loud thud, telling Gregori they are in the next room along and that he has enough time to climb through the window and cross the room to stand beside the door interior door.

The shouts and footsteps get closer, crossing the kitchen adjacent to the dining room within which he stands. The door bangs wide from a solid kick. Stupid people full of fear and panic, allowing their fear to channel into anger as they rampage about, telling any possible invader exactly where they are.

The front of the shotgun appears, waving left to right as the holder peers into the room. Gregori waits, holding position. The barrel sweeps left, right, left again. The person holding it can see the open window and knows someone is inside but not being able to see them, and it sends the panic and fear ratcheting up through his body. Gregori notices the tremble in the barrel, the slight shake as the sweeps become quicker.

'He's in here,' the voice whispers hoarsely.

'Get in there then,' the second male orders but with the same level of panic in his voice.

'Can't see 'im ... Oi, mate ... you in here? I got a shotgun ... Come out with your hands up!'

Pathetic. Adjusting position, Gregori faces the back of the door and pulls one leg back before sweeping it forward in a powerful kick that slams the door into the extended barrel. The holder clutches in fright, pulling both triggers in blind panic that sends a deafening boom into the enclosed space. Both shots negated, Gregori steps round, wrenches the door open, and grips the hot barrel with one hand to yank it towards him, pulling the man into the room and onto the point of the knife that stabs deep into the eye socket, driving through into the brain. With a low gurgle, the man drops down, leaving Gregori holding the shotgun and the knife in his hand, facing the second man who pisses himself in terror.

Gibbering with fear, the man stays rooted to the spot as the ugly man advances with frightening speed. He has sickly, grey, pock-marked skin, greasy, brown hair, and eyes that seem to bulge from sunken sockets. A rough hand clamps over his mouth, and his eyes widen as the knife drives into his gut, twisting, cutting, shredding, and spilling the sticky, hot innards onto the floor. Dead in seconds, and the man slumps down to join his mate.

Gregori drops to wipe the blade on the t-shirt of the corpse. His eyes already up and on the next open door. Head cocked to one side–voices, scared, and worried. Female, male. He moves off into the hallway, and instead of booting doors open with raging fear, he silently opens each in turn to check the inside.

The last room. The one the orange light was coming from. The doorknob squeaks as he turns it; the hinges creak as the door swings inwards to reveal three women and a man. Two of the women are young, in their twenties. The last are an old couple, grey-haired and staring as wide-eyed as the others. Silent and terrified, they stare at the blood-soaked vision of a nightmare that enters the room.

'Children here?' Gregori asks softly.

'What!?' the old man gasps. 'Children? No ... no children ...'

'No boys?' Gregori asks just as softly.

'No,' the old man shakes his head, 'no boys ... no children here ... Who are you?'

'I Gregori,' Gregori announces, 'I need the pajajamamas.'

'What?' The old man stares in horror.

'Pajajamamas,' Gregori repeats, 'the boy wears the pajajamamas ... I need these ...'

'Pyjamas?' the old man asks, aghast at the surreal shock. 'No ... no, we don't have any ...' he glances at the others as though utterly confused.

Gregori shrugs and closes the door behind him, sealing them in the room.

Minutes later, the last of the bodies is shoved down the stairs, into the basement. He took care killing those in the front room to prevent too much blood loss. Quick kills with stabs to the heart, and the old couple had their necks broken. They tried to scream and fight, but fighting against Gregori doesn't work. It just makes his job easier.

With a grunt, he shoves the old man roughly down the stairs and closes the door to the basement, turning the key in the lock before pocketing it in his trousers and heading for the front door.

'Come,' he says as he opens the door to reveal the boy staring up with wide eyes.

'You were ages and ages,' the boy says reproachfully as he crosses the threshold. Gregori checks the view–no sign of the infected, no sign of anything. The shotgun blasts were loud, but from a distance, they might be muffled enough to confuse the exact direction. Door closed, bolted, and locked, he turns to see the boy waiting patiently in the hallway.

'Are there people here?' The boy looks round at the doors.

'No, they go,' Gregori replies.

'Where did they go?' the boy asks innocently.

'They go,' Gregori shrugs. 'I ask, and they go.'

'Oh,' the boy looks up at Gregori, 'do they have pyjamas?'

CHAPTER FIVE

'Ready?' Clarence takes a deep breath.

'Yep, you want me to take the lead?' Paula asks. 'Might be less threatening than some giant bloke holding an axe.'

The big man thinks for a second while glancing down at the double-headed axe held in one hand. 'Yeah, alright,' he nods, 'we need ammunition.'

'I know we need ammunition.'

'And we'll offer to escort them back to the fort.'

'Yes, Clarence, I know that.'

'Tell them we've got a sanctuary and that it's an island now. Tell 'em we've got loads of people there ...'

'Clarence! Yes, I know.'

'And we're desperate for ammunition. We need 9 mil for pistols, 5.56 for the assault rifles and ...'

'Okay,' Paula snaps. 'I've got it. Just let me do the talking at the start. Come on,' she takes the lead, moving away from the group sat forlornly near to the still prone form of Howie. Threading through the quality control section of the factory, they pass small side offices used by the shift supervisors and admin staff before reaching the big double doors at the back. Windows, toughened and set high into the walls, allow the bright moonlight to bathe the room in a silvery light.

Reaching the doors, she pauses, clears her throat, and knocks gently on the thick wood,

'Hello? Anyone there?' she calls out in a polite voice, taking care to keep her tone respectful yet firm. Years of dealing with accountancy clients, stressed from impending cutoff dates for tax returns and VAT inspections, have equipped her with proficient skills in negotiations. She knocks again, a symbolic gesture of waiting to be invited in instead of just barging through into the next section. These people will be shocked and terrified to the core. Having had their almost fort-like building rammed by an army truck, then attacked by a screaming man, well, they'll be less than hospitable.

She knocks again after getting no response. 'Maybe they're further back,' she murmurs to Clarence.

'Maybe, let me try,' a huge, bunched fist thumps on the door a few times. 'HELLO?' he bellows.

'Clarence,' Paula groans.

'What?'

'You'll terrify them.'

'Stop saying that. I'm not that bad.'

'You are,' she looks up at him. 'In this light, really, you are,' she nods seriously.

'Well, they're still not answering,' he huffs. 'Just go through.'

'We should wait,' she points out, 'until we're invited or ...' She tuts as he pushes past to stride through the doors. 'Or we could just go straight in,' she mutters to herself.

'Hullo!' Clarence tries to adopt a less threatening, more jovial form of greeting that has Paula wincing at the sight of him lumbering through like some cheerfully psychotic lunatic. The lack of response is concerning, but it gives her a chance to swiftly move in front and take the lead. 'Stay behind me,' she whispers.

'Haven't got much choice, have I really?' Clarence mutters. 'Where are they?'

'I don't know,' she replies quietly as they make their way down a darkened corridor, pausing to check inside the side offices and staff rooms. 'Probably right at the back, away from us.'

The signs of habitation are everywhere, with offices converted and used as living quarters complete with makeshift beds, shoes, clothing, books left lying open and half burnt-down candles. It smells of people too, of people living close together, of sweat and food, feet and the scents of the living.

'This doesn't feel right,' Paula whispers quietly. 'It's like the Mary Celeste.'

'Nah, they're at the back like you said ... having a meeting probably,' Clarence says, giving up on the whispering.

Another set of double doors indicate the end of the office and administration section. Paula gets there first, knocking and calling out with her body positioned to block Clarence. There's no response, and after a few more knocks, she gently pushes the door open to peer inside.

'Factory floor,' she whispers back to Clarence. 'Can't see anyone, though.'

'Go through, then,' Clarence urges. She does, stepping into the room and calling out a greeting. Machinery, large and small, dominate the huge hangar-size room. Stainless steel surfaces with inert, red warning lights cover the area, and the walls are adorned with safety notices informing staff that full protective equipment must be worn at all times. Conveyer belts, processing plants, machines to spin, crush, wash, and do a thousand other tasks in a few minutes that would take human hands many hours to accomplish hulk down in the shadows. Wars are supplied from this room, and the effect is not lost on Clarence. His nose fills with the smell of gun oil, lubricants, hot brass, and the distinct smell of casings. The rounds he has laid down in service for his country in war zones all over the world, the rounds fired back at him, the friends, colleagues, and enemies he has seen cut down by the tiny objects were all mass-produced in this room. Millions of them, billions, and every size and calibre are made here to be sent out simply so men can kill other men.

He thinks of the muted conversation in barracks and mess rooms, and the angry, bitter words spoken right after firefights when they realised the bullets sent at them were also produced in British and American factories, only to be sold by lucrative contracts to supposedly stable countries that then sell them on for a further profit.

This one building, this one room must be responsible for the deaths of millions of people worldwide, and now, in the desperate hour when their species face extinction and they need it the most, the machines lie quiet and useless. Hunks of metal, plastic, and electrical wires all leading to other useless lumps of metal and plastic. This room should be functioning night and day, non-stop, with a queue of people outside lined up ready to take arms against those things.

'There's no one here,' Paula looks round, then up at Clarence with a searching gaze.

'Keep going, then,' he mutters back and steps in behind as she walks down the central aisle, towards the rear end.

Their heavy boots sound out each step on the bare concrete surface of the floor, echoing round the room with a noise that only serves to increase the eerie silence.

To the end, they go, traipsing past the silent machines that glint moonlight from the polished sections on display. Doors lead off to offices once again converted into living spaces, but all are empty, devoid of life, and soundless. Without a word spoken, they move from room to room, checking, looking, and searching. Through another set of double doors, with a sign that indicates they are heading towards the storage and distribution sections. Another corridor, but this one with bare concrete walls and unadorned with any furniture. Red lines painted on the floor indicate the track marks for the machinery used to haul the heavy pallets, boxes and cases from the factory to the areas set aside for sorting and distribution.

Another hangar-style room lies through another set of heavy double doors, but this one is devoid of machinery other than electric forklift trucks, mobile jacks, and haulage devices. Cranes fitted to the solid metal girders overhead rest quiet to gather dust. Sections are marked with letters, stencilled high onto the walls, ready to be piled onto trucks and sent out to the many police, armed services and conflict zones around the world.

Clarence picks out the stacks of boxes and crates identical to the ones seen on the naval supply ship they boarded just days ago. Stacks and columns of them. Cases of small and large calibre rounds, sniper rounds, heavy machine gun rounds, fifty calibre rounds, and within a sectioned-off area complete with signs warning of *explosives,* rests cases of hand grenades, mortars, and mines.

'Dave is gonna love this,' Clarence breaks the awed silence.

'Are they all bullets?' Paula whispers.

'Yep, rounds of every size and shape. See that?' he points off to the explosives section. 'Grenades, mortars and mines.'

'Wow,' she recoils at the sheer amount of stock waiting to be shipped out, but instead of the link to death being made, her mind works another route. What are the processes here? How is each round and each case accounted for? What is the flow from production to shipping them out to clients? The paper and audit trail must be immense. Whatever accountants work here must be flat-out from the minute they start work.

'It's incredible,' she stares in awe.

'It is,' Clarence nods, thinking of how many infected they can cut down now and a sense of a definite shift in the balance of power from the things to the survivors.

'But still no people,' Paula starts walking through the room. 'HELLO? ANYONE THERE?' Her voice rolls round the room, echoing back from the high metal clad sides and reinforced concrete walls. 'This is ...' she pauses. ' This isn't right,' she announces firmly.

Clarence grunts while shining his torch to the sides as he walks down the length of the room. 'Know what I think?' he asks slowly.

'What?'

'They've gone.'

'Gone? Gone where?'

'Gone,' he shrugs, but the movement is lost in the darkness, 'left ... gone somewhere else.'

'Really? No way.' Paula walks fast to join him as they cross the expanse of floor. 'Where would they go?'

'They aren't here,' Clarence states matter of fact. 'So if

they ain't here,' he looks over at her, 'then they're elsewhere.'

'Yes,' she bites the urge to snap at him, 'I get that, but why would they go?'

'Why? Why d'you think?'

'We scared them off? No ... no way.'

'Down there,' Clarence shines the torch beam to yet another set of double doors, but these ones fitted with the standard health and safety fire exit sign above. Huge things, thick metal panels fitted with iron bars and a lattice of studs with sunken hinges, fitted with alarms and deadbolts the size of car irons.

'Yeah, I see it.' Paula sighs at the sight of the objects left strewn across the floor up to the double doors. Teddy bears, books, toys, bags, rucksacks, bedding, and objects too bulky to move fast with. An image works its way into her head of men at the doors ordering the women and children to dump anything non-essential as they chose the danger of the night and the darkness outside to the threat of the maniacs within.

'They don't know what's out there,' Paula whispers sadly. 'They've been here the whole time.'

'Maybe they haven't,' Clarence replies weakly, 'but still ...'

'They chose *that* over us,' Paula finishes the sentence. 'I ...' shaking her head from the surge of guilt flooding through her body. 'I ... What are you doing?' she asks as Clarence pushes the solid bar down to find the door swings easily outwards. He steps out with the axe held ready, staring into the moonlit landscape of the cultured grounds surrounding the building.

'Tracks.' He shines the torch down onto the distinct area of flattened grass that cuts across the once perfect lawn as it undulates gently into the darkness and out of sight.

'Fuck,' Paula sags on the spot, 'could we catch them up? Talk them into coming back?'

'No, we get the ammunition and go back,' Clarence about-turns, heading back into the storage room.

'But we can't leave it like that. We're responsible for them ...'

'No, we're not,' Clarence snaps, baulking at the suggestion. 'They chose to go. It's up to them.'

'They left because of us ... Families, Clarence, whole families turfed out because we ...'

'We?'

'Howie then,' Paula snaps, 'but yes, because *we* bust in here.'

'Why? Why did we come here?'

'The ammunition,' she replies, missing the point.

'Because we've run out,' he answers with forced patience, 'because we used them all up ... killing the things ... fighting against them ... while they stayed in here, safe and sound.'

'Even so.'

'No even so,' he cuts her off. 'They could have let us in or just as easily put some cases outside for us ... They *could* have done many different things, but they chose to stay locked up and forced us to break in. Howie gave them a choice.'

'Did he?' Paula asks. 'He was on his own when he spoke to them ... I didn't hear it and neither did you.'

'What?' Clarence screws his face up in irritated confusion. 'What's that mean?'

'He's being going downhill all day ... His mental state, I mean ... How do we know what he said into the intercom?'

'Paula,' Clarence reaches his spare hand round to rub at

his own neck that feels so tight and bunched up, 'don't ever question Howie ... I've been with him for–'

'Six ... seven days? Maybe just over a week?'

'Eight or nine,' Clarence mutters, 'but it doesn't matter. I would trust that man with my life ... Hell, I *have* trusted that man with my life ... We all have ... Everyone has, which is why he's like this now.' Clarence trails off.

'Yes,' she draws the word out, 'but all I'm saying is, we don't know exactly what Howie said to them.'

'So what? What does it matter?' Clarence groans. 'Howie could have told them we'll get inside and burn them all alive, for all I care ... Fact is fact, Paula, Howie has had one bad day since this began, but even on his worst day, he's still the best human being I have ever met ... and fact is fact that they were locked in here ... Fact is fact that we've been outside, fighting and risking our lives while they stayed locked in here ... Frankly, I couldn't give a rats arse to what he did or didn't say ... We needed the thing they had, and they didn't want to share, so we did what we needed to take it.'

Paula opens her mouth to reply but finds his words strike a chord of common sense. It doesn't feel right forcing people out of their safe place, but the safe place *is* a munitions factory, and the stock they held inside could make the difference between life and death for so many.

'I get what you're saying,' Clarence says after a pause. 'And we did say we would offer them the chance to come back with us, but ...' he adds slowly. 'What can we do? We aren't splitting the team up to send people out looking for them, not at night.'

'Okay,' she nods to herself and realises he won't be able to see the movement. 'Yes,' she says abruptly with a tired finality to her voice, 'what now?'

'Wait till morning to load up and head back. We'll need another vehicle but ...'

'We can get some ammunition now, though, can't we? For our weapons, I mean.'

'I'll send the lads back down here to bring some cases back.'

'Why don't we just take a case back with us now?' she asks pointedly.

'Because we've only got little torches and ...'

'I can see fine,' she moves off, hovering the beam of light from her torch as she moves quickly to the first stack, all wrapped up tight in thick layers of clingfilm-type packaging. Drawing her knife, she slices through the outer layer, digging the blade against the taut plastic until it cuts, and she can tear it away with her hands.

'What we looking for?' she tries to ask with the end of the torch clamped between her teeth.

'Maybe ask that before you start taking them apart?'

'Then how do we see what's on the boxes inside the cling wrap?'

'On the manifesto,' he replies too quickly.

'What manifesto? Can you see a manifesto? I can see a big, printed barcode waiting to be scanned onto a computer system ... You could get the power running, then work out how to operate the computer systems, then find the barcode reader, scan the barcode, and maybe then we'll know what's in each pallet.'

'They always had manifestos when they were delivered to stores,' Clarence grunts.

'And I'm guessing once the army take possession, they issue their own paper manifesto, seeing as maybe it'll be hard to operate a barcode scanner in the middle of Afghanistan.'

'And you'd know that, would you?' he asks bluntly. 'Seeing as you served with distinction in overseas combat zones.'

'No, but I bloody worked with enough delivery companies to know how they establish stream-lined and paperless systems.'

'Oh, the stream-lined and paperless systems,' Clarence says scathingly. 'Yeah, we're all for that in the middle of a big firefight. Don't worry about the bullets and bombs flying everywhere, but for fuck's sake don't cut a tree down.'

'And back to the matter at hand,' Paula cuts him off. 'What are we looking for?'

'Looking for? You should know, seeing as you–'

'Clarence ... why are you being like that?' she snaps.

'Five point five six for the assault rifles and nine mil for the pistols ... Look for seven point six two for the big gun. It should be stencilled on the side of the cases ... unless they're a new paperless and streamlined service too,' he adds with an edge to his voice. 'You know, so we make life easier for the paper pushers who don't have to worry about the bullets and bombs flying about ...'

'Here,' she says, ignoring his caustic comments. 'Five point five six ... Christ, this is heavy,' she grunts trying to lift the solid metal crate.

'Allow me,' he reaches past one-handed to lift the case from the stack and lower it to the floor.

'Wish I had your strength,' she mutters.

'Bollocks,' he curses. The top opened up to reveal layers of shiny brass rounds looking innocuous under the torch light. 'No magazines ...'

'Oh ... will they be here too?' she asks, standing over his crouching form.

'I don't know, Paula,' he bites, 'I've never worked in a

fucking munitions factory ... I don't know who makes the magazines or if the fucking munitions factory makes the fucking magazines ... I'm a fucking soldier, not a–'

'And I was an accountant, and Howie was a manager at Tesco, and Lani worked in a nightclub,' she says abruptly, 'so you and Dave are ...'

'Me and Dave?' he looks up with scorn. 'Dave would know less than me ...' Paula notices his hand once more starts rubbing the back of his neck in a tell-tale sign of tension. 'And which is why,' he stands up to look down at the woman in the shadows, 'I suggested we send the lads down with torches to look properly.'

'You never said that,' she prickles at his tone. 'You said you'd send them down to bring them back ... not look for magazines.'

'I never fucking said that,' his voice rises in volume.

'I know you didn't,' hers matches his as it ramps up, 'and don't swear at me.'

'I wasn't swearing *at you*. I was just fucking swearing.'

'You're confusing me,' she shakes her head disdainfully. 'Fine, we'll come back with more lights and ...'

'Oh really? Shall we? That's a good idea,' acid drips from his tone.

'What the hell has got into you?' She demands with eyes widening in anger. Both of them hold their torches pointed down, and the reflected light casts their faces in terrible shadows that make their eyes appear more sunken, their cheek bones more pronounced, and their lips thin and cruel.

'Me?' he blanches. 'You're being difficult and snappy, for fuck's sake.'

'What? I am not. You're trying to control everything and be the ...'

'Be the what? Go on ... Be the what?'

'Stop rubbing your bloody neck.'

He freezes on the spot with one hand giving a self-message, and if truth be told, he didn't know he was doing it. Memories surged up of Chris and Malcolm taking the piss when he started rubbing his neck, and then Malcolm and Clarence doing the same to Chris when he rubbed his beard. What did Malcolm do? That was it, he cracked his knuckles. All three of them had a tell-tale sign of when the tension got high.

'It eases the tension,' he grumbles, continuing the massage. The fleeting hurt across his face is evident. A huge man full of strength, both physical and mental, but barely coping with his own anguish. He blinks several times and looks away, lost, forlorn.

'Turn round,' she finds her own voice is now softer than it was as the anger starts to ebb.

'Eh?' He glances down with a puzzled expression.

'I said turn round,' she nods for him to do so, motioning with her head.

'What for?'

'Fine, stay there then,' she tuts and moves round to face his back. Pocketing the torch, she reaches up to grasp his shoulders and gently slaps his hand away. 'Relax,' she orders gently.

'What you doing?'

'What does it look like?'

'I don't know. It's dark,' the feeble joke is weak, but it helps break the tension. His hand drops down to his side as her own hands start kneading at the trapezius muscles stretching from his neck to his shoulders.

'You're too tall,' she says. 'Sit down.'

'Here?'

'No, outside.'

He sits down, easing his bulk to a childlike position with his legs curled round in front and his centre of balance aided by his hands gently resting on the ground either side.

'That's better,' she moves in closer to rest the front of her legs against his wide back. Clarence is so tall she doesn't need to bend over that much to start working on his neck and shoulders. 'They're really tight,' she mutters.

Clarence sits rock still, uncomfortable to be touched in this way. It's too much of an intimate gesture, done at a time of great worry, and it feels wrong, forced, contrived. But he takes a deep breath and slowly lets the air out as her hands work harder to massage the bunched muscles. Seconds is all it takes, and he presses the button on his torch to switch it off and save the battery. Their breathing fills the air, soft inhalations and slow exhalations. She grunts gently as her hands work harder, digging her thumbs into his muscles. 'They're rock hard,' she mutters. 'Can I hit them?'

'Hit them?'

'Beat them,' she gives a dry chuckle.

'Go for it,' he shrugs, and she senses the great power in his body as her hands rise several inches from the movement. Using the blade of her hand, she rubs it side to side, down the right trapezius muscle before starting gentle taps along the muscle. Those gentle taps get gradually harder as she starts beating the muscle with hammer fists to loosen the knots and ease the cramping-like feeling within them.

His eyes close at the feeling. Endorphins flood from the muscle and the completely painless beating on his shoulders. She drums again and again, using both hands on the same muscle with hard karate chops that send minute shockwaves through the nerves and sinews.

'God, that's nice,' he mutters.

'Drop your head a bit,' she starts kneading at the back of his neck, using the flats of her palms to generate the force necessary.

Clarence snorts with a low grunt of laughter, 'This is when Roy walks in and shoots me with his bow.'

'I don't think he'd mind,' she replies quietly.

'You, er, you getting on okay, then?' he asks carefully, not wanting to pry but feeling a need to fill the silence.

'Me and Roy? Yeah ... yeah, I think so. He's nice. Strange but ... well, strange times,' she trails off.

'Say that again,' he rumbles.

'You worried? About Howie, I mean?' She asks.

'Course,' he nods, 'very.'

'He'll be okay,' she says softly. 'He just needs rest and quiet, and maybe ... maybe this is the right place for him to have it.'

'Hope so.'

'Everything he's been through ...' she talks quietly while working on his neck and across his shoulders, and like kneading pizza or scrubbing work-surfaces, the repetitive action soothes her as much as Clarence. Doing something simple with her hands lets her mind ease down a few gears and allow natural thought processes to flow. 'Everything *you've* been through ... all of them ...'

'And you,' he adds.

'All of us,' she agrees. 'I try not to think about it.'

'About what?'

'About ... you know, those that didn't make it.'

'Family, you mean? Like friends and ...'

'Yes,' she whispers, 'I saw my mother, she was turned ...'

'Christ, Paula,' his hand lifts across his chest to cover hers that rests on his shoulder.

'We've all lost,' she mutters.

'We have, but it doesn't make it easier.'

'It kind of does,' she counters gently, 'knowing that we're all in the same situation and that none of us have lost more than others ... Probably doesn't make any sense.'

'No, it does,' he squeezes her hand. 'Howie saw his sister get killed by Dave. Me and Sarah were ...'

'A couple?'

'No, nothing like that ... I liked her, and ... I think she liked me, but ... there was so much going on, and ... well, I never really got the chance to talk to her properly.'

She tuts softly, shaking her head at the sadness of it all. Her hands fall still as they both brood in silence for a few long seconds, remembering those they have lost.

'They're feeling less tight now,' she remarks with a final rub along his shoulders, getting ready to make a move again.

'Feel much better,' he replies.

'We've got to take comfort where we can now,' she says slowly. 'I'd never go with someone like Roy in ... well, in the other life like before, ... but now, I know he's kind, and he's strong, fit, and healthy ... Plus, he's on our side, which helps,' she gives another dry chuckle and abruptly slides down to sit behind Clarence and rest her own back against his. The big man stays still, feeling the warmth of her back against his.

'We had sex,' she announces softly, craning her head back to rest against his shoulders.

'Thanks for sharing,' he chuckles.

'Sorry,' she shrugs. 'The end of that storm, when we went back to our rooms ... we had sex.'

'Again, thanks for sharing.'

'I haven't had sex in ages,' she continues, 'too busy at work, too busy at life ... too busy for anything ... The world ends, and I have sex with the first man that comes along.'

'Like you said, you got to take comfort where you can,' he replies. She feels the rumble of vibration through his body when he speaks, his voice so deep and low, like a talking bear.

'It was nice,' she sighs, 'just having someone else there.'

'So it wasn't Roy so much as his penis,' he jokes.

She bursts out laughing, her back thudding against his as the room fills with the sound of chuckles. 'Clarence!'

'Sorry, couldn't resist ... Squaddie humour and all that. You're not offended, are you? You know, being a paperless, streamlined paper pusher and all that.'

'Cheeky sod,' she laughs again, 'and yes, I'm deeply offended that you'd think I just wanted cock.'

'Paula!'

'What?'

'Don't say cock.'

She laughs again in delight at the obvious discomfort in his voice. 'You started it.'

'Yeah but ... you can't say cock.'

'Why not? Cock ... There, I said it again.'

'Stop! Say penis or ... or something else ... stop saying cock.'

'Why?' she chuckles. 'I want squaddie humour too.'

'It doesn't sound right when you say it.'

'Why not? That's sexist. You're sexist.'

'No, I'm not ... just ... well, yes ... okay then, I am sexist but ...'

'Cock.'

'Stop it!'

'Why do I get the feeling you're blushing ... In fact, I think I can feel it from here.'

'Rude,' he mutters, 'I'm sat in a pitch-dark room with a beautiful woman saying cock ... so yes, I am blushing.'

'Beautiful?' she asks quickly. 'You think I'm beautiful?'

'You are,' he says firmly, 'very beautiful and a lovely person ... Roy is a lucky man.'

'Thank you,' she says sincerely.

'You're welcome.'

'So ...' she says after a pause, 'when was your last time?'

'For what?'

'Sex.'

'Huh?'

'The last time you had sex?'

'Bloody hell,' he shrugs, 'almost had it a few days ago in the fort, but that was with an infected girl so ...'

'Yeah, I heard about that.'

'I broke her neck.'

'Good,' she replies quickly, 'don't feel bad about it.'

'Other than that ... maybe a month or so ... Something like that.'

'Not that long ago then. Did you have a wife or girlfriend?'

'Nah, just a, er ... you know.'

'One night stand?'

'Sort of, this girl I used to see every now and then. Nothing special or ... dunno really, just ...'

'Comfort?' she asks gently.

'Yeah, guess it was.'

'No shame in it,' she muses. 'I wish I'd done more ... They say that, don't they? People who are dying–they don't say they wished they had worked more or spent more time at work or making money ... but more time with their family and doing things ... nice things ...'

'I've heard that,' he nods, 'so you wish you had more sex, then?'

She chuckles. 'Yep. I had this friend who never hesitated ... We'd go for drinks or coffee, and she'd regale me with stories of these crazy encounters she had with men. Always made me laugh.'

'Good for her,' Clarence chuckles.

'Do you really think I'm beautiful?'

'Eh?' he laughs. 'You fishing for more compliments?'

'I am,' she announces. 'Make a lady feel nice.'

'I thought you were a feminist.'

'I was. No ... the office I worked in was full of dirty, old, pervy sods.'

'Well, I ain't a pervy, old sod.'

'I know,' she says quickly. 'I know that ...'

'Right,' he says firmly, 'let's see.'

'See what?'

'Your hair is very nice,' he starts, 'er ... dark and nice ... and I like the way you pull your hair back into a ponytail.'

'Oh, I see,' she nods, 'keep going.'

'And er ... your skin is nice, looks soft ... like nice and soft ... clear too.'

'Okay, so far so good. Keep going.'

'I am, I am. Er ... you've got a cracking figure, or does that make me sound like a dirty old sod?'

'No, you're alright. You can keep going.'

He laughs gently, shaking his head at the absurdity of it all. 'Like,' he pauses and thinks, 'your boobs are nice.'

'My boobs?' she laughs. 'How would you know?'

'No, the outline of them ... Like, they look nice.'

'I'm joking, so ... keep going.'

'Nice shoulders, slim and toned ... but your stomach isn't too flat or ...'

'You saying I'm fat?'

'No!'

'Joking! Keep going.'

'It's nice and soft, like womanly soft ... and your legs are nice too ...'

'Keep going.'

'I've run out.'

'Really? What about my nails?'

'Nails? I can't say I've ever noticed your nails. Men never look at nails.'

'True,' she admits ruefully, 'and mine are all broken and chipped now.'

'Never mind.'

'Lani is very pretty,' Paula stares into the darkness.

'She is,' Clarence agrees, 'fierce too.'

'Beautiful hair.'

'Lani's? Yeah, I guess it is.'

'Oh, it is, so silky and black ... She's flawless. Not an ounce of fat on her body.'

'I like a bit of fat,' Clarence admits, 'something to hold.'

'Yeah?'

'Definitely.'

'That woman, then? Was she curvy?'

'Actually, no, she wasn't. She was skinny ... too skinny, but she was a nice girl.'

'You strike me as being an old-fashioned kind of guy.'

'Maybe,' he shrugs, 'more like a freak or a dinosaur or ...'

'Freak? Why?'

'Cos I'm so big.'

'Yeah, but bloody hell, Clarence, where would we be now without you?'

'Now is okay,' he admits, 'and when I was serving, but after the army, it was ... hard. I know Chris struggled too, and Malcolm.'

'I've heard that,' she says softly, 'service people struggling to cope to civilian life.'

'It's true. Very true. The army does everything for you, and there's a code, like ethics ... You know who you can trust and who your mates are. You know where to get food and clean your clothes. They take care of everything so we can do the nasty stuff, but on the outside, there's no respect or decency, no ... no discipline or unity, and the only work I could get was security staff, and that was bloody awful.'

'These are new times, alright,' she says with a sigh. 'Come on, we'd better get back.' She turns to help him up.

'Are you holding your hand out?'

'Yes.'

'I don't think you quite realise how heavy I am ...' he laughs whilst grabbing her hand and attempting to pull himself up. Paula staggers forward and only avoids face-planting the floor by using Clarence's massive shoulders to prop herself up on.

'Steady on,' he supports her with one hand on her shoulder. 'Almost sent you flying.'

'I would have got you up. I was just resting.'

'Sure you were,' he chuckles. 'Thanks for this.'

'For what?'

'Talking and the massage.'

'Anytime,' she says softly. 'Come here.' She steps in to wrap her arms round his torso. Pressing her body close into his, she rubs his back with one hand. 'You okay?'

'Yeah,' he relaxes into the hug, his own arms dwarfing her body.

'Everyone needs a hug,' she murmurs.

Taking comfort where they can, they stay close and silent in the dark, silent room surrounded by bullets of every shape and size.

CHAPTER SIX

Flickering orange lights of flames, candles, and lanterns illuminate the ground yet cast the shadows to the sides deeper and longer. Children sleep fitfully, grouped together in small groups, with the best of the bedding given over so they can rest. The weather is still hot, so they sleep without covers but rest on soft blankets, clothes, and the sparse bedding remaining in the fort.

A crew at the back gate talk in muted tones, careful not to raise their voices above a whisper. With the original gate destroyed by the force of the storm, this crew were tasked with rebuilding it. They combined their limited knowledge and taught themselves what they needed to know in order to fix it. They worked tirelessly, sustained numerous injuries, and made hundreds of mistakes before they learnt enough to make it secure. Even with it locked and bolted, the fort has fallen before, so a crew remain constantly at this position. The crew leaders take care to run their teams proficiently under the ever-watchful eyes of Maddox and Lenski.

Adults, many years senior to the two young people,

defer to their decisions and words without argument. The force between them is palpable, a bond that runs deep from mutual respect and trust.

The newly arrived doctors soon had their hands full with queues of injured, sick, and worried survivors making a beeline to be checked. Between the four of them, the doctors took stock of the equipment and medicines available, making constant lists of items needed. At the top of every list was the urgent requirement to locate and bring back a pharmacist.

Wounds are checked, washed, and dressed. Antibiotics are given out. Penicillin administered to those sure of not being allergic. Vast quantities of aspirin, paracetamol, codeine, and anti-inflammatories are handed out. Reassuring words, uttered by professional doctors wearing white lab coats with stethoscopes hanging from necks, have a profound calming effect on the camp.

The few beds they have are given over to those most serious cases only and those requiring constant observations. Survivors with an aptitude for care are drafted in to help organise the queues, keep people calm, and assist with washing, cleaning, and the hundreds of small tasks that keep a medical facility running.

With the sky darkening, the hustling fort gradually slows down, and the exhausted bodies can slump down to talk in soft tones, drink fresh water, eat canned food, or just simply sleep the pain away.

Maddox walks with long, relaxed strides that take care not to snag or trip on the many obstacles littering the ground. A pistol strapped to his belt is the only weapon he carries–such is the trust in his crews stationed around the fort. He checks in on the crew at the rear gates, then makes his way slowly towards the vehicle ramp and up onto the walls, checking the crews along that section, exchanging words, and offering his ready smile.

He makes his way down to the front and checks in at the hospital, nodding respectfully at the people waiting to be seen. The doctors glance up, and any puzzlement they feel at how such a young man can take lead is kept hidden behind masks of faces that smile and nod.

Next, he goes to the front gate and the crew positioned on the inside. He checks that they have eaten, had their vitamins, have drunk plenty of water, and that their weapons are nearby and ready.

Through the gates and across the narrow strip between the inner and outer gates, he steps out onto the small beach so formed after the storm.

'What's up?' Darius offers the familiar greeting as Maddox strolls over.

'Nuffin, you?'

'Nuffin, bruv,' Maddox replies. 'Anything going on?'

'Here?' Darius glances up from his position seated upon a folding picnic chair, his shotgun resting on his legs. 'Nuffin here, bruv ... Move along, innit? Nuffin' to see.'

'Fact,' Maddox nods.

'They due back by now,' Darius shifts in the seat, the street slang dropped as he expresses concern.

'Yeah, maybe,' Maddox stares out over the still waters and to the darkness of the land beyond.

'In there?' Darius tilts his head back towards the fort. Friends for years, and the inflection of tone given by years of closeness means whole sentences can be conveyed by just a few words.

'Good,' Maddox replies, 'Lenski's all over it.' He grins, showing a row a white teeth and an expression that animates his face from the usual brooding intensity.

'Three immune,' Darius remarks slowly as Maddox sits down in an empty chair.

'Four with the dog,' Maddox says. 'Fucked up.'

'It's all fucked up,' Darius nods in agreement. 'Howie, Lani, and Cookey. You think the others are immune too?'

'I've been thinking about that,' Maddox says quietly. 'It doesn't make sense that they would pass any immunity between them.'

'What d'you mean?'

'Howie and Lani kiss and probably have sex, so they would pass fluids, but Cookey? How would they get their fluids into him?'

'They cut themselves,' Darius reminds him, 'when Cookey went down. They cut their hands and pushed them into the wound.'

'Not convinced,' Maddox shakes his head. 'For something to work that fast would make it incredible. I've never heard of anything like that. Vaccinations can be made from cells but not that way.'

'So you think Cookey was already immune?' Darius asks.

'I do,' Maddox presses his fingers together under his chin, 'but how would three people who are naturally immune find each other in all this shit going on?'

'That's why you the Bossman now–you get to figure that shit out,' Darius smiles.

'Something is going on,' Maddox nods with a long look over at his friend. 'Something we don't realise ... That's for sure.'

CHAPTER SEVEN

Dark. Pitch-dark. The absence of light. A vacuum. Nothing exists here, yet I do. I am here within this place alone. Where did the light go? I have no knowledge of where the light went. It's just not here anymore. Standing still, I can feel the space around me, but not like I'm outside, more like a room with a high, vaulted roof. My footsteps echo with resonance that bounces off the walls. There's a dripping sound coming from somewhere, and each plop of liquid that falls unseen seems to come from every direction at once.

My breathing is audible, and not just to my own ears, so I keep moving. I take one step at a time with my hands stretched out in front of me. I can't lift my feet high for fear of tripping on something, so I sort of shuffle my foot along a few inches at a time, redistribute the pressure and do it again while all the time my head cranes to the left, then to the right as I strain to listen.

There is airflow here, a slight breeze wafts by, but again, I cannot tell where it comes from. I was in that ruined street before, trapped amidst the destruction of whatever foul landscape I was in. I could hear voices, Lani's and Dave's, but they went, just went. I closed my eyes because I was so scared, and when I opened them, I was here, wherever here is.

Step after shuffling step. Tiles. I'm walking on a tiled floor–that's the sound I can hear from the water dripping. That distinct bathroom sound of water on tiles, except this is no bathroom It's huge. I drop down to feel around, and sure enough, I can just about grope the odd bit of ceramic type tile here and there. Most of it is broken, fractured, and I can feel the thick dust coating my fingertips.

It takes forever to move just a few steps, but then no time at all. Time does not exist here because, in order to be time, there would have to be light. Without light, there is no life, so therefore there cannot be any time. Interesting. Maybe I am dead then. I died back in the munitions factory, and this is the afterlife. How did I die? Did Dave shoot me? Probably.

This afterlife is a bit shitty, though. It's not what I imagined heaven or hell would be like. What's that other place you can go? Purgatory? I don't even know what that means. Something to do with hanging about for unfinished business?

Fuck knows. Deep down, not that I would admit it to myself. of course, I don't think I died in the munitions place. I think I passed out, and now I'm having some fucked-up dreams.

This means that if this is a dream, I can do what I want. You can't get hurt in dreams, can you? You always wake up at the point where the thing will hurt you. Fuck it, then. I start walking faster, grimacing as I wait in expectation of walking into something.

I get faster. Striding out, then jogging, then running. Running faster as my feet trip and slip on the broken tiled floor. Ha! I'm dreaming and running in the pitch black of nowhere. Nothing can happen because this is a dream.

'Arghgh!' my own scream scares me. The sudden arrival of a human voice, despite it being my own, scares me. I trip on a loose tile and spin off to hit a very hard wall, bounce along a bit, and end up crumpled on the floor. It's not meant to hurt in dreams, but that bloody hurt. It really hurt.

Rubbing my knee, I roll about a bit, feeling woefully sorry for myself that even in my dreams I seem to hurt myself. I can't even tell if my eyes are open or not. It's that dark. I physically make myself squeeze my eyes closed, then open wide, trying to see any difference. There is something. Not a light as such, more of a very slight change to the shade.

Sore knee forgotten, I clamber up, constantly opening and closing my eyes. There is a definite change when I open them. I start walking again, not fast but not shuffling either. Ten steps, then twenty, thirty, and I lose count, but I start shutting my eyes for long seconds, then opening them up to see there is a subtle change. Like the black isn't quite so black now.

I keep going. Eyes squeezed shut as I count my steps. Twenty, thirty, forty steps, and I open my eyes. Ha! A definite change now. Lighter. I'm heading towards light.

'Stay away from the light ... come back from the light,' I say to myself in a pathetic attempt at humour, but again my own voice scares the shit out of me, so I shut up.

I close my eyes again, and this time I don't count but keep walking for what seems like hours but is in fact probably only about a minute. When I open them, I feel a flood of relief. I can see my hands, only just, but I can see the outline of them. I move faster, desperate to be away from the darkness and into the light.

Wherever this place is, it's very bloody long. Suddenly, there's a change in the sound of my footsteps, and after fifteen days of surviving on my wits, or rather, surviving on Dave's wits, I stop to take stock and work out the difference. The shape of the place I am in is changing, the acoustics are different. I keep walking, straining to see or hear anything. There's something dark and shadowy ahead, solid and unmoving. Slowing down, I hold my hands out ready to touch it. It's weird and soft, like hard rubber and smooth too. I recognise it but ... Stepping closer, and the realisation hits me. The underground. I'm in the underground. The Tube network in London, or something very much like it. Long, tiled corridors, and the smooth, black thing is the railing edge of an escalator. Edging forward, I realise it sweeps down and away from me, and that's where the light is coming from.

The metal steps are quite steep to walk down when they're not moving, and my footsteps clunk despite trying to tread quietly.

Down I go, my hand moving gently over the old, worn-out rubber safety rail. The light at the bottom is distinct and orange, flickering too, so I know it's made from flames.

Torches, to be precise. Old-fashioned torches stuck to the wall with some kind of burning oil coating the top to produce a smelly yet constant light source. On the floor, there are dirty oil stains, and the walls surrounding the torches are smoke blackened from long use.

Another corridor stretches away, and a fractured, old sign on the wall points to east and west platforms with the place names of locations I can't quite read.

There are more torches to the east but not to the west, so east I head. Stepping into the tunnel and walking along the same broken tiled floor. Reaching another flaming torch,

I glance down at the ground to see dried oil stains and the smoke-blackened wall and curve of the ceiling is also old. These torches have been here a long time.

The corridor leads out onto an old, wide platform that stretches off left and right. Ahead is the drop down onto the tracks, and the sputtering torches are fitted at irregular points, giving light in an otherwise black existence.

It reminds me of the fort. The way tiny sections have been set aside with bedding and a few personal objects. Blurred lines of boundaries between living areas, but whereas the fort was at least moderately clean, here is filthy. Along the platform are blankets, rags, old mattresses, and all manner of things, but everything is filthy. Not just dirty but filthy beyond description. The type of filth that would have people in white biohazard suits picking them up with those grabby sticks to shove in yellow bin liners ready for incinerating. It stinks to high heaven with the putrid stench of old oil, faeces, body odour, stale breath, and unclean bodies that have spent far too long pressed together without access to washing and hygiene.

But there are no people. Just the empty bedding areas. A few paperbacks lie dotted about, well-thumbed with ripped and torn edges. I bend over to pick one and read the cover, The Second Reality, a story about people descending into double lives within a dream world. The irony is not lost, and I cast it aside with a snort. Stepping closer to the edge of the platform, I look down and see the tracks have also been given over to living areas. Ply board, old doors, metal sheeting, and anything large and flat have been used to lay across the uneven and rutted surface of the racks. There's more bedding and filthy rags of life, and even in this god-awful place, I can see there is a difference between the quality of items possessed by those that reside on the platform proper and those that dwell on the tracks. The platform residents are obviously the more affluent residents, the equivalent of detached houses with big gardens while the track dwellers are the council estates who scavenge amongst the filth.

Human nature is unstoppable, unceasing and as relentless as the infection. Not to survive but to carve out a meaning to our lives. I'm better than you are. I live higher up and have more bedding. The roles of existence that serve to validate who we are and why we're here. The possibility that we're just another species scrabbling for survival with the rest of the food chain is rarely considered.

So this is what we've become, is it? Living here as the last few of our numbers dwindle and die out in the darkness of the old tunnel network. Shaking my head, I look about, letting my eyes linger on objects that reflect the decline of mankind.

But why am I here, and where are the people? Just like the last place, this is a reflection of the future, and I'm in some fucking Dickens tale of scrooge, being shown what the future looks like without the brave efforts of a few to stem the flow of the infected.

Clumsy and ham-fisted. My own sub-conscious is creating this world. *Howie ... you have to keep going ... don't stop now, Howie!*

Bollocks. All of it is utter bollocks. This bedding isn't even really here. This place isn't here. It's made up in my head while I lie flat out in the munitions factory while Dave pokes the side of my head with his pistol.

To show my generalised disdain, I start kicking at the bedding, toeing it across the platform with the mad glee of an idiot trying to argue against his own dreams and the make-believe world he just created. Blankets get cast down onto the lower tier of the tracks, and in a way, it feels like retribution, like an act of anarchy to bring down those who are powerful and redistribute the wealth among the classes. Yeah, communism. Bring on the revolution. I work harder, using my hands to fling the shitty, nasty, lice-covered stuff away as I power along the platform.

A sudden coughing fit brings me to a stop. Someone fights for breath nearby and suffers from lungs too tight to let his body draw proper breath. Spinning round, I trace the noise to the far end of the tracks, by the entrance to the tunnel proper. I jump down, threading my way through the bedding and crap as I peer into the gloom and listen as the dry, hacking coughs get closer.

'Hello?' I call out to the huddled shape swathed in filthy blankets.

He tries to respond with a voice that starts to call out, but the coughs take over, wracking his body that heaves and writhes in situ. I stop a few feet back, letting my eyes adjust to the gloom until I can make out a haggard face with deep, sunken eyes and skin the colour of death. A grey beard, straggly and unkempt, frames his face, and his wild hair is patchy in places with clear bald spots. The lice are visible from here. Tiny, maggot-looking things that crawl through the greasy hairs of his beard. A shaking hand lifts between coughs to scratch at the hairs, delving deep to agitate the skin in response to the vermin infesting it. He has filthy, blackened fingernails and looks ready to die as he fights to gain breath with a horrible, ragged sound of air being forced through something constricted and broken.

'Where is everyone?' I call out, not bothering with the pleasantries, seeing as this is a dream and the old, dying man doesn't actually exist.

'Gone,' he wheezes into the air, not bothering to turn or even glance in my direction.

'Gone where?'

'Tunnels,' he points off to the looming tunnel mouth just yards from his prone form.

'Why?'

'Not safe here anymore,' he finally turns his head to stare at me, and for a second, I wait for the recognition of it being someone I know, but it isn't. It's an old man getting ready to die in the squalor of an old Tube station.

'Oh,' I can't think of anything else to say, fighting the urge to offer help while remembering this is all made-up shit and is meaningless. I've just got to ride it out until I can wake up.

'I'm dying,' he wheezes dramatically and somewhat predictably.

'Looks like it,' I reply.

'Take me up top,' he doesn't so much ask as demand.

'Do what, mate?'

'Take me up top,' he forces the words out while fighting off another coughing fit.

'Top where?'

'YOU BLOODY IDIOT,' the bellowing voice startles me enough to step back, the power and depth thundering from the old bugger who descends into another round of coughing. 'Up ... top ... outside ... bloody outside, you blithering fool.'

'Er, right ...' I nod slowly, 'yeah, that's not really gonna happen, mate.'

'I want to feel the sun on my face.'

'It's nighttime,' I shrug at him. 'No sun.'

He glances at the watch on his wrist. 'It's three thirty in

the afternoon,' he says in a voice that speaks of culture and education. 'It is not nighttime; it is daytime ...'

'You are covered in lice, mate.'

'Am I?' he asks with another long and thorough scratch at his beard. 'Can't say I noticed.'

'And this is a dream so ... so no, I'm not carrying you anywhere as you don't actually exist so ... er ... bollocks.'

'Yours or mine?' He glances up at me.

'Eh?'

'Blithering fool,' he tuts, 'your dream or my dream?'

'Mine, obviously.'

'Why obviously? Just because you are there talking to me doesn't mean it's your dream ... This could be my dream.'

'What? Get off, it's my dream ... I've passed out in the munitions factory, and I'm having weird dreams ... I saw Paco and Chris a few minutes ago.'

'And I am at home ... Well, not my home but a care home. It's a bloody awful place, run like a blasted concentration camp, and worst of all, they serve weak tea. And I can't abide weak tea ... We're all dreaming, young man,' he adds wistfully, 'so rather than standing here, arguing who is having this blasted dream, I suggest you take me up top.'

'But ...'

'The lice? We've just established that one of us is dreaming ... The lice, therefore, are not real.'

'Oh ... shit.' He's right. This is a dream, and as disgusting as he looks, I don't really feel that I have much of a choice. With a sigh, I step closer, grimacing at the stench coming off him. It's an actual wall of stench that is so foul it has me gagging on the spot.

'Stop your bloody malingering,' he chastises me with a

mean look. 'Young lad like you can hoist me up and carry me on your back. Here,' he holds a hand up, 'help me up.'

Clasping the hand, I'm surprised at the strength in his grip as he clamps on tightly. Coughing, spluttering, wheezing, and fighting for breath, he gets free of the bedding and slowly gets to his feet while I bend over closer to give what support I can.

'You're naked,' I observe quietly.

'That I am,' he replies proudly, 'naked as the day I was born.'

'Where are your clothes?'

'Gave 'em away,' he wheezes. 'I'm going out nuddy as a baby.'

'Right ... awesome ... so I'm going to have a naked old man on my back, is that right?'

'Sharper than a knife, aren't you?' he replies in a cutting tone. 'Turn round and crouch down.'

'Oh, for the love of god,' tutting with disgust, I do as bid, turning on the spot and dropping down to present my back to him.

'Closer, you bloody fool,' he snaps. 'I'm not a blasted gymnast ... That's it. Now hold steady.' Bony hands grab my shoulders, pulling me back as he heaves himself up. His digits dig into my skin, and I can feel the sharp nails cutting me. His rancid breath blasts past my ear, and the greasy strands of his beard start tickling the back of my neck. As his hot, feverish, naked body presses against mine, the stench of shit and stale urine brings tears to my eyes, and the thought of his dirt-encrusted penis rubbing against me makes my stomach flip over.

'Hold my legs,' he demands in a hoarse whisper that is way too close to my ear for comfort. My hands reach down and loop under his bare thighs that feel wet and sticky.

'Hoist me up, then,' he continues giving orders, as though this is entirely natural, and I am his to do with as he pleases.

Why am I doing this? I could just drop him and walk off. He isn't real but a figment of my imagination. Except he feels real, and that bloody smell is far too real. All of it is too real.

'Which way?' I gasp. Unfortunately, the way our bodies are designed means that air is blown out when we speak, which then means that air has to be pulled back in. Breathing in, with his whole foulness so close, is too much for me at the moment.

'Are you sick?' he barks when I bend forward to retch, strands of spittle drool from my mouth as I fight the urge to vomit.

'Which way?' I ask again through blurred eyes.

'The way you bloody came in, you blithering fool,' he chastises me with that same withering tone. 'Come on, I ain't dying on your puny back, you know.'

'Puny back?' I start walking, treading carefully through the flotsam and jetsam of the abandoned platform.

'Down there,' one of his hands reaches past my head to point towards the end of the platform and the set of steps leading up.

He isn't heavy so much as disgustingly fucking gross, and I move fast, kicking stuff out of the way until I clamber up the steps and start down the platform.

'Ah,' he sighs with too much hot air going into my ear again, 'I'll miss this place.'

'Here?' I ask incredulously.

'Not here, you bloody idiot,' he snaps. 'How anyone can actually like *this* place is beyond me, and truth be told, I was bloody glad to see the back of them.'

'Who?'

'Who, he asks! The people that lived here, you bumbling halfwit.'

'Why did they leave?' My god, he stinks so bad. So, so bad.

'Why? Why do you think?'

'I don't know. This is a fucking dream,' I remind him harshly.

'Those blasted creatures, that's why,' he shakes his head in despair, brushing his beard against my neck and no doubt tumbling a thousand lice down my back at the same time.

'The zombies?'

'Yes, the zombies ... What else would I mean? The aliens? The mutant fishmen that crawled out from the sea ...?'

'How ...' I cough up a lump of phlegm which gets ejected off to the side, 'how long have you been here?'

'What are you? A bloody policeman?' he tries to shout, but the action renders him into a coughing fit again, and being as close as he is, I can feel the rattle of his bones and the wheeze of his lungs as he fights to draw breath. Fear grips him, fear that this is it, the final few seconds, and his hands dig tight into my shoulders while I feel his heart thudding erratically.

'Hold on,' I speak softly now, feeling a great sense of pity for a man that knows he is dying and has one last wish to see the sun. Moving faster, I start back down the corridor with the flaming torches towards the escalator.

The voice that comes from the old man is whispered and weak. 'A long time,' he says with regret and pain, 'years, many years.'

'Why? Why down here?'

'Last place,' he takes a ragged breath. 'We barricaded and sealed off a section and came down here to live.'

'Why here? There's got to be loads of places they can't get in.'

'They got clever; they worked things out,' he explains, 'and those of us left just couldn't find anywhere else. Nothing was left ... tower blocks were useless, castles and old forts all fell ...'

'Forts?'

'All of 'em,' he wheezes into my neck, 'everything.'

'Didn't you fight back?'

'With what?' he snaps with a show of strength. 'With who? Against so many? No, we ran and hid like rats down a sewer, getting filthy and diseased from the lack of sun and food.'

'You should have fought back.'

'Old men and women, mothers with children? You expect them to fight and charge into battle and die like everyone else did.'

'Not everyone who fought back died,' I point out.

'Didn't they? Then where are they? Where are the saviours of our species come to cast light upon our sorrowful eyes.'

'Very dramatic.'

'They died ... or they gave up ... or more likely they gave up and then died,' the old man speaks the bitter words so harshly they set him of coughing again, and this time it goes on for minutes while his lungs fight a desperate battle of their own to draw air.

At the escalator, I pause, not knowing if I am meant to ascend or go somewhere else. Common sense dictates the surface will be up, but its pitch black up there and not somewhere I fancy going. But again, between the coughs, a trembling arm reaches out to indicate we need to go up.

Climbing broken escalators with an old, dying man having a coughing fit in the dark isn't as easy as you might think. Halfway up, my thighs are burning and my own chest is heaving from the exertion. I'm having to keep a tight grip on his legs to stop him slipping off, so I can't use my hands to pull me along on the railing either.

I stumble forward into the darkness and feel warm, wet liquid spraying the back of my neck. He coughs harder, and I'm guessing it's blood mixed with phlegm and spit being sprayed out. A few times his whole body tenses and shakes from the exertion of the coughs that refuse to stop. Eventually, they ease off, dying down to the odd spasm, and we walk in near silence for a few minutes until he recovers breath to talk.

'There was hope,' his voice comes out weak and strained, barely a whisper uttered into the darkness, 'when it first happened. Oh, don't get me wrong, millions were dying and being turned, and a few were fighting back here and there but ...'

'But what?'

'Rumours ... stories and ...' he takes another few ragged breaths, 'just whispers really, but we heard of a group in the south who were not only fighting back but winning ... inflicting huge losses on the other side ... Trained and armed they were and moved about in an old army truck, wreaking havoc. We heard about it, many did ... and we all said that if they come our way, we'd join them ... Some even left to head south, trying to find them ... We kept seeing the turned ones leaving, and they headed south too, so we figured there was truth in it ...'

'What happened?' my voice seems unnaturally loud after his muted tones. 'And am I going the right way?'

'Yes, you are, you blasted fool. Where else is there to go?' he groans at my evident ineptitude.

'So what happened?' I press when he doesn't continue.

'Impatient as well as stupid,' he tuts. 'Nothing happened, the rumours stopped ... and hope stopped too. The survivors began to realise there was no help coming, so they descended into the usual human fall-back positions of squabbling, killing, and stealing.'

'What happened to the group? The ones who were fighting back?'

'I just bloody told you! I don't know ... The rumours stopped; the stories stopped ...'

'There must have been a reason?'

'Of course, there was a blasted reason, you halfwit, but damned if I know what it is ... Hurry up, I can feel death's icy hand gripping my heart.'

'Alright, Shakespeare,' I snort, 'doth thy icy hand clasp at thy heart, doth it?'

'Don't mock your elders, you impudent sod,' he smacks the side of my head with a solid thump that makes him start coughing again.

I speed up, stretching my stride out as I barrel down the pitch-dark corridor, and like before, I start seeing the first hints of the darkness lifting.

'It's not going to work,' I say once the coughing fit passes, but I can feel his grip is weaker now, and his breath too shallow and rapid.

'What isn't?' he asks, almost slurring the words from fatigue.

'All this shit about there being a group that could have

saved everyone, but they stopped, so the whole wide world just gave up because they did ... It's not going to work.'

'Don't know what you're on about, you crazy, blasted halfwit. Jabbering on about god only knows what ...'

'I was that group,' I inform him and give an audible groan when we reach the base of another inert escalator. 'I led that group, to be precise,' I inform him while my own breathing gets harder, 'for over two weeks ... We cut thousands down ... more than that ...'

'That was years ago,' he whispers.

'Not to me, it isn't ... It's now ... My dream, you see.'

'*My dream,* the blithering idiot says, *my dream.* That's an assumption, not a fact. An ideal, not a reality ... I can't abide this filthy, darkened place,' he spits. 'I'm glad to be dying ... You hear that, my boy? Glad to be leaving this cursed and wretched land so full of darkness and ...'

'Take it easy, Shakespeare, you'll set yourself off again.'

'Do you know the last time I saw the sun?'

'Yesterday?'

'Don't be flippant, you blasted fool,' he snaps with some energy back in his voice, and despite the circumstances, I can't help but smile. 'Years ago,' he adds in a whisper. 'Became too sick to walk myself, and none of those sick buggers would carry me.'

'Sick?'

'Sick, yes, sick ... What do you think living in the darkness does to you ...?' the words hiss out with a wheeze that I've already come to recognise as the precursor to a fit and one that is much worse than the others.

I can feel him dying on my back. Literally dying as he struggles to breathe air into his body. Each breath taken in irritates whatever infection is inside him, and he can't help the reflex action of dry-coughing over and over with such heaving intensity it shakes his whole frame.

We get to the top, and instead of waiting for instructions, I head down the corridor towards the light. It becomes a race of life and death. To get this old man outside, into the sun before that final breath is expunged from his body or his heart gives out from the fitting coughs.

'Hang on,' I gasp and hoist him up higher before breaking into a steady jog. The coughing gets worse as the once tight fingers on my shoulders start losing grip, and his body starts sliding down my back. I drop down to a crouch, giving him less space to fall as there's no way of stopping him falling off.

On the floor, he rolls side to side, writhing in panic as the coughs just keep coming. His frail frame is such a pale, grey pallor, like there's no blood flow to his skin. Instead, it sprays frothy and bright red from his thin lips, dripping into his beard and coating his hands. His eyes flicker open, searching for the light ahead of us with such desperation that I don't hesitate but gather him up in my arms and start walking again. The coughing disrupts my gait, and my arms ache from the heavy pressure of his body heaving and shaking.

The light gets stronger, blinding almost in its purity and strength. Sweat prickles my forehead to drip down onto the naked man I carry in my arms, but there it is, the latticed gate pulled close across the entrance with a huge padlock and a thick chain holding it shut.

Realising we're sealed inside, I flounder about, trying to work out a way of positioning his body so he might see a glimpse of the sky through the gaps in the metal strips of the gate. His hand thumps the side of my head again and again with nasty little knocks that make me almost drop him to the ground.

'THE BLOODY KEY, YOU BLITHERING IDIOT,' he thunders with a voice of power snatched between the gasps for air and once again descends into coughs. On the wall, well out of reach from the gate, is a hook screwed into the old grout between the tiles, and a large key is hanging from it.

I have to put him down, but I do so gently, then scrabble to get the key, and work to undo the padlock, unclasping the looped metal bar and de-threading the chain to wrench the gate open. It takes time as someone has put a lot of effort into looping the chain round the frame to keep it as secure as possible, and by the time I turn round to pick him back up, he's already dead.

Lifeless. Eyes open and staring into nowhere. The chest that was heaving doesn't move, nor do the arms that thrashed with the spasms that took over his body. A great shame settles on me, that this was somehow my fault. Gently, I lift him back up and step out through the gate and into the bright sunlight of a ruined street where I lay him to rest on the old paving thick with weeds growing through the cracks.

Death. Final and resolute. Without doubt as to its intentions or motive. Simply to take life and never give it back. He is just one old man that passed away in a coughing fit, but it's more than that. It's what he represents. The final throes of a humanity that has given up and made a choice to dwell in the blackness of tunnels rather than fight back.

This is all a cheap shot. I know that, but it doesn't take away the emotion of the moment at seeing his lifeless body so pale and weak lying naked on a pavement.

Choices. That's all we are, a stream of decisions and

choices. Of choosing what to do, where to go, and the self-justification that we're making the right choice. They went into the darkness to escape the infected because they lost hope. Too weak to fight back, too ill-equipped to make a stand, so they took courage from the snatched whispers of a group doing that for them.

Like I said, it's a cheap shot.

But it still bloody stings.

CHAPTER EIGHT

Day Sixteen

A new day dawns with the solemn promise from Mother Nature that life will go on. Perhaps not the life of our species but life nevertheless.

Jess and I made camp in an old barn set down a country lane and bordered by flat fields. Jess ate her oats and was given a good brush-down, which she suffered with the regal grace that only a pure blood animal can muster and with a wholesome belief that I am to perform in servitude for her needs.

Before the night grew dark, I made a small fire and heated water to enjoy a refreshing Earl Grey tea. My rations were opened, and a good meal was made of them, and it was as the last of the tea was drained that I became aware of Jess showing signs of nervousness.

. . .

Horses have strong instincts of flight. She is not a guarding animal but one born to have constant awareness. With outstanding hearing and a keen sense of smell, she is a lot more in tune with the surroundings than I am. Having spent so much time together now, I have become acutely aware of when she is unsure, scared, terrified, or building up for a tantrum.

She was flicking her head up, and her eyes were somewhat wider. They were gentle movements but enough for me to be reaching for the assault rifle and making it ready before heading outside. After my last debacle of entering the house of the first man I was supposed to find who was immune, only to find he was not only not immune but very infected and shut in an upstairs room with his infected family–I did kill them but only after stumbling back to fall on my arse. So after that too-close encounter, I was now ready with the weapon held properly and my feet treading carefully.

It was fog. Fog made Jess nervous. A bank of fog heading towards us like a somewhat translucent wall of scentless, white smoke. To watch such a thing is to feel the hairs on the back of your neck prick up, and a creeping urge to run and flee builds. I knew it was fog for I have seen fog before; however, this was thicker, more dense, and higher than anything I have previously known.

It was silent too, for it swept upon me like a noiseless entity that absorbs sound. Not only did it make no noise, but it seemed to take noise from all around and make it seem, I don't know ... deader? Emptier? Less resonant?

My guess is that the particles in the air, the trillions of tiny water droplets hovering in a suspended stasis somewhere between a gaseous vapour-like state and a physical molecular form, somehow do absorb noise.

Sound is created by the air around us and the differences in friction, heat, and speed. There is no sound in space, for space is a void that is empty of air. With no air, there can be no sound.

The fog thickens the air and therefore reduces the shockwaves needed to create sound. I know this. I am a scientist.

But science and mythology are two different things. I know what the fog is, but I can't see through it, and that scared me. It scared Jess too.

For some long minutes, I remained kneeling in the doorway of the barn with the weapon held up and ready, as though I were expecting the infected to come blundering into view, having walked silently across the fields.

My mind sought to create form where there were none. Instead of the rolling mist, I demanded to see monstrous shapes of horned beasts with wild, red eyes looming from the depths. I twitched, flicking my aim wherever I supposed they would be. I tried to remember the exact layout of the land around me and aim the weapon to where I supposed the entrance gateway must be, but it could have been metres to the left or right. So there I stayed while Jess ferreted about behind me, dropping splatting dollops of horseshit that nearly sent me into apoplexy.

It was the noise of her defecating that eventually prompted me to turn and face her, and in so doing, I observed that, although she was watchful and alert, she was now not showing signs of concern or anxiety.

If something were to come towards us, she would hear it or smell it, and in her heightened senses I must place my trust, or I shall become a nervous wreck within a day or so.

I found some rope and looped a loose collar round her neck and fastened the other end to my wrist. Being tethered in such a manner meant I could sleep easy, knowing I would either be jerked by her head flicking up or dragged along if she gave flight.

As I drifted off, I did hope she did not choose to enjoy a midnight gallop.

The morning came as mornings do, and I awoke with Jess first blasting my face with warm horse breath. After not getting the reaction she so desired, I was prodded, pushed, and finally bit on the shoulder. On seeing me awake, she then decided I needed a walk and proceeded to toddle off towards the door while I got jerked by the tether.

The fog was still as thick as the previous evening but seemingly denser or perhaps thicker.

We knew that weather changes would happen, but without real data, we were unable to predict exactly what those changes would be. The only like-event ever to take place was the extinction of the dinosaurs, but without finding a way to go back and ask them what happened, we had no real way of knowing for sure.

. . .

Predictions were made as to the expected changes as a result of the cessation of humankind and our species' immediate impact on the planet, and the storm at the two-week mark was, although a lot stronger than we thought, was not without some sense of expectation.

The thought of setting out in this fog is, frankly, quite terrifying. I know the direction to take, and I have maps, a compass, and can navigate the route, but we will be walking into the unknown without any idea of what lies immediately ahead of us and solely reliant on Jess's sense of hearing and smell.

Thinking back to those days within the complex, it now seems like a lifetime ago. The sheer wonder of having the greatest of minds together in the same room and access to unrestricted data was something none of us had ever envisaged before.

Panacea. Even saying the word now sends shivers down my spine. The ability to end all suffering. All diseases and all illnesses cured, and propel our species to that next step on the long road towards immortality.

We knew alright. Oh, we knew this was something beyond mere hypotheses. To gather the greatest of professionals and experts in one place, regardless of country of origin or political affiliation–and to enter a research programme to determine the cause and effects of a "hypothetical" scenario???

No. We knew. All of us knew they had something real.

. . .

Where did the finance come from? Who paid for us? And how did they get access to all the restricted data? Our primary objective was one thing, but the secondary principles we established were ground-breaking.

We were the first group in the history of humankind to correctly calculate the population of the planet, and further, we were able to break those populaces down into age ranges, gender, and then further into a matrix that determined health, education, and ability to survive in differing scenarios.

We were the first group that went beyond the use of mere statistics to correctly calculate the projected annual population increases. We knew what effects the introductions of certain diseases would have in certain areas. To release the Influenza virus in one place would have the same fatally catastrophic effect that, say, the release of Smallpox would have somewhere else. More than that, we knew how differing strains of viruses would have differing effects within populaces that held either natural antibodies or had access to First World medical facilities.

We compiled the first fully accredited list of the stockpiles held by each and every country. Be that food, weapons, or medicines. Surprisingly, the First World countries all topped with weapons but not food or medicines. It was the devel-

oping nations that were paying attention to their evolution and economy that held the best balance.

Enough for now. My mind is finding ways to delay the inevitable, and we must now venture into the fog to continue our search.

Today is Emma Ford. Emma is twenty-five years old and works as a shop assistant in her local town. She has a boyfriend called James who is a local mechanic. An ordinary person of no special concern.

Apart from being immune to the virus, that is.

NB

CHAPTER NINE

'Slow down,' a voice winces in the darkness, 'my fucking leg is broke ... Derek ... Derek?'

'What?'

'Fucking slow down.'

'And wait for that lunatic?' Derek whispers hoarsely. 'No way.'

'They got him down,' another voice speaks out too loudly, and the others shush and wave for him to be quiet. Panic ripples through them as they flee the munitions factory into the dark night, fleeing from the deranged man. Shushing each other, they gasp in pain from the broken limbs wrought by a deranged Howie battering anyone close enough to strike. Noses that gushed with blood now drip silent as the blood congeals. Fingers snapped out of sockets are held steady as tears of fear stream down the faces of men, women, and children.

Derek and the men gathered round the intercom, listened as Howie demanded bullets be brought out. That they wanted a fair exchange of trade in return was a perfectly acceptable situation to them. After all, they were in what they thought was one of the most secure buildings in the country.

The munitions factory boasted state of the art security and permanent on-site armed personnel. The walls were re-enforced with steel bars. The windows were toughened to withstand explosive detonation. There was simply no way of getting in.

Or so they thought. The over-reliance on a nation running as it should. They had been relying on the fact that any attack coming would be withstood by those security measures and buy time for the authorities to scramble and counter that attack. The confidence that they were secure was falsely given as, without the authorities responding, they had but time to wait until Howie repeatedly rammed the Saxon into the re-enforced wall.

Over ten tonnes of generated energy against an immovable object. Friction. Speed. Power to weight ratio. And a dangerous man descending into a state of mind that meant he would never stop. Each impact shuddered through the walls. Each impact sent shockwaves of dispersed energy under their feet, and their terror grew as the brickwork and plaster gave way and finally the steel bars were bent, screeching and straining until the snapped.

A hole was formed, and through that hole, there came a nightmare of the darkest, longest nights. A man torn and bloodied with dark eyes that blazed with fury.

The men inside could have repelled that attack. Howie was one, and they were many, but the pure wildness that Howie brought cowered them back.

Panic exploded as more came through that hole. Men and women who knew how to fight. Men and women now lean from fifteen days of solid combat. They screamed and shouted at those inside to stop, but the confusion was increased as they screamed and shouted at each other and at the one called Howie.

When they finally brought him under control, the damage was done, and no sooner had the violence abated, the occupants were surging through their building, gathering whatever they could carry to run out and into the dark night.

Now they are stretched out in a straggly line as they run, walk, and limp. Children cry and sob, women weep, and men grunt in pain. They send whispered shouts to *hurry up, slow down, stay together, don't bunch up, keep watch, but stay quiet.* Orders and commands conflict and only serve to exacerbate the confusion and panic.

Into the night they run. Desperate to be away from the factory and the rogue group of mercenaries who destroyed their safety.

Into the night and shadows of the countryside.

Away from the insurgents.

Away from the danger.

One race.

The infection is not driven nor relentless, in the way the ocean is not driven nor relentless. It simply is what it is.

The wind is not relentless. The sun is not driven. The moon has not ambition nor motivation.

The infection is not bound by the same paltry attempts humans make to apply emotion and reason to every process of life.

The infection must survive as the oceans must follow the pull of the moon.

Howie leads the growing resistance, and the weapons

they carry inflict sustainable losses now, but the resistance will reach a number that can inflict such losses that are not sustainable. The chain has to be broken, and the infection understands this.

Break the chain and take away their ability to inflict great losses. Take away the tools they use so well.

As the shared consciousness gathers greater hosts, so the memories and knowledge contained within those hosts are put to use. The munitions factory is explored through the architect's memories who drew the blueprint. The types of machinery and what they produce are understood by the engineers who built them.

Every round within that factory represents the loss of a host. Those rounds must be destroyed. Every bullet and every bomb must be rendered unusable.

The infection sends hosts towards the munitions factory. Hordes of silent infected, *bound by a discipline that means they do not whimper, gasp, cry or, make any utterances of noise, move stealthily through the countryside towards the fleeing group running from the objective.*

The infection hears them before the unmistakable stench of blood and fear rides the warm thermals of air that precedes the survivors.

As one, the horde ceases movement and remains still. The direction of the fleeing group is tracked and calculated. The horde break from the wide country path to slide silently into the undergrowth to the sides.

'Derek,' the voice rolls down the lane, 'for fuck's sake, slow down.'

Red, bloodshot eyes turn towards the noise, and the infected saliva glands pump infected drool into mouths, already preparing for the bite.

CHAPTER TEN

DAY THREE

Silence in the room. He breathes slow and easy, but forever alert and watchful. Any thoughts on his mind are masked by a face that shows no outward expression.

The index finger on his right hand slowly lifts from the handle of the ceramic mug, holds in the air, then drops down to tap silently back on the handle.

Gregori draws an inhalation of breath that fills and stretches his lungs, before being slowly released. He does it again, drawing breath in, but this time, pushes his stomach out to stretch the taut muscles. On exhalation, he contracts his lungs to push every last bit of air out through his mouth. Again. In through the nose–his stomach expands–out through his mouth.

It's a quick fix designed to flood the body with as much oxygen as possible. If Gregori had closed his eyes and re-opened them once the breathing exercise was complete, he would notice a sharper sense of vision and a greater clarity of view. He continues his breathing exercises until he hears the creak of bedsprings, followed by the thud of two small feet hitting the wooden floorboards above him.

A slight frown crosses his face, and Gregori's lips tighten. Why is he here? Why take care of the boy? Why?

There is no objective now. No mission to complete and no pickup point arranged. No safe house to hide away in before he can be covertly extracted and sent onto the next mission arranged by his Albanian mafia Bosses.

He looks round the old kitchen, at the plates and cups stacked up beside the sink. England was a strange country at the best of times, but here, surrounded by vast landscapes of countryside broken only by the squalor of ruined industrial cities and towns, those places were ruined well before this happened.

The toilet flushes, and he hears taps being twisted on, then off. The boy works unseen round the bathroom, going from toilet to sink to shower, and those actions alone make the hairs on the back of Gregori's neck stand up.

Children were small people. That was all. They were people who were smaller. Everyone was born, everyone had a childhood, and everyone became an adult, so there really was nothing special about them. It was the facts of life, and to Gregori, a target was a target. If he was instructed to kill just one, he killed that one. If he was told to kill many, then he killed many. If those many consisted of children, women, elderly, sick, infirm, or disabled, then he did it.

The boy was no threat to him. He could move silently from this chair, cross the floor, go up the stairs, into the bathroom, and emerge five seconds later, leaving the corpse of the boy behind him.

Only he couldn't do it. No, he could do it, except he

couldn't do it. He wanted to do it but ... what? What was that?

How did the boy know the things were going to howl like that? Gregori's hearing is exceptional, and he didn't hear a single sign of what was about to happen. How did the boy know the howling was going to end? How did the boy know they were coming? Why wasn't the boy gibbering with terror and fear? Why was the boy getting up in a strange house and going for a shower without any obvious signs of fear?

The plan had been to find a group of survivors and leave the boy with them. Gregori had also factored in that, by having a small child with him, he would appear less threatening. Those reasons were now gone. He'd found survivors last night, but instead of handing the boy over, he killed them and hid the bodies in the cellar.

He was going to head south and find a way back to Albania. Back to his people and the safety they would offer. No, not the safety *they* would offer as Gregori would be the one giving the safety. It was the order and structure of life he was going back for.

'Gregoreeeee?' the boy's singsong voice calls out into the silence of the old house. Footsteps thud on the stairs as the boy runs down to jump two-footed into the hallway. He spins and heads straight towards the back of the house and the kitchen.

'Gregoreee,' he grins wide, bursting into the room, claps his hands in excitement, 'Gregoreee.'

'What?'

'Guess what, Gregoreee.'

'What?' Gregori stares hard at the boy, once again trying to muster what he knows is his most terrifying glare, but it goes completely ignored.

'S-sunday! Sunday! Sunday, Gregoreee,' the boy skips and laughs up to the table. 'It's Sunday today, Gregoree.'

'What?' Gregori widens his bulging eyes and makes his lips pursed and thin in the pre-murder look he reserves for those marked for special treatment.

'Ha!' The boy laughs. 'Can I do it?' The boy makes his eyes wide but pushes his head forward too far. He stretches his lips out into a wide smile, thinking it's the same as Gregori.

'Did I do it?' he asks in a muffled voice, holding the pose.

'No.'

The mimic is forgotten as the boy jumps up and down on the spot, 'Sunday, Sunday, Sunday.' Clapping his hands, he takes the final step towards Gregori and grabs his big hand between his own, 'Sunday, Sunday, Sunday,' he sings and swings Gregori's left hand side to side.

'What Sunday?'

'Today is Sunday.'

'Sunday?'

'Sunday, Gregori.'

'Why is this good?'

'Happy Meal!'

'What?'

'We're gonna have a Happy Meal.'

'What is appymill?'

'Happy Meal! We have a Happy Meal on Sunday. Mummy always gets me a Happy Meal.'

'I not know this. No appymill.'

'Happy Meal!'

'You said this. I not know this. Not this thing. No.'

'You can have one too,' the boy gasps, as though this is the best idea he has ever had. 'Mummy always has coffee, but you can have a Happy Meal ... What one do you want, Gregori?'

'No. Not this appymill. Not do this. We go.'

'Fish fingers,' the boy holds one finger up, 'or ... or ... chicken McNuggets or ... fish fingers or ... burger ...'

'We go. You get ready.'

'Yay, we gonna get a Happy Meal ... me and Gregoreeeee.'

'Boy. I not do this. We not go this place appymill.'

'It's not a place,' the boy giggles. 'It's food!'

'Food? What food? Come. We go.' Gregori ushers the boy towards the front door, mindful that the heat will cause rapid decomposition of the corpses in the cellar, which, in turn, will stink the house out and attract unwanted attention.

'Fish fingers!' The boy states with a disdainful shake of his head, 'Gregoree ... Mummy said they're not really fishy fingers ...'

'Ssshhh, Boy. We quiet now.'

'Oh, they're not here,' he says lightly. 'They gone far, far away.'

'Who not here?' Gregoree pauses at the front door to glare down at the boy.

'*They're* not here. I've never seen a fish with fingers, and Mummy said they're not reeeaaalllly fish fingers, but then why are they called fish fingers? Do you like the chicken nuggets?'

'Boy,' Gregori snaps, 'how you know they are not here?'

'Because they've gone.'

'Where?'

'Far, far away.'

'How you know this?'

The boy's attention holds long enough to give Gregori a false sense of hope that he will explain how he knows the things are not here, but that attention soon wanes as he looks up brightly. 'Cheeseburger! You can have a cheeseburger.'

'Chisburger?' understanding finally dawns. 'Burger with chis?'

The boy nods quickly. 'Cheeseburger ... and you get a toy.'

'Toy? This is the quick food?'

'No,' the boy shakes his head sadly, 'sometimes the queue is soooo long and soooo boring, and Mummy says I got to stop fidgeting.'

'Come,' Gregori leads the way, feeling the comfort of the two pistols in his waistband but knowing they've each only got one full magazine each. Two new knives are taken from the kitchen to complete his arsenal of weapons that are now gripped and ready.

'But I like it when it's busy,' the boy chirps up, 'cos Mummy and me go to the car, and we eat in the car and listen to music.'

Gregori leads them down the path they ran up last night. Watchful as ever, he scans the grounds off to one side and the entrance that comes into view ahead.

'Do you know where it is?'

'What?' Gregori whispers.

'McDonalds!' the boy giggles.

'McDonalds? Appymill? Chisburger? I know this now. No.'

'We can find another one. Mummy said there are lots and lots of McDonalds all over the world.'

'No world. No McDonalds.'

'McDonalds didn't go anywhere,' the boy states knowingly.

'It go. Everything. It go, or it dead.' From the entrance lane, they emerge slowly into the street, with the *ugly man* peering left, right, ahead, and behind while listening, scanning, and sniffing the air.

'But the houses are here,' the boy points out.

'So? Houses not people. People die. Everyone dead.'

'McDonalds didn't die.'

'No people to make the chisburger.'

'Oh, that's alright,' the boy smiles. 'Mummy made burgers at home. You can make the burgers in McDonalds if you want to, Gregori. I don't mind.'

'I no make chisburgers,' Gregori stands upright to glare down at the boy again. 'I Gregori,' he says, tapping his own chest with the hilt of a knife. 'I kill. I ugly man. I no make chisburgers. I Gregori.'

'Silly billy,' the boy giggles, 'Mummy said *anyone* can make burgers or fish fingers...'

'Not Billy,' Gregori snaps, 'Gregori. I kill. No make chisburgers.'

'But it's Sunday,' the boy explains. 'We have to have a Happy Meal.'

'No Sunday,' Gregori stands his ground.

'Yes, it is,' the boy stands in front of him.

'No. Monday.'

'Yesterday was Saturday and today is Sunday because it is Monday, Tuesday, Wednesday, Thursday, Friday, Saturday, and Sunday ...'

'Wrong. Monday.'

'Sunday,' the boy's face flushes red.

'No appymill. No quick food. Quick food bad,' Gregori

prods the boy in the stomach. 'Fat. Bad fat. No quick food. No Chisburgers.'

'But,' the boy folds his arms, 'it's Sunday, and we always have a Happy Meal on Sunday.'

'Boy. Everyone dead. Look,' Gregori points round at the road and the few corpses dotted about, lying festering in the hot morning sun, 'dead. They die. No one make the chisburger. Come, we go.'

'No!'

'Boy,' Gregori hisses, 'we go. NOW!'

'No.'

'I go,' Gregori takes a step away. 'I go, and you stay.'

'Don't care,' the boy pouts.

'Good,' Gregori nods, 'I go.'

'Don't care.'

Gregori walks off, knowing the boy will chase after him. A knowing sense of predictability that the boy will not want to be alone. After a few steps, and he allows himself a rueful smile. A few more, his eyebrow twitches as he prepares for the sound of running feet. A few more steps, and the smile fades, but he doesn't turn to check–that would be weakness, and this is the game of life.

Gregori gauges the distance at fifty metres and growing. Sixty now, which, he knows, to a child must be like a mile. He keeps walking, and at the one-hundred-metre mark, he stops, spins, and draws breath to bellow for the boy to move. But seeing the boy standing still in his shorts, red shoes, and his little arms folded, he snaps the words off before they leave his mouth.

With blonde hair and tanned skin, the child could be in the Hollywood movies, but even from this distance, Gregori knows the boy will not budge. His face is set in stone; the little eyebrows down to form a fierce scowl.

'HAPPY MEAL,' the boy yells.

'NO.'

'HAPPY MEAL.'

'NO.'

The boy cocks his head to one side and half-turns before rotating back to face Gregori with a small smile on his face. 'Happy Meal?'

It's a question this time, a loaded one too by the sounds of it.

'NO.' Gregori folds his own arms, taking care not to cut himself with the knives held in his hands.

'FINE!' The boy lifts his folded arms a few inches and drops them down with a visible sign that he isn't budging.

Gregori does the same. A slight lift and a drop. The boy plants his feet wider. Gregori does the same.

Seconds tick by. There's no movement from either of them. The boy turns his head to the right, then back at Gregori, who swivels his eyes, trying to see what the boy keeps looking at.

The first one comes from the smashed-in doorway of a house. An adult female, obese in size, with long, dark hair and dressed in shorts that are way too tight. Rolls of fat hang over the waistband as she staggers slowly onto the road and shuffles round to face them.

Gregori's eyes narrow as he flicks back to the boy, who is watching him intently from across the distance. The boy doesn't turn or look but somehow knows that the woman was there, and she would be coming. Gregori holds position and, in turn, watches the boy and the woman. That she is obese is considered as the reason for the slow movement. They were fast last night, but then yesterday daytime they were slow too.

He looks up at the sky and considers the change in day to night having an effect on the speed of motion.

Behind the obese woman, another shuffles into view, then another from across the street. A door bangs open with a thud as an infected stumbles out onto the pavement. There's four now with eyes locked on the boy. He looks back to the boy to see him staring off to the other direction. Gregori looks to see a handful from that side. Four. No, five. All adults and all covered in dried blood.

He shows no reaction. Not a flicker of emotion as he watches the boy watching him. The things shuffle and stumble with stiff legs that seem unable to bend at the knees. Heads loll side to side as they walk in a tick-tock fashion towards Gregori and the boy.

Gregori feigns boredom and taps his foot as though killing time.

'HAPPY MEAL?' The boy shouts across.

Gregori inwardly winces and pauses before shouting back, 'NO.'

All eyes are on them, and the first sound of a drawn-out, grumbling groan comes from the things.

'THEY EAT YOU,' Gregori shouts, then instantly wishes he hadn't as even shouting that makes it seem like he's getting ready to barter.

'DON'T CARE,' the boy shrugs. 'HAPPY MEAL.'

'NO. THEY KILL YOU.'

'NO. YOU'LL KILL THEM. HAPPY MEAL!'

'NO APPYMILL.'

'FINE.'

'I NOT KILL THEM. THEY KILL YOU.'

'FINE. DON'T CARE. IWANTMYSUNDAYHAP-PYMEEAAAAALLLLL!' The veins in his neck bulge as they pump the blood into the boy's face, burning crimson from the effort of the screech.

'BOY ... COME,' Gregori shouts the command. 'COME,' he shouts louder. 'NOW!' He slaps his legs and even goes to whistle.

'IWANTMYSUNDAYHAPPYMEAAAAALLLL-LL.'

'NO APPYMILL. COME NOW, OR I GET YOU.'

The boy's face screws into the darkest, most malevolent look Gregori has ever seen. It's dark and brooding, with eyes fixed on the Albanian hitman. A switch is flicked, and Gregori strides towards the child. Neither of them pays the slightest heed to the infected shuffling ever closer as they continue in their battle of wills.

'I SAY NO,' a bellowing roar from Gregori.

'HAPPYMEAL,' the boy roars back.

'I COUNT THREE ... THREE, BOY ... YOU COME. I COUNT THREE,' Gregori tucks the knives away and holds out his right hand showing three extended fingers while the other jabs the air and points at the boy.

The boy doesn't reply but stares with eyes ablaze with rage.

'ONE,' Gregori strides forward on powerful legs and holds one finger up.

The boy's face grows darker still.

'TWO,' two fingers held up, and the distance is closed. The boy drops his folded arms to make tiny fists as he prepares for the fight.

'THREE,' Gregori is on him. Grabbing the boy's ear, he tries to twist it in the same way his own ear was twisted as a child. The boy flails and kicks, refusing to yield to the pain of a gripped ear. Gregori spins on the spot as the boy turns and kicks hard at his shins. Fists pummel his stomach, hips, and groin. One connects to the right, sending a shooting, sickening pain through Gregori's gut. He grunts and drops to his knees as the boy spots the new target and aims for the head.

Gregori reaches out to grab the back of the boy's shirt. In one swift motion, he drags the boy in, bends him double over his bent leg, and raises his right arm ready to deliver the first smack on the boy's backside.

A growl sounds as the first lunge comes in. A quick glance, and several are on them–teeth bared and hands clawed into talons. Wrapping an arm under the boy's stomach, he explodes back from the power of one leg and sends himself sliding back with the boy held safely to the front. Landing on his back, he's gained three feet before the infected turn and lunge after them.

'HAPPYMEALLLLL,' the boy squirms and fights without heed of the danger. A deft twist, right hand down, left arm wrapped round the boy, left foot sliding forward, and the Albanian is up in a perfect position to deliver a driving kick of the right foot into the stomach of the closest infected who folds double and staggers back into the next.

Gregori spins, and having already identified the next target, he lashes out with a fist into the face of the obese woman. The density of her absorbs the blow. She's got legs like tree trunks, and although her nose bursts open, she doesn't flinch or rock. After a quick adjustment of pace and position, a blade appears in Gregori's hand and whispers across her throat as the metal slices through the layers of skin, fat, and tissue of the neck.

'SUNDAYHAPPYMEALLLLL.'

With the knife in hand, the Albanian makes light work of the slow beasts. One-handed, with the squirming boy held tight in his other, his movements are neither rushed nor hurried but exactly where he needs to be with the most minimal of effort and expenditure of energy. The fresh kills seep and spurt blood onto the already hot surface of the road, and the air fills with the metallic tang of iron.

With the grunting infected slain, the only noise is that of the boy huffing audibly as he squirms to be released from Gregori's grip. After a final check round, he releases the child who drops, spins, and comes back for another attack with tight fists and hard feet raining blows into the now passive serial killer.

Gregori takes the pain without reaction. That most rare pulse of anger he felt just seconds ago is now entirely gone as he stares down dispassionately and takes care to hold the dripping blades away from the child. Life is not a precious gift to Gregori, and he has taken it so many times that the very act of killing is a job done by a professional without regard for the moral consequences. Yet he holds position and lets the boy beat him. He allows the fists and feet to pummel until the boy exhausts the pure fury pent up inside, and the crimson, flushed face sweats freely. The boy's arms drop, and he stands back with a heaving chest and eyes still brooding with flashes of temper.

'You finish now?'

The boy nods and looks up with not a flicker of apology but pure defiance in his eyes, 'It's Sunday,' the boy pants. 'I want my Happy Meal.'

Gregori stares round at the death surrounding them. The torn flesh lies so ripe and open, and the flies already settle to lay eggs within the warm, moist bodies. A corpse lies with intestines strewn behind like a string of glistening sausages. Red, bloodshot eyes glare lifelessly into the sky, and mouths, encrusted with blood, hang open as the deadly drool still drips out. He takes the sight in and looks back to the boy who stares up. Not round at the death, not at the corpses but up at Gregori. The boy pays no heed to them. The concept of death comes with age, but a child of this age should be screaming with terror at the sight.

The boy swallows once, blinks, and looks back up as though pained. 'Please,' he murmurs, 'please can we have a Happy Meal?'

Gregori lifts his eyebrows at the boy showing no sense of remorse or guilt or apology or worry or concern, apart from having the thing he wants.

'Yes,' the word comes out from Gregori before he realises it, 'yes, we do this.'

'Really? Can we? Really? Really, Gregoreeee?'

'Yes ... but ...' Gregori holds a hand out, then stops to stare at the dripping knife held there, 'but ... we need the rule. You no do this again,' he points round at the bodies.

'I didn't kill them,' the boy says innocently. 'You did it.'

'No. No shouting. No hitting.'

'Okay!'

'This I mean,' Gregori says. 'You make noise ... They come ... You die.'

'Noooo,' the boy laughs with delight, 'you're here, silly.'

'No. They come. You die.'

'No, no, no,' the boy sings and reaches out to take Gregori's hand, 'they can't kill me.'

'Off,' Gregori tugs his bloodied hand free before swapping it over with his non-bloodied hand. 'They kill you. You die.' He starts walking with the boy holding his hand. 'They bite. You die. They cut. You die.'

'No,' the boy laughs and skips, 'you're here, Gregoreeeee. They can't kill me.'

'I not always be here,' Gregori says firmly. 'I go toilet. I go sleep. I go away. They come ... You die.'

'Are you having fishes fingers, Gregoreee? Do they have fishes fingers in Albaniania.'

'Albania. No. You listen. I go. They come. You die.'

The boy giggles with a skip and swings the hand he grips so tightly. 'No, no, no ... You can have chicken nuggets if you like.'

'Chisburger.'

'You want a cheeseburger?'

'I eat chisburger.'

CHAPTER ELEVEN

'Is he alright?' Jagger asks as Lani heads back into the main room and walks over to the hole in the wall created by the Saxon.

'Blowers,' she calls quietly.

'What?' his voice sounds through, muted and strained.

'You okay out there?'

'Yeah, fine. How's the Boss?'

'Still the same,' she replies, raising her voice enough for everyone to hear, 'asleep, I think ... or ... yeah, just asleep.' She bites the word unconscious off before it spills from her mouth. Howie isn't asleep. You can be roused when you are asleep, and the prospect of him being unconscious is too worrying to contemplate. Being unconscious means you can't be woken up as something is wrong with you. It means your body or mind is fucked up and has shut down. Howie isn't fucked up. Howie doesn't get fucked up. Howie is just resting.

'He's sleeping,' she reaffirms. 'He'll be okay.'

'What if he isn't?' Nick says from the shadows behind

her. She turns to see his face flaring in light as he ignites the end of another cigarette.

'He is,' she replies quickly.

'We gotta get him back to the docs. We grab what we can and get the fuck out of here.'

'He just needs rest,' she repeats.

'I'm with Nick,' Blowers calls through the hole. 'We've got the Saxon. We fucking load up what we can and fuck off out of here. What if the Boss needs medical help?'

'Clarence will be back in a minute,' Lani says with a glance towards the end of the room. 'We'll ...'

'He's not asleep,' Roy's voice joins in the conversation as Lani winces at the blunt words. 'Sleeping people can be woken up. He's unconscious.'

'Lani?' Cookey calls through the hole. 'Is that true? Can't you wake him up?'

'Cookey, Mr Howie needs rest so ...'

'Yeah, but I heard you shouting at him,' Cookey blurts. 'Everyone was bloody shouting, and he didn't wake up ... so he's unconscious, which means something isn't right with him. We gotta get back ...'

'Cookey, calm down,' Lani says softly. 'He's not injured ... He didn't hit his head or anything so ...'

'How do you know he didn't?' Roy says, stepping closer to the gathering group. 'Head trauma can manifest in unusual or aggressive behaviour. He could have a blood clot for all we know.'

'Roy!' Lani hisses.

'Fuck,' Cookey exclaims, 'I'm coming through ... We're getting Mr Howie back right now.'

'Alex, just slow down,' Lani moves back as Cookey's head appears through the hole.

'He's got a fucking blood clot ... That shit kills people.'

'He doesn't have a blood clot,' she says softly.

'He might,' Roy says matter of fact.

'He doesn't have a bloody blood clot,' she snaps. 'He's exhausted ...'

'Yeah, but Roy knows shit like that,' Cookey grunts as he gets through. 'He's like the doc in our group ... so ... so like, if he says Mr Howie might have a clot, then we gotta get him back.'

'You've been fighting non-stop for what? Two weeks?' Roy asks.

'More than that,' Nick says dully, 'and we've all got hit, whacked, and fucked up ... but we all watch each other like fucking hawks, and Mr Howie hasn't had a big bang to the head.'

'What about the car park?' Cookey asks. 'He was out of sight and had that heart shoved in his gob ... He could have had the shit kicked out of him then ...'

'It doesn't take a big bang,' Roy keeps going as Lani stares daggers in the darkness. 'Any trauma to the head can cause that, and we've all seen him fight ... *The way he fights* ... The man is unstoppable ...'

'Exactly,' Lani grabs the opportunity. 'Mr Howie is different ... He doesn't get hurt or stop ... He keeps going and nothing ... nothing will stop him ...'

'But what I'm saying,' Roy steps closer, 'is that, when he gets in that zone, anything could happen, and he probably wouldn't notice it ...'

'Dave's always with him,' Nick says. 'Dave would see if the Boss got hurt.'

'The Boss has got hurt,' Cookey's voice rises in panic. 'You seen all those bruises and cuts on him? He doesn't feel pain like we do. He's got fucking bite marks all over him and–'

'Cookey,' Lani cuts him off.

'No, Lani ... Mr Howie takes more punishment than all of us put together ... He could get hit round the head with a house brick, and he'd keep going.'

'What?' Roy sneers. 'He's only human.'

'Say that again, you fucking prick,' Cookey snaps. 'Mr Howie is better than any one of us.'

'Calm down,' Roy groans. 'Howie is the same as the rest of us.'

'He fucking isn't,' Cookey's voice drops dangerously low, 'and it's *Mister Howie* ...'

'Roy,' Nick gets to his feet, 'I like you, but say another word like that, and I'll knock your fucking teeth out.'

'Grow up,' Roy snaps, 'listen to reason ... Howie ... okay, *Mr Howie* is a human being, and human beings are all subject to the same laws of science ... If he gets hit in the head, it hurts him like it would the rest of us.'

'No, you cunt,' Cookey takes a step towards the older man. 'Mr Howie isn't a human like the rest of us ... You weren't there, Roy. You didn't hear him in our heads that day.'

'The prayer?' Roy asks somewhat too lightly.

'Everyone heard it,' Nick says. 'Every person on that field heard it ... One man stood in the middle of thousands, and every man, woman, and fucking child heard it ... You telling me that every fucking human being can do that?'

'Well, no, but ... maybe ...'

'Maybe what? Maybe we all fucking imagined it? That it? Maybe we all had a shared fucking phenomenon? Thousands of people all fighting to stay alive and–'

'Okay, okay,' Roy waves them down, 'but that doesn't detract from the fact that, if Lani and Dave can't wake him up, then he must be hurt.'

'Where's Clarence?' Cookey heads off towards the rear exit doors. 'CLARENCE?' he shouts.

'Cookey,' Lani jogs after him, 'they're sorting the people out.'

'Fuck the people! Fucking cowards hiding in here,' Cookey's voice breaks with emotion concealed by a rising anger and panic. 'CLARENCE?'

'What?' Clarence strides through with Paula right behind him. 'What's happened?'

'Mr Howie's probably got a blood clot. We need to get him back.'

'Blood clot?' Clarence says.

'No, no, he hasn't,' Lani interjects. 'Roy said he could have a blood clot if he's asleep and not waking up.'

'Roy,' Paula says in a warning tone, 'what did you say?'

'Nothing,' the man replies, 'just that confusion, aggression, and changes in behaviour are all signs of head or brain trauma and that Mr Howie might have a blood clot.'

'Roy!' Paula snaps. 'You don't say things like that.'

'Why not? He might need medical attention.'

'He's just exhausted,' Lani stresses. 'Look what he's been through.'

'Fuck it,' Clarence mutters. 'He might be right. We should have thought of that.'

'Clarence,' Lani takes a breath. 'Howie does not have a blood clot. He is just–'

'None of us are doctors,' Clarence cuts her off, 'and Roy makes a good point.'

'Oh fuck,' Cookey reels on the spot, 'he's got a blood clot... Oh fuck ... oh fuck ...'

'Cookey!' Nick grabs him by the arm. 'He's fine, and Roy is bang out of order for saying that.'

'No, he's not,' Paula steps in. 'Yeah, Roy is too blunt, but he's also a complete hypochondriac, which means he's clued up on this sort of thing.'

'Hang on,' Lani says. 'You just said Roy shouldn't say things like that.'

'Yeah, but he might also be right, Lani,' Paula says. 'Howie changed today ... We all saw it. He could have a brain trauma and ...'

'Fuck's sake,' Nick growls, 'Mr Howie doesn't have a fucking brain injury.'

'Right, listen in,' Clarence booms. 'The other people here have legged it and ...'

'Eh? Legged it?' Jagger asks. 'Legged it where?'

'Just legged it,' Clarence shrugs, 'gone out the back door at the far end.'

'Seriously, bro?' Jagger clucks his tongue. 'S'fucked up, innit?'

'All of them?' Blowers asks. 'They all legged it?'

'That's what I said, isn't it?' Clarence snaps. 'So we get loaded and go ... Blowers, I want you to–'

'We going after them or what?' Mo Mo asks.

'No,' Clarence says with forced patience, 'we are not going after them. We are loading what we can and going ...'

'We should go after them,' Nick says. 'We can't leave 'em out there ... They won't last five minutes.'

'We are not going after them,' Clarence sounds each word out carefully. 'We are loading up and getting the Boss back to the fort.'

'Mr Howie would go after them,' Nick continues. 'You know he would. I'll go ...'

'I'll come,' Mo Mo adds quickly. 'Can't leave 'em alone, bruv.'

'Me too,' Blowers shouts through the hole.

'No,' Clarence says firmly, 'we're loading up and going.'

'Clarence, you can't leave people to die,' Nick says equally as firmly.

'We can, and we will ...'

'I didn't sign up for that,' Nick retorts. 'Mr Howie came after me when I got isolated, and you know he'd fucking go after them.'

'Don't swear at me, Nick,' Clarence shifts his gaze to look down at Nick.

'What? I always fucking swear so don't start that shit.'

'With the Boss down,' Clarence glares round, 'I give the orders ... and my order is that we load up and go.'

'Er,' Paula speaks out clearly, 'firstly, no one agreed that you take command, and secondly, we're all adults, and we all have valid opinions.'

'This isn't a fucking meeting for accountants,' Clarence growls. 'This is ...'

'I know what it is,' Paula snaps back.

'Guys,' Lani says quickly, 'get a grip. We can do both.'

'Both what?' Paula asks.

'Go after the people *and* load up *and* get Howie back to the fort.'

'I thought everyone had to call him *Mr Howie,*' Roy states.

'I think,' Lani says hotly, 'that, given the fact I'm his bloody girlfriend, I can call him Howie.'

'So I'll take Mo Mo and Blowers after the people, and you lot load up,' Nick stubs his smoke out and grinds the ember under his boot, 'Blowers, you coming through?'

'Yes, mate.'

'I said no,' Clarence's voice drops. 'We're loading up and going now.'

'And you can't go with just you three,' Lani says. 'You got to have Dave or Clarence with you.'

'Why?' Nick asks pointedly.

'You know why,' Lani replies.

'Dave won't leave the Boss,' Cookey says quietly. 'Clarence, you going?'

'No. Nobody is going. Blowers, I want you to take Nick, Cookey, Jagger, and Mo Mo down the end to sort out the ammunition we need. Roy, you and Lani head outside to see if you can find another vehicle, preferably a van or something big that we–'

Nick interrupts quickly, 'I can take Mo Mo and Blowers after the group. Cookey, Jagger, and Paula can sort the ammunition out, and Roy and Lani can find the transport.'

'Stop fucking interrupting me,' Clarence seethes, 'there is a chain of command and ...'

'We've all got voices, Clarence,' Paula cuts in, 'and we're *not* soldiers.'

'We bloody are,' the big man finally raises his voice. 'We are bloody soldiers, and we'll act like bloody soldiers and do as we are fucking told.'

'Say something?' Mo Mo cuts in with a surprisingly tactful tone to his voice. 'Mr Howie said, if he wasn't here, then Clarence and Dave were in charge. He said that to me and Jagger.'

'Swear down,' Jagger nods.

'So's, if he's out of it, then it's either Clarence or Dave, innit?' Mo Mo adds.

'Dave's out of it with the Boss,' Jagger says.

'So's it's Clarence,' Mo Mo shrugs. 'Like, I wanna go after them people cos, like, that's what Mr Howie would do, but ... but like Maddox always says we look after ourselves first ... so ... What I'm saying is that we do what Clarence says, you get me?'

'I get it,' Nick speaks before anyone else, 'but they'll die. We fucked up their safe place and made them leg it so ...'

'They shouldn't have been hiding here in the first place,' Cookey points out, 'and Mr Howie asked them to put the rounds outside, but they fucked us over, so it's their fault. Fuck it, we've got to get Mr Howie back to the fort in case he has a blood clot.'

'Why don't we vote on it?' Paula asks.

'VOTE?' Clarence booms. 'Soldiers don't vote.'

'Okay then, we vote on who is in charge, and all agree to do what that person says,' Paula says calmly, too calmly.

'I just said soldiers DON'T FUCKING VOTE,' Clarence explodes. 'We are a disciplined group, and we work with discipline. That means we get on with it. Blowers, take them down and get the ammunition sorted. Roy, outside with Lani ...'

'We should ask Dave,' Paula interjects. 'He was a soldier too.'

'Yes, but not that kind of soldier,' Clarence hisses.

'What kind of soldier was he, then?' she asks pointedly.

'He killed people.'

'That's what soldiers do.'

'No. Soldiers follow orders, and the very last thing is to kill people. Dave *just* killed people. That's all he did,' Clarence reaches up to rub the back of his neck.

'Dave?' Paula calls out. 'Can you hear me?'

'... Yes ...'

'What do you think we should do?'

'...'

'Dave?'

'Yes.'

'I said what do you think we should do?'

Dave sits on his haunches with one hand resting on

Howie's chest, feeling the rise and fall and the solid heartbeat within. In the darkness he remains, ever watchful, ever present, and never resting. One hand grips the pistol with the index finger held extended over the trigger guard.

'Dave, what do you think we should do?'

Dave doesn't reply but knows that he should. He knows Mr Howie would go after the people and do what it took to get them to safety. Mr Howie would give the orders, and everyone would respond instantly. The ammunition would be loaded, the guns made ready, guards and lookouts posted, and they'd be gone within a few hours. His eyes flick over to Meredith lying at Howie's feet. Her ears pricked and twitching at the rising sounds of the conversation in the main room.

Dave knows he could stand up and walk into that room and assume control within seconds. They'd all listen to him, even Clarence.

'You just going to ignore us then, Dave?' Paula snaps.

'Don't talk to Dave like that,' Cookey responds instantly.

Meredith twitches her ears with a soft whine coming from deep within. She lifts her head to look back at Dave, who is crouched down, one hand on Howie's chest and the other gripping his pistol.

CHAPTER TWELVE

'Lenski.'

'Mmmm.'

'You awake?'

'No.'

'I was thinking.'

'I not awake. Shush.'

'About Howie and the others being immune.'

'I not awake.' She stretches a hand from beneath the thin blanket and feels her way up Maddox's chest to his mouth, where she presses her fingers onto his lips.

'Howie is immune. Lani is immune,' Maddox moves his head to free his mouth from the pressing fingers, 'and Cookey is immune.'

'Fine. I awake now,' she groans and rolls over to face him. Blinking heavily, she props her head up on one hand and yawns. 'I hear you.' She taps the side of his head, 'In there ... you never do the switching off.'

'There's no way they'd make each other immune,' Maddox turns to stare at the sleepy Polish woman.

'No?'

'No way,' a tiny shake of the head. 'Lani was the first, wasn't she?'

'Urgh,' Lenski stretches, 'that is what they say, yes.'

'Lani was turned but went back to normal. Then Howie. Then Cookey.'

'Yes.'

'Howie and Lani could have kissed or had sex ... but Cookey?'

'Yes. They touch him,' she says softly, 'when he bit. They touch the place he was bit.'

'Yeah, I saw it, but ... you don't pass immunity like that.'

'No? Maybe it happen now? Maybe they do this.'

'Pass disease but ...' Maddox trails off. 'I need to see the doctors.' He sits up in one fluid movement.

'Are you sick?' she asks quickly as she sits up with a worried look.

'No.'

'Why you see doctors? It early. Doctors sleep now.'

'They were immune before this happened,' Maddox sits on the edge of the bed and twists his upper body round, 'Lani has a different immunity ... but Howie and Cookey were immune before this happened.'

'I, er ...' Lenski blinks again and shakes her head. 'I not know ...'

'They didn't share immunity,' Maddox explains in a rare show of talking more than one sentence at a time. 'They already had immunity.'

'Oh,' Lenski nods, still not quite sure she understands.

'If Howie, Cookey, and Lani are immune,' Maddox states, 'how are they together? Everyone else dies if they get bitten, but three people in the same group are immune.'

'Oh,' Lenski nods slowly, 'yes, we know this, they know this, the doctors–they know this. Everyone they know this.'

'It's bugging me,' Maddox sighs softly, 'really bugging me.'

'You not fix everyone,' she reaches out to touch his muscled shoulder. 'You young but old ... Everyone, they look to you ... You not fix everyone.'

'They look to you,' Maddox replies, 'and Howie when he's here.'

'Howie–yes,' she nods. 'Me–some. You they see the next Howie ... You and Howie.'

'Me and Howie,' Maddox repeats the words. 'Howie ... where did he live?'

'Howie? I not know this.'

'Lani? Cookey?'

'Lani is from the, er ... Isle of, er ...'

'Wight, Isle of Wight,' Maddox nods. 'Cookey was in the army, and Howie worked in a supermarket. So they didn't know each other. They had no connection. Not related.'

'Hmmm,' Lenski lets her fingertips glide slowly down his shoulder to the back of his arm holding his upper body still. She fingers the shape of the triceps muscles and round to his biceps, then down to the smooth skin on the inside of his elbow. Smiling coyly, she sighs and looks up to see him grinning, his white teeth showing clear in the gloomy, dark room. 'You see doctors now?' she asks.

'You said they're asleep.'

'They asleep,' she nods and reaches forward to loop her hands round his neck. 'All asleep.'

He lowers down back onto the bed and gently pulls the blanket away before tracing a soft path across her naked stomach.

'Maybe I'll wait ten minutes,' he grins.

'Ten minutes?' she arches an eyebrow at him. 'You do this twice, then?'

Laughing softly, he lowers down and allows the warmth of a woman to soften the hard edges of reality and the constant whirring of his mind.

CHAPTER THIRTEEN

'Dave ... Dave ... Get out there and tell them to go after the group ... DAVE!'

Why am I still here? I can hear them perfectly, the whole bloody squabbling lot of them. I can hear everything they say. Weird, ghostly voices float about in this shitty, broken, ruined, empty street I'm in.

I keep pacing up and down on the spot, wondering why I'm still here and haven't woken up yet.

'DAVE?' I shout into the grey skies way above my head. 'YOU TAKE NICK AND PAULA AND BRING THE OTHER GROUP BACK, GET BLOWERS AND CLARENCE SHIFTING THE AMMO AND ROY AND LANI TO FIND TRANSPORT WHILE EVERYONE ELSE KEEPS WATCH.'

Nothing.

'... Dave, what do you think we should do?' That's Paula's voice. Bollocks, I know Dave, and I know he won't bloody answer, the stubborn shit. He'll be sitting right next to me, no doubt, with either a knife or a gun in his hand or a knife between his teeth and a gun in his hand. Maybe a gun between his teeth and a knife in his hand?

'You just going to ignore us then, Dave?' I wince on the spot at the scathing tone of Paula, then listen to Cookey's quick rebuke before it once again descends into a bloody mess of arguing.

I swat my chest again and look down, as though something is pressing against it, but there's nothing there. And the bottoms of my legs feel hot too.

Am I unconscious? I'm definitely not asleep as I can't wake up, but I don't feel unconscious. I feel *very* conscious, in fact.

'STOP BLOODY ARGUING AND GET ON WITH IT,' I bellow at the sky. Roy is winding everyone up with this bluntness. Nick sticks to his principles, which is good, but he should also be doing what Clarence says, and Paula is treating the whole thing like it's a managers meeting. Cookey thinks my head is about to fall off with a blood clot, and Lani is desperately trying to convince herself I'm having a nice nap.

Mo Mo sounds very calm, though, for such a young lad. Maybe we've underestimated that one. Nodding to myself, I turn on the spot and sigh.

'This is shit,' I say glumly, 'really bloody shit.' The houses–or rather, what were the houses–are all in ruins. Like something from post war Britain or Berlin. Everything is scorched, busted, ruined, rusty and just generally all a bit fucked up and messy. How do you wake yourself up? Pain?

No, hang on, I ran into that wall in the tube when I found the old man and that bloody hurt, *and* it didn't wake me up. What else can I do?

I start jumping on the spot, trying to jig my body. Maybe an increase in heart rate will do it?

I start jogging, heading down the middle of the broken street at a steadily increasing pace until I'm pretty much running. This feels too real, even to the extent my eyes are blurring from the wind in them as I run.

Bloody hell I've got so much fitter now and can run for ages. Two weeks ago, I would have collapsed by now and be almost puking from the exertion. Mind you, Cookey does think I'm some superhero mega god, bless him.

I know they all heard me pray that day, and I have no bloody clue how that happened, or anything else, but I'm not anything special, and quite frankly, it's getting a wee bit annoying that everyone thinks I am.

Even that old man who died when I carried him out was saying how there was this group led by Howie that *could* have changed the world. Changed the world, my arse. A ragtag bunch of bloody misfits all thrown together and led by a twat Tesco night shift manager.

'Fuck!' I slow down to a stop and stare ahead. I know that place. A squat, brick building that looks intact with open ground all around it that leads into the countryside. That's the munitions factory. Fuck me.

I turn back to face up the street I just ran down. It's still the same shitty residential street, but when I turn to face forward, instead of more shitty residential streets, I can see the ground simply changes into the open land surrounding the munitions factory.

'DAVE?' I try again, screaming his name in the hope he'll hear me. I walk forward steadily, keeping a close eye as the building comes clearer into view and wince again at the sight of the busted-in reception area and the Saxon within it. I instantly feel a surge of guilt. What was I thinking?

'Sorry about that,' I whisper.

When I turn to look back at the street, it's not there

anymore. Just more open ground. Shaking my head, I head towards the building as the sky above me darkens quickly into night.

This is here. I mean, this is here and now. I'm inside that building now, and the team are in there now, and I'm outside ... now.

It's so real that even the steps of my boots on the roadway seem too loud, so I move quickly over to walk silently on the grass. The moon is high and bright, casting the squat building in a silvery shade.

I head down to the reception and spot Blowers leaning against the wall, next to the hole I made. A red light flares as he inhales on a cigarette, but he pays no attention to my boots scraping and crunching the debris underfoot as I trample through towards him. The Saxon looks huge inside this room, almost like a museum piece reflecting the carnage of war in the corporate world.

Mind you, this place made the bullets which made the wars, so fuck 'em. One trashed-up reception room is a small price to pay for all the lives they have taken.

Whoa, this is weird. I'm standing right next to Blowers as he leans against the wall and listens to the arguments within. His face looks strained, far more strained than I have ever seen him look. This lad is tough as old boots, as hard as they come, but he looks ready to cry right now and sucks on that smoke with trembling fingers.

I peer down through the hole into the main room, and after a few seconds, I start clambering through, then worry that one of the others will clamber through at the same time, which would mean we'd go through each other. That wouldn't be so bad if it was Lani but not one of the others.

I make noise and grunt with the effort, but not one of them even glances towards me, not even when I drop down on the inside and stand up while rubbing my hands together to rid the gritty dust.

Nick, as ever, is smoking. Cookey is smoking. Jagger is smoking. Mo Mo is leaning against the wall, and everyone is sort of stood round in a rough circle as they argue and bicker.

'... And the longer we stand here arguing, the longer it takes to get anything done,' Clarence says, seething. I can see it from here, but he also looks defeated too, in the same way the fight looks like it's gone out of Blowers outside.

'Why is Blowers out there, on his own?' I ask out loud, but of course, no one pays any attention. 'You should have two out there with Meredith keeping an ear on things.'

Nope. Still no reaction, so I move into the centre of the group and position myself so I can see everyone. Then I stamp my foot.

'OI,' I bellow as loud as I can.

'Clarence,' Paula places her hands on her hips, 'it's not an automatic right to take charge, and yeah, you were a soldier, but this isn't a war ... This is something no one has done before, so we've all got skills that matter now.'

That's a fair point. This isn't a war zone with generals and armies running about.

'But we still have to have a chain of command; otherwise, the whole thing turns into a pile of shit,' Clarence growls.

Fair point too. In a perfect world, everyone can sit down and agree everything way in advance. But this ain't a perfect world. This is the end of the world.

'Why are we still here?' Cookey groans. 'Mr Howie could be dying ... Please ... can we just get him back ...?'

Bless him. Cookey has a special place in all our hearts. Fuck it. He is the heart of this group, and any one of us would die for him. The lad is so open and so honest he has no idea of his own worth. He's sees himself as the joker and fool when he's so much more than that.

'He's not dying,' Lani repeats. 'He'll be fine in a bit. We can get loaded up, and then he'll probably just wake up.'

Her loyalty is unfaltering, but that sheer ferociousness of her character is crumbling away at the thought that, perhaps, I am not just resting and that something far more serious could be wrong. She falters and bites her bottom lip, and even in this gloomy light, I can see her blinking back the tears.

The big man rubs the back of his neck and glances over to the room where I lay protected by Dave. His face a mask of worry, confusion, pain, hurt, and loss. He can't hide his emotions either. 'We've got to the get the ammunition and get back,' he says again. 'The fort is full of people relying on us.'

The soldier. Strong and resilient, but now he too seems almost consumed with worry. He should be the one in charge–not *because* he was a soldier but because he will always be a soldier. That some of the others aren't doing as he says angers me.

I admire Paula immensely. She not only survived on her own but slaughtered a whole town of the bloody things in the process. She is tough, quick-thinking, and an amazing asset to our team, but she has to realise that not every idea she has is the best one, and she needs to listen.

'SHIT,' turning round, I spot Mo Mo standing but a few feet away and staring hard at me with his eyes fixed on mine. He's looking at me. Half-hidden in the shadows, but he's actually looking right at me.

'Mo Mo?' I call his name softly, my heart hammering in

my chest at the fright of seeing him staring at me. His head tilts slightly, and he goes to speak.

'Mo,' Jagger prods him in the side, 'you got any smokes, bruv?'

'Huh?' Mo Mo blinks and stares round as though snapping back to reality. 'What?'

'I said you got any smokes or what, bruv?'

'Smokes? Nah ... Nick's got 'em.'

'Mo Mo,' I call out louder this time and step towards him, 'Mo Mo, can you hear me?'

His head tilts again, and his eyes go slightly glassy as though unfocussed. 'Mo Mo! Can you hear me?'

He blinks and lifts his eyebrows. His soft, brown, Arabic complexion is so clear in this light now. He goes to say something, then shakes his head, and looks round at the others.

'MO MO,' I shout, 'LISTEN TO ME,' his gaze flicks back to the place I am stood–not at me but where I am.

'Mo Mo, tell them to get two outside with Meredith. Blowers should not be on his own.'

He opens his mouth as a look of intense worry crosses his face. He looks round at Jagger who is occupied getting a smoke from Nick; then, I watch as his eyes track round the rest of the group still bickering.

'MO MO,' I shout, and again, his head snaps to where I am. 'Blowers must not be left outside on his own. Two outside with the dog ... Tell them ...'

'Yous,' Mo Mo speaks, then clears his throat as everyone looks round at him.

'What?' Clarence asks bluntly.

'TELL THEM,' I roar, 'FUCKING TELL THEM TO GET TWO OUTSIDE WITH THE BLOODY DOG.'

'Two outside,' he snaps. 'Get Meredith outside. Blowers shouldn't be on his own.'

'Good lad,' I shout, 'now get some fucking energy into that voice and do it again ... like this ... JAGGER, OUTSIDE WITH BLOWERS AND KEEP THE DOG FACING OUT ...'

'Jagger,' Mo Mo turns quickly, 'get Meredith and get outside with Blowers. He shouldn't be on his own. Keep the dog facing out ...'

'We need her senses, Mo Mo,' I prompt him.

'She can hear things we can't,' he adds with a growing energy to his voice.

'Mo Mo?' Clarence asks gently.

'Tell him enough of this,' I snap.

'Enough,' Mo Mo states.

'And stand up straight ... Look people in the eye when you give orders,' I step closer and watch as the young lad stiffens to straighten his back, 'say it like you mean it but be polite. Politeness counts.'

He strides into the middle of the room and glares round at the shocked faces all looking at him. 'I want Clarence, Nick, Cookey, and Paula getting the ammunition stacked and ready to be loaded ...'

'Clarence,' Mo Mo spins to face up at the huge man, 'take Nick, Cookey, and Paula down to get the ammunition loaded ...'

'Our weapons are still empty, Mo Mo,' I move closer and speak clearly. 'They should be loaded with spare magazines at hand by now.'

'Why are our weapons not loaded?' he glares round at everyone. 'We've been here a long time and still have empty weapons? We should be loaded and ready by now.'

'GOOD LAD,' I roar, 'Roy and Lani, go find another vehicle ...'

'Roy,' Mo Mo spins to point at the shocked bowman, 'and Lani, we need another vehicle to carry the ammunition back ...'

'BUT,' I cut in, 'only after they've got fresh magazines and loaded weapons.'

'Get your weapons loaded first,' Mo Mo snaps.

'Shame on you,' I roar at the group.

'Shame on all of yous,' Mo Mo spins round with fire in his eyes.

'Bickering when there's work to be done.'

'Yous bickering when yous should be working,' Mo Mo fires the words out.

'Clarence is in charge.'

'Clarence is in charge,' Mo Mo points at him.

'He was a professional soldier and knows more than the rest of us about how to accomplish our task.'

'He knows this shit,' Mo Mo roars.

'We will find the people who ran off ...'

'Oh, we will go after those people that legged it,' Mo Mo grows taller with every word uttered.

'But after we've got loaded and ready.'

'But we get our shit done first.'

'Tell Cookey Howie is fine ... It's not a blood clot.'

'And the Boss,' Mo Mo faces Cookey, 'just needed a time out. He doesn't have a blood clot.'

'Er, Mo Mo,' Paula says slowly, about to start arguing with him. I grin as I spot Dave creep ever closer forward at hearing Mo Mo speaking.

'Do as he says,' Dave barks.

'No, listen,' Paula starts to speak but gets cut off by the low growl of Meredith now standing by the side of Mo Mo.

'YOU WILL FOLLOW THE ORDERS GIVEN,' the drill sergeant's voice booms round the room.

'Well done, Dave,' I grin.

'Well done, Dave,' Mo Mo booms. Everyone starts moving, apart from Dave and Clarence who both stare hard at Mo Mo. As one, they both turn to look at my body lying flat out in the room behind, then back to Mo Mo.

'Innit, blood?' Mo Mo grins with a slightly crazed expression on his face. 'Swear down.'

CHAPTER FOURTEEN

She draws a breath and works to keep any expression of frustration from her face. Only when she is sure her tone and manner will be completely neutral does she speak, and even then, she watches him carefully.

'James, I love being here with you. I really do ...' she nods emphatically. 'But ...' she stops mid-sentence when he turns to stare. He doesn't portray anger but a completely normal look of interest in the words she speaks, but the fact he turned is enough for her to choose each word carefully.

'Go on,' he nods for her to continue, 'but what?'

'Nothing,' she smiles.

'What? Say it,' he smiles back. 'You can talk to me. You know that.'

'Yeah, of course,' she nods again. 'I don't know what I was saying,' she shakes her head and gives a light laugh.

'You said,' he smiles gently, 'that you love being here with me but ... What was the but?'

Panic starts to rise that he smiles so gently and speaks so softly. His soft, blue eyes settle on her face, and she swallows nervously. 'I ... I mean ... You're hungry,' she looks up with a sudden idea, 'and I'm worried about you.'

'Worried? What for?'

'Because you're so hungry, and you're doing all the work and ... and you need to keep your strength up.'

'My strength is fine.'

'Oh god, I didn't mean that ... I just meant ...'

'What's wrong with my strength?'

'Nothing! James, nothing is wrong, but ... you're hardly eating anything and...and not now, god, not now but later ... like ... in days or weeks, then.'

'What's wrong with my strength?'

'James! Nothing,' she rushes towards him, sensing the atmosphere dropping through the floor. 'You're so strong and,' she puts her hands on his shoulders. She feels the hard bones and sinewy muscle. 'I mean, wow, James,' she squeezes his thin arms, 'you're *so* strong. Forget it,' she tries laughing again. 'I'm just being a worrier as ever.'

'Warrior? You want a warrior?'

'What? No! I said worrier ... I worry ... You know I worry about you.'

'Yeah right,' he says quietly, and her heart drops through her stomach at the way he says it. It's a quiet, muttered response, and his eyebrows lift up. She watches his blue eyes, and maybe it's just her perception, but they now seem more grey than blue.

'James,' she whispers and swallows again before casting her eyes round the spotless kitchen.

'A warrior,' his head tilts to one side, 'a warrior.'

'No, I said worrier ... I worry, James ...' she closes her eyes in resignation and knows it's already too late.

'So ...' he falters and stops, as though he is the victim. 'I'm not a warrior, then? Is that what you're saying?'

'No,' she whispers and keeps her eyes closed.

'Yeah,' he snorts a dry laugh, 'a mechanic isn't a warrior, is he?'

She stays silent now. Nothing she can say will make a difference to the outcome.

'It's not like I paid the rent, is it?' he says conversationally. 'Or put food on the table?'

She waits.

'You want to go with them, don't you?' he asks gently. 'Say it, tell me the truth. You want to go with them.'

She waits. Silently, she waits.

'Go on,' he urges, 'you know you can be honest with me.'

She doesn't reply but holds still.

'You want to go with them. Why?'

She wishes he would just do it. The waiting is harder than the inevitable action. The fear of thing is greater than the thing itself.

'Why?'

Like walking a tightrope. One wrong step, and you plummet. She can't show reaction or speak for fear her tone will be wrong.

'Tell me, Emma.'

She suppresses the wince when he uses her name. The build-up has started. This slow, gentle questioning as he seeks answers to questions that cannot be answered.

'I asked you a question.'

Even when his hand softly brushes against her cheek as it reaches round to gently cup the back of her neck, she shows no reaction. She can't allow the shudder to show, so she breathes instead. In and out she breathes.

'Emma,' his voice is that little bit firmer now, 'I asked

you a question.' The pressure of his hand on her neck increases by the tiniest increment.

'Why,' he sounds the words out, 'do you ...' She braces and prays the injuries won't be so bad this time. '... Want to go with them?'

The silence is heavy and loaded. A fizzing, bad energy seems to fill the room, and she knows that if she opens her eyes now, she'll see his steel cold eyes boring into hers, and he'll look that much paler than he did before and that much bigger too.

'Him?'

The word is spoken softly, but the impact of her forehead against the table is jarring, and for seconds, she sees stars behind her closed eyes. His hand holds her down. An act of power and control as he pins her upper body to the kitchen table.

'Him?' he asks softly again, and she dares not breathe.

'I asked you,' he lifts her head up and strikes it back down. Not hard, but a display of utter control that she is a plaything to be toyed with. 'Do you want to go with him?'

Him? She knows who he means. Brian. But to say that name will invoke a vicious beating.

'Is it?' he demands, still so softly.

The name is on the tip of her tongue. She wants to say it simply so the beating comes sooner and ends sooner. The hits and kicks she can take, for they give physical pain, but this, this precursor build-up of control, power, and domination is far worse. She bites it down and stays still.

'Brian? Have you seen him?'

'No,' she blurts.

'Eh?' he lifts her up by the fistful of hair he grabs. 'What?'

'No,' she shakes her head.

'Open your eyes.'

She screws them tightly closed.

'Open your eyes.'

She shakes her head. 'I haven't seen him. Stop. Please, James. Please stop.'

'Open your eyes,' the voice growls out now low and close.

Piss threatens to spill out when she opens her eyes and looks at him. That terrible expression etched on his face. The ginger hair now looks so much deeper in shade, and his skin so pale it makes the freckles that much darker. He believes that, by staring into her eyes, he can see the truth.

'Now, I'll ask you again. Have you seen him?'

'No,' she glares back, trying with every ounce of strength to convey a look of honesty.

'LIAR.'

And so it starts. The explosion of violence erupts in the spotless kitchen of the spotless house in the ruined street of the apocalypse.

As she sails through the air towards the sink, she almost gives thanks that she can at least shut her mind down now. He'll deliver the beating until he tires, and she can curl up and wait until the anger abates.

Her knees slam against the cupboard doors as she bends double. He's right there, grabbing the back of her head and forcing it down into the stainless-steel sink.

'Lying cunt,' twisting the tap on, he starts soaking her head, and again, she gives thanks that, at least with the power now gone, he can't use scalding hot water anymore.

'Wash you,' he hisses, 'wash those fucking lies out of you.'

She doesn't even like Brian. Yeah, Brian is big and handsome, but any sense of self was beaten out of her a long time ago, and there's no way Brian would ever look twice at her.

'Wash ... fucking wash ...' grabbing the bottle of washing-up liquid, he squirts it into her hair, then her face and forces the nozzle between her teeth.

She didn't leave the house either, so how would she see Brian? Or any of the other survivors? James went out foraging and locked all the doors.

She gags on the thick liquid and feels the chemical sting in her eyes, but that's just physical, and she can handle the physical, and as his fingers pry into her mouth to force her jaw open so he can rinse the lies away, she thinks of what life would be like living with the other survivors in the church hall.

James used to show restraint in the sense that facial injuries led to people asking questions and the police calling. So he learnt to strike the body where the bruises wouldn't show.

Now there are no police, so it doesn't matter if he hits her in the face. He hits her in the face.

On the floor, with the blood pouring from her nose, her mind turns to how she'll have to scrub the stains from the floor now; otherwise, he'll get angry again.

'Did you see him?' he drops down to sit crouched over her, his body weight pinning her down. Reaching up, he grips her wrists and pulls them high so she gets stretched out. 'Did you see him?' he glares down into her bloodied face.

'Brian?' Defiance flares, and that look of shock on his face as she utters the forbidden name is worth it. 'Brian?' she spits blood from her mouth and gags as a thick dollop hits the back of her throat.

'Emma!' he snaps as though hurt at what she said.

'You're going to beat me anyway,' she spits again, 'big man.' The defiance grows stronger as it surges up from her gut. 'Go on then, big man,' she urges, 'beat me.'

'You said his name,' James whines.

'Brian? I haven't seen Brian in months. I've never spoken to him, and I'M LOCKED IN,' she screams, 'SO HOW CAN I SEE ANYONE?'

The backhander stings and snaps her head to one side. She pants from the exertion of shouting and the adrenalin coursing through her system as she slowly turns back to stare up at him.

'What's got into you?' he sneers with distaste.

'Not you. That's for sure,' she hisses the words out in a scathing tone and watches as the look of hurt morphs into one of rage. As the blows start falling, she takes that nugget of pride that at least she got to him.

'Hello? Anyone there?'

James freezes with his fists held mid-strike as his girlfriend of five years lies unconscious between his legs. Her nose and jaw broken, and her left eye socket fractured. Blood lies deep around her head and spattered against the white tiles and beige linoleum floor.

'Hello?'

He looks down at Emma, then at his fists dripping red blood. His heart hammering in his chest.

'My name is Neal Barrett. I'm a scientist with the government. I urgently need to speak with Emma Ford. Is she here?'

The voice comes from the locked, bolted, and nailed front door. A man's voice, clear in inflection and tone. Well-spoken and clearly educated. The type of man that always used to make James feel so inadequate and stupid he'd add fifty pounds to their bill and make sure their cars failed the MOT just for the spite of it.

Is she dead? He peers down to watch her face, but the pulped mess gives nothing away.

'I thought I heard someone in there,' the voice calls again. 'Is anyone there? It's vitally important that I speak with Emma Ford.'

Oh shit. He looks around frantically, then remembers he was checking if she was still alive. He drops his head to her chest and presses an ear close. A heartbeat, slow and faint, but a heartbeat, nonetheless. Emma is alive.

'I say,' the voice calls out again, 'I'm from the government. We are working on the spread of the infection, and we have urgent need to speak with Emma Ford.'

Government? Shit. That meant the government was still running, which meant the country still had laws, which would mean they'd do him for beating her. No. They wouldn't put him on trial but summary execution and just shoot him or something.

Easing himself up, he peers round the edge of the open kitchen door, into the gloomy but spotless hallway and the barred front door. James moves down the hallway, into the lounge, and over to the curtained, barred windows.

'Hello? I think I can hear movement,' the polite voice calls out. 'Do not be alarmed, I am here to help.'

James eases the edge of the curtain back and winces as his fingers leave a crimson stain on the heavy cream material. Emma will have to scrub that out. With the thick planks nailed in, he angles for a gap to look through.

A horse is in the street. A big one too, with a saddle and leather bags hooked on. James moves over, desperately craning to see as a man steps back from the door and looks up at the front of the house.

James stares with wide eyes at the assault rifle ready. He's seen them on movies and television but never in real life, and it looks so brutal. Black and heavy, with a magazine jutting out the bottom. The man looks like he knows what to do with it by the way he holds it too. And a pistol on his belt! This man is armed to the teeth, with a fucking horse and calling for Emma by name.

'Emma Ford,' the man shouts, stares at the house, then turns to quickly view the street behind him. 'My name is Neal Barrett,' the man calls out again. 'I'm a scientist ...'

He doesn't look like a scientist, James thinks frantically. He looks like a soldier. He has a thick, brown beard and a high forehead, but he looks fit too, fit and strong. Panicking, James eases the curtain back gently and creeps away from the window and into the hallway. He freezes at the solid thumping on the barred door and the voice calling out again.

Staring hard at the front door, he backs into the kitchen, hardly daring to breath. He turns and again freezes at the empty, bloodstained spot where Emma was lying a few minutes ago. Turning quickly, he spots the flash of metal in her hand as the carving knife sinks deep into his gut. A hand lashes out, gripping her throat as she grunts from the effort of twisting the handle.

Pain sears through his mid-section as he feels a growing wetness spreading down his stomach and groin. Emma grips and turns as his hand squeezes to block the airflow to her already weak and dizzy brain. She falters and steps into him, pushing the blade an extra two inches deeper. She gasps as her legs give out. James gasps as the blade bites deep, and suddenly his legs don't work anymore either.

Down they sink. Entwined and killing each other as she

uses the final seconds of her life to twist the handle back the other way.

'I ...' she barely gets the word out, but his grip on her throat weakens.

'I ...' she looks up into those blue eyes and the palest of skin, now draining of colour, as his life blood seeps out through the ragged hole in his stomach.

'Emma,' blood oozes thick and fast from his mouth.

'I ...' she grins a macabre smile, 'fucked Brian.' Yes! She said it. She got the words out. They aren't true, but it doesn't matter. The victory in death is there as his eyes go wide with fear, loss, and hurt.

'Fucked him good ...' the last word chokes off as the final breath of air exhales from her lungs.

Tears prickle the wife-beaters eyes as everything starts turning dim. The edges of his vision blur, and the last thing he hears is the final hammering of Neal Barrett at the barred front door.

CHAPTER FIFTEEN

Day Sixteen

A quick entry, for I do not have time to make detailed notes after each event.

The address for Emma Ford was found quickly enough, but despite repeatedly knocking and calling out at the address, I could not elicit a response. However, I swear I had heard noises from within.

Consideration was given to forcing entry at the time of calling, and knowing what I know now, I wish I had taken that course of action. I must be more decisive in future and trust my instincts.

. . .

I faltered and became hesitant, and once that seed of doubt had taken root, I scuttled away while telling myself there could be anyone inside the address, including the infected. If Emma was there, then surely she would make herself known on hearing her name? I had considered greatly what to say on calling and decided I would announce myself as a scientist, which is truthful, and that I worked for the government, which is not truthful in so much as there is no known functioning government within this country.

On moving away from the address, Jess and I picked out a natural route through the outskirts of the small town towards the centre. It was during that short and somewhat tense journey that I began to notice signs of habitation and organisation.

Certain houses had red crosses spray-painted on the doors and windows. Clear, large, and distinct and obviously some kind of warning. Others had a blue cross. What these signs meant, I could not fathom. Red means danger, so I could only assume the red cross was a signal not to enter the address, but what did the blue cross mean?

With my senses becoming more alert, I then noticed that the main road had been littered with objects in a very careful manner. A vehicle on the right, then at a set distance another on the left and arranged in such a manner to obstruct the road.

This meant that I had to zigzag down the road, weaving through the vehicles. I further noted that the tyres had been punctured and, in some cases, the wheels removed, and the vehicles filled with heavy objects, such as house bricks and debris.

It occurred to me at that point that I was heading down a road designed for a dual purpose. First, anyone travelling at speed would have to slow down to navigate the obstacles, and second, anyone fleeing down this road would have solid objects of cover from which to fire from.

There were no corpses rotting in the street either, which was a first. It was highly apparent that someone or some persons had taken time and effort to clear them away and create this bi-functioning roadway.

Jess alerted me that we were being watched. Her heightened senses of hearing, sight, and general threat-perception told me there were people to the left and right. Her breathing changed, becoming somewhat faster, and her ears swivelled frantically, trying to find a source to noises she could hear, but I couldn't.

At such a slow walk, I simply put into practise what I had trained for by wedging the reins underside my right leg to hold them in place and riding by the strength of my legs only. This allowed me to bring the assault rifle to bear and held ready. The bolt was engaged, and the safety clicked off.

We stayed like this for several moments, and the tension within me was palpable. Jess maintained a solid course, weaving gently through the vehicles until I observed ahead that the road ended at a T-junction. Straight ahead of me was a high-spired church and a man standing in front of it, staring down the road at me.

I could see he was armed with a long-barrelled weapon, but I could also see that the weapon was lowered and not pointing at me. That told me two things. First, that he did not want me to see him as a direct threat, and second, that others were training weapons on me. As an overt sign of compliance, I simply lowered my assault rifle and held it away and pointed down in my right hand while I took up the reins in my left hand.

No sooner had my weapon lowered, and he raised a hand. I could not tell if this was in signal to me or to the others clearly watching me from covert positions.

'I mean you no harm,' I called out to the male and could see as he nodded in return and motioned me to come forward.

'I am Neal Barrett. I am a scientist,' this I shouted ahead and again watched him nod. I say I shouted this, for this is not a verbatim account but a representation of what was said.

The man made motion to lower his weapon even further and started coming forward. He told me his name was Brian and asked me the reason for my journey through the town. This was a point of great care as I did not know the intentions of this man, and this is something I had fretted about and worried greatly about during my planning phase.

To say I was from the government could elicit a dangerous response. They could be angered at the government for what had happened. They may kidnap me in the hope of a ransom. Even saying I was a scientist could be worrying as they may consider me skilled in the ways of this pandemic and demand that I do things beyond my means or capabilities.

In the end, it blurted out of my mouth that I was a scientist, and no sooner had I said it, and I was cursing myself inwardly.

I told him I was a relative of a girl called Emma Ford and that I was trying to find her. He asked me if it had anything to do with me being a scientist. I said no. He asked why did I say I was a scientist, then? I said so he did not think I was a threat to them. He then looked at the assault rifle and the pistol on my belt and said I did not look like a scientist and asked me where the weapons came from.

I said I was working on a routine research project for the Ministry of Defence when the outbreak commenced, and I had simply been fortunate enough to find these as I fled.

He didn't believe me. I could see it in his facial expression, and the silence between us grew until I really felt the need to say something to fill that gap.

Fortunately, Brian called out to some people behind him. Women and men then came into view, and amongst them, I saw a veritable collection of shotguns and single-shot rifles held by farmers.

I was told that Emma lived in the village with her partner James, and from these people, I gleaned that James had been seen several times since the outbreak commenced, foraging in houses for food and supplies, but that Emma had not been seen.

Brian said some of his group had spoken with James and urged him and Emma to join them at the church, particularly given that James was a mechanic and his skills were in demand. He refused.

I also gleaned that James was "heavy-handed" to Emma, in that he beat her regularly. This was worrying as I knew I had heard noises from within and now drew the thought process that perhaps Emma was being prevented from coming out to me.

I thanked them for their time and made motion to leave. On doing so, I asked what the red and blue crosses were for. The red crosses, as I predicted, signify a property considered dangerous, either by heavy blood loss of the infected, corpses stacked within, or dangerous structure due to damage sustained. The blue crosses represented a house that had been cleared of usable supplies and one that also had a fortified room within–such as a bedroom with a sturdy locking bar and bolts.

This simple meeting gave me hope that mankind will find ways through the very worst of times. What I also noticed was the haggard look of the group. They appeared thin, weathered, pale, and grey, and despite being several in number, it was clear they were surviving but not thriving.

. . .

On returning to Emma Ford's house, I left Jess secure a few doors down and made my way on foot to the back of the house. There I found the windows barred and secured and the back door fixed with several thick, wooden planks across it. However, on closer inspection, I observed the planks were only fastened to the door and not the wall. To any casual glance the door appeared secured and strong, but in reality, it was held in place by a single lock.

I did not knock but kept my resolve and quickly forced the door open, intent on finding Emma and possibly James and making them listen–even at gunpoint if the situation called for it.

I found them immediately. I say I found them, for I could not recognise Emma due to the disfigurement of her face from a vicious beating. Her nose, jaw, and eye socket were visibly broken. Blood was everywhere. There were old bruises on her arms and legs too.

She was holding the hilt of a large carving knife that was embedded in the stomach of a ginger-haired male I can only assume was James.

They were entwined in a murderous act of death in a kitchen that was once spotlessly clean but now dripped with blood.

My heart sank, for I knew within myself that I had heard the noises of the struggle while I was outside. If I had taken action quicker, I may have stood a chance at protecting her. But then, if I am to be painfully honest, I am not a brave man, and even the confrontation with Brian and his group has left me shaken and worried.

Jess and I are resting in a field to the side of the country lane that leads from Emma's town. Our, or rather, my nerves are frayed to the extent my bowels have been loosened and my stomach churns.

I will have a cup of soothing tea, then start again.

List entry for Emma Ford: Deceased.

Cause of Death: Suspected Homicide.

NB

CHAPTER SIXTEEN

'What can I do for you, young man?'

Maddox stiffens at the patronising tone of the bearded Doctor Heathcliff Stone.

'Maddox,' the younger Doctor Andrew Stone moves swiftly towards him. 'How are things?' he adds quickly, with a warning look at his husband.

'Good,' Maddox nods. 'My name is Maddox,' he says to Heathcliff, 'not young man.'

'Oh, come now,' Heathcliff rocks on his heels, 'it was a term of greeting and not something to be offended at.'

'Nevertheless,' Maddox slides effortlessly into slowly increasing cultured tones, 'I do not appreciate being called young man. I could withstand it, of course, but that would lead to ill feeling, so I feel it is better to inform you now that I wish to be called Maddox and not young man.'

'Oh,' Heathcliff blinks sharply.

'I have many younger people under my care,' Maddox continues with a stark contrast between his appearance and tone of voice, 'and many older people who look to me for guidance. Calling me young man denotes me of someone younger and in less of a position than others. It gives distinction to my age where there should be none.'

'Good god,' Heathcliff blinks.

'That's why he's in charge,' Andrew grins. 'I think you've told him,' he whispers audibly to Maddox. 'Come on, I'll make a cuppa.'

'Right,' Heathcliff nods, 'cup of tea, yes ... splendid idea.'

'Are the other two doctors here?' Maddox asks.

'Sleeping,' Andrew replies, 'they took the night shift.'

'Things okay?'

'Okay as they can be, given the circumstances,' Andrew sighs as he leads them into the back room set aside as an office, rest room, day room, and general storeroom.

'Looks cleaner,' Maddox stops at the door to peer round at the interior of the makeshift hospital. It's set deep within the walls of the fort, and there's no natural light, but the air smells clean, and there's not a trace of dirt to be seen.

'Scrubbed and scrubbed, and it will keep being scrubbed,' Heathcliff joins the conversation. 'I was a surgeon,' he adds, 'orthopaedics ... you know, hip and knee replacements, but I'm from the generation that insisted on the highest standards of hygiene when we still had ward matrons. Not one,' Heathcliff holds a finger up for emphasise, 'not one of my patients ever developed a hospital-based infection, and that is a record I intend to maintain.'

'Good,' Maddox nods, 'if you need help, speak to Lenski.'

'Er, the other girl has been organising it ... Lilly? Blonde girl, very pretty,' Andrew says while igniting the gas stove.

'Lilly,' Maddox nods. 'Lenski said she was doing well.'

'Well?' Andrew scoffs. 'Well is not the word. That

woman is a godsend, let me tell you that, and intelligent! My god, she's bright as a button.'

'Worth training?' Maddox asks.

'Ahead of you on that one,' Andrew laughs. 'Once we've settled down a bit, we will need to identify those that can undertake training. Anne was a training doctor, so she's pretty good at that kind of thing.'

'What am I good at?' Anne appears behind Maddox, yawning while casting a professional eye over the hospital, 'and you lot make enough noise to wake the dead.'

'Anne!' Andrew stares in horror.

'What? Oh, yeah,' she chuckles. 'Bad joke ... sorry,' she shrugs, no hint of apology in her voice.

'I need to speak to you,' Maddox cuts to the point, 'all of you. Is Lisa awake?'

'Lisa?' Anne calls down to the next room. 'Maddox wants a word.'

'Hang on,' Lisa's voice floats up. 'Yeah, what's up?' she rushes up the short corridor while pushing her arms into the white lab coat.

'It's not urgent ... No! No, it is urgent,' Maddox corrects himself. 'Everyone, come inside and close the door.' He is a teenage black male from the streets with no formal education, but Maddox commands an air of respect, and the four experienced doctors shuffle into the small room, close the door, and wait with interested expressions.

'Howie is immune,' Maddox says firmly. 'Cookey is immune. Lani is immune. You know that, right?'

'We do,' Andrew speaks first.

'There's no way they passed the immunity to each other,' Maddox states.

'Are you telling us or asking us?' Anne asks.

'I'm telling you,' Maddox replies in a tone that does not

invite a response. 'Howie and Lani could have kissed or had unprotected sex, but that would never be enough to pass whatever antibodies are needed to gain immunity. Lani turned. She became one of them but then came back,' Maddox explains and again holds the four doctors' interest with ease. 'Cookey was bit. I saw it. We all saw it. I saw the actual bite too,' Maddox adds. 'So there is no doubt he should have turned. I saw Howie and Lani cut their hands and press the cuts to Cookey's wound ...' Maddox imitates the slits they both made on their hands. 'But again, there is no way that would have passed the immunity.'

'It's very symbolic, and yes,' Lisa nods, 'it shows the closeness of that group but ...'

'But we don't know anything,' Anne cuts her off. 'This virus has no known rules. So until we have more knowledge ... anything is possible.'

'I accept that,' Maddox holds a hand out before they descend into a protracted medical discussion. 'But there is something else. I did not witness it,' he says clearly, looking each of them in the eye, 'but everyone has told me that there was a big fight here on the seventh day after the outbreak started ...'

'Again very symbolic,' Lisa mutters.

'And Howie was beaten down, properly beaten down,' the tone he projects piques their interest. 'Many saw it,' Maddox looks to each in turn. 'Then ...' he gives a tiny shrug of his shoulders, 'then he got back up and started reciting the Lord's Prayer.'

'Wow,' Anne blinks, 'who heard him?'

'That's the thing,' Maddox smiles like a wolf. 'Everyone did.'

'Pardon?' Andrew steps closer.

'Everyone,' Maddox repeats with a nod. 'I'm told that

every man and woman on that field heard those words. They heard the Lord's Prayer as Howie said it ... It turned the battle and–'

'No,' Anne cuts in with a firm shake of her head. 'Sorry,' she holds a hand up. 'I'm sure several people heard him, and it became one of those things whereby everyone wants to say they heard it.'

'Maybe,' Maddox shrugs again. 'Speak to the lads that were with him. Speak to Clarence ... You know him? The big one ... ex-paratrooper that served in nearly every conflict in the last fifteen years ... He heard it.'

'He was probably close enough to hear it.'

'In his head,' Maddox gives the slow wolf smile again and projects a cold, ruthless exterior that silences the four doctors. 'Clarence heard it in his head.'

'Right,' Lisa says slowly, 'in his head?'

'And there's more yet. Howie has this way about him ...'

'Way? What way?' Anne asks bluntly.

'I will tell you if you will allow me,' Maddox says politely, but his smile hangs past the point of comfort.

'Please,' Anne nods.

'The things, the infected people–whatever you want to call them–they are scared of him ... Do not interrupt me again,' he fixes Anne Carlton with a glare that immediately stems the words about to fall from her mouth. 'I have seen this. With my own eyes. He fights them like you could never imagine. We fought against thousands of them. We were so few in number, but we won, and the only reason we won was because of Howie and Dave. He ...' Maddox glances down, trying to find the right words, 'he just transforms into ... I don't know ... I don't know what to call it ... He moves so fast, faster than anyone I have ever seen, and they wilt back from him, and there's this power like ... like an energy that flows and ...'

Heathcliff clears his throat, 'There are accounts of famous military leaders that inspired their men to the greatest of victories against really terrible odds ...'

'Yes,' Maddox nods, 'Alexander the Great was such a man, but no, not like this. My point is this, and the task I have for you–'

'Task?' Anne scoffs. 'You don't task us.'

'Yes, I do,' Maddox cuts her off. 'Howie, Cookey, and Lani were always immune. We need to know if the rest of their group are also immune. I want to know who else within this fort has immunity. Then we need to understand how these people came together when so many millions had died. What is it that draws them together? Why are they different? I need you to work out a way of testing people for immunity ...'

'I beg your pardon?' Anne explodes. 'We're in a fucking old fort, hardly coping with basic triage and ...'

'You are doctors,' Maddox states. 'You have the knowledge and training to build on. You are the only known hope this country has right now, and you will do this.'

'Or what?' she glares at him. 'Is that a threat?'

'No. You'll know if I ever threaten you,' Maddox replies softly. 'Work together and find a functional test. Tell me if you need more equipment or supplies. This is the priority right now.'

'We'll do our best,' Andrew nods sincerely.

'What? With what? How?' Anne pushes her head forward as the veins in her neck stand proud. 'This isn't an episode of fucking CSI or a Hollywood movie. Have you any idea how much research and specialist knowledge goes into the most basic of understanding of viruses and retro viruses? We,' she motions to the other three with a frantic wave, 'are general doctors ... medical doctors ... We are not scientists.'

'On you,' Maddox nods to the four and quietly walks out of the room, 'and I'll expect a status update every twelve hours.' Closing the door behind him, he strides down the makeshift hospital and out into the early dawn with a mind that is already working on the next task at hand.

CHAPTER SEVENTEEN

Derek leads the group further down the path as the first prism of light heralds the new dawn. The path is bordered by dense thickets on both sides, and the verges are deep, with luscious ferns, grasses, and thick-stemmed plants, making a dog walkers dream.

There's not a sound ahead of them. Not a stirring in the rushes as the infected remain still. Silent drool drips from mouths crusted with scabs. Skin, drawn and beyond deathly pale, now mottled with deeper greys, and the veins within show through the thin skin. So organically deathly they are, but the red of their eyes splashes colour like the hint of poppies within the greenery of the country path.

The escaping group breathe hard and grunt as broken limbs repeatedly strike the ground. Grown men weep audibly at the pain of having to run with such injuries. Women cry at the pain their husbands are in, and children whimper at the confusion harried rush from the place they thought was safe.

'Right,' Derek turns to face the group and drops his mouth at the sight before him. Men and women red-faced, and others so pale they look like they'll pass out any second. Blood drips freely from wounds, not given time to clot. His heart sinks at the view, and although he knows they need to keep going, he also knows that, without a break, they will start dropping to die where they stand.

'Everyone, take a break.' No sooner are the words from his mouth, and those that can fall without pain do so instantly. Those with injuries are helped down to the ground, and the groans, winces, and yelps of pain echo down the almost enclosed path.

'Piss,' a gruff-voiced man brushes past Derek and heads to the side, already pulling the zipper down on his jeans.

'Good idea,' Derek mutters to himself and walks over to join him. Other men spot the action and join in.

'What about us?' a woman asks.

'Go the other side,' Derek replies as he releases his penis to aim deep into the ferns and deep ditch hidden from view.

Jets of piss start streaming out as the men shuffle feet and grown from the agony of having to run so far after sixteen days of relative inaction.

Stage fright hits Derek, and suddenly the thought of pissing in front of other men stems his urgent need to go. He closes his eyes and takes a breath, willing his bladder to just open and let the gush out, and when it finally does come, he gives a small sigh of satisfaction. His piss arcs out and down, splattering the broad-leafed plants, but the noise is too weird, so he adjusts aim and points the jet through the gaps where it rains down on the greasy, grey hair of an infected. The piss rolls down the filthy, long strands to pour over the grey forehead and into the red, bloodshot eyes. A black tongue darts out to lick at the urine and the taste of human it brings, and suddenly the restraint cannot be held.

As one, the infected rise to surge from the ditch and up,

towards the standing men and the squatting women. Shock hits. Silent, stunned terror ripples down the line.

A woman screams. Several women scream. Men scream and children scream until the lane is a cacophony of sounds tearing the air apart.

The surging mouths are open, and the teeth bared as they sink into the closest flesh they can find, and several men find their cocks bitten clean off as the infected sink deep into their groins. The bare backsides of the women are chomped, and in fear they break away from the sides, into the main group in the middle. People trip over the injured, who scream in pain as broken limbs are kicked and trampled.

The infected surge ever on from the ditches and into the group. It's a pulsing, ragged attack as the deadly, diseased mouths bite and the clawed hands rake open the skin of the living. With each bite and cut, the infection is passed and storms through the veins as it resumes the battle within the new hosts' bodies.

Hearts pump strong and fast in panic and only serve to increase the speed in which the infection is delivered to every organ and cell within the body. The survivors flail, fight, and some try to flee, but the infection works faster than they can ever imagine. The first goes down with a sickening pain to the stomach that has them dropping to bend double. Others follow, and one by one, the thumps and groans spread down through the group as they topple and gasp from the agony.

The first goes still. Derek clutches his stomach as the pain cramps with agony he has never experienced before. On the floor, he writhes as his vision blurs until it darkens, and the screams of the dying from all around him are blotted out as his heart ceases function, and his brain dies.

So fast was the attack that for one minute there is nothing other than the infected standing drooling amongst the dead bodies. Low growls, hisses, and snarls start to echo up and down. Then the first twitches happen, followed closely by the next and another after that. Electric currents passed through muscles that spasm back to life as the infection restarts the heart in the true state of living.

Brains are accessed, and any thoughts, other than the sole desire of the infection, are quelled and suppressed. The whites of the eyes of the freshly dead bloom with blood as the visible tell of the infection takes over. Saliva is produced, thicker than before, copious in amount and laden with the deadly virus. Fleshy hands that just seconds before were soft and flaccid now curl as the tendons lock the claws into the place. Eyes snap open. Heads roll as mouths open and snap shut. Slowly they rise to their feet and gone are the uncontrolled infected of the beginning when they would stagger on stiff legs and spasm with uncontrolled bursts of energy sent into muscles foreign to the infection.

These infected are understood, and the infection is now experienced. The infection has them standing as one. Without motion. Without movement. Eyes fixed and open. Drool forming to drip.

There. The infection rifles through the recent memories of the reactivated brains, and hundreds of heads snap to the side as the infected stare down the lane, towards the munitions factory.

There. Howie. Dave. Clarence. Blowers. Lani. Cookey. Nick. Paula. Roy. Jagger. Mohammed.

There. They are there. Those that defy are within the munitions factory. Those that refuse to die are here.

The infection is within every brain, and the decisions are collective as the hive mind sorts through the knowledge of the newly taken hosts. Within seconds, it knows the inside of the munitions factory, the layout, the exits, where the stairs are, the ruined reception area, and the hole leading in.

It feels, hears, and sees the memories of those that cowered inside as a raging Howie broke through the supposedly reinforced wall.

The infection examines those memories without mind or conscious. Howie is raging. Howie is broken and dangerous. He attacked innocents and was taken down by Dave. The infection hears the screams of Howie as he battered the Saxon back and forth. It watches from many points of view as Howie first appeared grinning through the hole. A different Howie. A broken Howie. A Howie pushed to breaking point, and he lies unconscious and prone within a side room as the group falter and panic without their leader.

Bullets. Rounds. Shots. The factory made the bullets, and within those walls are millions of bullets. Enough bullets to stem the tide of the infections desire for one race.

One race.

Bullets.

Without Howie, the group are leaderless but still dangerous. With their leader down, they will fight harder than before to protect him, and the infection knows that Howie commands greater love than any man alive now.

They will fight, but without the heart of their group, their strength will diminish. The small one, Dave, will stay by Howie's side and only fight if Howie is threatened. But they have millions of bullets and the weapons to fire at them with.

The infection desires a frontal charge with a growing urge to attack and end this now, but the infection also knows this has failed time and again.

As one, the infected snap their heads back to face the other direction, towards the town from whence they came. As one, they start running towards they town. Broken legs no longer give pain. Broken limbs do not cause an issue now, and those wounds that bled freely now clot to congeal the flow.

Drumming feet sound along the earthen path as the infection sends them down the country lane, and as the sun lifts free of the horizon, so the first break free from the path and into the streets and houses.

Fine motor skills are easy for one infected, but with so many, the infection cannot control those fine skills. As one, the hosts *could* drop down to tie their shoelaces, but only if they all did the same motions at the same time. The infection knows there is a balance between maintaining complete control and having a basic tool to work with and drawing back to allow a greater conscious entity within each host. That balance is yet to be found, but the infection works and practises with every minute of every day.

Cars' windows are smashed as dead arms reach through to drop handbrakes. It takes time, but the vehicles are shunted and pushed onto the main road leading to the munitions factory.

The infection then holds the hosts still and silent as it works with the least injured of the newly taken hosts.

Derek stares at the car in front of him, then walks quickly to the rear quarter panel where he levers the fuel cap open and turns the plastic cap within. He grabs his shirt, rips it from his flabby body, and shoves it, bit by bit, into the fuel cap. Then he draws it back out and lets it hang sodden with fuel down the side of the vehicle. Derek goes still.

Bob repeats the actions. Getting the fuel cap open before using his own clothing to form the wick.

Jennifer is next. Then fourteen-year-old Danielle. Fuel caps opened. Material soaked and primed. Jonathon does his; then, each goes still and obedient.

The infection sweeps an examining ripple through the newly taken hosts. One man moves to draw his lighter from his pocket. He thumbs the wheel, and a spark is made, but no fire. He tries again and this time holds the little, black lever down. A small flame is made. His spare hand makes a flat palm which is held low, over the flame until the skin blackens, burns, and finally blisters as the heat burns through the layers of epidermis.

One by one. Four more draw lighters, and one by one, those four ignite the flames. They each move to a vehicle. Five vehicles. Five bombs made. Five infected holding lighters.

The infection takes the many and sets them against the weight of the vehicles, which move instantly from the combined strength of so many.

The country path is too narrow, so the infection takes the main road and brings the motion up from a walk to a jog to a sprint as the five vehicles are swept towards the munitions factory.

The infection evolves.

One race.

CHAPTER EIGHTEEN

Day Three

A killer of men. A killer of women and children. A killer with no compassion. Ruthless beyond compare. His name brought fear throughout the criminal underworld. His was a name synonymous with retribution. The *ugly man* meant the end. If the *ugly man* came for you, then it was already too late.

His hands have wrought death, and he views the human body as a surgeon would: a cut here bleeds out quickly, a bullet in the gut right here means a slow, painful death, and like a surgeon, he can remove organs from the still living and show it to them as they die.

He fears nothing. He is nothing. Void. Empty. A machine disguised as a human but with no emotions or sentiment attached.

'Gregoreeeeee,' the boy looks up at the pock-marked skin of the *ugly man*.

'Gregoreeee,' the boy says more urgently and tugs at the hand of the killer as he speaks.

'What?' Gregori scans. Always scanning. Always watching. Forever watchful. He knows the distance to the first hard cover and the time it would take to get there. He knows the exits and paths leading from the immediate vicinity and which vehicles would be easiest to take. His senses are always heightened.

'Need a wee-wee.'

'What?' he glances down with irritation. 'We?'

'Uh-huh,' the boy nods, 'need a wee-wee.'

'What we-we? We here ... We go there,' Gregori points ahead. 'We find the chisburger.'

'I need a wee-wee.'

'What? What we? What is we?'

'Toilet!' the boy giggles.

'Toilet,' Gregori repeats the word and shrugs. 'Go then.'

'Where?'

'Anywhere. Go anywhere. I not care.'

'But,' the boy looks round with suspicion, 'where, though?'

'Here,' Gregori shrugs and scans the area. 'There,' he points to one side. 'Or there,' he points to the other side. 'I not care. Go toilet.'

'So I can wee-wee here?' the boy asks through narrowed eyes, as though this is not possible.

'We-we? What? Yes ... yes, go.'

'Right here?' the boy looks down at the pavement, then up at Gregori, then round at the road littered with bodies, pools of blood, the ever-present signs of carnage.

'Yes,' Gregori huffs his first ever huff and rolls his first ever roll of the eyes, 'go ... I not care ... Poop on the street,' he shrugs.

The boy bursts out laughing. 'You said poop,' he giggles.

'What?' Gregori sneers. 'Poop is not funny. Poop,' he repeats and looks down in distaste at the boy cracking up in fits of giggle. 'What?' he snaps. 'Poop ... is not funny ... poop, poop ... Is a word ... poop ...' he shrugs with each pronunciation, 'poop ...'

'Poop!' the boy wails with a face flushed from laughing. 'You said poop, Gregoreee.'

'Yes. I say this. You poop now,' he nods down at the boy.

'I don't need a poop,' the boy roars in delight. 'I need a wee-wee.'

'Piss?' Gregori asks. 'Wee-wee mean piss, yes?'

'Oh no!' The boy stares up with a look of pure delight on his face. 'You said a rude word.'

'What?' Gregori huffs his second ever huff. 'I not understand.'

'Mummy said that is a rude word.'

'What is this?'

'Don't look,' the boy suddenly turns round and bends slightly forward as the pressure on his bladder increases. 'Can I really wee-wee here?'

'Yes. Yes, you do the wee-wee and the piss and the poop ...' Gregori, already turned round on request of the boy, darts a quick look over his shoulder to see the boy shuddering with laughter as the jet of piss sprays everywhere, 'Poop and piss and poop,' Gregori shrugs. 'I not care.'

'I'm weeing in the street,' the boy laughs and leans back to aim higher. 'Ha-ha, I can wee in the street ... Can I wee on that dead man?'

'What? No!'

'Will he know I wee-weed on him?'

'No.'

'Then why can't I wee on him?' the boy gasps as he

stems the flow and hops forward to the corpse lying face down a few feet away.

'*I'm weeing on a dead man*' the boy singsongs as he resumes the urination on the head of the corpse.

'Boy. No,' Gregori snaps, 'not do this.'

'You said he was dead,' the boy half-turns to glance at Gregori, 'and you said dead are dead, and they are dead, and they ...'

'I know what I say but ...' Gregori pauses, trying to think of the right word in English. 'This not ... It not ...' he screws his face up, 'bad ... bad to piss on dead man.'

'Finished!' The boy announces. 'You can wee-wee on the dead man too if you want to, Gregoreeee,' the boy offers with genuine sincerity.

Gregori looks over at the wet puddle forming on the ground beneath the corpse and the dribbles across the tarmac. 'Come ...'

'We go,' the boy mimics a deep voice as he skips over to the Albanian. 'Come ... we go ...' he makes his voice deeper. 'When we will have the Happy Meal?'

'We find it,' Gregori replies instantly but doesn't know why he replies or why they are looking for the MacDonald's. He doesn't know why they don't take a car and head somewhere. Anywhere. Where? Why?

Where and why?

A prickling within him. A feeling he never experienced before. Uncertainty and hesitation. Go where? Why?

He is the *ugly man,* and he always knows what to do. Someone always tells him what to do, but then nobody ever tells him what to do. He is tasked and left to it, but the parameters outside the actual mission are very closely defined. He is collected from the airport or seaport. Delivered to the target, then collected from the target, and extracted to a safe house until delivery back to the port.

He stops in the street and stands staring ahead; then, just as quickly, he starts walking again. Where? Why?

'Are we there yet?'

Where? Why?

There is no mission now. His natural instinct is to head home for Albania, and he knows he could take the boy with him. But they'd kill the boy at the first display of temper or tantrum the boy shows. Children in Albania do not behave like that. Not ever. They get beaten until they stop, and if they die, they die.

He could leave the boy. He should leave the boy. He can't leave the boy.

He stops and stares; then, just as quickly, he starts walking again.

'Why we going so fast?' the boy asks. 'Can you see it? Pick me up.'

'No. I not see it. Shut up,' Gregori hisses.

'I want my Happy Meal.'

He drops down and grabs the front of the boy's t-shirt in a clenched fist, dragging the child to within an inch of his face. 'Shut up,' the gun is in his hand and pressed against the boy's temple before Gregori realises.

Where? Why?

'Shut up,' Gregori whispers again.

No mission. No objective. Freedom escalates past uncertainty towards fear. He examines the boy's face. The blue eyes framed by golden skin and the blonde mop of hair. A child. A tiny child with eyes that hold him rooted to the spot. There's defiance within them. A daring for him to pull the trigger. The boy shows no fear but simply leans left to look over Gregori's right shoulder. 'Up there.'

'What? Where?' Gregori stands and spins in one fluid motion.

'MacDonald's,' the boy groans, as though the answer is obvious. 'It's up there ... Mummy used to come here, and she went into that shop to look at the shoes, and she always said shoes first and Happy Meal second ... It was soooo boring,' the boy rolls his eyes.

'Come. We go,' Gregori grasps the boy's hand and tugs him along. Everyone is scared of him. Everyone fears the *ugly man*. Women scream. Men weep and children cower.

'Fishy fingers, fishy fingers, fishy fingerrrrrrsssssss,' the boy skips and sings while swinging Gregori's hand. 'And Gregoreeee is having a cheese burgerrrrrrr ... Come, we go,' the boy mimics the deep voice again, 'cheeseburger ... come ... we go ... I Gregori ... I shoot you ... Gregoreeee?'

'What?'

'Can I shoot the gun please, Gregori?'

'No.'

'But ...but ... please, Gregoreeee ... Just once ... please ... just once ... I promise I'll be good and everything ...'

'No.'

'Please, Gregoreeee ... I'll be good and quiet and ... and ... and ... please let me shoot the gun and make it go bang-bang.'

'You be quiet?'

'Yeah, soooo quiet ... like a mouse that is asleep cos the mummy mouse read him a story and gave him warm milk and ...'

'You'll be quiet? You promise this?'

'Yeah! I promise and double promise and ...'

'One bang ...'

'One bang ... just one bang ... I'll be quiet and ...'

'Okay,' Gregori stops and looks round. 'What? Shoot what? Window? You want break window?'

'A dead man,' the boy announces and earns a hard look.

'You shoot window.'

'A dead man.'

'No dead men. Window. Car. Look, you shoot car.'

'Dead man,' the boy says firmly.

'No. No shoot car ...Shoot window, shoot ...'

'Dead man,' the boy goes to fold his arms.

'Okay, okay,' Gregori says quickly, 'dead man. You shoot dead man.'

'In the head.'

'In the head? You want shoot dead man in the head?'

'Make his brains come out,' the boy nods, 'like you did.'

'You see this?' Gregori asks with raised eyebrows. 'You really do this?'

The boy nods and points further down the street, to the unmistakable mound of a body lying prone. 'That one.' He strides off with confidence, leaving Gregori to walk behind and watch as the boy gets to the body, stops, and turns back. 'His head came off already.'

'Shoot chest.'

'No. I want to make brains come out.'

'No head,' Gregori points down at the mangled body.

'What's that?'

'What?'

'That ... They look like sausages.'

'Er ... I not know the word ... inside here,' Gregori taps his own stomach. 'They in here.'

'Why did they fall out?'

'The stomach,' Gregori motions his own stomach, 'you cut here, and they come out.'

The boy watches Gregori make a slicing motion across

his own belly, then looks down at the body. 'Does your heart come out too?'

'Everything, it come out.'

'Can you put it back in? Can that man have his sausages and head back in?'

'No. They come out–you die. The head, it come off–you die. The heart ...'

'Gregoreee,' the boy cocks his head to one side, 'does the man be dead when the sausages come out?'

'I think ... You mean, you mean he see them? He see them, and then he dead?'

The boy nods.

'Yes,' Gregori says matter of fact, 'you show them to the man. He see them. Then he die.'

'And when his brains come out, can he see them too?'

'No. The heart you show ... Seconds ... one second ... two second ... three seconds, and he die ... The things in here,' Gregori taps the boy's stomach lightly. 'You show, and he die ... The brain–he die and no see.'

'Will the man always be dead?'

'Yes.'

'Mummy said you go to heaven, but the man is there,' the boy points down to the corpse.

'Not the body. The body is ...' Gregori frowns. 'The body is like car ... Yes, like car ... but inside is not the car ... Inside here,' Gregori taps his chest, 'is not ... I not know the word ... Soul? You hear this?'

'Mummy got soles for her shoes in that shop,' the boy points across the street.

'What?' Gregori glares over at the looted shoe shop.

'Mummy got her sole in the shoe shop.'

Gregori stares in fascination at the shoe shop, then round at this weird and strange land. 'Come ... we go.'

'But ... there's one,' the boy spots the feet poking out from behind a car and runs ahead giggling. He darts out of sight, then runs back laughing and waving at Gregori to hurry up.

'What?' Gregori looks to the boy and follows him round to see the infected turning slowly round on the spot. Both legs broken at the knee joints and splayed out from the mangled pelvis, but the thing groans at the anticipation of being so close to a fresh host.

'Can I shoot its head?' the boy jumps up and down with excitement.

Gregori watches the creature closely and waits until it has snaked round on its stomach. He takes in the red eyes, the drooling mouth, and the long hair that was once so pretty and blond.

'Woman,' Gregori states dully.

'Where is it?' The boy moves to Gregori's side and starts patting for the pistol.

'Here,' Gregori slides one out and holds it firmly in his hand. 'You listen?'

'Okay,' the boy nods eagerly.

'Do what I tell?'

'Okay,' he nods again.

'It heavy.' Gregori steps behind the boy and shifts it into the child's small hands. 'Use two ... like this ...' the Albanian manoeuvres the boy's hands to grip the pistol. 'I hold too.'

'No, let me.'

'Boy! It hurt you when it shoot. It hit you in nose.'

'Okay,' the boy goes silent and still as he lets Gregori move his hands into position.

'This,' Gregori tilts the gun to one side, showing the safety switch. 'This here ... gun not work. This now here ... gun work ... Not work ... work ... not work ... work ... Yes?'

'Okay.'

'Trigger,' Gregori gently shifts the boy's finger over the trigger, 'touch not heavy ... like this.' Gregori taps his finger lightly to show how little pressure he applies. The boy copies him.

'We go back,' Gregori walks the boy back and away from the oncoming infected now holding her mouth open as she prepares for the bite. 'Do not close eye,' Gregori whispers. 'Not movie, not one eye ... two eyes ... aim ...' he points the gun down at the head, 'but if you shoot, the bullet, it go through, and it come back up and shoot you ... no shoot down ...' Gregori moves the boy to the side and lowers the stance so they are aiming at the side of the head. 'Now the bullet go through and away, yes?'

'Okay,' the boys whispers.

'I say three–you shoot. One ... two ... three.'

The gun fires a solid shot that strikes the infected female in the side of her temple. A small hole forms as the bullet goes through the skull, but the back of the skull explodes in a pink mist of flying blood and brains that showers the road beyond.

'Brains!' the boy exclaims. 'Did you see the brains?'

'I see,' Gregori thumbs the safety and slides the pistol from the boy's hands, noticing the boy didn't flinch at the huge retort and nor did he brace so hard his arms were rigid. The child absorbed the retort, as though he had done it a hundred times.

'Make her sausages come out now,' the boy looks up and smiles at Gregori.

'No,' Gregori shakes his head, 'she dead. Dead is dead.'

'Aw, but I want to see her sausages.'

'Chisburger.'

'Fishyfingers!' The boy forgets the brains in an instant

and rushes after Gregori. Eyes up and watchful as he reverts to the base state of being. With no traffic or ambient sounds, the single retort of the pistol will have echoed for miles in this near silent landscape. It was a risk, but one calculated and stupidly taken. Things are changing. Gregori is changing. He would never risk a shot like that under any other circumstances, so why do it now?

The boy chatters non-stop. He talks breathing out and gets so excited he talks while breathing in. He swings Gregori's hand as he walks and skips. Nonsensical mutterings that Gregori only half understands from the language and age barriers between them.

Gregori has never had a cheeseburger. He has never eaten food in a MacDonald's. He eats food that provides nutrition and nothing else. Food is fuel and not for the delight of tasting or the enjoyment of gorging. Water hydrates. Food nourishes. Clothing protects. Exercise prepares the body. Constant vigilance keeps the mind sharp.

'THERE,' the boy skips ahead and dances on the spot at the sight of the golden arches fixed to the wall above the restaurant. 'Gregoreeee, there it is,' he points needlessly up the street.

'Boy,' Gregori stares at the child, 'quiet now. I listen ... You listen.'

'But ... but ...'

'Boy. You shoot head and see brains. Quiet.'

'Okay,' the boy swallows the excitement while shuffling impatiently from foot to foot.

'We go in,' Gregori points to the front of the restaurant, 'but we make sure no one here ... No one follow.' He turns slowly to view all sides. 'We listen ... sounds ... We use nose,'

Gregori makes a show of sniffing the air. 'We listen ... use ear ... use nose ... use eyes ...'

The boy turns slowly in a mimic of the big man. He stares at every house, entrance, car, and shop before tilting his head to sniff at the air.

'What hear?' Gregori cups his own ear.

The boy cups both his own ears, 'Nothing.'

'Hear nothing?'

'Birds!' the boy exclaims.

'Good. More?'

'Er ...' the boy slowly turns in a circle while pressing his hands behind his ears, 'nothing?' He looks up.

'Good. Nose? What your nose tell you?'

'Tell me?' the boy giggles softly.

'I smell,' Gregori sniffs the air, 'what? What I smell?'

The boy sniffs again, then again before his face changes with a sharp focus. 'Smoke?'

'Good,' Gregori whispers, 'smoke. I smell smoke. You smell smoke. What smoke?'

'I dunno,' the boy shrugs.

'What smoke come from?'

'Fire?'

'Good. If smoke, then fire. Where is fire?'

'I dunno,' the boy looks everywhere.

'Can you see fire?'

'No.'

'Is fire close?'

'No,' the boy completes the turn and looks up at Gregori.

'Fire somewhere,' Gregori motions the surrounding area, 'but not close ... We know this. We careful of this. If smoke get more in our nose, then fire get closer ... Fire makes you die.'

'Okay.'

'How many dead bodies?' Gregori asks the boy while holding eye contact. 'Here, this place–how many dead?'

'Um ...' the boy again turns slowly. 'One ...' he points to the one they shot. 'Two,' he points to the headless one further back. 'Three ... four ... five ... Five, Gregoreee.'

'Good,' Gregori nods. 'We know this–five,' he holds the fingers of one hand splayed out. 'We watch this ... We smell smoke, and we watch dead bodies ...'

'Why?'

'If body moves,' Gregori shrugs, 'it not dead. We eat chisburger and come out, and now there is six bodies ... Where number six come from? We come out, and four bodies. Where did body go? We know this, and we not be dead. We remember.' Gregori taps the side of his head, 'In here ... We watch ...' He holds two fingers towards his eyes. 'We listen,' he cups his ear. 'We use nose,' he sniffs. 'We remember,' he taps the side of his head again. 'We live and not be dead.'

'Okay.'

'You do this,' Gregori prompts the child and points to his own eyes, ears, nose and taps the side of his head.

'We watch,' the boy presses his fingertips against his closed eyes. 'We hear,' the boy cups the backs of his ears. 'We smell,' the boy shoves a finger up each nostril. 'We remember,' he finishes with a tap to the back of his skull.

'Good,' Gregori almost grins, which involves a twitch at the side of his mouth. 'Now,' he holds the boy's gaze, 'now we not be dead.'

'Fishy fingers now?' the boy asks softly but hopefully.

'No,' Gregori scowls, 'not fishyfingers ... chisburger.'

'No!' the boy laughs and pushes Gregori playfully. 'Not cheeseburger ... fishy fingers!'

Gregori leads the boy to the front of the restaurant and takes in the smashed plate glass window giving way to the chairs and tables lying scattered across the floor.

'Behind,' he pushes the boy behind him and steps over the window frame as he draws a knife from his waistband. 'We watch ... We hear ... use nose ... Remember,' Gregori threads a path through the strewn floor as they head to the counter. 'You play game? Game where hide and other child find?'

'Hide and seek?'

'Yes. This game. If play now. Where you hide?'

'Um ...' the boy looks round, then points to the door leading to the toilets, 'there.'

'Place you hide ... is place they hide,' Gregori first peers over the counter before heading towards the wooden swing door. 'Look place where you hide. Check place. Not be dead.' He leads the child into the corridor and checks the disabled men's and women's toilets, 'Is empty?'

'Yes,' the boy nods, 'but ...'

'What? Speak.'

'I could hide in the kitchen,' the boy says.

'Good,' Gregori says softly, 'this good. Very good. We check kitchen, yes?'

'Okay,' the boy heads towards the door.

'I go first,' grabbing the small shoulder, he eases the boy back, then heads out into the restaurant and through the gap at the end of the counter. 'Where we see?'

'There,' the boy points to a side office. Once cleared, Gregori lets the boy find anywhere a person could hide. Cupboards, fryers, shelves, and cubby holes.

'Is clear,' Gregori announces. 'No ...' he turns, 'food here ... Food kept cold ... Where this place?'

'What place, Gregoreeee?'

'Place food stay cold. Milk in this place.'

'The fridge?' the boy starts looking and finally points to a metallic door fitted into the far wall.

Gregori pulls the door open and sniffs the first release of air. Meat is held in here. Cheese. Vegetables, but the air is still cold, and above his head, a green LED light flashes.

'Power,' Gregori points to the light, 'they have way to make power.' He heads over to the griddle and searches for an on switch. This being MacDonald's, and with the high turnover of staff employed, everything was designed to be easy and fast, and the big switches marked "on/off" made it easy.

He goes round the room, activating everything he thinks they might need. 'Boy, you watch door.'

'Okay,' the boy turns to stare at the way they came in, 'I can't see.'

'You small,' Gregori hoists the boy up and carries him over to the countertop. 'You look out now.'

'Come ... we go,' the boy mimics the deep voice.

'You want go?' Gregori asks. 'Okay,' he says with a shrug, 'we go.'

'No,' the boy giggles, 'make Happy Meals, Gregoreee.'

'Okay, I make appymills,' Gregori turns back to the kitchen.

'Come ...' the boy affects the deep tone, 'we go ...'

'Okay,' Gregori turns back to the counter, 'we go.'

'No, no, no! Make Happy Meals.'

'I make appymills,' Gregori turns back.

'Come ...' the joke is repeated as the boy descends into fits of giggles as the knife-carrying *ugly man* turns first one way then the other.

'Enough,' Gregori snaps. 'I Gregori. I hungry. You watch. I make.'

Gregori has never cooked before. Everything was done and provided for him, and now, in this most foreign of places, he causes chaos and disarray as he works out what should be cooked and how it's cooked. Burgers are put in the deep fryer. Fish fingers are placed on the griddle where they get charred and burn. Fries are heaped on top of the burgers, but they cook too fast, and everything has to be turfed out onto the draining side. Smells fill the room as the heat rises from the machines.

He finds knives and spends minutes weighing each one and scowling at the blunt blades; then, more minutes are wasted as he finds a knife sharpener and brings each blade to the exact specification required by a killer.

He stares at lettuces and tomatoes, gherkins and seeded buns. Machines start bleeping. Food litters the floor, and several times, he winces at being splashed with hot oil or touching the griddle plate.

With the concentration of a man determined to succeed, he finds the flat-packed boxes for the Happy Meals and spends another ten minutes working out how to push them in from the corners so they pop into boxes. A magical thing that has his eyes going wide in surprise, so he makes more. Squeezing the corners and lifting his eyebrows as each new box is made. The boy said there was a toy. He hunts the kitchen and the side office until he finds a huge box full of the plastic-wrapped toys, ready to be dished out. He takes the box and pours the contents on the counter as the boy stares in delight.

'Find toy,' he mutters, then walks back to his glorious creations burning and sizzling.

The boy, left to his own devices, jumps down from the counter and drags a chair over to make a step to get back up. Then he heads into the kitchen and remembers watching the people take the cups from the tube and press them against the plastic lever to make the drinks come out.

He finds the cups and selects the biggest one; then, realising he can't reach the drinks dispenser, he goes out and drags another chair into the kitchen. Standing taller, he pulls a face as he tries to decide what to drink. He pushes the cup and makes Coca-Cola come out. Then he gets another cup and makes diet cola. Then Fanta and 7UP. He sips from each and smiles at the sugar-laden fizzy sensation in his mouth. He tries combinations of several, then all until his mind is racing from the influx of so much glucose.

With the sugar driving him on, he prods and presses the milkshake machine, but nothing happens. The lights are off, so he goes back to the counter and starts unwrapping the toys. Gregori makes a mess. The boy makes a mess, and if the health authority should visit now, the place would be condemned instantly.

Crunching glass underfoot, and the boy looks up to spot the lumbering infected trying to navigate the step up and over the windowsill. With a toy in hand, the boy frowns, 'Gregoreee.'

'What?'

'A dead man is here.'

'What man? Oh,' Gregori leans round to spot the infected, scowls, and grabs one of the newly sharpened knives. 'Don't move, boy,' he launches the knife through the air and nods in satisfaction as the body is slammed back from the blade driving deep through the right eye socket.

The boy stares dispassionately and goes back to

unwrapping the next toy, which he sorts into colours and places with the rest he's unwrapped.

'Another dead man,' the boy announces a few minutes later and stays still as the knife sails by to strike clean and true into the head.

'What toy do you want, Gregoreee?'

'No toy.'

'You can have a green one or a red one ... or a ... Another dead man, Gregoreee,' he pauses as the knife hits the head, 'or a yellow one ... Do you want a car?'

'Yes. Yes, I have car.'

'What colour car? Do you want a green one or a red one? Gregoreee ...?'

'Dead man?'

'Yes, Gregoreee.'

'I cook now,' Gregori huffs his third ever huff. 'I no time to kill,' he flicks the knife out and doesn't watch to see if it strikes home as he has just figured the burgers are cooked on the griddle and the fish fingers can be deep-fried. 'They come up.'

'Pardon?' the boy looks up politely.

'Fishy fingers, they come up ... They done–they come up ... Good,' Gregori watches the floating fish fingers sizzling in the oil and gives a scowl at the mound of wasted, burnt, and undercooked food stacked high on the drainer.

'Boy.'

'Yes, Gregoreee.'

'I thirsty. You have drink?'

'Hang on,' the boy ditches the latest toy and hops down to run over and clamber back up to the drinks dispenser, where he stares until deciding that Gregori is an adult and should have Coca-Cola.

He fills a large cup, then spills most of it down himself

and on the tiled floor as he heads deeper into the steaming kitchen.

Gregori takes the cup and a big swig. His eyes widen as he pulls the cup away to stare in horror. 'What this?'

'Coca-Cola.'

'You drink this?'

The boy nods, 'Fizzy pop.'

'No drink this,' Gregori shakes his head at the vile taste of so much sugar. 'No. No drink this. Water. Where water?'

It takes time, but the food is made and piled into the cardboard Happy Meal boxes. No wrappings or greaseproof paper but just lobbed in and piled up until the fries and fish fingers spill out over the rim, and the pair of them are sat on the counter, amidst a sea of Happy Meals toys arranged by colour.

They eat in near silence. Munching fries, fish fingers, and slightly burnt burgers covered in too much cheese and slurping drinks. Water for Gregori and a mixture of Coca-Cola, Fanta, and 7UP for the boy.

Several bodies lie outside the window, and each with the hilt of a knife poking out of its head.

The boy nudges Gregori in the side as another one shuffles into view. An old man wearing a striped pyjama top but no bottoms, and a deep, festering wound on his right thigh.

'How many?' the boy leans round to count the knives stacked to Gregori's side.

'Two,' Gregori grabs one, flicks it out, and watches as the body spins round and slumps down. 'One.'

'Okay.' The boy shoves another handful of fries in his mouth. 'Moffterfor,' he sprays fries out as he nudges Gregori at the next one.

They watch with interest as the infected woman trips and staggers over the already downed bodies before finally getting to the windowsill. She tries to step up but doesn't lift her leg high enough.

They eat fries and watch.

She tries again and again, each time staggering back a step as she fails to navigate the sill.

They slurp drinks and watch.

The woman changes tack and just walks forward so she falls through the window to land on a heap on the inside.

'She got in,' the boy remarks in a contented tone. 'Can I shoot her brains?'

Gregori thinks for a second, then shrugs, and pulls the pistol from his waistband, 'Remember?' He passes the gun over and shuffles closer to the boy.

'Um ... work ... not work?' the boy presses the safety switch.

'Other way.'

'Work ... not work?'

'Yes. Now gun shoot.'

Holding the pistol two-handed, the boy lifts it up and taps his finger gently on the trigger, 'Will it hurt my nose?'

'No,' Gregori puts his hand on the boy's back to stop him being sent back and off the counter, 'hold arms out.'

The boy stretches his arms out, 'Will the bullet hurt me?'

'No, no, come up ... It go that way ... See?' Gregori motions the end of the barrel and sweeps his hand towards the infected woman now on her feet and groaning audibly.

'Okay,' the boy takes aim and fires a deafening shot that booms in the enclosed space. The bullet sails past the woman as the boy frowns, 'Her brains in her head.'

'You miss. Try again.'

The boy aims again.

'Breathe,' Gregori advises quietly, 'not hold breath ... breathe out as shoot.'

The boy breathes out and fires. The woman staggers back from the shoulder hit and lands crumpled amongst the tables and chairs. They both watch as she writhes and spasms to get upright.

'Aw,' the boy groans as she sits up, and he spots the fresh blood seeping from the wound in her shoulder.

'One more,' Gregori knows he should not be wasting bullets like this. He should not be firing a loud weapon like this. He should not be sat here, eating bad food like this. He shrugs. 'Again,' he prompts.

The boy takes his time and holds still until the woman is back on her feet and swaying less. Gregori takes in the focussed look on the boy's face as he tracks the head and gently pulls the trigger.

'YES! I DID IT,' the boy bounces on the spot as Gregori deftly takes back the pistol.

'Good.'

'I did it. I did it, Gregoreee. Her brains came out ...'

'Yes. Good,' Gregori thumbs the safety on and glances back across at the child. The kickback didn't bother him, and Gregori felt the force of the recoil through the boy's body as he held a steadying hand on his back. He didn't blink or flinch either. Not a flicker of concern.

'Night soon,' Gregori remarks to fill the silence after the shot. 'We go.'

'Where?' the boy asks.

'Find place. Sleep. We hide and sleep.'

'Hide and seek?'

'No. Hide and sleep. They danger in night,' he points down to the now still body.

'Will I have pyjamas?'

'We look,' Gregori replies. 'We try. If no, then no. If yes, then yes.'

'Okay,' the boy burps and giggles as he hops down from the counter to venture forward and peer down at the grey matter spattered across the floor, 'can we see her sausages?'

'No.'

'Can I see her sausages?'

'What?'

'Can I get her sausages out?'

'No!'

'Can we eat her sausages?'

'No. Not say this. Not ever. You eat that, you die. I kill you.'

'Have you eaten sausages?'

'Not from dead man. Eat dead man and die.'

'Okay ... Is it here?' the boy points at the woman's stomach.

'Yes.'

'How?'

'How?' Gregori walks over and crouches down. 'Cut like this,' he slices his fingers left to right over the top of the woman's midriff. 'They inside, but ... but she down, so they not come out.'

'Do it,' the boy nods. 'I want to see her sausages.'

'Boy. She dead. Dead is dead. There no ... Why take insides out? She dead.'

'Show me,' the boy urges. 'Can I see her heart?'

'Heart?' Gregori stares at the child. 'Why?'

'I never seen one,' the boy shrugs.

'No. She danger. Her blood–it danger. Her blood touch–you die.'

'Why?'

'She has, er ... She has sick ... She sick. Her sick touch you, and you sick ... then die.'

'They're going to howl now.'

Gregori snaps his head up at the boy, then out to the now dark sky outside. How did he not notice it's so late? How did he let this happen? A chill runs down his spine as he glances back to see the boy's head tilted up, as though he too is about to howl.

Lights on in the restaurant. Discrete and soft, and he failed to see the day was going faster than he thought.

On his feet, and he draws both knives, 'Come! We–'

His words cut off as the howling hits the air with a sudden screeching that comes from every direction. The night fills with noise from the hundreds of voices that give sound. A chilling noise that has Gregori racing to leap over the windowsill and into the street. Hundreds of them. More than that. Solid ranks on either side, and they scream into the night as one drawn-out sound.

'BOY,' Gregori yells, 'WE GO ... NOW ...'

The boy ambles and gently steps over the sill while staring with amazed interest at the two sides trapping them.

'NOW,' the boy shouts up at Gregori at the second the howls end, plummeting the scene into a deafening and oppressive silence.

Only one way out, and that's straight across the road and through the shops on the other side, and hope to hell there is a back entrance. Gregori sweeps his gaze across the frontages of the stores and turns back to face the stores right behind him. If he could funnel them, he could hold them off, but two knives are not enough for a group that size, and the pistols only have one magazine each, not even that after the shots taken by the boy.

He squats quickly with his back to the boy. 'UP,' he

snaps and waits as the boy jumps up to wrap his arms round Gregori's neck. 'Tight ... TIGHT,' he roars.

'We will see their sausages?'

Gregori doesn't reply but starts running. The infected start running. Everyone starts running. He aims for the stores and curses his own stupidity as the boy whispers in his ear, 'I need to poop.'

CHAPTER NINETEEN

Day Sixteen

I have but a snatched few minutes. I stumbled into an awful situation. I don't have time to make a full entry, but if this becomes my last notes, then head back to my base–the address is at the front of this book, complete with GPS coordinates and postcode. Find my diaries and know what happened and how this came to be.

There is a gathering in this town. A mass of the infected all holding position in the central square. Hundreds of them. We walked right into them!!! We turned a corner, and there they were. I don't know why. Jess did not smell them, but that I put down to the wind direction or simply that she is not bothered by them as they want humans to infect, not horses.

We scarpered pretty darn quickly from that place and cantered down side streets, into the maze of alleys of this blasted old town. Why didn't we build towns in a grid formation like the bloody yanks!? Alleys and twisting lanes and avenues that don't blasted lead anywhere.

We found an old quay with warehouses next to it. One of them is converted into an arts centre, and it's in there we hide. The old doors were big enough for Jess to get through, and I can only hope we've found somewhere they won't look. I don't know if they're coming to search or even if they saw us. I saw them. Turned Jess round, and we got out of it. I should have gone back the way I came, but fear and panic had gripped me, and I don't know ... I just took lefts and rights in a blind worry that they were right behind me.

Why are they here? What's here that they want? Why gather in one place? This does not fit the information we knew about. I should try and find out, but I have my objectives to accomplish, and me being dead serves no purpose. This is recorded. Everything I do is recorded, but ... but the chances of a vastly reduced population and someone finding these books are unlikely ... Should I run? But where? How do we get out of here? I must be calm and think clearly. Jess is faster than they, but ... but only if we know the way out.

Okay. Calm down, Neal. I must calm down. I must calm down. My heart hammers so much, and it feels like my chest is restricted. Is this a panic attack? I knew I should have recruited guards or soldiers to work with me. This is too much for a scientist to do.

I must calm down and find a way out.

NB

CHAPTER TWENTY

'I'm bored,' I turn round from the window and face Dave, who faces me. The me on the floor, that is, not the me at the window.

'A new day,' I say glumly. 'A new dawn heralds the start of another fine morning in the apocalyptic world. How can Mo Mo hear me, and you can't?' I ask the small man. 'You're Dave. You're like this magical being that can do everything ... Well, apart from hold a sensible conversation, that is.'

He doesn't reply but stays where he is, sat on the floor, next to my body, one hand resting on my chest.

'Is this an out-of-body experience?' I ask no one in particular. 'It's a bit shit if it is. I thought it would be flashing lights and music and ...' I shrug, 'some other cool shit. *Come back from the light, Howie ...*' I snort and look away when even my stupid ghost voice doesn't get a response.

The old man in the tube station I can understand. That was a representation of bad shit to come if we don't do our good shit now. Wow, that's a lot of shit.

He was showing me what will happen if we don't keep

going, if *I* don't keep going. What the hell is this? A cunning plan to bore me so much I want to go back?

Hang on. Go back? Does that mean I have a choice? Can I choose to go back or … ? What's the alternative? Be a ghost? Am I a ghost now?

I stride out of the room, looking for Meredith, then remember that I ordered her to be taken outside to keep watch, or rather, I suggested to Mo Mo who half-ordered, half-suggested it to everyone else.

'Where you go, I go.' The words stop me in my tracks, and I spin round to see Dave staring at the me on the floor.

'Say that again,' I stride back towards him.

'Hear me, Mr Howie? Where you go, I go …'

My god. The look of terror on Dave's face at the prospect of a future without Mr Howie. Not me. Not the me here, but the me down there. The me that leads and shows the path.

What does that mean? 'Dave,' I say gently, 'what does that mean?'

I'm in a place that Dave can't reach, and it's killing him more than anything we've done together. In his mind, I'm struggling and fighting and without him. He fears I will lose.

'You'll fix this,' he says quietly. 'Mr Howie, you'll fix this.'

'I don't think I can,' I say sadly. 'Got nothing left, mate.' As I say the words, I feel a sense of distance being created, like I'm falling away but without moving. It happens slowly and so organically that it feels entirely natural and even somewhat nice. I can let go. Just let go and fade away to somewhere warm and safe where none of this matters. I exhale slowly and feel the pressure of it all lifting, like a great weight being taken from my shoulders and mind.

Warmth spreads through me so gently it makes me sigh, and it feels like I'm falling but slowly, so slowly. Sinking down into a beautiful warm place of ...

'INCOMING,' the unmistakable tone of Blowers shouting in alarm rings out, but it's too late now–I'm too far gone. My heart ramps from serenity to explosive thudding, but I can't stop the descent. A huge bang shakes the whole of the building and sends juddering shockwaves through every beam and wall.

But I'm not there. I'm in the street where I started. I start running, making ready to shout orders for Blowers to get inside, for a GPMG to be placed covering the hole, and for someone to plan an escape route. I want to know the security of the building and have eyes on the point of attack. What exploded? The sound was two noises: an impact, then an explosion. Like a battering ram. A car set on fire and sent against the wall.

I want magazines laid out, weapons made ready and a ... I'm sprinting, but the street is the ruined street and not the munitions factory. It doesn't end like it did before. I reach the point where it ceased being the street, and it carries on being the same dismal fucking town, ruined and broken, blackened and in heaps of bricks and rusted metal.

Hands on my head, I spin round and round. The group are under attack from something concerted and organised. Something that has worked out to use a car as a weapon and send it against the walls of the munitions factory. My group are under attack. My team.

The tranquil state of being is gone. It's replaced with an utter desire to be back in their midst so I can lead the charge with my axe held firm. So Dave and I can loop out from that hole and attack them from the rear or the flank. I want

Meredith with us so her teeth can tear them apart, but I can't do anything.

'COME ON,' I scream into the air, fists clenched, and arms locked, 'COME ON ... SEND ME BACK ...'

Why won't I go? Why can't I go? 'LET ME BACK ... DAVE ... HIT ME, SLAP ME ... WAKE ME UP ... DO SOMETHING ...'

Nothing. With a frizzed blurring, the air shimmers all around me, and the street is how it was before this happened. The houses no longer destroyed, and people walking about their business. The sun shines bright and high in the sky. Cars move slowly past, and children laugh as they play in the park.

'NO! NO,' I rage and run through the street as it flickers between the destruction of the future and the hope of the past. I don't care one shit about this fucking street. Put me back in the fight. Give me my team. Let me lead like I was.

Static electricity makes me gag and drop to my knees. My hair stands on end as the street blurs faster than it was before. Then it settles, and the silence is only broken by the fetid, ragged breathing of the infected.

I stand slowly, sensing them behind me. Knowing they are there.

'No,' I mutter the words through gritted teeth, 'not now ... not fucking now.'

Growls ripple through them, and I turn slowly to find the whole of the street behind me rammed from left to right with rank upon rank of the infected.

I stand straight and stare them down.

'Not happening,' shaking my head, I look up to the grey, streaked sky as the first fat drops of rain fall heavy to land on my face.

'Send me back. Please. Please send me back.'

There's movement within them. Their ranks are deep, but there's a flash of long, black hair.

'Marcy? MARCY?' I run towards them. They close tighter and prevent me getting in but make no move to attack.

'MOVE! MARCY ...' I grab the first and send it staggering from the front rank with a heave, but they close up. Another I tackle and start fighting them harder and harder. Fists slamming into noses and jaws. I kick and gouge and drop them one by one, but the ones are few and the masses are many.

Panting hard, I step back and fix my eyes on the now solid front rank. Hands are not enough. I need a weapon. My axe. Knives. Anything. Give me something.

She moves towards me like water flowing through rocks. 'Marcy!' She doesn't reply, and I only get glimpses as she moves round and between them but coming ever closer.

'Fuck's sake,' I attack the front rank again with renewed purpose and manage to get two ranks deep before they force me back out to stagger and drop to my knees.

'Force isn't always the answer.'

'Fucking is,' I'm on my feet, staring at the woman who tried to save me, tried to kill me, then saved me again. 'Are you here?'

She looks down at her ample cleavage and smiles coyly. 'I think I am.'

'I'm knocked out. In the mun– ... Fuck it! In the munitions factory. They're being attacked ... Send me back.'

'What makes you think I can do anything?' she asks lightly, but the words are cut off by my hand gripping her throat.

'I will end you whether this is a dream or not,' I increase the pressure. 'Know this. Can you send me back?'

She shakes her head as a tear rolls free down her cheek, and one hand lifts to gently cover my wrist.

'Fuck ... FUCK ... FUCKFUCKFUCK,' I let go and spin round as the rage burns through me. I end up punching an infected in the face just for the hell of it.

'You wanted out,' she speaks softly, and her voice sends shivers racing up my spine.

'Don't talk to me.'

'Why? Why not, Howie?'

'Your voice is like fucking treacle. It ... it does something to me. Just ... fuck off.'

'Howie. Come find me.'

'Find you. You're right there ... How do I get back? Tell me?'

'You're so lost,' she takes a step closer, 'so lost.'

'Don't,' I growl.

'You carry the world on your shoulders. You take the burden without complaint.' I glance up at her to see a look of complete pain etched onto her face, but other than the red eyes, there's no sign of the infection. Her skin is as tanned and lustrous as ever. Her hair shines and shimmers with waves of midnight raven. Her lips look as full and sensuous as her hips and breasts. I swallow and breathe out slowly while forcing my eyes away.

'They're right, Howie.'

'Who are?' I ask without looking but sense her getting closer by the second.

'They told you to see it through. They're right. This–'

'Don't touch me.'

'This is a dream,' she whispers, so close to me now I can sense the warmth of her body. 'This isn't real.'

'Feels real.'

'Howie,' she reaches out to touch the side of my face,

and no sooner do her fingers brush against me, a fat tear wells in my eye to fall singly down my cheek.

'This is not about you. This is about what you are, what you can do.'

'No,' the word comes out muted and torn.

'The weight of the world is upon you. You falter one step and berate yourself so harshly,' her tone is so soft and compelling I can't make myself move away from her. 'Your team needs you. They all need you ...' I half-turn and find myself sinking down into her warm embrace. Hands wrap round my back as I rest my forehead on her shoulder.

'You faltered, but you will be stronger. You have to see this through. You have no choice. Listen. Listen to me,' she lifts my head to stare deep into my eyes. 'You've done more than anyone could ask ... but this isn't over, and you have more to give.'

'I can't,' I gasp as the tears run free.

'You will,' she says gently, with an almost maternal essence. 'You must. *You* do not matter. What you *can do* matters most. It matters more than anything.'

'... Stay here ...'

'With me? You want to stay here with me?'

I nod, and she laughs a pained sound full of remorse. 'Oh, Howie,' she pulls me in for another tight embrace, 'no, you cannot ... but ... you have to find me.'

'I tried but ...'

'But what?'

'But I broke ... and I'm scared. I think about you and ... I love Lani, but sometimes I think about you.'

'You will be strong,' she pushes me to arm's length and holds me there. 'I do too. All the time. But ...' she pauses and sighs, 'close your eyes.'

I do as told without question, for there is no danger

here. Marcy would never hurt me. I don't know how I know but I do.

'When you open your eyes, you will rise, and you will fight. You hear me?'

'No ...'

'You will fight as you have never fought before. Your team are strong, but without you, they falter and bicker and argue. Clarence has the strength of five men, but he cannot carry what you can. Paula is smart, but she lacks the humility of your touch. They cannot win without you. The infection is throwing so much at them right now, right as we speak ... Cars laden with fuel are being sent flaming against the walls, and a hole has formed. Your team are strewn throughout the building, fighting separately without cohesion while Dave remains by your side, staring into the darkness. The infection aims for the ammunition and is working route towards blowing it up. If it wins, all your team will be killed. One has already suffered a bite. Without you and Dave, the group lacks the heart to keep going. Howie,' she pauses and steps closer, 'your team are the hope. They are the future. You cannot go on without them, and they cannot survive without you. Dave will close his eyes and accept death as a means of being with you. You will die. They will die, and with you, the hope of mankind dies. So when I say you will fight, you will rise up and fight, and your voice will carry throughout that building. They will rally on you, and you will blaze a path through them.' Her breath on my face now, and her hands cup my cheeks. 'Lani is torn. She knows the team need her, but she longs to be by your side. She is at the far end, at the most dangerous point, and she covers a gap in the wall. She's alone and scared, but she knows, if she turns away, they will break through. So again, when I say you will rise, you will rise, and the strength will be there again. I promise. All of this doubt will be gone.'

I nod and weep, but it's as though her strength flows into me with a calmness I have never felt before.

'When you open your eyes, you will lead. Do you understand?'

'Yes.'

'When you open your eyes, you will not falter again. Do you understand?'

'Yes.'

'You will fight and win, and you will find me.'

'I will. I swear it.'

'Good. Now, keep your eyes closed ... There's one last thing to do.'

I stiffen as her lips touch mine but only for a second. Within that second, a whole barrage of thoughts race through my mind. That this is wrong. But I'm dreaming. That she's infected, but I'm immune, *and* I'm dreaming. Everything is wrong, but everything is right, and that second passes as I sink into the kiss of her full lips against mine. My heart surges with power, and the strength I felt flowing into me before is doubled, tripled, forced through every vein in my body until my muscles feel like they'll burst with energy. Her hands grip the back of my head as her tongue darts between my lips. The flow increases until I'm no longer human, for surely no human has ever felt like this. She breaks and breathes a long, contented sigh.

'I'm still a woman,' she whispers. 'Now go ... go ...' she pushes me roughly away, 'but remember me ...'

CHAPTER TWENTY-ONE

'Lilly!'

She turns and smiles as Maddox threads his way through the moving crowds of the fort's survivors.

'Hey, Mads,' she blows a strand of hair from her face and stands waiting for him, 'everything okay?'

'Yeah, listen,' he stops and offers a wry smile at the sight of the clipboard in her hand, 'Lenski's at the gate. We've got more survivors turning up.'

'More?'

'Word's spreading,' he replies. 'We've sent two crews out in boats to the shore on the other side ...'

'Are they being checked?' she cuts in quickly.

'Darius and Sierra are there,' he nods, 'and that nurse has gone over, but I don't like putting him at risk.'

'We can't send one of the doctors.'

'I know. Lenski wants you down with her for processing.'

'At the gate?'

'Yeah, why? That okay?' He notices the fleeting glimpse of a frown creasing on her forehead.

'No, no, it's fine,' she says. 'I was arranging a rota for childcare but ...'

'Anyone can do that,' Maddox says and looks round to see two women stood nearby talking. 'You two, are you assigned a task?'

'I beg your pardon?' the older woman blanches in surprise.

'We need a rota for childcare. Can you do that?' he speaks fast, firm yet soft, with a perfect blend of respectful, commanding authority.

'Er, I suppose ...' the older woman blinks a few times.

'I worked in a nursery,' the younger woman offers. 'For childcare,' she adds quickly with a nervous glance between Maddox and Lilly.

'You did? Brilliant!' Lilly beams. 'Right, we need a safe area made for the children. It needs to be checked for anything that can cause injury or harm, and we need people to be with them, make sure they eat, drink water ... have rest time, not too long in the–'

'In the sun. Yeah, I was thinking that,' the younger woman interjects. 'Who is doing it now?'

'Now? No one really,' Lilly says with an imploring look.

'What's your name?' Maddox asks.

'Angela.'

'Angela, you are now in charge of childcare for the fort and act on my authority. Get what you need from the stores. There'll be a radio somewhere for you, and we'll get you a few guards assigned. Got it?'

'Wow,' Angela offers a nervous smile, 'really?'

'Yes, really,' Maddox says seriously. 'You get any problems, you find one of the crews ...' He turns to spot Ryland patrolling nearby with a shotgun held across the crook of his arms.

'Ryland, your crew on now?'

'S'up,' Ryland nods in greeting. 'Yeah, we're on.'

'Angela,' Maddox nods at the woman, 'she's in charge of childcare now. Get her a radio and stay with her.'

'Sweet,' Ryland smiles at the woman. 'Ryland,' he nods with a grin. 'Yous better come with me, innit?'

'Lilly,' Maddox motions for her to fall in beside him as he starts striding back towards the front. 'You cannot do everything yourself.' She watches as his eyes dart to every corner of the fort. Nothing escapes his attention, but he takes time to look at her and show his interest. 'Delegation is the key to leadership.'

'Delegation. Right.' She nods and hurries alongside and notices again how people seem to step out of his way, and he rarely has to swerve or deviate. The power of the man exudes utter confidence, that nothing is beyond him, and unlike the crews and guards who hold long-barrelled weapons and stare with fixed expressions, Maddox has a single pistol in a holster on the back of his belt. Unassuming, yet it only serves to increase his control. 'You're one of us now, Lilly.'

'Am I?' she asks with a surprised look.

'You are. Howie goes out and does what he does out there,' Maddox nods forward. 'And we run this, so you're one of us that run this. As such,' he spares her a glance amidst the chaos around them, 'you need to assert control and authority.'

'I'm only fifteen,' she blurts.

He stops and stares at her with a poker face, 'How old am I?'

'Pardon?'

'How old am I?'

'Er,' she concentrates, 'I would say ...'

'I'm eighteen,' he resumes walking.

'What!?'

'Howie is twenty-seven, yet he commands everyone, and do you know what Howie did before this?'

'Worked in Tesco, didn't he?'

'He did. I was in a gang that grew cannabis. Howie worked in a supermarket. Lenski is a Polish immigrant … You get me?'

'I think so,' she nods and sidesteps a man carrying planks of wood.

'It's in your voice, your manner, your bearing … Look people in the eye when you talk to them and assert the authority in your voice but …' he spares her another glance, 'only shout or raise your voice when you have to.'

'But you and Howie can fight,' she says. 'Everyone says how tough you are. So by the masculinity of your toughness, you command that respect.'

'Ever seen Lenski fight?'

'Well, no, but …'

'Lenski doesn't fight.'

'Right.'

'Does Lenski command respect?'

'Oh god, yes, but then she's got that Polish look, you know, she doesn't show her emotions or …'

'Do I show emotions?'

'No, no, you don't … but Howie does. Howie isn't like that.'

'Everyone's different. Make no mistake. Howie is special, but he's also got the ability to be utterly ruthless when he needs to be. You have to find your way, but you're too valuable to do that slowly, over time. Find it. Assert control.'

'I'll try,' she bites her bottom lip, then stiffens to show resolve.

'Maddox!'

'Yes,' Maddox holds a hand out to show the approaching Doctor Andrew Stone he is aware, but he is also busy. It works too. The eighteen-year-old simply stops the doctor and looks back to Lilly. 'Everyone speaks well of you.'

'Do they?' Lilly blushes from the praise.

'One of us. Go find Lenski.'

'Okay, and er ... thanks, Maddox.'

'Anytime. Doctor Stone, what have you got?'

'Right,' Andrew steps in and rubs his hands, 'we've inventoried the equipment, and we have enough to start some basic analysis ...'

'Good. What do you need?'

'Need? Who says we need anything?'

'You need an infected?'

'Well, yes. Yes, actually we do ... or rather, not an actual infected person, but we need infected blood.'

'Got it,' Maddox nods. 'I can do that. I can get you an infected person.'

'Is that safe?'

'No. Nothing is safe, but I'll make it safe enough. It won't be brought in here, but we can bring one close enough so we can get samples, and you can do whatever tests you need.'

'For a thorough analysis, we'll need the ones we know are immune, some we know are not immune, and obviously the infected. Also,' Doctor Stone steps in to lower his voice, 'the one that turned but stayed normal?'

'Lani?'

'No ... the other one. The woman ...'

'Marcy?' Maddox lifts his eyebrows in surprise.

'Yes, yes, her. We need her too. We need every known type so we can get a cross-section of all the blood types and ... Well, to even begin to understand how this infection works is way beyond us, but we may be able to identify certain things within the blood that are different across that spectrum. Listen, we are just general doctors. You understand that, right? We'll do our best, but we've also got sick, injured and ...'

'I get it,' Maddox cuts him off. 'You'll get Howie and his team when they return. As for an infected,' the youth pauses to think for a second, 'that will have to be Howie too. Marcy ...? Marcy I can get.'

'Really? How?'

'Ears are for listening, eyes are for watching, and the brain does everything else. Thank you, Doctor. You'll have what you need as soon as possible.'

Maddox strides off. Not because he has another specific task, but because he needs time to think, and he thinks best whilst walking. Also, it makes him look busy, which means people don't interrupt unless it's important.

The immunity is beyond his control, so that is pushed to one side of his brain. An infected he can get, but again, that is a task best completed by Howie, so that too is segmented to one side. Marcy. He's heard the story and knows who the woman is, and from what he can gather, she's close too. Whatever happened between her and Howie is unfinished. He could wait until Howie gets back and ask his group to find Marcy, but that will take time, and he couldn't be sure that Lani would agree to it. Not that it would really matter. Howie would see that it was for the good of the fort and get the job done, but he wouldn't like to cause unnecessary upset between those two.

'Maddox, we need more fuel for the generators ...' a man rushes up with a harried look on his face.

'For cooking? There's more fuel in the storeroom at the far end. Find Ryland. He's the duty crew chief.'

'Got it, thanks, Maddox.'

Weigh up the risk and the threat. He can take a crew with him to find Marcy, but that exposes that crew to unnecessary risk, and he knows he can move faster on his own. The Bossman used Maddox as an enforcer to collect debts, and it was a skill Maddox honed over several years. Finding people and making them want to do the right thing. Opposition doesn't faze him. Maddox knows he's fast at running and capable in a fight. But then he leaves the security of the fort to someone else, and if he was to die out there, then it leaves this fort without an established leader.

'Mads, we got anymore suncream?'

'Stores. You know that,' he casts a searching look at the young boy. 'Carl, you getting enough water?'

'Yeah, swear down, Mads,' the youth nods his head eagerly.

'So what's up?'

'Nuffin,' the boy looks down and fidgets.

'Carl, you know where the suncream is kept. You wanted to speak to me. What's up?'

'My stomach hurts,' the boy blurts with a flush of embarrassment.

'You told your crew chief?'

'Can't find her,' the boy mutters.

'Skyla? Where she at?'

'Dunno.'

'How bad is it?'

'Fucking hurts,' the boy winces, 'like fucking proper.'

'Let me see ...' Maddox sees the shame on the boy's face and guides him over to one side out of view. 'Come on.'

'It's like ... in here,' the boy lifts his t-shirt and rubs across his abdomen, 'and it hurts when I piss.'

'You sure you drinking water?'

'Swear down,' the boy nods.

'Carl, I ain't angry. You get me? How much you had today?'

'Water? Some at breakfast.'

'You on the early crew?'

'Yeah.'

'Go see the doc.'

'But Skyla said I had to stay by the gate.'

'I'll do the gate. Go see the doc, and if anyone says shit, then tell 'em I said so. You get me?'

'Yeah, thanks, Mads,' the boy goes to walk off, then stops. 'Is it bad?'

'What? Your stomach? Nah, is it fuck,' Maddox grins. 'You probably dehydrated. Stay in the shade. Tell you what, see the doc and tell 'em I said you got to stay in there and help them today.'

'Okay, Mads,' the boy runs off, stops, and runs back before handing over his rifle with a sheepish grin. 'Loaded, and the safety's on,' the boy runs off again, leaving Maddox holding the weapon.

'Mads, we got two boat loads coming in,' another young voice calls out from the gate.

'Carl has gone to the hospital,' Maddox announces on stepping through into the middle section. 'Keep this gate locked and stay alert, you get me?' He looks to the crew standing ready with shotguns. 'You lot been here all morning? You had a break yet?'

'Nah, Mads, but wes okay.'

'Skyla, this is Maddox. You hearing me?'

'Alright, Mads.'

'Your crew needs rotating. Where are you?'

'Toilet.'

'Sort your crew out.' He clips the radio back on his waistband and walks out to the small beach. Two boats move slowly, laden with survivors. Maddox nods to Lenski and Lilly waiting to receive them and casts his eyes over the watchful crew. He stays a few feet away from everyone else in yet another subconscious but overt display that he is in charge.

'We bring them in or ...?' Lenski turns to Maddox.

'DARIUS,' Maddox shouts across the still water, 'HOW MANY?'

'ELEVEN,' Darius shouts back. 'ALL CHECKED. NO WEAPONS. NO BITES.'

'BRING 'EM IN.'

Lenksi watches the boats as they ground out gently in the shallows. The crew ranges out into a wide semi-circle, weapons ready but lowered. All eyes scanning the new arrivals.

A few men, more women, and yet even more children. All of them bedraggled, sunburnt, filthy, and completely terrified. The refugees take in the youths holding the weapons and the distinct lack of friendly faces ready to greet them. A weighted silence, heavy and oppressive.

'Lilly,' Maddox says softly across, 'they need a warm welcome.'

She beams with genuine sincerity, 'Hi. I'm Lilly. This is Lenski ... You're all safe now.'

As she speaks, Maddox waves his hand low, signalling the crew to ease back. They respond instantly with smiles and nods as a palpable relief sweeps the occupants of the two boats.

'We're going to get you out of the boats, but we need to process you before you can go inside ...' Lilly steps into the smooth explanation as Maddox turns to look out to the still water and the land beyond.

The golden, beached bay sweeps inland gently, and the blackened stumps of the ruined estate look stark and ugly as they protrude above the water. His eyes follow the bay, towards the houses set back. They're expensive beachside houses and the only place left close enough that could house someone.

That's where she'll be. Watching the fort. Is she watching now? Staring at the tiny figures on the beach.

'Where's the adults?' a rough voice snaps his attention back to the group clamouring from the boats. 'They're just bloody kids ... You seeing this?' A bearded older man shakes his head in distaste. 'Bloody kids with guns ... Where's the grown-ups? Where's this Mr Howie and his army gone?'

With an inward sigh, Maddox knows Marcy will have to wait, and as he steps towards the man, his mind shifts into the task at hand and the diplomatic skills he'll need to keep the day running smoothly.

CHAPTER TWENTY-TWO

'Down.' Gregori turns from the back door and squats in the narrow corridor. The boy slides down and gets pushed quickly into a corner. 'Stay here.' The Albanian ducks out of the back door, checks both directions and quickly gets back inside before closing the door quietly.

'Boy,' he squats down to face the child, 'they come ... I fight ... You stay ...' He speaks quietly and urgently, 'Yes? You do this?'

'Okay,' the boy replies without fear.

A narrow corridor runs from the front of the building to the rear. Locked doors lead off to storerooms, offices, and staff rooms. A recessed side door sits next to the plate glass display window and double doors of the clothes shop. It's painted white but with black scuff marks down both walls, indicating this is the service entrance, but the walls are solid and high. The floor is concrete, which gives good grip. The width doesn't allow more than two at a time to come down.

An egress point is behind them, so this makes a perfect tactical point to hold them off for a while. He can kill. Let the bodies mount up and cause an obstruction. The rest will ram in behind; then, he can use the egress point and take the boy into the dark shadows of the night.

He draws both knives and holds them with the blades pointed down while he breathes slowly in through his nose and exhales out through his mouth. His heart rate lowers instantly, and the running with the boy has warmed his muscles and expanded his lungs to drive more oxygenated blood to his body.

He glances back to make sure the boy is staying put, and as the sound of drumming feet and snarling voices gain ever closer, he once again wonders what the hell he is doing. But that thought vanishes as the first infected arrives square in the purposefully left open doorway.

A calm descends. The calm he has been trained for since a child. The resonance strikes him, and again he turns to look down at the boy standing quietly behind him. The beast snarls with wild abandon at seeing the prey is close. The boy stares with interest as Gregori feels a prickle of discomfort at realising he was the same age as the child when he started his training.

He looks back at the oncoming infected, then back to the boy. He was young, young like the boy is, and he too was unafraid. That's why they chose him. His father's debt had to be paid, but they could have taken that payment in many different ways. His father could have been put to work; his mother used as a sex slave until the debt was paid off. Property or what little they had could have been taken, but they took the boy instead.

He remembers it, that day they came. He remembers hearing his mother sobbing and his brothers and sisters cowering in fear while he stood at his father's side, waiting for the unsmiling men. His father was stoic, firm, and so full of pride, but ultimately, he was weak. He gave up his own child, but he did it to protect the rest of his family. Weakness and strength. Honour yet servitude.

The men had already chosen Gregori. They knew he was different from the stories in the local school. How Gregori got into fights with much bigger boys and never backed down. How Gregori never cried and never told tales.

The transaction was simple. The men came in and waited. Then the old man came in and stared down at Gregori before nodding without a flicker of emotion. That was it. He was chosen, and he was taken.

The years after stream through his mind in an increasingly rapid succession of images. He views himself as a third person and never through his own eyes. He sees the small child being taught the ways and the beatings he took when he got it wrong.

The boy looks up to lock eyes on Gregori as the beast surges down the passage with the uncontrolled blood lust of a newly turned infected. They are approximately three days old, and they are strong and wild and have yet to evolve into the coordinated monsters they become.

'Watch,' he turns back to the boy, 'watch me.'

'Okay,' the boy nods.

'Learn,' Gregori has time to nod once before slamming the impaled infected into the wall and wrenching the blade free with a vicious twist. Blood sprays from the arterial cut and soaks against the wall, but not one drop touches the Albanian. The passage fills as they charge down, but Gregori has chosen his ground well and takes one small step back. The already downed body impedes the next, who trips, staggers, and has her throat cut as she falls.

With two down, Gregori holds his position. Using the

minimal amount of effort, he slices and stabs into the seemingly never-ending supply of bodies.

'Neck,' the single word rings out, and Gregori quickly glances back to make sure the boy is paying attention, 'neck ...'

'Okay,' the boy repeats.

'Slice,' Gregori slices. 'Slice,' he does it again. 'Slice,' he keeps sweeping the blade across throat after throat. The sharpened steel whispers with the faintest of brushes but enough to go through the seven layers of epidermis and rupture the artery in the side of the neck.

Hot, crimson blood pumps high and to the sides, but the position of the cuts, the bodies, and the killer means never a drop touches him.

'Stab,' Gregori sticks a blade into the larynx of a fat male, 'stab, twist ... See?'

'Yes.'

'Stab ... twist,' he turns his wrist while pulling the blade out, thereby destroying the windpipe and causing a massive loss of blood, which runs down into the lungs of the infected, 'stab, twist ... slice ... stab, twist ... slice ... See?'

'Yes ... sausages.'

'What?'

'Sausages.'

Both hands blur as he moves forward in a sudden charge, and the passage becomes clogged with bodies downed with slit throats and ruined necks. He stabs one through the eye while easing the blade across the throat of another. He ducks to avoid a hand scything through the air and, while low, aims for the hamstrings and Achilles tendons he can reach. Growling snarls, grunts, and howls sound out as body after body falls to land noisily in the deepening pools of blood.

Those dead start to get punted across the floor, and a wet, scraping sounds adds to the noise. Gregori gets pushed back as the onslaught keeps coming. He moves faster, but they push harder. He kills more, but more keep coming. Thousands upon thousands have perished in the densely populated working towns packed into the north of the country. Thousands and more that are fresh and driven to take more hosts, and this is a foe the like of which Gregori has never seen before.

A light sweat breaks out on his forehead as he grunts from the exertion of the work at hand. He takes what cuts he can, slicing open stomachs to release their contents, and in the heat of battle, he hears the boy give a cheer at the sight of the glistening "sausages" being spilled.

'BOY,' Gregori hacks left and right in the final blur to gain a vital few seconds, 'Come ...' Breaking from his spot, he runs to the boy, squats down, and then launches off, towards the back door. With a swift kick, it opens, and he's out into the sultry night, running down the rear service lane. The corridor behind him fills with the infected pushing and driving forward until those bodies are disgorged from the doorway to spill left and right. Legs and ankles are broken as the raged beasts surge over and through the obstacles. They fall with twisted limbs but instantly start crawling.

Gregori spares a glance back and immediately increases his speed as the first runners break free from the pileup and start after him. The service lane is blocked on both sides by the high walls of buildings, and the only doors and windows are secured with metal shutters or thick iron bars.

With no choice, he pounds the road with the boy gripping his neck. Holding the knives ready, he can't spare a hand to help secure the boy, which factors into the speed he can go. Another glance back, and the runners are gaining.

Pistols wedged into his tight waistband, a knife held in each hand, and a child clinging to him. He could ditch all of them and sprint safely away, and that thought is considered along with every other option that presents itself.

Diversion and distraction is called for. When faced with overwhelming foes and unable to find a safe extraction point, you must give the pursuers something else to worry about, but until such an opportunity lends itself to use ... you just run.

He does run. He runs as fast as he is able to, given the circumstances, but he knows they're gaining. At the end of the service lane, he takes a right, knowing this will lead him away from the area of the town he was in.

More shops, stores, charity shops, bookies, dry cleaners, shoe repairs, and the hundred and one other independently owned shops found on the edges of every town centre. Sounds from every direction speak of danger close. Screams and wails of utter pain, misery, and terror. The growls of the infected heard close but not seen. Glass being smashed. Thumps and bangs as objects are thrown.

The deeper into the town he heads, the more he hears, and all the time, those behind him charge after in a long procession that will simply never tire or run out of steam.

A woman runs across the road ahead of him screaming at the top of her voice at being chased by the small horde of infected hot on her heels. She aims for a doorway as Gregori watches, knowing the mistake will cost her life. She slams into the door, hammering and screaming, and suddenly it opens with a sliver of orange light. She's pulled in as Gregori instantly changes direction.

'WAIT,' he bellows ahead, 'CHILD ... I HAVE CHILD ...'

Five ahead of him. The five that chased the woman. He

slows enough to be able to fight without fear of tripping and gauges the positions of each. The first is a male with a balding head that deviates from the door and heads straight towards Gregori, only to slew off to the side from the combined shoulder barge and laceration to the artery in his groin. It's a difficult cut to do at the best of times, given the thickness of the thigh muscles, and on a moving target at that. But it works, and the blood sprays down onto the pavement as Gregori swivels and backsteps. The remaining four charge through the freshly laid pool of blood to be cut down by vicious hands holding vicious knives that give vicious cuts.

'CHILD ...' Gregori roars. 'I HAVE BOY ...'

The door opens again, just a fraction, but it's enough for Gregori to slice the last one down and charge across the short distance. With a half-turn, he aims the solid muscle of his shoulder into the door and powers through.

'Get in,' a man hisses as others grab his arms to pull him clear. In a split second, Gregori has taken the sight in. A packed room full of survivors. Some dressed in evening clothes of dresses, trousers, smart shirts, and others are workmen in thick, blue cotton trousers and polo shirts. A bare concrete room with one other door leading out, and several candles flickering violently from the drafts of air created by the opening and slamming of the door.

'You alright?' a man with a deep voice asks Gregori. Others appear in front of him, and a woman starts to ease the boy from his back.

'Let him down,' she whispers urgently. 'Get the bloody door closed!'

'It is closed.'

Voices in accents speak back and forth, and Gregori reverts to type. Head down, avoiding eye contact in case they should recognise him in the future. He counts the pairs of legs–one, two, three ... Nine people. Five men and four women.

'Is he your son?' a different woman asks.

'Give them water.'

'Are you bit?'

'They're at the door.'

'That door is solid. Nothing'll get through that.'

'Here, mate, have some water.' A bottle is thrust under Gregori's nose, which he takes with a curt nod and drinks deep. Fluid must be taken on board. Enough to prevent dehydration but not so much it bloats or causes cramps.

'Boy,' he turns and spots the child's face being cleaned with a wet wipe. The boy watches Gregori closely and doesn't utter a word. There's a connection between them as though the boy knows what's about to happen.

'Drink, boy.' Gregori hands the bottle over and watches as the boy takes a few glugs.

'Fuck me ...They're going fucking nuts to get in,' one of men whispers in a terrified voice.

'Ssshh,' another one says too loudly, giving away his own panicked state.

'Can they get in?' a woman asks.

'Helen, how many were coming after ya?' the man who gave Gregori a drink speaks to the woman who got in just ahead of him.

'Fucking hundreds,' she gasps out between ragged breaths. 'Few ... a few after me ... but he had tons ...' she points at Gregori.

'They can't get in, can they?' the woman cleaning the child's face asks.

'Back?' Gregori nods to the other door.

'Leads to the front of the building and the High Street ... Fucking crawling with 'em, mate.'

Gregori nods and affects to wipe the sweat from his forehead while all the time checking, scanning, and thinking. They won't be at the front. They all came after him, so he knows there won't be any at the front, and now they know this once concealed entrance holds fresh meat, they won't stop until they get in.

Thumps and bangs at the door confirm his thought processes. Solid bangs as infected launch themselves against the solid wood of the door that vibrates and rattles the frame. Showers of dust sprinkle down from the plaster above, glittering in the candlelight, and each fresh bang elicits a worried gasp.

'He's got guns. 'Ere, mate, you got two fucking guns ...' a man points to Gregori's waistband. 'Where you get them from?'

'I find,' Gregori shrugs.

'Find? Find where? Tom, you're ex-army ... You know how to fire guns?'

'What, pistols? Yeah, did 'em in basic ... Never used one, but I remember. 'Ere, mate, you'd best hand 'em over.'

'No. I keep,' Gregori keeps his tone low and his eye contact down.

'Listen, mate. You said you found 'em. Tom there is ex-army, so he'd better have 'em.'

'No,' Gregori shakes his head and gently slides the knives back into his waistband so the blades run parallel with his legs.

'Mate, we're not fucking asking,' the man whispers urgently. 'Give 'em to Tom. We need them guns, and they best off with someone who knows how to use 'em.'

'I know,' Gregori replies.

'No offence, mate, but you don't look like a soldier ... You Polish or sommit?'

'Yes. Polish,' Gregori nods. 'Polish army.'

'Polish army? Nah, mate, hand 'em over. You can stay with us, but we're having the guns ... Come on,' the man holds an expectant hand out as Gregori weighs the options while remaining devoid of expression.

He half turns at the loud thumps coming from the door. He listens to the cracking of the plaster above the door and knows the door will yield within fifteen minutes. The plaster will fracture, which will loosen the frame, and it'll be that frame that gives.

Hundreds. Maybe more. Maybe a thousand. Just in this one area, and no doubt more rushing to join the frenzy. Diversion and distraction. Nine people. Thousands of infected. The odds are not good, but they're enough.

'Mate,' the man snaps, 'guns ... NOW!'

'Yes,' Gregori nods but doesn't move as he looks down and clocks the positions of each person and calculates the way they are likely to move when he starts. 'Boy?'

'Yes, Gregoreeee.'

'Stay still.'

'Okay.'

'Still for what? Mate, we're having them guns,' the man moves first with what he thought would be a warning hand gripping Gregori's shoulder. He's several inches taller than the Albanian and outweighs him by at least thirty kilos. Bigger. Heavier. Stronger and with people he already knows.

But slower. His wrist is broken first, followed, a split second later, by a loud crunch as Gregori slams his open palm into the back of the man's elbow. He lets that strike carry through with a fluid movement that he reverses, and he strikes back to slam the blade of his palm into the man's voice box.

'FUCK!' Tom shouts and lunges to grab at Gregori, who sidesteps and holds a foot out to trip the ex-squaddie. With one hand, he gently reaches out to snuff the closest candle, then darts round the back of the now screaming survivors to the next candle. One only remains, but the light is now poor enough.

Old habits die hard. He draws one knife and blinks slowly. 'I Gregori,' he announces to the room and starts stepping through them.

The first cut is the woman who ran in ahead of him. A deep slash across her stomach, and the blood oozes out thick and fast as she screams. Gregori knows the closest man will lunge at him instead of backing away. He has that look about him–clean shaven, tidy hair, and serious eyes. For his efforts, he gets his hamstrings severed and falls crying to the ground. Tom, back on his feet, forgets every part of his training and rushes forward with a furious yell. Gregori, anticipating the attack, backsteps and flicks the blade gently across Tom's outstretched arm. The deep cut to the wrist sprays blood high and wide as Tom spins, screaming as his blood drains faster than he can cope with.

Round the room he goes, cutting, slashing, disabling, but not killing. He doesn't want to kill. He wants blood, as much blood as can be spilled without causing instant death.

Nine people down. Five men and four women screaming in pain as they beg for him to stop. He has stopped. The knife is away as he steps towards the boy.

'LEAVE HIM,' the ex-soldier screams and tries to scrabble across the concrete to protect the boy.

Gregori squats. 'Up!'

The boy doesn't speak or show emotion but reaches out and wraps his arms round Gregori's neck.

Stepping over the bodies, he moves to the door and first pulls back the thick top bolt, then the bottom bolt. With only the middle one left holding the door, he gently prises it back until only the smallest amount is keeping it shut.

'Come ...we go ...' the boy mimics Gregori's deep voice, and as he moves deftly to the interior door, the boy turns to smile at the dying nine bleeding out on the floor.

The door bangs and gives a little. It rattles hard in the frame as chunks of plaster fall from the wall above. It bangs again as the snarling from the other side increases. The nine weep and cry, holding each other tight as they listen to the impending death about to be wrought upon them.

As the interior door closes and Gregori disappears from view, so the outer door gives, and the nine face the onslaught of infected, pumped to a frenzy by the stench of blood and piss. The last thing they hear is a small boy speaking in a low voice, 'Come ... we go ...'

CHAPTER TWENTY-THREE

Day Sixteen

They saw me. Of that there is no doubt. Hundreds of them, maybe more, possibly thousands.

My god, I am so terrified. Utterly terrified. My chest feels so tight I can hardly draw breath, and my heart is hammering so much I feel dizzy. My stomach is knotted into a tight ball. I'm not suited to this type of activity. I can't cope with it. I fear I shall die here today.

We hid in the arts centre, but now, looking back just that short time ago, it shows me of the poor decisions my panicked mind is making. Hiding in a blasted arts centre with a horse!!! What was I thinking? There was a big enough door to get Jess into the place, but none of the other doors were big enough to get her out.

We stayed quiet for a while, but Jess sensed them getting closer. Maybe she doesn't perceive them as a direct threat to her, but the general alien sounds they make or their predatory nature certainly spook her, for no sooner had I realised they were drawing closer, she was snorting and slamming one metal shod hoof into the tiled floor–a nice clanging sound that echoed round the old warehouse.

They heard us and came running. I mounted Jess, secured my assault rifle across my chest, and just had time to grip the reins when they started beating in the big door. The poor horse was skittish, terrified of hearing the beasts outside but being trapped inside a blasted building. We cantered and slid round the inside, looking for a viable alternative exit, but on finding none other, we knew we had to go out that main door. The problem was that the door was locked on the inside by me when we came in, which meant I would have to get off Jess, unlock the door, get back on Jess, and get out before they got me. There are thirty or so rounds in the assault rifle, and even assuming I got clear shots with each, it would never be enough to stem the tide coming against us.

So the only option was to wait and stand a few metres back from that door and listen to the constant hammering as they beat it down from the outside. Every single bang and thump made me want to puke, and I think it was a combination of my fear and the whole situation that added to the panic Jess was feeling.

I must, for the sake of posterity, say now that, once again, I owe my life to that horse. She's big and clumsy, highly strung, overly sensitive, and stubborn as a mule. But she's also exceptionally strong and very well trained by the police that owned her before me. I understand that horses will naturally shy away from tightly packed groups of people that present a wall. Police and military horses are trained to go through such things and use the power of their size and strength to do so.

There we waited. Slowly those doors started to give. The noises were indescribable. Snarling and growls like wolves or beasts from nightmares, and in my frightened state, I knew the noises were done on purpose to generate more fear so the infection could pick up on the hormones and scents released. Even knowing that did not stop me from being utterly shit scared. Listening to such a thing but being unable to flee or do anything other than wait until the inevitable. I knew my time had come. I knew I was going to die and even contemplated sacrificing myself in the hope they would leave Jess alone, but that same fear kept me rooted in the saddle.

The doors finally gave way with an almighty splintering of wood and tearing of bricks that created a cloud of dust and debris spewing into the centre. There they were. A solid mass of old and freshly turned infected hosts.

What struck me was that they paused. Only for the briefest of times, but they held back as though taking it all in. Scanning the room to see what the opposition was, and it was as though a combined effort was being undertaken ... No, that is unclear. I am a scientist and must ... must make accurate records ... Forgive my shredded nerves.

The door was broken down. There then stood approx. one hundred infected persons within line of sight and so densely packed it was hard to gauge the specific quantity of them. They were clearly ranged from hosts taken days ago with old, festering wounds to newly taken hosts still with colour in their cheeks and hair on their heads that wasn't greasy, greying, or falling out.

Every mouth had bared teeth. Every mouth was drooling, and I know the infection is contained within that drool. Every hand was clawed so not only could they bite and pass the infection, but they could claw and rake to open the skin and pass the infection that way.

Every pair of eyes was on me and Jess. The eyes were red from the blood being forced to surround the pupil.

**** IMPORTANT*** The red eyes are the only visible sign of an infected person. The appearance of clawed hands, drooling mouth, and sickly-looking skin colour is a by-product and secondary in terms that it is a behavioural manifestation done as necessity. The blood in the eyes is the only known irreversible side effect.*

I have been a scientist long enough to know when a visual examination is taking place. That pause WAS a visual examination of me, of Jess, of the scene, the place, the locality. That concerns me greatly as it means the intelligence of the infection is growing. They did not simply charge, but they assessed first.

When they did charge, I clamped my muscles and waited to die. Jess did not. Jess had other ideas, and her training kicked in. The charging beasts were no different to her than a solid line of student protesters or football hooligans. They were screaming, wailing things to be gone through, and my god, that horse went through them. As a side, I am rather glad the place was a warehouse as the ceiling beams were high. So when Jess reared up on her hind legs and kicked out with her front legs, I did not strike my head on the ceiling above but rather whimpered in abject terror while the horse did the work.

She kicked out, sent a good three or four of them flying away, and timed her landing to perfection so that another one was trampled down. This gave her space to gain purchase as the tiled floor was slippery, but the body she landed on was not.

Then she went forward. She did not walk nor run, but ... well, she ploughed ... Yes, that is the best word I can think of to describe it. She put her head down and simply powered through them. Several times she reared up, but she did so less than before and only enough to batter them aside. She used her head too. Thrashing side to side and using that solid bone to beat them away.

Horses are docile herd animals, but remind me never to get into a fight with one. She was a ferocious animal that could not be stopped.

It was only when we were halfway through that horde that I recalled having the long-bladed machete with me. I did not draw it. I did not do anything other than hang on for dear life, and quite possibly I closed my eyes for some bits and prayed Jess would get us through.

Going through the doorway was the worst point, but she seemed to sense the resistance would be harder, and I felt a surge of speed as she aimed for that gap and charged through them. Of course, I feared getting bitten or scratched on the legs, but her head, neck, feet, and sheer immensity of her removed them from our path. She did not falter or become skittish but showed a tremendous ability and confidence in her own size.

Once outside, I glimpsed both sides of the street and felt my stomach churn once again at the clogged streets.

At this point, I thought Jess was losing control as she started moving sideways. After a few seconds, I realised this was just another tactic of using her ample behind to trample them down. She stepped high too. Like they do in dressage. Her high feet came down heavy, and I even heard the snapping of bones as she landed on legs, ankles, and feet. With space gained, she powered on and gained speed to get through them.

Street after winding street, we went through, and every single one of those streets was full of infected, but I did notice that after the initial density of the group coming through the doors, the rest were almost in pockets or distinct hordes. Like teams as it were. Groups moving together. Seven or eight in one group. Twenty or more in others, but I confess that in the chaos, I could not detect if each group had an alpha leader or if they were each still controlled by the hive mind.

With Jess taking control, I let her ... I say I let her, I had no choice in the matter ... Jess led us out and ran down a street building at a gallop. It was about halfway down the street when I realised she was aiming for the five-bar gate at the end. I think my maximum level of fear had been reached as I do not recall feeling an increase in terror but rather a continuation of sustained terror. I think I gripped correctly, and I know my backside was off the saddle as she leapt, but everything seemed to go in a sort of Hollywood slow motion from then on. The landing was solid. She did not miss a step but just kept going, and once on the turf of an open field, she ran like the wind. Her stride opened, and although it felt she was at her fastest before, she found an extra gear and moved up until the wind was roaring past my face and whipping the tears from my eyes.

I could not have stopped her if I had wanted to. Jess was in charge, and it was Jess that ran until she could either run no more or felt sufficient distance had been gained.

Once she slowed and gently eased down to a canter, I looked back and sat amazed at the great distance now between us and the town way back. The infected were coming after us, but they were small and in the distance.

It was right at that point I knew I had made the right decision in not only choosing a horse as my transport, not only in choosing a riot trained horse, but in choosing Jess.

We moved some miles until finding this old stable block in the lee of a hill. Running water and equipment in their tack room meant I was able to give Jess a cooling wash and brush down while she drank deeply and ate food.

It is here I make these notes while constantly watching

the land around me for signs of movement. Will they keep coming, or is there another purpose to the gathering I have found in that town? If I were a brave man or a trained soldier, I may find a way to deplete their numbers with bombs and such like. But I am not, and my mission is one of the upmost importance.

Greater care MUST be taken. I MUST not allow myself to get into such dangerous points again ...

I must go. Jess has lifted her head high and is giving that snort of worry. Something is coming after us.

NB

CHAPTER TWENTY-FOUR

Jagger glances across at the stony-faced Blowers. Only a few years between them, but the battles, fights, deaths, and constant striving for survival have etched a mask of years on the team's corporal. He stares ahead, then off to the left, to the right, then back to ahead. He listens intently and constantly glances down to watch Meredith strolling about, sniffing the ground.

He's deeply unsettled, yet he shows no outward sign of the troubles in his mind. Being separated from Cookey was difficult. He's always teamed up with Cookey. Why not now? They've been together from the start. They know how each other move, and they work together instinctively to cover each other's backs. Cookey is a dick, but he makes everyone laugh, and yeah, the constant barrage of jokes gest a bit much sometimes, but Blowers wouldn't change it for the world and, without doubt, now counts Cookey and Nick as his best friends.

Jagger stays as stony faced. Years of living in a hard council estate teaches you not to betray your emotions. He's different from Blowers, and he looks with his eyes instead of moving his head.

Why did Mo Mo send him outside? Why did Mo Mo shout the orders? That wasn't Mohammed. Jagger shifts position and goes to say something, then stops when he realises he doesn't know what to say without sounding a twat.

'Shit, isn't it?' Blowers mutters.

'Huh?'

'I said it's shit,' Blowers sighs. 'Mr Howie down ...' he stops and sighs again, 'and what was all that with Mo Mo?'

'Dunno, bruv,' Jagger blurts, 'he ain't done that before.'

'No?' Blowers turns to stare with his mouth turned down. 'He sounded like Mr Howie. Like ... that's what Mr Howie would say ... I mean ...'

'Yeah, I get it,' Jagger murmurs. 'Shit, innit?'

'Say that again.'

'So is Clarence number one now?'

'Eh? Number one?'

'Yeah, like the Bossman? Is he in charge?'

'Should be,' Blowers nods, 'but ... he ... he didn't look too good just then.'

'Stress,' Jagger nods knowingly.

'Stress?'

'Yeah bruv, stress,' Jagger replies. 'It's fucking way worse than people think.'

'Right,' Blowers remarks.

'We going back, then?' Jagger asks for the sake of the comfort of speaking.

'Yeah,' Blowers sighs again, 'Cookey will keep on until they see sense. Lani's fucking losing it ... Paula thinks we're in a managers meeting, and Roy just talks bollocks.'

'Yeah,' Jagger nods slowly, 'Maddox is like Mr Howie ...

He's like ... got that way, innit? You get me? Everyone *wants* to do what he says cos–'

'Shush,' Blowers holds his hand up an inch. Jagger goes instantly quiet and knows better than to ask what Blowers heard. Instead, he strains to see anything different while noticing Blowers motioning towards the dog who stands taut and alert, with ears pricked.

She sniffs the air. Dissecting scents as they carry through her nasal passage, into the olfactory senses of her brain, forty percent of which is given over to her ability to smell.

She glances back to Blowers, to the member of pack with her. She knows her sense of smell is greater, but she also knows his height and advanced vision of his species outmatch hers.

She separates the scents hitting over two hundred million receptors. Badgers. Foxes. Species of birds. Old carrion meat and the now ever-present smell of blood, piss, shit, and fear. She picks up on the scent of Nick smoking within the building. She smells the nerves given off by Lani and Clarence. Wood smoke hangs unseen from a great distance. Burning rubbers, chemicals, and a hundred other scents. A hidden world of messages, knowledge, and understanding, and there, right there, is the smell of the things. They're coming. Coming this way.

The pack leader is down but not dead. She felt his heart beating as it was before and knows his body is still strong. Either the pack leader comes back or another steps forward to challenge for the role. She senses Mo Mo, Clarence, and Nick for the role of leader for those have the energy. Dave is the same as her, a member of the pack, and one given to a set of skills but not given to lead. A protector, not a leader.

But the pack leader is down, and the pack are not

together as they should be, and there is danger coming. The things that tried to kill her little one are coming. She can smell them. She is repulsed by that stench, and images of sinking her teeth into their flesh flood her mind. An urge to attack and drive them off. She gives voice. A warning first to the pack. She smells something. They have to listen and smell too. The voice she gives is quiet but steady, and she feels the hand on her neck. She knows the message has been passed, and now she gives her big voice.

She stands proud, with the hairs on her back standing up. She shows teeth. Big teeth. Teeth ready for killing. She roars in defiance, warning them to stay away, stay back, do not come here, for I am here, the pack is here. You threaten the pack, and I will not let you pass.

'Oh fuck ... Not now ...' Blowers stares hard as the massed snake on the road comes into view. Vehicles are being pushed by the many figures running alongside. No noise. Silent. An approach of overt stealth that steals into view.

'Fuck ... Jagger, get inside and warn the others. Fuck.' Blowers raises his rifle and takes aim as the first rag hanging from the first vehicle is ignited. Spotting the plume of smoke, he lowers the assault rifle and stares intently as his heart booms through his chest. He draws breath, and in that second, he knows everything has just changed.

'INCOMING ... INCOMING ... INCOMING ...' he roars the words over and over. Without hesitation, he raises the rifle and fires single shots into the dense crowd. Jagger is in an instant behind him, and the air fills with the rapid pop, pop of the weapons. The vehicle gains speed. The infected sprint flat out with everything they have to send the vehicle against the building. Down the access lane they surge, aiming for the reception building and the already weakened wall.

Blowers empties the first magazine, rams the next one home, and flicks the weapon from single shot to fully automatic. He aims and fires a solid, withering stream of lead, but the effect is negligible as but a few fall.

'GET IN,' Blowers grabs Jagger's shoulder and sends him staggering towards the smashed-in wall of the reception. He shoves in his third magazine and fires again before turning to race behind the lad.

'MEREDITH ...' He forces the dog into the room, past the Saxon, and into the hole of the wall. 'COVER ME,' he shouts ahead as he throws his assault rifle through first and starts the mad scrabble.

The vehicle gains momentum and, timed to perfection, slams into the ruined wall. The rag ignites with a flickering, blue chemical flame that flares up the material to the fumes seeping from the fuel inlet. The gases ignite and plume down the tube into the tank. The chemical reaction finds resistance in the membrane of the tank, which is pushed beyond the limits of its construction. As the fuel ignites, it heats the air which expands with such force it blows the tank and the vehicle surrounding it in a filthy black cloud of flaming smoke.

Blowers grits his teeth and feels first the impact of the vehicle, then, a second later, the heat, noise, and shockwave of the explosion. Wide-eyed, he scrabbles to get his legs and feet from the room before the twisted, super-heated fragments of vehicle strike the wall.

Two hands reach in to grab his wrists as Jagger tugs the older lad free. Dropping down the safe side, they rush to pick up their assault rifles and aim on the hole.

'Back,' Blowers waves Jagger to fall away. 'Give me your weapon and go tell the rest,' Blowers snaps.

'But ...'

'NOW!' Blowers unleashes a furious roar as he snatches the weapon from Jagger, lays it down on the ground, and slides the box of magazines brought up from the back of the factory. One by one, he takes them out to place them bullet end up and ready for a rapid change.

'DAVE,' Blowers shouts. 'We've got incoming, Dave ...' He works fast, checking each weapon and getting ready for the flow he knows will be coming any second. Glancing round, he spots Dave staring intently down at the still unconscious form of Mr Howie, and with a scowl, Blowers snaps back to the problem in hand.

Thick smoke starts pouring through the hole as the burning rubber of the tyres melts along with the chemical fluids, seats, and other materials of the flaming car. Brickwork falls from the weakened wall.

The smoke hits his eyes, which immediately fill with tears to rid sensitive organs of the particles carried in the air. He coughs, blinks, wipes his face, and grimaces while taking aim down the hole.

'Come on, you fuckers ...' he mutters and blinks again. 'Dave ... Dave! We've got incoming, Dave ...' he spits and waits, feeling the greatest sense of fear so far.

'What the fuck got into Mo Mo?' Nick asks Cookey as they carry another box of ammunition to the thick metal shutter earmarked by Clarence as the place for stacking.

'Fuck knows,' Nick says quietly.

'We should just get what we can carry and go now,'

Cookey looks round at the others working. 'This is fucked up ... What if the Boss has a blood clot?'

'He doesn't,' Nick repeats again. 'Mr Howie is fucking indestructible.'

'You heard what Roy said, though.'

'Fuck Roy–the bloke is just rude.'

'Yeah, I know, Nick. But he's got a point ... He's just blunt.'

'Blunt? Fuck blunt ... Dave is blunt ... Roy is fucking rude. Lani is blunt, but Roy ...' Nick shakes his head, 'that's not our way.'

'What ain't?' Cookey asks.

'What?' Nick puts his case down and lights a cigarette, knowing it'll earn him a bollocking from Clarence for smoking in here.

'Our way,' Cookey says. 'What's that mean?'

'S'wot Mr Howie says,' Nick blows the smoke out. 'We got our way of doing things ... and that ain't it. We've got to be polite and nice. Fuck, Cookey, we're the authorities now, mate.'

'You reckon?'

'Cookey, for fuck's sake, Mr Howie has told us a hundred times. We do things the right way. We stay polite. How many times did he tell us to smile and look nice?'

'Yeah,' Cookey's face brightens at the memory. 'Ha, you remember when we formed a chain to get that shit to the top of the wall, and you were on the Saxon loudspeaker?'

'Yeah,' Nick chuckles, 'see, that's our way.'

'Yeah, I get it,' Cookey sags with a crestfallen look. 'I'm shitting it,' he whispers.

'Shitting what?' Lani walks over.

'Nothing,' Cookey mutters, knowing to give voice will only worry the woman even more.

'Howie? He'll be fine,' Lani says too brightly. 'He's resting.'

'You're fucking losing it, Lani,' Nick stands up straight and waits for the backlash, but she doesn't reply. She just smiles softly. 'Lani, fucking get a grip,' Nick whispers urgently.

'I'm fine,' she shrugs, 'so is Howie.'

'This is fucked up,' Cookey groans. 'Don't be like that, Lani,' he pleads. 'You're scaring me.'

'Why?' she asks. 'Scared of what?'

'You, being all weird and shit.'

The mask slips, and the girl shows her emotions but for the briefest of seconds.

'What if he's not?' she asks softly.

'The Boss?' Nick asks, and she nods. None of them reply but instead watch the burning embers of the end of Nick's cigarette.

'Thought you were going for transport?' Cookey finally asks.

'Guess,' she shrugs.

'Where's Roy?' Nick asks.

'Here,' Roy says from behind him.

'Thought you two were getting the transport?' Nick asks again.

'We were,' Roy casts a loaded look at Lani, 'but er ...'

'What?' Nick presses. 'We need to get the fuck out of here.'

'I figured we'd wait a minute,' he says quietly.

'What for, Roy?' Nick demands. 'Mr Howie needs help, and we ain't got time for a fucking rest.'

'Lani seems a bit odd,' he says with a quick lift of his eyebrows as he struggles with the insurmountable task of using tact and diplomacy.

'Eh?' Nick glances from Roy to Lani, 'oh ... fuck ... yeah, right ...'

'We'll get this done, then come with you,' Cookey cuts in quickly.

'Sounds good,' Roy offers a fake smile that does nothing to hide the worry etched on his face.

'We'll be alright,' Nick says to all of them. 'We got through worse than this before.'

'Sure,' Cookey walks off to get another case.

'I'll give you a hand ...' BOOM. 'What the hell was that?'

'That's gunfire,' Nick snaps back. 'CLARENCE ...'

'I can hear it,' the big man strides from the back of the room.

'Fucking automatic,' Nick tilts his head at the sound of Blowers firing on automatic from outside. A muffled sound comes through, muted through the thick walls, all too familiar to them.

'Make ready,' Nick blurts the order without waiting for Clarence. Grabbing his own assault rifle, he checks the magazine, then quickly pats his pockets to make sure he's got spares.

'Blowers,' Cookey is already off and running.

'COOKEY WAIT,' Clarence booms. 'We go together.'

'Fucking hurry up, then,' the normally smiling lad snarls with impatience at the thought of Blowers on his own.

'FUCK,' he drops low at the explosion of the vehicle against the reception as it sends a vibrating shockwave through the building.

'GO,' Clarence orders at Cookey's already retreating back.

. . .

Blowers stares into the smoke, waiting for the next explosion to come, but it doesn't. The infected, on seeing the lack of damage sustained at the reception building, change course to send the next vehicle into the metal shutters at the far end. Blowers feels the impact and twitches with concern.

'Dave ... what the fuck is going on?' he calls out and stares into the hole, through the tendrils of smoke billowing through. 'Where are they attacking?'

Cookey races through the rear section, through the factory floor as he charges hell for leather towards the far end. As he reaches the next set of doors, the second impact slams behind him into the thick metal shutters. It's closer now, and the noise against the steel bounces, echoes, and rolls round the huge chamber-like rooms. He stops with a hand on the door and pauses to turn back, 'CLARENCE?'

'GO ...' Clarence roars, 'GET TO BLOWERS ... WE'LL COVER HERE ...'

'Fuck,' Cookey jumps back as Jagger pushes through the door, breathing hard.

'Incoming,' Jagger gasps. 'They got cars ... on fire ... cars on fire ... fucking hundreds of them ...'

'We need height,' Nicks snaps, 'to fire down on them.'

'The shutters are the weakest point,' Roy interjects. 'If they get through, we're ...'

'COOKEY,' Clarence booms, 'GET TO BLOWERS ... JAGGER, GO WITH HIM ... EVERYONE ELSE, BACK IN THE SHUTTERS ROOM.'

There's another explosion as the third vehicle slams into the shutters; then, the fourth and fifth are sent rolling and ablaze to join the awful cacophony of noise.

The group split, running in different directions. Cookey goes towards the front to be with Blowers. Lani runs back into the ammunition storage room, towards the exit door at the far end. The rest go for the shutters, now buckled and groaning under the weight and heat of the blazing vehicles on the other side.

A dull roar reaches them as the massed infected outside scream into the air. They surge towards the munitions factory. Breaking into pre-set groups, a large section veers off towards the reception building and the hole they know is there. Another breaks off towards the rear emergency exit doors the survivors used in their panicked flight just a short time ago. The main bulk goes for the shutters.

Through the many pairs of eyes of the hosts, the infection quickly established that the reception building has not sustained any further damage, and it also knows there will be people inside aiming weapons at the hole made by Howie. What it does notice is the Saxon standing silent and brooding on the once pristine tiled floor of the reception area.

The power of the vehicle is well known to the infection from the countless battles, fights, and skirmishes done since this began, and as Cookey races through the building, he hears that dull roar from the infected suddenly cease.

Blowers holds his aim, with his finger ready on the trigger. The succession of explosions told him the attack was being focussed on the shutters, and the hairs on the back of his neck prickled at the sound of the feet charging.

He listened with increasing concern as they breached the reception. The snarls, groans, and hisses sound clear as he increases his grip and makes ready to cut them down. The sudden cessation of noise stopped his breath in his chest. Silence from the other side. Complete silence.

'Come on,' he mutters under his breath, 'come on ... get it started ...' The waiting was the hardest bit. Waiting meant they were planning. Planning meant the infection was getting smarter.

'Dave,' he whispers over his shoulder, 'they're planning something.'

Dave doesn't respond but stares fixed at the prone form of Howie.

Clarence heaves the General-Purpose Machine Gun over to the shutters and moves quickly to get the thing loaded and positioned. The others open cases to grab magazines which they rest on the ground, ready for rapid changes. Roy lays his bow on the ground next to him and takes up the assault rifle.

'What the fuck?' Nick is the first to voice his concern at the sudden drop in noise from outside. There's just the crackling and spitting of the vehicles on fire as thick, choking, black smoke seeps through the gaps of the damaged shutter.

'Oh no ... no ... no, no, no,' Blowers feels the panic rise harder on hearing the unmistakable sound of the Saxon firing up. 'Dave ... they've got the Saxon ...'

Still no response as Dave refuses to budge from his position. One hand clutches the pistol, the other rests on Howie's chest, and his eyes fix unblinking on Howie's face.

'Blowers,' Cookey bursts into the room, running flat out with his assault rifle already up and aimed.

'Saxon,' Blowers calls back, 'they've got the Saxon started.'

'Fuck no ...' Cookey drops with heaving chest next to his mate and starts laying out his own magazines. 'They'll get in,' he adds quickly.

'Was it the shutter they rammed?' Blowers asks without moving his aim from the hole.

'Yeah.'

'Is it holding?'

'Dunno ... I was running here.'

'The Saxon will get through it.'

'Yep,' Cookey lifts his rifle to aim through the hole, 'we're fucked.'

'Where's everyone else?'

'Dunno ... at the back,' Cookey whispers.

'Dave, for fuck's sake,' Blowers snaps as Cookey looks round to catch glimpse of them in the side room. 'He won't move ... doesn't even reply,' he adds to Cookey.

'Like I said,' Cookey replies, 'we're fucked.'

Both lads fire as one at the fleeting glimpse of a body on the other side of the hole. A shadow passes but enough, and the booming shots echo round the room.

The infected hold still as the infection works the controls of the heavy armoured vehicle. It's a tiny, old woman at the steering wheel, which would be comical if it wasn't for the dire threat of the situation. The size and age don't matter, just the ability to be controlled. She shunts the vehicle back, turns the wheel and shunts forward and, in turn, slams the rear and front into the walls as she slowly gets it facing out.

A shadow passes in front of the hole, and the infection hears the weapons opening up. There's two of them, which means maybe only two are covering that hole.

They have enough for a few sacrifices to be made, and it sends one into the hole, moving as fast as possible before being cut down by a hail of bullets. But the view was enough. Blowers and Cookey are on the other side, but no more. The rest must be at the rear.

The Saxon bursts out of the reception, into the open air, where it gathers speed and powers into the grounds, churning divots of once perfect lawn up. It turns slowly, almost lazily, back to face the building and starts the journey towards the shutters and the fiery wrecks slowly melting to fuse against it.

The old woman bounces on the cushioned seat. Her wrinkled, gnarled hands clutch the steering wheel as her red eyes stare fixed at the weakest point of the building. The gathered hordes part as the vehicle lumbers towards the building, gathering speed as it goes.

Inside, Clarence racks the bolt back on the GPMG.

'There's grenades over there,' he shouts to Roy. 'Bring 'em over.'

'Is that wise? What if they throw them back in?' Roy shouts back.

'Fuck it,' Clarence grimaces at the realisation that the ammunition and explosives are a very dangerous thing to be near during a fire fight.

'What's that?' Nick steps closer to the shutters. 'An engine ... shit!'

'WHAT?' Clarence barks.

'The Saxon ... That's the fucking Saxon.'

'Blowers must have got out,' Paula says.

'No,' Nick shakes his head, 'he wouldn't leave that hole unprotected.'

'Dave and Howie?' she glances round to Clarence.

'No,' he mutters, 'we'd know ...'

'Who, then?' she asks with a puzzled frown, which quickly morphs into shock. 'Oh ... oh no ...'

The engine they have heard so many times, which was normally a comforting roar, now turns into a defiant scream as it thunders towards them.

'Will it get through?' Paula shouts.

'It'll get through anything,' Nick yells back. 'We need to–'

'FALL BACK,' Clarence is on his feet, lifting the GPMG and the case of ammunition. He strides away from the shutters as the rest follow suit.

The old lady shows no reaction until the last second; then, she bares her teeth. The Saxon impacts on the shutters as the old lady slams her foot down to drive increasing power to the wheels.

There's huge bang from the initial impact. Metal grinds and compacts as the front of the Saxon drives the flaming vehicles harder against the already yielding shutters. She backs up, pulling way back onto the churned-up lawn, before changing gear, and slamming her foot back down. The Saxon's wheels spin on the soft mud but find traction, and it roars as it goes forward to once again smash into the vehicles.

The shutters buckle inwards. Bricks fall from the walls as the solid steel bolts pop from the solid steel frame. She backs up again and takes another run up while the massed hordes remain silent and still.

Blowers and Cookey fire and fire into the hole. The first one through was cut to ribbons, but even now, after already exhausting several magazines, they can see the pulped body being slowly pushed forward. They shoot at it, through it, through the gaps, and keep killing, but the infected on the other side keep pushing the bodies through, using them as shields.

Clarence lifts the GPMG to hold at waist height one-handed while clutching the magazine with his free hand. A shiny ammunition belt links the two together, and he waits with his heart racing and the awful, growing feeling that everything just went very horribly wrong. This fight isn't like the others. The infection is using tools and weapons, and the spirit amongst the team is already broken. Every person in that room clutches their weapon and stares in horror as they listen to the Saxon reversing, then screaming forward to drive the shutters in a few more inches at a time.

The infection gains the knowledge of the motions needed to pull the Saxon back and forward. It takes the horde at the back door and eases back to give them a greater degree of free thought while still pumping them full of hormones to build them into a wild rage of unleashed thirst and blood lust. As one, they race to the door and start beating themselves against it. Slamming fists, feet, legs, arms, and heads smash against the wooden doors until those limbs become battered and bloodied.

The munitions factory was never designed to withhold sustained attacks. In the event of a strike, they simply had to wait until the authorities arrived.

The shutters yield with every impact, groaning as they buckle ever inwards. The rear doors rattle in their frames as the hinges are loosened. Blowers and Cookey fire and fire as the completely ruined and pulped body is forced through the hole to drop down in a mangled heap.

The old lady pulls back further this time. Taking the Saxon onto fresh lawn, she changes gear and gently eases her foot down as the vehicle rumbles forward. Steadily, she pushes her foot down harder, and with the extra space, the Saxon builds greater speed until it crashes jarringly into the vehicles, and the shutter bends in by almost a metre. She pulls back, and as the infection draws its attention from her, it releases the horde to charge. And charge it does.

At the hole they slowly push through as the ammunition is being used so very quickly. At the rear door, they loosen the hinges and vibrate the doors in the frame so the brickwork starts to give. As each inch of movement on the doors is gained, so the greater motion they can use.

At the shutters, they aim for the metre gap on either side, plenty of room to get through. Clarence opens fire on the left gap, a sustained but controlled burst that destroys the first bodies. He starts to rake across the doors, hoping to fire through and kill more, but the shutters are thick steel, and the rounds ricochet on the inside to ping back into the room. Shouts of warning sound out from Nick and Roy.

'I'LL TAKE THE LEFT SIDE.' Clarence roars, knowing he can't afford the time to switch aim at the exposed gaps on both sides, but also, he can't risk striking the shutters for fear of the bullets coming back in to kill his own team.

Nick, Roy, Jagger, and Paula focus their small arms fire on the right side, but the fleeting glimpses of bodies are few and far between. A taunting begins. Dead body puppets are propped up and presented to be peppered and pummelled by the persistent pounding given by the weapons.

The rear door starts to buckle as Lani takes aim and makes ready to fire. The room fills with the deafening thuds of rifles and machines guns. Shouts are given and ignored. The heat of battle builds as sweat starts to flow, but the energy is different. The bond between them is weakened by the bitterness of Howie going down. Tiredness from the previous day spent running, fighting, and hiding shows, as do the nerves–frayed by the vigilance needed during the journeys through the fog. After a night and day awake, they have to give what they can to stay alive.

'BLOCKAGE,' Blowers casts the weapon aside and grabs the one taken from Jagger. He aims and fires.

Cookey screams, 'MAGAZINE!' and loads yet another one into his rifle.

Round after round is fired. Magazine after magazine is emptied, and although they are but metres away from thousands of bullets, they cannot stop to get more. Worrying glances get cast down at the rapidly depleting stacks at their feet.

'SINGLE SHOT!' Blowers turns his weapon over and makes the change before raising, aiming, and firing with greater care. Cookey does the same. They disgorge from the hole in a never-ending vomit of pulped bodies shot to bits in an effort to waste ammunition and energy.

The infection forces the team to split. Attacking three points at once, and without the cohesion given by Howie, without Howie shouting at Dave to give orders, and without Dave giving those orders in such a manner that everyone hears–they become fractured, broken, and the fear saps at their energy reserves.

The rear doors give as Lani opens up with a withering volley of automatic fire that shreds the first comers to bits. But the infection watches through those that die and sends more from the shutters round to the rear doors. The hive mind tells those at the hole there is a breach, and those in the reception push harder and make more noise to drive the panic and fear higher.

Still Dave watches enraptured at the sleeping form of Howie. To anyone, his face a mask that is devoid of expression, but Howie would see the concern there. He would see the slight narrowing of the eyes and the gentle crease across Dave's forehead. He clutches that pistol but does not for one second glance anywhere else other than at the man he watches. The heart is strong beneath his hand, and Dave feels that heart as it speeds up and slows down. Dave watches the rapid eye movement of Howie's sleep and the twitches and silent murmurings given. Dave knows Howie deals with something, battles with something, fights something but that he does it alone.

'FUCK ...' Cookey yells in pure frustration as he snatches a glance round in the vain hope others will be coming to support them, but the room is empty. 'DAVE ... WE NEED HELP!'

Dave doesn't flicker but rests that hand on Howie's chest as though driving energy into his beloved leader.

'LAST MAGAZINE,' Cookey screams. 'FUCK YOU ...' he adds in a voice that breaks with emotion.

'Easy, mate,' Blowers pulls the trigger and hopes to hell the bullets are killing something on the other side of that hole.

'Not like this ... not like this ...' Cookey repeats over and again. 'Not here ... not like this ...'

'DAVE,' Blowers yells, 'we're running out ...'

Nick snatches the magazine out and slams a new one home as he dares to step forward and rake the gap with thirty rounds of fully automatic gunfire.

'GET BACK, YOU BLOODY TWAT,' Roy lowers his rifle a second as he curses the stupidity of the action.

A huge bang sounds out, and the shutters give another three feet as the old lady slams the Saxon back into them from the other side, the noise of the engine lost in the constant thunderous noise of the fire fight.

Lani steps back to buy time as she changes magazine and starts firing from the hip as they burst and push to gain a footing within the room. As the gun clicks empty, she knows the time it will take to change again is enough time for them to gain the room. The gun is cast aside, the meat cleaver is drawn, and a tear rolls down her face as she knows she will die here. The urge to turn and run to be with Howie is so strong, but she has to hold position for his sake. The noise is so great she cannot call for help, and the air is so thick with smoke and fumes that any effort to shout will break her down in coughing. She needs to buy time for the others, but more importantly–Howie. Hopefully Dave will finally realise how dire the situation is and get Howie out of here. If they all die, if all of them lay down their lives to buy enough time for Dave to get Howie out of here successfully, it will have been worth it.

'Fuck you,' she snarls her upper lip up and rotates her wrist as the first one comes in for the kill. A twirl, and the innards are spilled as she drives deep into the horde in a desperate fight to hold that rear door.

Nick backs away from the shutters and glances down to see Lani firing from the hip. With a shock, he realises the immensity of the foes she faces and starts towards her.

'HOLD YOUR GROUND,' Clarence, unaware of Lani's plight, roars the order at Nick. He pauses and, glancing down, spots Meredith raging with barks at the shutters. One hand reaches to grab her by the neck as he forces her round to show her the back door. As Lani throws the gun down to draw her hand weapon, so Meredith spots a fight she can join, and she's away, sprinting across the distance of the room as she fixes eyes on a big male aiming for Lani's back.

As Lani severs a hand and spins round to open a throat, so the male lunges and is taken neatly away by an airborne Meredith attaching her teeth to his face. She drops, and her body weight takes him clean down to the floor. She rags once, twice and removes enough flesh to ensure he bleeds out; then, she's off, snaking and leaping to fight back-to-back with Lani.

Lani senses the presence of the dog, and that act of kindness both increases her fortitude to hold the door until she dies, but at the same time, it presses an almost overwhelming sadness through her. They are dying for him. They are giving their lives in the hope Howie will live.

'HOWIE,' she screams the name and feels the pressure building as she is driven further back into the room. She cannot falter now. She cannot give ground, so she fights, and her long, black hair swishes left to right as she dances and swirls in an ever-pressing circle of death. Meredith senses the desperation and goes up a gear. She becomes faster, biting harder, ragging quicker, and killing with everything she has.

Not enough. It's not enough.

They break through the shutters as the Saxon once again pummels them inwards. Surges of infected pour through the broken sides, and the desperate group fight a backwards retreat as they fire into the thick ranks of incoming infected.

Clarence knows they have to stop shooting. The further back they go, the greater the risk of a stray bullet igniting something or exploding an exposed round in a case or a magazine. A horrible thought crosses his mind. They're fucked. They stand no chance of winning this fight. But they could draw as many in as possible before blowing the place to shreds. It would be a final "fuck you" to the infection, and it means they could choose their own manner of death and die proud, the way Chris did. He glances back towards the huge pile of explosives, and the temptation is there. Except for one thing. Dave. Dave will never let harm come to Howie, so even if they all die here, they do it one by one to buy time for the man they all follow. More determined than ever, he lets out a roar and tries to fight harder.

But the feeling isn't the same as it was before, the energy wanes, and he fights with a wildly increasing desperation.

The infection gains the shutters and the rear doors as the two lads in the room covering the hole fire their last magazines. They drop the rifles to draw handguns and fire two-handed in perfect synchronised movements.

Three breaches. Three points of entry. The pistols click empty, and the time for shooting is over as the time for fighting begins.

'WEAPONS DOWN,' Clarence roars the order, drops the GPMG, and grabs his double-headed axe, pausing for the briefest of seconds to make sure the rest have finished firing. As one, they drop firearms and take up hand weapons. Nick rams the butt of his rifle into the face of one running faster than the others. As it goes down, he drops the rifle and gets his toes under his axe. Flicking it up in the air, he catches it by the handle and spins round to remove the head of the next one coming.

The roar of the infected increases tenfold as the infection senses victory, and from all the glimpses through all the eyes, there is no sight of Howie or Dave.

Lani is cut and bitten, but she fights on. Meredith is kicked and raked, but she fights on. They hold their door with a viciousness of epic proportions as pure stubbornness keeps them alive.

Blowers slams his axe down and takes a pulped head clean off, but the body is pushed through with such force it slams into Cookey and drives him back. A never-ending flow pushes and pushes until the strikes given by Blowers and Cookey lose aim and strength. They no longer give killing blows, but they break shoulders and sever arms. It's not enough to kill, and the infected cram and force each other through that gap.

Clarence fights, but his aim and focus are off. His energy not right. His rage is there, but it's fuelled by fear and not the righteous glory it was before. Roy and Paula fight back to back. Jagger and Mo Mo the same. Nick is the only one that keeps hope alive in his heart. He was alone in that house and without hope, but despite the most awful of circumstances, Howie came for him. Howie will never leave them to suffer. Howie will come.

'Keep coming, you cunts,' he mutters and glares, but somewhere, deep down in his soul, the first prickle of hesitancy creeps in. A blood clot on the brain. A medical thing. What if Howie doesn't come back? What if this truly is it?

Fuck it. These last sixteen days have been better than all the days of his life before. He belongs somewhere now. He is part of something, and no fucker will take that away.

Cookey goes down under the weight of an infected slamming into him and feels the teeth sink into his shoulder. He grimaces and screams with rage as he drives his thumbs deep into the eye sockets before twisting round to kick at the next one coming through the hole.

'DAVE ...' the smiling lad screams without humour now, 'GET THE BOSS AWAY. GET HIM AWAY ...' The thought of dying is real. This is it. They are overrun and losing, but it's not help he calls for but the protection of Howie. 'DAVE ... TAKE HIM ...'

'COOKEY, GET UP ... YOU CUNT,' Blowers slams his foot down on the neck of the one surging through the hole.

'BLOWERS ... I THINK WE'RE FUCKED, MATE.' Cookey heaves the body off, gets to his feet, and winces as Blowers grabs the one halfway out and shoves him over to Cookey.

'I'll grab 'em ... You kill 'em,' Blowers shouts and spins as

Cookey goes down again from the weight of the body hitting him. Both of them are bleeding, cut everywhere, eyes sore and stinging from the dust and debris. Voices break and give out. Limbs get heavy and weary as they fight a battle that goes against them.

As Blowers turns to help his best mate, the hole is left unprotected. The infected surge in, one after the other. Blowers grabs the neck of the one on Cookey and slams it to the side. He turns back and curses at the sheer numbers getting through the hole.

Cookey jumps to his feet, and the lads spare a glance at each other. It's a fleeting meeting of eyes, but the decision is mutual. With a nod, they charge. Without axes. Without knives. They charge with bare hands.

Blowers reverts to his boxing training and lashes out with hard punches that break noses, jaws and slams his foot down onto knee joints. Cookey fights like a bastard. Biting, gouging, and strangling anything that comes at him. Back to back, they are pressed and ready to die. The skin on Blowers knuckles open, but it goes unheeded as he punches and punches. Pain radiates from the blows he gets back, and one gets past his guard to sink teeth into his arm.

Pure anger erupts, and he beats the thing off. 'I'M BIT,' he screams, 'GET OUT. GO BACK. I'M BIT ...'

'FUCK OFF,' Cookey yells back.

'GO ... I'LL HOLD 'EM. GO ...'

Cookey doesn't reply but feels Blowers pressing harder against his back. He pushes back, the only comfort he can give, and he fights with blood pouring down his face, with blood seeping from his hands. With his legs growing heavy and his arms hurting, he fights.

'I'm sorry, mate,' Blowers mutters.

'Don't be,' the only words Cookey can get out.

Meredith bleeds from open wounds. Lani bleeds from bites. Roy fights to defend Paula, so not used to hand-to-hand combat. Jagger and Mo Mo feel the tide of the battle turning so badly against them. Clarence falters and grows weary.

Nick smiles.

'Now,' he mutters, 'now. For fuck's sake, Howie ... NOW!'

'I'm still a woman,' she whispers. 'Now go ... go ...' she pushes me roughly away, 'but know this–not everyone will survive this journey, Howie ...'

A kiss, and the energy pours through me. Into my lips, my limbs, my muscles, and my chest burns like an electric rod is pressed against it. Energy flows into me. Pure energy. Energy unlike any that has ever been experienced before. Marcy pushes me away and gives me a stinging, open-handed slap across my face. My eyes snap open, but it's not her I see.

Dave. Dave stares down at me with eyes ablaze, and his hand ready to hit me again.

'GET UP!' that voice drives me up, and without movement, without motion, without leverage, I am on my feet and burning with a fire which heats from my gut. My heart roars, and lungs fill with air.

'We fight,' I shake from head to toe as I lock eyes on Dave. 'WE FIGHT. FIGHT, DAVE ... WE FIGHT ...'

He nods. Words are not needed, and it takes minutes, hours, days, and weeks to turn from facing him to look through the doorway, into the room. I see my lads pinned back to back and surrounded by the filthy beasts that dare touch them, and that sight, that view of my team being beaten down, is enough to make me know I will never, never stop fighting.

'MY BOYS,' I roar with a voice that matches Dave's, and two terrified heads snap round to face me, but I'm already running.

The pure hatred is balanced by the purest of love for my team. Fuck mankind. Fuck everyone. I fight for these boys that were prepared to die as I lay sleeping in that room.

'Back to the others ... NOW,' I roar at the lads.

'MOVE ... GO, GO, GO ...' Dave repeats the order in only the way Dave can, and together, me and the small man, launch into those beasts.

'THEY GOT THE SAXON,' Cookey blurts as he and Blowers back away.

Now that only makes me worse. The thought of it. The intrusion that our machine has been used against us and defiled in such a way.

I don't use weapons. Not my axe or a knife, but I snap necks one after the other with hands that I didn't know could do that. Each head is gripped and simply twisted to the side as I feel the spinal column snapping. Again and again. Like water, I move through them. Fluent and graceful. Dave matches me. Kill for kill, we go one for one. Snap and drop. Dead and drop. They do not touch us, for they are slow, and we are far, far faster than they ever will be. Hands out. Head gripped. Neck snapped with ease. With insulting and offensive ease, we kill those that got through until around us lie only the dead and nothing else. I glance round and see the lads standing at the far end with open mouths.

'Still here? I gave you an order,' I smile gently. 'Go on ... We'll be right down.'

They turn and run as I bend over to smile at the infected coming through. He turns to look up at me, but it's not him I see but the thing inside.

'One race, is it?' The energy blazes dark in my eyes as I snap the neck and stand up.

'Which way?' Dave asks with a nod at the hole.

'You that way,' I give my own nod at the hole. 'I'll go after the lads.'

'Okay, Mr Howie.' He grabs the body and pulls it clean through before diving in headfirst, and God help the thing that meets him halfway.

I glance round and see my axe is back in the side room. After a quick deviation, I'm running after the lads. I go through doors I didn't know were here, but I remember Marcy's words that the team are in the room at the far end, and Lani is on her own, protecting the rear door.

At the mid-point, I catch up with Cookey. He's bent over Blowers on the ground clutching his left arm.

'What? What's happened?'

'Bitten,' Blowers gasps.

Shit. The realisation that Marcy was right hits me hard. 'Where?'

'Arm,' he looks up at me, 'sorry.'

'Let me see,' I gently lift his hand away to reveal the punctured teeth marks. 'Any pain?'

'Hurts like a bastard,' he grunts.

'What's this?' I turn his hand over to see the opened wounds on his knuckles. 'You're cut to bits.'

'Punching,' he says apologetically.

'When?'

'Back there,' he nods at the way we just came from. I don't say anything for a second but wait for his own brain to catch up.

'Oh ... oh shit.' his eyes go wide, 'fuck ...'

'What?' Cookey looks terrified, pale, and drawn.

'Huh,' Blowers snorts with laughter as he gets to his feet, 'didn't realise.'

'You too then,' I nod at him.

'Looks that way, Mr Howie.'

'What?' Cookey repeats, 'fucking what?'

'You're such a twat,' Blowers shakes his head but can't keep the grin from his face.

'Eh? What!?' Cookey looks down at Blowers knuckles dripping with blood and the visibly open cuts. He stares hard for a second, then up at the bite mark.

'Oh ...' he says softly, 'oh, right.' The grin that spreads across his face changes his whole appearance. 'You're immune.'

'Yeah,' Blowers replies just as softly, 'think I am.'

'Mate,' Cookey stares in shock.

'Later.' I pat Blowers on the shoulder and start running again. They fall in beside me, and I don't need to look to know the relief they feel or see the grins on their faces. They fade though as they remember the dire situation we are running towards and the unknown of what we might find.

I remember yesterday and forcing these lads to run because of my own obstinate issues. They're exhausted, drained, wounded, and I can see they hardly have anything left to give.

'Lads, drop back and let me do–'

'No chance,' Blowers gives a burst of speed with Cookey right at his side. Through the double doors, into the factory section and sprinting flat out down to the next set of doors, and already the sounds of fighting are reaching my ears.

Lani is torn. She knows the team need her, but she longs

to be by your side. She is at the far end, at the most dangerous point, and she covers a gap in the wall, and she knows if she turns away, they will break through. The words given to me by Marcy fill my mind, and as that image, that emotion, and feeling settle inside my mind, so I find greater speed, and opening my stride, I outstrip the lads as I aim for the last set of doors.

She is at the far end, at the most dangerous point. There's something in her voice. A warning. A tone of inflection, and suddenly the fear is upon me. *Lani is torn. Torn?* The word has more than one meaning. No. Please no.

The doors burst open as I charge into them and head straight through without slowing.

'STAND YOUR GROUND AND FIGHT ...' The words spill from my mind, and I can see Nick with a wry smile on his face as he fends off several infected. Clarence swings his axe to cleave two in half as he turns with a slow grin spreading across that broad face glistening with sweat and filth. Paula sags with relief as Roy turns, sees me running, and goes back to the fight. Jagger and Mo Mo suddenly get faster and fight harder. Nick is possessed, and Clarence roars with glory as the energy of the team becomes one again.

Behind me, the lads burst into the room as a cheer erupts. Now we are whole, and together we fight. Except two are missing. *Lani is torn. At the far end. Lani is torn. The most dangerous point.*

I hammer through and pass the group, swerving round cases and stacks of boxes, and there it is. The light pours through the smashed-in emergency exit door at the far end.

A horde, thick and fast, are spilling through, and I watch as though time slows down as she fights with a speed and dexterity I have never seen from her. The light glimmers and catches on her raven black hair, and that golden skin seems to glow, but on her face, there are tears that stream, and her heart is broken. The tide against her is too great, far too great, but she tries to dominate that central ground. The ground about her feet is littered with the dead and dying.

They converge on her and, as one, engulf her. I watch helpless as she's torn from her feet. Teeth and nails gouge into her arms, legs, and torso. She screams and bucks, but the bodies swarm, and she's taken out of sight.

Meredith attacks, with blood spraying from her mouth, and I scream, oh, I scream and demand my legs go faster. I cross that ground with every ounce of strength, willing Lani to just hold on.

'LANI ...' If she hears me, she will know I am coming, she will know to fight and keep fighting and to never give up. She held this door on her own, at the most dangerous point to protect those she holds most dear.

I cannot speak nor form words, but the passion spews forth as a howl of utter frustration, and then I am amongst them and upon them. I grab bodies and heave them aside with a strength that flows and burns. One after the other, after the other, is wrenched from that writhing bundle. I see dark hair, raven black and silky straight, and down I go after her, stamping and kicking while my hands grab at body parts to cast them aside. I get bitten and scratched, thumped, kicked, and battered, but the pain does not reveal itself until I see her slender arm and grab a firm grasp of her wrist. I heave and run backwards to free her from the massed pressing bodies, but they cling and bite into her. I kick down to free the dirty infected from her blessed skin, but hands that are broken and ruined cling on until I can stamp and wrench. Meredith is within them, biting and ragging furiously but never quickly enough, and then she's free, and I'm dragging her body across the floor.

They're up and surging towards us, intent on finishing what they started, but Lani is no longer alone, and like fuck will I let one of these bastards get past me. Meredith is at my side, and we bring a frenzied death down on them. My axe was dropped somewhere, but my hands do the work. Their skin is soft and yielding, and I tear throats out with my bare fingers, snap necks and arms. A leg is torn free by the dog, and I take it up to use as a weapon. A human leg complete with shoe that I grip and swing out to take more of them down.

Dave appears behind them with a roar that has every head in that building turning, and it's enough for me to drop the leg, grab Lani, and drag her further into the room as Dave shows them what dangerous really looks like.

'Lani ... Lani ...' I'm dragging her by the arm, but she doesn't answer. Her face is covered in blood. Her clothing torn and ripped. Her body torn. *Torn. Lani is torn.*

Free from the melee, I drop down and force myself to stay calm. I start checking for injuries, but she's bleeding from so many places. The infection can't hurt her, but the wounds are so many. Bite marks, grips marks, bruises, and cuts to her neck and cheeks.

'Lani ...' I try to identify the worst injuries, but the blood covers nearly every inch of her exposed skin, and I can't see anything other than blood through the blurred tears that I blink furiously away.

Time ceases, and I have no idea what goes on around me until suddenly hands are touching me, and the team are dropping down to my side.

'Move, Mr Howie, move ...' Roy's tone is urgent, and I let him take over. He drops down to inspect the wounds.

'Water,' his tone is calm, and bottles are handed over. He pours them over bite marks and identifies the ones bleeding the most. 'Bandages.'

'Where from?' Nick asks.

'First aid kit. Find one,' Roy calls back, and several of the team burst away as Roy goes back to gently pouring water over the wounds. He lifts her head and starts pouring the liquid down her forehead. She murmurs and twitches as the water hits her mouth, an instinctive reaction to take fluids in, and one that has me gasping in hope.

Roy holds the mouth of the bottle to her lips and lets the tiniest trickle in. Just a drop, which she takes without sound. Then a bit more, and he waits, watching for any reaction before doing it again.

'Give her more,' Jagger urges.

'She could drown,' Roy replies softly, 'little bit at a time.' He eases some more into her parched lips as I take hold of her hand and rub it gently.

'Here,' Nick drops down, breathing hard and holding a large, green box with a white cross on the front.

'Bandages. Get the wounds covered,' Roy instructs. Paula and Nick work fast, opening the box to take the clean, sterile bandages from within. The plastic covers are ripped open with teeth, and the dressings applied by Roy as he starts on the ones bleeding the worst.

A deep cut to her right thigh is bound first, and we all help to raise the leg so Roy can loop the bandage underneath. Her left calf is next. Her right arm, her left arm, and her stomach.

'Dave, get outside with Nick and get our fucking Saxon back.'

'On it,' the pair race off.

'Everyone else, get ammunition stacked and ready to go.

Reload the weapons and make ready in case they come back. Hang on, Dave? Did you kill 'em all?'

'Yes,' he shouts back.

'Cookey and Blowers, you cover the outside of the shutters. Jagger and Mo Mo, face down to those rear doors. Paula, you watch the top section. Roy, once Lani is finished, check the dog next, then everyone else in turn.'

'On it,' he nods with the same prompt reply the others give.

'How is she?' I ask in a quieter voice.

'She's lost a lot of blood,' he turns to glance up at me. 'There's a lot of wounds. Her heart and pulse are shaky. We have to watch for shock now.'

'Shock?'

'Her body is shutting down to protect the vital organs,' he explains slowly, 'which is why she's passed out. Her mind doesn't need to be working for her to stay alive. The danger now is her core temperature will plummet, and that makes it harder for her whole body to work. Worst case is she goes into cardiac arrest.'

'Okay,' I nod quickly, 'you mean her heart could stop?'

'Yes, if it does, we can do CPR or find a defib machine. She needs emergency medical care.'

'Everyone,' I shout, 'fuck covering the doors. We get loaded, and we go as soon as possible ...'

The Saxon is found and put to use, battering the vehicles away from where the shutters were and then backed into the building. The rear doors are opened, and Clarence carries Lani to lie in the back while the ammunition crates are stacked and shoved into every possible place.

'Car park round the corner,' Nick runs back in. 'Want me to grab something?'

'Get what you can. The bigger the better ... Dave, go with him. Roy, please stay with Lani.'

'I can, but you said the dog needs checking.'

'I'll do it,' grabbing bottles of water, I head over to the animal still standing and still alert as she flicks her head to look from the shutter entrance to the rear. 'Good girl,' I drop down at her side to stroke her huge head. Her tail wags, and she whines softly. I pour water into my hand which she laps and keeps lapping until two bottles are drained. Her wounds are checked. She bleeds but not badly, and she takes the pain without complaint when I pour clean water over the worst injuries. We need to go. Go now. But the fort needs ammunition, and that value is greater than one life, which is something I will be discussing with the team when the time is right.

Once cleaned and checked, Meredith deftly jumps up into the Saxon and lies down next to Lani with her head resting on Lani's chest.

The only words spoken are those from necessity. Nick comes back with a small van that gets jammed full of ammunition crates, boxes of grenades, and everything else we can fit in. There's plenty left here, but with two vehicles loaded with as much as we can carry, we finally load up.

Nick and Dave stay together in the van as I clamber into the driver's seat and cast a quick look back at Lani. She's being watched so carefully by everyone perching on and wedged between crates and boxes. Clarence takes the front with me, another two crates on his lap, and a curt nod.

The engine fires up, and the machine that was turned against us pulls away to start the journey back to the fort.

CHAPTER TWENTY-FIVE

Day Sixteen

Jess and I remain in the stable block we found after fleeing the horde that found us hiding in the arts centre.

On higher ground with a good view, and damned if I'm going back out there today. It's too much. All of it is too much, and as my panic subsides, so I am left with frayed nerves and my stomach cramping in fear.

My god, I knew it would be hard but nothing like this. How can I even hope to continue my search for those with immunity if I am to face such peril at every turn? Writing these diary entries is the only way to calm my thoughts and bring order back to my mind.

. . .

Besides, and I know this is a reason I cling to and a process of self-justification for my paltry cowardice, but Jess galloped flat-out for a great distance, and resting her now is the right thing to do. I rely on her for survival, so even if I wanted to go back out there, which I do not, but even if I so desired to venture out into that danger, it would be on a tired horse. Having said that, Jess appears not the least bit tired. If anything, she appears somewhat pepped up by the whole experience.

I must take this period to reflect on what I have learnt:

**They are massing in a town.*

I do not know the reasons for this massing. It could be something as simple as there having been a festival or event within the town at the time of the infection being released, and therefore a greater population within one place.

However, their desire to infect should be driving them to seek more hosts. Therefore something is holding them there. They are there for a reason.

**There appeared to be smaller groups noticeably separated from each other, but all within the greater nucleus of the horde.*

The virus will evolve. We knew that.

The virus will also be manipulated and changed as it evolves. What infects one person may be changed to something different within another. There will be many millions who suffer the same symptoms and change in exactly the same way. But we also knew there would be fewer numbers within the population who would not be affected in the same way, those who's natural antibodies would cause a slower rate of infection or repel the virus to an extent the virus would change, and they too would change.

Like the cup of coffee I am drinking now. The coffee was one thing. The water another. They were separate and unique, but once put together, the chemical reaction changes them both to produce something else.

Those manipulations are the most dangerous, the single most dangerous threat to our species that has ever been known.

Only one test subject showed a manipulation, and that was terrifying beyond compare and was the reason I reached my decision to bug out from the project and undertake this perilous activity.

Even the thought of that test subject sends shivers down my spine as the memories come spilling back. The intelligence. The cunning. The emotional range that could be understood and played with. The absolute lack of hesitancy for the sanctity of life.

If there is one here, within that town, that has that form of manipulated virus within him or her, then to be blunt, we are all ~~fucked~~ doomed.

. . .

But the plan must remain. I must seek the immune and work through my list.

But not today. Today I have done enough, and today I will cower in this stable block until my stomach cramps ease, and I can hold the coffee cup without trembling so much it spills out.

NB

CHAPTER TWENTY-SIX

'Shit ...'

'WHAT!?'

'Go faster.'

'Why? Roy ... why are you telling me to go faster?'

'Focus on the road, Boss,' Clarence twists in his seat to stare back into the rear of Saxon.

'What?' Gripping the wheel, I try and peer behind me, but the speed I'm travelling at makes it too dangerous to take my eyes off the debris-strewn road.

'KEEP IT STILL,' Roy shouts.

'Fuck ... what's happening?' I ask Clarence. 'Clarence ... tell me ...'

'Looks like she's stopped breathing,' Clarence's voice is calm, deep, and measured. 'Pull over, let me drive.'

The urge is to stamp on the brake, but that will send everyone flying forward, and the Saxon is weighed down with tons of ammunition crates, plus most of the team. I ease my foot off the accelerator and gently apply the brake.

'Roy's working on her ... chest compressions ... He's

doing well. Paula is doing mouth to mouth ... Let me drive,' he repeats.

'No,' I know this beast, and even though the dirty hands of the infected have defiled her, I have faith in the countless hours I've spent behind this wheel.

The engine roars as I increase the pressure of my right foot on the accelerator, but the noise has become so familiar to me now that I don't hear it. Just the silence of the vehicle as all eyes rest on Roy.

'Try now,' Roy says in measured tones.

'Try what?' I ask Clarence, urging him to give me a commentary.

'Paula's checking for a pulse ... One of you, find a mirror,' Clarence calls out.

'A mirror?' Cookey replies. 'What for?'

'See if it mists,' Roy says. 'The vibration of the vehicle is making it hard to feel for a pulse ... You saw that movie too, then?'

'I did,' Clarence says. A brief exchange by the two older men that conveys a competence and unflappable nature to the younger members of the team.

'Where the fuck we gonna find a mirror from?' Cookey asks.

'My bag or Lani's,' Paula replies. 'Women always have a mirror.'

'Got it,' I hear Jagger's voice exclaim, then people shuffling as the mirror is passed along the chain.

'Anything?' I ask Clarence, forcing the same level of calm into my voice.

'Hang on,' he says quietly, 'Paula is checking now ...'

Seconds. That's all it is, but they go on forever. I grip the wheel and focus on the road ahead. Cars, vans, and all manner of vehicles left abandoned. Tree trunks, power cables, and telegraph poles ripped up by the storm and dumped in the carriageway. The big wheels of the Saxon have no difficulty dealing with the millions of bits of shit littered about, but the bigger stuff needs negotiating, and if I go fast, it will cause the vehicle to swerve, but going slow feels the wrong thing to do.

'Yes,' Paula says, 'misting ... but only just.'

'Thank fuck,' I let out a gasp of air as I realise I was holding my breath.

'Listen,' Roy speaks up so we can all hear him, 'she's only just hanging on ... so be prepared.'

'For what?' I call back.

'Losing her,' he replies in a tone of voice so matter of fact it makes my stomach flip.

'Not happening,' I mutter the words under my breath and focus on the road. Gentle movements as I steer the heavily laden vehicle down the main road, towards the motorway. Silence. Nobody speaks.

Lani is torn ... but know this, not everyone will survive this journey, Howie ...

How did she know? Was it even Marcy or just a manifestation of my own mind? But how the hell would I know Lani was at the back door or that someone would get bitten.

'How's your arm, Blowers?'

'Fine, Boss.'

'Arm? What's up with your arm?' Clarence calls back.

'Got bit,' Blowers says in a clipped voice.

'Bitten? You got bitten?' Clarence twists to see the young lad better. 'Are you okay?'

'Immune,' he gives the one-word reply, too bereft with worry to say more.

Clarence's jaw drops for a second before he recovers his wits. One big hand reaches up to rub the back of his neck.

'Five now,' he says.

'You sure you were bitten?' Roy asks. 'Can I see?'

'I was bitten,' Blowers says. 'The fucker put his teeth on me.'

'And it broke the skin? Yes ... yes, I can see,' Roy must be examining the wound. 'You were bitten,' he says dully.

'Five of us,' Cookey says. 'What does that mean?'

'What?' Blowers asks.

'Five of us in one group. Why us? Why are we immune?'

'Roy,' Paula's voice is urgent, 'look.'

'At what?' I ask Clarence.

'Can't see,' Clarence twists round to lean over the back of the seat. 'What is it?' he asks.

'Yes. Yes, I see,' Roy says.

'See what?' I call out.

'Her wounds are congealing faster than they normally would,' Roy replies. 'They're fresh wounds that should be bleeding, but ... but they're not.'

'You dressed them,' I shout back. 'How can you tell?'

'The blood should have seeped through, especially the deep one on her thigh. I've just checked it.'

'And?'

'Like I said, it's already scabbing over.'

'Scabbing?' Clarence says, 'that wouldn't happen.'

'It is happening,' Roy says. 'Her body still carries the infection.'

'Mate, that's an assumption to make,' Blowers says.

'Blowers, show Roy your knuckles,' I shout.

'Knuckles?' Clarence asks. 'Why knuckles?'

'Blowers was punching them,' I reply for him, knowing Clarence and Dave had already told Blowers never to use his fists to fight the infected, 'but to be fair, Dave was in the room, punching me in the face while I was sleeping so …'

'Scabs,' Roy says.

'Scabs? Fucking scabs?' I call back. 'Mate, I cannot see what you are doing … Be more specific, please.'

'Sorry,' he says. 'I am examining Blowers hands. The knuckles are cut in several places from punching. Those cuts are scabbed.'

'Is that not right?'

'No, Mr Howie. They're small cuts, so they would heal quickly, but the scabs are drying out, as though these wounds are maybe one or two days old.'

'Anyone else cut?' I ask.

'Yeah, everywhere,' Mo Mo says.

'Me too,' Jagger adds.

'My hands are cut,' Clarence looks down at the backs of his splayed hands.

'Are you scabbing yet?' I glance across.

'Shit!' Paula shouts. 'Not breathing.'

'Okay, hold her head,' Roy shuffles into place as he starts the chest compressions for the second time, and once again, the tension in the vehicle ramps up.

'Come on, Lani,' Paula speaks softly with her head bent down to Lani's ear. 'Come on, love. Breathe … you've got to breathe … Cookey, hold that mirror there.'

'No point,' Roy says quickly. 'The compressions will be forcing air out of her mouth.'

'Sorry,' Paula says, 'I didn't think.'

'How far?' Roy calls out louder.

'Er …' Christ, I have no idea where we are and have just been following the road.

'*Nick, you hearing me?*' Clarence grabs the radio handset from the front.

'Has he got a radio?' I ask.

'I gave him one,' Clarence replies.

'This is Dave. Go ahead, Clarence.'

'Dave, ask Nick for an ETA.'

'Standby ... Nick says ten to fifteen minutes.'

'We don't have ten to fifteen minutes,' Roy says calmly. 'We're going to need a defib.'

'Options?' Clarence asks the vehicle.

'Find a hospital,' Jagger shouts out.

'No power,' I call back.

'Nick can get the power on,' Paula says.

'Too long, it means finding a hospital, finding a defib ... getting the power on and ...'

'Police cars got 'em,' Mo Mo says, 'and custody blocks too.'

'Shopping centres,' Blowers says.

'I'm hearing you,' I say, 'but we don't have time to find one. We need doctors, and the only place we know where there are doctors is the fort. We head to the fort. Roy, keep working. If the infection is in her, she–'

'She's back,' Roy announces, 'again.'

'Fuck me,' Blowers says, 'is she breathing on her own?'

'Yes,' Roy says, 'and to be honest, this is unheard of.'

'What is?' I ask.

'CPR can keep a body functioning until medical help arrives, but it doesn't normally bring someone back when they've stopped breathing. Not like that ... not twice ...'

'Infection?' Clarence asks, as if Roy suddenly knows all the answers.

'I don't know,' Roy replies, 'but if we think it through, we can inflict serious damage on the infected, and they pay no heed at all. Their wounds heal faster, or at least they clot faster, so they don't bleed out, and they have no known pain threshold.'

'I don't think now is the time for this, Roy,' Paula says gently. 'Not right now.'

'Why not?' he asks.

'Because one of our team is badly hurt,' she says.

'I am merely trying to work out her chances of survival.'

'Do it in your head, then, mate,' Blowers says, and I was expecting a tone filled with aggression, but instead, he's as exhausted and drained as everyone else.

'Boss,' Clarence speaks over the small gap to me, 'is it worth getting Nick to go ahead so he can get a boat ready and ...'

'No, mate, we're not splitting up.'

'Boss,' he says seriously, 'Dave is with Nick, and you're with us ... Nothing can hurt us now.'

'Fuck, mate,' I glance across. 'You being serious? I'm not like Dave.'

'Better get ready to sack me,' he lifts the handset up. '*Nick, Dave ... Lani is in a bad way. Get there and arrange medevac ... Receive?*'

'*Roger. Understood,*' Dave's flat tone amplifies over the speaker, and we watch the small, lighter van gather speed as the distance between us gets larger.

CHAPTER TWENTY-SEVEN

'And then what?'

'Like I said. It was so clear. So very clear. Like it was actually happening. Do you ever get that?'

'Me? Gosh no. Oh no. No, my dreams invariably have me running *from* something or hiding from something,' he tilts his tidy head to one side, 'or running *and* hiding as some beastly monsters get closer and closer and ...'

'Reggie!'

'Reginald. My point is, Marcy. It was a dream. Just a dream.'

'Perhaps,' she sighs, 'but I knew. I knew where Lani was. I knew she was in danger, and I knew she would be hurt ... How did I know that?'

'A dream, my dear Marcy. Just a dream. I should imagine Mr Howie and his intrepid group are holed up somewhere, being heroic while slaughtering the living challenged with blunt teaspoons,' Reginald sighs for effect and adjusts his tie to make sure the knot is just so. 'Anyway, what are we to do? You are looking much better, really much better.'

'Thank you,' Marcy smiles.

'Really, the infection shows no signs on you. Other than the red eyes, of course, but ... no ... no sickly grey pallor. In fact, if anything, my dear, you look positively radiant. You're not pregnant, are you?'

'Pardon?'

'Pregnant. I read somewhere that pregnant women get the same healthy glow about their complexion. Probably from an influx of hormones or some such thing.'

'No, Reggie. I am not pregnant.'

'Are you sure?' he persists politely, adjusting his glasses and once again checking his tie. 'I mean. You and Darren had relations, didn't you?'

'Relations?'

'Yes, relations.'

'What are relations?'

'You know full well what relations are. You are teasing me again, which is most unkind of you.'

'Truly, I don't know the term.'

'Marcy, that innocent look will not work on me.'

'Reggie, I do not know the term. What does relations mean?'

'You know,' he flusters. 'The thing a man and, er ...' he blusters. 'The interaction between members of the opposite, er ... gender ... that, er ...' he blushes and checks his tie, 'that results in offspring.'

'Sex. Sex, Reggie. You can say the word sex.'

'Good lord, woman, no need to go blurting it out a hundred times. Is there no decorum left?'

'Did you mean sex?'

'Yes!'

'Reggie, men and men can have sex, you know.'

'I beg your pardon!'

'You said it is a thing that members of the opposite gender do. Men and men have sex just as much as women and women.'

'No. I meant they do it for the result of offspring. To copulate. To reproduce.'

'Oh. Not for pleasure, then?'

'Oh, the thought of it,' he squirms and looks away with distaste. 'All that sweating and grunting about like animals. Gosh, gosh no.'

'Hmmm, yes, Darren and I had sex, but no, I am not pregnant.'

'Are you sure?'

'Yes, Reggie. A woman has ways of knowing.'

'Ah, the menstrual cycle. You have commenced your menstrual cycle.'

'My menstrual cycle, as you put it,' she smiles warmly, 'has been and gone.'

'Good lord,' Reginald sits bolt upright, even more than his naturally perfect posture, 'you mean to say you are still having menstruation?'

'Yes, Reggie. I am still a woman.'

'Well,' he snorts as though having been told something incredible yet somewhat slightly distasteful, 'indeed. Yes, it appears the infection has had very little effect on you.'

'Lucky me,' she smiles wanly.

'I say,' the dapper little man rallies with a burst of energy, 'I have a grand idea. A positively grand idea if I may be so bold as to ...'

'Is it the one that involves you and me going north?'

'North?'

'Yes. North. The northern plan that takes us away from the fort and this area. The one that involve finding a nice, little cottage in a valley, where we can rest and recover from this horrid little event.'

'Well,' he huffs, 'yes, that was my grand idea, but I can see you still have the same level of scorn as previously.'

'Not scorn, Reggie. I am not scornful of you, but we are waiting here.'

'For what, my dear Marcy? What are we waiting for? For Mr Howie? No good shall come of this.'

She stays quiet in reflection, unable to explain why she waits or indeed what for. A factual certainty within her that compels them to remain close.

She looks down at her hands and examines the skin she knows so well. The ridges and bumps of the knuckles and the smooth, almost perfectly unblemished skin that remains a healthy olive complexion. Turning her hands over, she looks down at the veins visible on the inside of the wrist and how normal they appear. Not a sign on her. Other than the red eyes, of course.

Her hair is as lustrous as ever. Her lips as full. Her skin as soft and radiant as it was before. The bite mark on her backside caused when Darren turned her is almost healed.

She shudders at the memory of it. Like any woman with a mistake in her past, she cannot fathom what the attraction was.

He turned her, so in effect he controlled her. But when he died, that connection ceased. Since then, she has felt a growing sense of her own mind being in control of her body.

What she is. What she carries. It is the answer. How she can remain herself, with no desire to kill or hurt. No thirst for blood or drive to pass the infection on. She heals faster than she should do. She is healthy and feels physically well. Her heart beats strong.

The infection is wrong. The minute the last human is turned is the first minute of the beginning of the end.

But what she has, what she carries is different, and she knows Howie is the key.

Or is he?

She shifts position and stares out of the window of the top floor of the three-storey house on the edge of the bay. The surface of the sea glitters like diamonds with the reflection of the sun. The little boats in the distance that carry yet more survivors to the fort. The stick figures of people holding weapons that guard what they've salvaged in this torn world.

Lani is torn.

In the dream, she knew Lani was in peril and desperately wanted to warn Howie. The cryptic message was not of her own design but the words the Marcy in the dream uttered while the Marcy that slept murmured quietly while a fretful Reginald watched over her.

She knew Blowers would be bitten. She knew one would take him on the arm. She knew Dave was watching over Howie. She knew Clarence was faltering, and she knew Howie didn't want to go back. She sensed he felt compelled because he knew an attack was happening, but within his heart, he had given up.

The most enduring feeling of the dream was the tidal wave of energy that pulsed through her when she glimpsed him through the inert ranks of the host bodies.

It tingled and made her heart beat faster. Butterflies in her stomach that flipped over with a pleasant sensation. Her mouth was dry. Her throat felt a little constricted with an almost breathless dizziness that passed the second she stepped out to speak to him.

She could have taken him right there. He was ready for

the taking. He was ready to give up, and the right words from her would have meant he would never wake up.

'Hello?'

'Huh?' she shakes her head, then chuckles at the sight of Reggie rolling his eyes and sighing deeply.

'I was talking to you,' he says reproachfully.

'I know,' she lies. 'I was listening.'

'Were you? Indeed I think not. Moreover, I think perhaps your rather beautiful head was full of fanciful ideas of running through fields of flowers, hand in hand, with Mr Howie.'

She bursts out laughing and snorts through her nose, 'What?'

'Yes, well. Mark my words–no good shall come of this.'

'Reggie, your words are endearing, and if I did not know you better, I would say you were jealous.'

'Jealous? Good gosh, I am not jealous. I think you are beautiful, yes, but in the same manner I find a particular work of art beautiful. Just because I have admiration in the pleasure of a thing, doesn't mean I want to ... well, do what men do to other, er ... Well, that is to say men and men and women and women and, of course, the traditional men and women coupling that ... My point is–I rather pride myself that my emotions are not solely base emotions.'

'Did you just call me a thing?'

He stops talking and holds still for a second. 'The complexity of your gender will forever be beyond my understanding. Of all the words I uttered, and you heard only the part that may have caused you offence.'

'So, did you?'

'Yes,' he says with a firm nod, 'I called you a thing.'

'Reggie. I am not a thing,' she says with a mock cold edge to her voice.

'We are all but things, my dear.'

'A thing is an inanimate object,' she fixes him with a look.

He shifts and narrows his eyes. 'And surely, if you pursue this current course of action, I fear it will render us both as inanimate objects as we are clearly displaying an inability to think coherently.'

'Show off,' she tuts and turns back to the window. 'I bet you were a right pain in the arse in the old world.'

'So another day we shall spend gazing longingly out of a window,' he sighs again. 'My mind requires stimulation and exercise.'

'Go for a run.'

'My mind, not my body.'

'Go for a mind run.'

'What, may I ask, is a mind run?'

'I have no idea,' she stands up quickly. 'Come on, then.'

'What? Where? Don't just stand up and walk off without telling me why. Oh, you cause me palpitations, palpitations of the stomach!'

'Do you need the toilet?'

'No. I do not need the toilet.'

'Jolly good, I say,' she says in a voice that belies a decision made and a mind made up.

'Marcy ... Marcy ...' Reginald rushes from the room to traipse down the stairs behind her. 'Where are we going? Do I need to pack?'

'Pack?' she says without turning. 'We didn't bring anything.'

'I have been foraging, and as luck would have it, some of the menfolk of this region were of a similar size and taste of adornments as I.'

'No ... yes ... yes, if you want to pack, then do so.'

'Oh my gosh. Packing means moving. Moving means going to the fort. I do not want to go to the fort.'

'Stay here, then.'

'I cannot. You know I cannot. I am tied to you.'

She stops and examines the space between them with a raised eyebrow, 'You are not tied to me.'

'That is not what ...'

'I release you,' she states and starts heading down the next flight of stairs. 'You are free to go and find a Mrs Reggie to make baby Reggies with.'

'If only it were that easy,' he mutters. 'Really, do I have no say in our decision making?'

'Of course you do,' she says with a laugh, 'but whether I choose to listen is something else entirely.'

'To the fort, then,' he says glumly. 'We are going to the fort, where we shall either be executed on sight or held as medical and scientific subjects to be examined and prodded with sharp, pointy things.'

'Probably.'

'Probably? Which one?'

'Probably both. Probably executed *and then* prodded with sharp, pointy things.'

'I do not wish to be executed nor prodded with sharp, pointy things. I wish to remain here, in a calm and peaceful manner. I also do not wish to go in one of those little boats or be near the men and women armed with guns. I do not want to see Clarence or the other men after what happened. Really, I am ashamed at what happened. Really, I cannot ...'

'You got drunk, Reginald. Blind stinking drunk, and you were singing songs before passing out.'

'My dear Marcy. Please. Please stop and listen one last time.'

'Okay,' she stops and turns, with one hand resting on the lock of the front door, 'go ahead.'

'We have tried this,' he speaks openly, with genuine honesty. 'We went there and tried this. It did not work. It will not work now. We are not their kind anymore. They do not want us. They will kill us. Please. I am appealing to any sense remaining in your delightful head to reconsider this.'

'Reggie,' she reaches out to gently adjust his tie, 'you care for me, and for that I am eternally grateful. Please, you can go anywhere you want or stay here. I do not want to hurt you or be the cause of you getting hurt. But I have to do this.'

'Fine,' he sags and softly scoots her hand off his tie, 'so be it. We shall walk to our deaths, and ... of course, I will go with you,' he adds with a sudden earnest glance up at her face.

'Oh, Reggie.'

'But only because I am more terrified of being here by myself.'

'Fine!' She opens the door and strides out.

'I mean what if those awful things come back.'

'The zombies?'

'The living challenged,' he corrects her quickly, 'or people. Gosh, March. It appears both sides probably hate us equally now.'

'So you're as popular now as you were in the last life, then.'

'Cutting,' he tuts, 'wholly cutting. And besides, without Mr Howie there, how do you know they won't kill us on sight?'

'They will. But Howie is coming back now.'

'He is? And you know this how?'

'Because of the dream. They were in a munitions factory. I told you that.'

'We are basing everything ... indeed, the very basis of our lives on a dream.'

'Yes, Reggie.'

'Reginald ... Did you eat cheese before going to bed? I know cheese can cause lucid dreams.'

'There is no cheese, Reggie.'

'Or any dairy products in general?'

'No.'

'Perhaps you were dehydrated. Yes, a vision or hallucination caused by ...'

'I am not dehydrated. I drank a pint of water before going to sleep and woke up needing the toilet.'

'Well, perhaps you once took LSD then. Yes, I have heard accounts of people that have taken LSD later in life suffer severe delusional encounters.'

'I have never taken LSD. I have never taken cocaine. I have never taken any drugs.'

'We must surely reflect and find the root ...'

'Reggie!'

'Reginald.'

'Stop it, Reggie. We are going to the fort. Now, do I look okay?'

'I beg your pardon?'

'I said, do I look okay?'

'Oh,' he rolls his eyes, 'of course. Yes, of course. We want to look our best for the great Mr Howie.'

'Yes. Now, do I look okay?'

'Yes,' he sighs, 'you look splendid, but may I suggest you do one more button up on your blouse.'

'My boobs are too big,' she looks down at her own cleavage. 'It'll pop off if I breathe in.'

'Find a bigger blouse then.'

'I like this one,' she pouts playfully. 'It's got red checks. Red suits me.'

'Hello?'

They both spin at the voice calling out. An instinct to run and hide. Reginald freezes on the spot. Marcy grabs the sunglasses hanging from one stem on the back pocket of her jeans and makes as though to shield her eyes with her hand.

'Cover your eyes,' she mutters and watches as a man steps out from the side garden passage of a house. He pauses and goes to move back, then stops and holds position. Nervous. Worried.

'What with?' Reginald asks quietly.

'Can you hear me? the man calls out.

'Yes,' Marcy shouts back and quickly looks round to the sides, then behind.

'Are you going to the fort?' the man takes a step forward, then stops again. 'We got here last night and ...'

'You're survivors?' Marcy asks without thinking.

'Yes ... my wife ... and some others, er ... We heard about it. About the fort, I mean. Are you? I mean ...'

'Same,' Marcy says quickly. 'How many of you?'

'A few,' the man says, clearly not wanting to give too much away. 'Can I come over?'

'Of course,' Marcy takes a confident few paces towards him. 'Wait here,' she mutters to Reginald.

'They might be dangerous,' Reginald whimpers.

'I'm a zombie, Reggie,' Marcy says with a turn of her head towards Reginald.

'Don't say that word!'

'My friend is waiting there,' Marcy calls out, 'er ... We've had some pretty bad encounters on the way here.'

'Same,' the man says. He looks bedraggled, with several

days of grey-streaked beard showing on sunken cheeks and hooded eyes.

'You look exhausted,' Marcy says quietly. 'Are you all like that?'

'Yeah,' the man nods and stops a few feet away. Nervous and worried, he doesn't know what to do with his hands. Putting them first in his pockets, then on his hips before visibly sagging on the spot. 'Is it safe?'

'The fort?' Marcy asks. 'I think so.'

'Everyone keeps talking about Mr Howie and his army. You heard about them?'

'I have,' Marcy says.

'My daughter died,' the man blurts the words out with a choking sob, 'on the way ... She got bit and ... Christ ... I'm sorry.'

'It's okay,' Marcy steps closer again and watches the man crumble before her eyes.

'We've been walking so long ... My wife, she hasn't spoken since our daughter, and ... and everyone said the fort was safe, and Mr Howie can keep them away, but ...' he lifts a hand to point to the fort across the bay. 'And we're here ... fucking here ...'

'Do you have more children?' Marcy asks softly.

'Son,' the man clenches his jaw to stem the tide of tears falling down his face, 'and there's more kids with us.'

'Your son will be safe now,' Marcy speaks soft and earnest. 'I know Mr Howie, and I know his team. They'll never let anything happen to your family.'

'You know them?'

'Yes.'

'She died,' the man sobs again, 'in my arms ... I can't ... Oh my god, I can't ...'

He sinks to his knees at the realisation that the strength

he needed to get this far can be let go. A journey through hell, with death and suffering at every turn. Loss and deprivation with the constant threat of dying and walking miles every day on weak legs that have spent a lifetime sitting and resting.

'Come on,' Marcy grips his arm and starts to help him to his feet, 'you're almost there, but your family still need you.'

'I'm sorry ...'

'Don't be, get up, and take your people down there. Go on ...'

He gets up with a head lowered and takes a few steps on heavy legs. 'You're not coming?'

'Not yet, we're waiting for some others ... You go first.'

He walks back towards the house, and Marcy watches a man defeated forcing himself to take the final few steps before he can sink into the abyss of shock. Pain on her face that he doesn't even have the gumption left to ask *how* she knows Mr Howie and his team or why she's here.

She motions to Reginald to move back. The two of them retreating further away while the man disappears for a few minutes, then comes out in front of a ragtag group of men, women, and children. They stare round with expressions of utter terror and confusion, but with eyes that flick always back to the fort and the promise of the safety it offers.

'We're not going with them?' Reginald asks quietly.

'They'll see your eyes.'

'Ah, at least you have some small amount of common sense left.'

'Common sense?' Marcy says as an idea pops into her head. 'Wait here,' she says to Reginald before darting across the road towards the man she just spoke with.

CHAPTER TWENTY-EIGHT

'Almost there,' Nick focuses on the road as he feels the sway of the laden van through the frame as he steers round the debris on the road.

'Dave, did you know Mr Howie would be okay?'

Dave doesn't answer but watches out the front windscreen, his hands resting in his lap.

'I kinda had an idea he would be,' Nick glances across. 'Like ... fuck, I don't know ...' Nick shakes his head. 'I don't know how but ...'

Talking to Dave is hard at the best of times, but when he stays so silent, it makes it near on impossible. Nick sighs and navigates the vehicle through the narrow roads that feed towards the bay.

A journey of silence since Clarence radioed ahead. Nick driving. Dave inert.

'You are a good soldier, Nicholas,' Dave says without any preamble. 'I am proud of you.'

The tears prickle Nick's eyes the second the words hit his ears. A deep crimson blush spreads across his face at the overwhelming compliment paid by the most dangerous man any of them have ever known.

He doesn't know what to say or how to respond. He thinks of something to respond with. To say thank you would sound fake. To say anything else would be flippant.

'You survived in that house,' Dave says. 'You showed courage and fortitude in the face of an enemy far greater in number than you.'

'Jesus, Dave.' Nick whispers.

'That is all,' Dave nods with a signal that the conversation is over.

'Okay,' Nick coughs and widens his eyes while shaking his head, 'thanks.'

'And you did not falter when Mr Howie went down.'

Fucking hell! Nick glances across with the realisation that he is having an actual conversation with Dave.

'Do not falter,' Dave says.

'I won't.'

'I won't is not a good enough response. You will not falter because you will not falter. It is fact and not an attempt at something.'

'Okay.'

'We cannot falter,' Dave says quietly in a tone Nick has never heard before. 'Stop the vehicle.'

Nick starts at seeing the beach right ahead of them. With trembling hands, he steers the van onto the sand and brings it to a stop as Dave alights with fluid movements.

'YOU,' Dave bellows across the beach, towards the guard crew stationed there, **'WE NEED BOATS NOW … MAKE IT HAPPEN …'**

'Fuck me,' Nick says to himself, 'did that just happen?' He watches with the eyes of a man ever learning as Dave dominates the ground around him. Orders shouted and complied with instantly. There is no room for error with Dave. Simply no question of *not* doing what he says.

Nick rubs his face and yawns. The exhaustion evident in every movement from his bone-weary body. Without thinking, he tugs his packet of cigarettes out from his torn and bloodied pocket. The filter touches his lips, the hands find a lighter, and he inhales at the same second as realising he is sitting in a van full of live ammunition, grenades, and God knows whatever else was shoved in.

'Sorry, Dave,' the words spill out of his mouth as fast he scrambles from the van to pace away as though expecting it to combust instantly.

'Smoking is unlikely to ignite rounds,' Dave looks back, 'however, the embers from your cigarette could set fire to other flammable material that, in turn, could cause a fire which–'

'I get it,' Nick waves, then stops in horror. 'Sorry,' he winces. Shit, he just cut Dave off mid speech. The small man stares hard for a second and seems to take in the sorry state of the young man before looking away.

'Rest now,' he says simply, 'take fluids and rest.'

'Fuck,' Nick sinks down onto the soft sand and lets his over-tired mind ease down with the frantic thinking. He smokes and blinks heavily. He smokes and stares without looking. His hands are encrusted from the battle. Blood and gore spattered all over his clothing and up his bare arms.

He looks down at his own sorry state and winces but carries on smoking. Boats are rushed towards the beach from the fort. Voices calling. Radio transmissions, and Nick watches as Dave simply takes a radio from a youth and bellows an order into it before handing it back and knows he will never be as competent as Dave.

'Shit,' on his feet, and he crosses the short space of

ground to the van. Dragging his assault rifle out, he racks the bolt back and has the weapon up and aimed as he about turns and starts pacing towards the oncoming group heading across beach. 'STAND STILL,' Nick roars, 'STAND STILL NOW ...'

As one, the group freeze. As one, the guard crew spin with weapons being raised and made ready.

'YOU,' Nick points off to the guard crew, 'FAN OUT AND COVER ME ...'

'ON YOU,' Darius shouts back.

'SHOW ME YOUR HANDS,' Nick paces towards the group with long strides of his legs while the guard crew fans out. Dave watches without reaction or movement.

Arms shoot into the air with an instant compliance of the orders given.

'GOOD. STAY STILL ... ARE ANY OF YOU BITTEN OR SCRATCHED?'

'NO,' the man at the head shouts back quickly, 'we're survivors ...'

'Okay ... okay,' Nick lowers his voice but keeps the weapon raised, 'this is the Fort, and you will be safe here ... but you must remain still so you can be checked. Do you understand?'

Nods come back at him. Faces fixed on the young man that dominates the scene.

'You are safe,' Nick repeats, 'but you are safe because we have procedures ... Stay still and let me check your eyes. That's it... Everyone, look at me so I can see your eyes ...' He moves to the front of the group, and while keeping the weapon raised and ready, he peers from face to face.

'Good, you two go forward,' he motions to the first clear faces, 'then you ... and you. That's good ... and you, sir ....

and you, madam, take the child with you–I can see her eyes from here ... Okay, good ... DARIUS?'

'HERE.'

'ALL CLEAR.'

'GOT IT.'

Nick lowers the weapon and smiles sheepishly at the terrified group huddled together, 'Sorry about that,' he shrugs. 'Er ... everyone okay?'

'Jesus, mate,' one of the men says with a gasp, 'what happened to you?'

'Me?' Nick looks down and blanches at the state of his clothes. 'Oh, yeah ... we had a hard night.'

'Hard night?' the man whimpers. 'Doing what?'

'Killing zombies,' Nick shrugs again as he lights another cigarette.

'Are you with Mr Howie?' someone asks.

'Hmmm? Yeah, I'm Nick. That's Dave,' he points off to the small man watching him from his original position.

'Nick and Dave!'

'Where's Clarence?'

'What about the Chinese girl?'

'Thai,' Nick says, 'she's from Thailand, not China ... Er ... Mr Howie is just coming now, but ... but one of our team got hurt, so we're using these boats first ... You'll have to hang on for a bit.'

'Er,' one of them men steps forward, 'I got passed a message.'

'Do what?' Nick asks.

'Marcy. She said to tell Mr Howie or one of his team–'

'Marcy? Where?'

'Back there,' the man points back to the houses on the edge of the bay. 'She's there with a man ... She said to tell you that–'

'A man? What did he look like?'

'Small bloke ... er ... glasses and a tie ...'

'Reggie,' Nick mutters and stares hard at the houses. 'Okay, listen ... do not tell anyone else. You hear me?'

'Yeah, sure.'

'Cheers,' Nick walks off with a backward glance at the houses as the Saxon's engine roars into the vicinity.

'Dave,' he rushes over as Dave turns to watch the incoming army personnel carrier, 'that bloke just said Marcy is up there.'

'Where?' he turns to look at Nick's outstretched arm and up to the houses on the edge of the beach.

'Reggie is with her, or at least the bloke said there was a man with her with glasses and a tie ... She told him to tell us.'

'Okay,' Dave nods once as the Saxon slews to a halt. Doors burst open as Howie and the others burst into activity.

'BOATS?' Howie shouts.

'READY,' Dave replies.

'How is she?' Nick runs round the back to look inside the Saxon and Roy straddled across Lani doing chest compressions. 'Oh fuck ...'

'We need a stretcher,' Blowers jumps down, 'Roy's got to keep the compressions going while we move her ... Nick! Nick, we need a stretcher.'

'Fucking hell,' Nick drags his eyes from the awful sight of Lani being worked on by Roy and Paula. 'Stretcher. Got it,' he nods and runs down the beach to the boats waiting in the shallows.

He wades in, heading to the closest boat, and grips the edge to peer in. 'CLARENCE,' he turns to shout. 'Get this boat up on the beach,' he orders the youth waiting by the outboard at the back.

'What?'

'Fuck's sake, lift the prop up ... lift it ... pull the thing towards you. CLARENCE ...'

'What?' the big man runs down the beach.

'The middle section–we can make a stretcher.'

'Got it,' they heave the boat until it grinds on the beach. Clarence levers himself over the edge and shuffles over to stand straddling the thick board of the middle seating running width ways across the boat. He takes a deep breath, pauses, then heaves with an explosion of force that tears the plank free from the marine screws holding it in place.

'Here,' Nick leans in to grasp the end, pulls it closer, then starts running back up the beach, towards the Saxon.

'Any good?' Nick gets to the rear, panting from the exertion.

'Lay it flat,' Howie appears at his side. 'Roy, we've got a stretcher ...'

'She's breathing on her own again,' Roy jumps clear and moves up to push his hands under Lani's armpits. 'Quickly now! Someone, grab her legs. We've got to be quick but gentle.'

Cookey gets in and, on cue from Roy, lifts Lani's legs as Roy eases her upper body clear. Over the stacked ammunition boxes, they pass the unconscious woman out to the gentle waiting hands that lower her softly onto the board.

'Everyone,' Howie orders, 'she's not strapped in, so we move steady but quick!'

The board lifts with ease from the hands all jumping in. Howie at the head while Roy stays close to Lani's side, monitoring her pulse and breathing.

'Down!' he orders at failing to find a pulse.

'Onto the boat, mate,' Howie counters the order. 'First one is here ... Easy now ...'

Clarence in the boat, and he leans forward to grasp the offered plank as they work between them to get Lani down. Roy vaults the side to gain her side and once again check for pulse and breathing. Without a word uttered, he starts work, fingers interlinked palm to back of hand, and the first compression is given.

Clarence scrabbles over the edge, grips the front of the boat, and pushes it clear of the beach and back into the water.

'Darius,' Howie climbs into the boat as the youth gets the engine going, 'we go first, then the ammunition, then the people after that.'

'Got it,' Darius shouts back.

'And get the doctors waiting for us.'

'Done it.'

The team pile into boats that get swiftly turned round and pointed back to the Fort, each one opens up with whatever horsepower the engine can generate as they glide through the water.

Roy works steady, never ceasing as he pushes down, pauses, pushes down, pauses, and counts fifteen before nodding at Paula to give two breaths.

The lads watch quietly, and no one notices that Jagger and Mo Mo have chosen to stay with them in the boats rather than rejoin their old mates on the guard crews.

'We need faster boats,' Cookey says through gritted teeth in the second boat. 'This thing flat out?'

'Yeah,' the boy holding the rudder arm nods but dares not say anything else. The sight of these people is something else. Each one of them covered in gore, blood, and filth. Hard eyes, and the way they move and talk. Like a unit of professional soldiers. Even the smiling Cookey looks like something from a movie with his blond hair plastered to his head and covered in cuts, bruises, and fresh bite mark to his shoulder, exposed by the torn fabric of his clothes.

They still grip weapons as though only resting from the battle. They look round constantly, always scanning, always checking the positions of the others. Looks pass between them, and in those fleeting glances are messages and nuances of meaning that have built up over long days and nights of depending on the others for life.

'Doctors,' Nick nods ahead to the white lab coat wearing figures waiting to receive on the small beach in front of the fort.

'Did Darius tell them we need a defib waiting?' Blowers ask the youth.

'I dunno.'

'Dave, we need a defib,' Blowers shouts over the water. 'Can they hear you from here?'

Dave sits in the exact middle of the third boat, his hands gripping the plinth beneath his lap. He nods, draws breath, and shouts.

'DEFIB NEEDED.'

'Fuck,' Cookey says under his breath. 'They bloody heard him, though.'

A doctor lifts an arm and runs back into the fort as the boats glide so slowly across the expanse of water before finally hitting the shelving beach.

The lads jump out and wade over to the first boat, assault rifles pushed back on the straps to rest across their backs.

Orders are not needed as the plank is lifted and moved swiftly over the edge of the boat and into the hands of the waiting medics.

'Give us room,' Doctor Andrew Stone orders calmly as Anne Carlton runs onto the beach carrying a small plastic case.

'Tell me what happened, please,' Andrew asks without looking up at the group.

'She was bitten, cut and ... See the wounds? We dressed them,' Roy stands with hands on hips.

'Much blood lost?' Andrew asks.

'Not really ... Maybe at first, but the wounds have clotted really fast ... Do you know she was immune?'

'This is Lani, right?' Andrew says.

'Yes, but her wounds are already healing faster than they should ... She might be a carrier ...' Roy says.

'Face masks,' Andrew and the other doctors move back to quickly tug the masks up. They pull plastic safety glasses from deep pockets and quickly check their gloves are intact.

'No pulse, no breathing,' Doctor Franklin reports. 'Are we charged?'

'Wait,' Andrew opens the case and pulls two wires free. He moves quickly as he first fixes two self-adhesive patches to Lani's chest. He plugs the wires into the patches and checks the front of the machine.

'Clear?'

'Clear,' Lisa and Anne lean away as Andrew pushes a button on the machine. Lani jolts with a sudden pulse of electricity passing through her body.

Everyone stands together, watching and waiting and feeling useless as the doctors check for vitals and speak to each other in hushed tones. Once again, Andrew presses the big, red button on the machine that delivers a shock to Lani's body.

'Pulse ...' Andrew relays with a hand outstretched in

warning to the others. All three watch the screen on the front. 'Holding ... It's holding ... weak but ...'

'We should get her inside,' Doctor Franklin turns to the waiting group. 'Carry the stretcher straight into the hospital bay.'

With the defib still attached monitoring Lani's heart rate, the ad hoc stretcher is once again gripped, lifted, and carried by people almost too tired to walk but refusing to yield to the exhaustion sapping at their limbs.

Through the outer door and across the gap to gain the inside of the fort. Survivors stare in silence at the gruesome sight of the battle-weary men and Paula racing while taking the greatest of care of their own. Every one of them a sight that tells those watching survivors they have freedom this day because of the actions of this small group.

Men and women grip the hands of their children or avert their eyes because the sight of the young team tells them what they've been through. The cuts and bruises, the bite marks and blades still encrusted with blood. The hoarse voices that speak of constant yelling and shouting. The heavy way they move while laden down with weapons, ammunition, pistols, axes, and water bottles.

The doctors run ahead, clearing the way. Doctor Heathcliff Stone already having made a bed free for the incoming casualty.

'Hold it,' Lisa Franklin makes the team hold the stretcher next to the bed so Clarence can lift her easily from the plank to the bed. Once the transfer is made, the team immediately and instantly become redundant. Not needed. Not required. In the way.

Still they hover and wait. Desperate to stay together and watch as if moving away will break the bond and cause the death of Lani.

The A&E nurse rushes forward with a pair of scissors to cut away Lani's clothing. The doctors bustle with calm efficiency remembered from the years of their lives spent in casualty departments.

Hospital machinery run by thirsty generators run by valuable diesel are plugged in and connected to the Thai girl.

'You need to go,' Heathcliff asserts his seniority by ushering the team away. 'Being here is no good ... Let us work.'

'But,' Cookey is the first to give voice as he stares desperately at Lani.

'No buts, please ...' Heathcliff spreads his hands. 'We are the experts here, and we need the space to work without being watched ... especially by armed men ...'

'And you're all covered in shit,' Lisa Franklin says without turning. 'Get out of here now before you infect someone else ... I want those clothes incinerated and you lot scrubbed with antibacterial cleanser ...'

Howie nods, his dark eyes brooding as he glances round at the state of the people around him.

'Howie, what happened?' Maddox strides into the hospital bay with Lenski and Lilly hot on his heels. Lilly gasps at the sight and rushes to Nick.

'Lani got hurt,' Howie says quietly. 'We were overwhelmed.'

'Everyone else okay?'

'Yeah ...' Howie nods.

'Get out of my hospital!' Lisa snaps.

'Everyone out,' Howie says, knowing the team will happily ignore the angry doctor.

'Nick,' Lilly stops short of hugging him, her eyes

widening at the sight of his clothes and skin, 'my god ... Are you okay?'

'Me? Fine,' he says quickly, 'Lani's hurt ... They were ... I mean Roy and Paula were doing resuscitation on her.'

'You go,' Lenski motions to the door, 'go your rooms. I bring water, and you wash ...'

They file out in silence. Howie leading the way until they stand once again in the bright sunshine and warmth of the homely fort.

'Maddox, we've got loads of ammunition ... It's in the Saxon and the van on the beach.'

'Darius told me,' Maddox holds a hand out to cut Howie off. 'Leave it with me. Go. Go wash.'

Howie inclines his head in a sharp gesture of understanding. Still together they skirt the middle busiest sections of the fort and walk round the inner perimeter towards their rooms. No speaking. Eyes watchful. Hands held ready to grip weapons.

'Fluids first,' Dave orders, 'then wash and clean your weapons ... then sleep.'

'Dave,' Cookey and the rest nod in affirmation.

'You've all done well, very well,' Dave adds to another quick glance from Nick.

'Boss,' Nick takes a step towards Howie.

'I'll do it. Get washed,' Dave says in his monotone voice. Nick drops his head and joins the others filing into the rooms.

'Do what?' Howie asks.

'Marcy is back ...'

CHAPTER TWENTY-NINE

'Fucking what?' I blink in surprise as Dave delivers the news as deadpan as ever.

'Marcy is back,' he repeats.

'Where? Back where? Here?' I spin round as though expecting her to be behind me.

'The survivors on the beach were told to tell Mr Howie or his group that she is by the houses on the beach. They told Nick. Nick told me.'

I don't reply but take a deep intake of breath. Just me and Dave outside the rooms. The rest are inside, already glugging water into parched throats.

Lani is dying in a hospital bed. The team are the most drained I have seen yet. The fort is filling up with people again. We've got doctors and ammunition. We've got people in the right roles. Maddox and Lenski.

And Marcy is back.

Marcy.

'Okay,' I nod at Dave and head inside the old armoury, the space given over for us to use.

'Boss,' Clarence passes me a cold bottle of water, which

is downed in one go. Sighs and burps from all around as the water is taken on too quickly.

'Can I come in?' Lilly calls from outside.

'Yes,' I call back and watch as she appears with a polite smile and nod while gripping a handful of yellow bin bags.

'Sorry,' she winces, 'I've been told to collect your clothes so they can be burnt?'

'Sure, leave them there,' I nod at the table in the middle.

'Is there anything you need?' she asks the room.

'Coffee,' I mutter, 'lots of coffee.'

'Food,' Nick offers a weak smile.

'Sleep,' Blowers says quietly.

'Weapons first,' Dave reminds everyone.

Buckets of soapy water are carried over, along with a hose connected to clean, cold water. A folding screen is propped up outside, giving us some degree of privacy to wash instead of doing so in full view of the Fort's occupants.

The weapons are done quickly but competently. None of us need to be reminded how much we reply on them.

Belts are checked. Pistols cleaned and filled with fresh magazines. The blades of our hand weapons are sprayed with water, then scrubbed with antibac before being dried fully and resharpened.

Finally we file outside and drink coffee and eat food while stripping off to dump the ruined garments into the yellow bin bags.

We scrub and scrub. Arms and faces. Torsos, legs, and heads. Everything is cleansed, and as the filth comes off, we realise just how battered and bruised our bodies are.

There is no banter. No jokes. Not even weak ones. Faces are worried, and eyes constantly drift towards the hospital bay. Our team is down one member, and each one of us feels it more keenly than ever.

Clean clothes are laid out.

The lads can hardly keep their eyes open, but no one wants to break the spell of being together. Jagger and Mo Mo are with us now. Members of the team as much as anyone, and they learn fast, adopting the mannerisms of the others. Paula and Roy stay close together.

'Doc coming,' Blowers nods behind us as we stand outside. We all turn to see Andrew Stone walking quickly towards us.

'Right,' he says and nods seriously, 'Lani's body has taken one hell of a beating, but ... like Roy said ... she is healing far faster than anything I have ever seen. She is stable for now and ...'

'And what?' I prompt him.

'We don't know,' he shrugs. 'She's stable. Her heart rate is okay; she's breathing on her own ... Whatever the thing is inside her is changing the physical way the body responds to trauma,' he takes a breath before continuing, 'to the extent that it has probably saved her life. We cannot detect any broken bones, but then we don't have any X-ray facility. Her lungs are clear, and her heart is strong, and that's half the battle. The rest is down to her to heal. Until she comes round and tells us where it hurts, there's not a great deal we can do.'

'At least she's stable,' Paula says. 'That's brilliant news.'

'Yeah,' Cookey says, 'she'll be alright now.'

'Maybe,' Andrew offers a wan smile. 'Early days, but at this stage, yes ... it's looking okay but,' he tilts his head as though to emphasise his point, 'we do not know how she has changed or ... well, until she wakes up and can tell us. The visible wounds are stitched and cleaned but ... er, is anyone else hurt?'

'Blowers got bit on the arm,' Cookey says.

'Snitch,' Blowers replies quickly.

'Let me see,' Andrew takes Blowers' offered arm and checks the bite marks. 'Does it hurt?'

'Yes.'

'And the skin has been punctured ... broken through ... Open wound ... Did it bleed?'

'Loads.'

'Show him your knuckles,' Clarence says.

Blowers turns his hands over to present his bruised and cut knuckles.

'Old wounds?' Andrew asks as through unsure why he's being shown them.

'Same time as the bite ... Same time as Lani got hurt,' Blowers says quietly.

'I see,' Andrew mutters. 'And ...? Well ... I, er ... bollocks, I have no idea what's going on,' he admits quickly. 'These wounds are scabbed and healing. I would date the bite mark at two days at the least.'

'Cookey got hurt too,' Blowers says.

'Show me,' Andrew looks over the cuts and marks on Cookey's arms, hands, and face.

'Right, then. Howie is immune. Cookey and you,' the doctor points at Blowers. 'Lani and ... Anyone else?' he looks round.

'We don't know,' I say.

'Hmmm, you're all carriers then until we can prove otherwise. You are not to share any food, washing water, drinking water, or anything that can transmit the disease by way of bodily fluids.'

'Doc,' I say softly, 'we've been bleeding over each other for the best part of two weeks now.'

'We have no idea what this infection is,' Andrew says

firmly, 'and until we know, you will ... You must adhere to the basic principles of–'

'We get it ... and we've been around loads of people, and no one has caught zombie from us yet.'

'I understand that, Mr Howie, but until we're in a position to understand–'

'Doc, sorry to keep cutting you off, but they need sleep. Anything else?'

'Er,' he blanches slightly. 'No ... Do you want updating with any changes? Right, yes ...' he becomes visibly nervous at the hard, flat stares of the killers around him. 'Of course, yes ...'

'Weird bloke,' Cookey says quietly as the doctor rushes away.

'Him? Us more like,' Blowers says. 'I'm fucked ... Can we turn in?'

'Go for it ... Oh, hang on ...' they turn back with tired faces. 'Nick was passed a message earlier,' I say while Nick lifts his eyebrows in surprise. 'Marcy is at the houses by the bay ... She told some survivors to tell us.'

'Fuck,' Cookey says, 'never rains, does it?'

'We going then?' Blowers sighs but straightens up as though ready to move back out.

'After we've slept.'

'Thank fuck for that,' Blowers sags again with a wan smile.

'Sleep.' The order isn't needed, and as one, we head inside the walls of the old fort to our bare concrete bunkers and the space we call home.

Paula and Roy have rooms elsewhere. Jagger and Mo Mo were in the space reserved for the crews, but we've been through too much together to be separated now. Everyone finds a bed or something soft, and within minutes, they're all crashed out and falling into silence.

My mind spins for a few minutes. Thoughts of seeing Lani go down, and the image in my head of Roy straddled across her body while doing chest compressions. Guilt mixed with despair. Guilt that I kissed Marcy in my dream, and guilt from the sensation of my stomach flipping when I heard the message she passed. Despair that Lani almost laid down her life for mine.

There is another emotion mixed in with the guilt and despair. A feeling that has come from the fucked dreams I had and the things I saw. Not just the old man I carried out from the underground train station or the meeting with Marcy, but watching the team argue and bicker. Seeing Blowers and Cookey fight with bare hands as they sought to cover the breach in the wall.

A sensation. No. A gripping, icy hand that rips through every other feeling that I must have fortitude. That we're at a turning point, and right now is the time to make a decision. We can stay within the fort now. We have ammunition, weapons, doctors, medicines, fuel, people, skills, and food.

We can focus on building a place of safety and refuge to protect our species so they may survive and continue our race.

The infection told me there can only be one race. The infection won't allow us the peace to live quietly. It will mass and attack again, and it won't stop.

The thought of the infection making an infected drive the Saxon is terrifying. If it can do that, what else can it achieve?

Staying here and hiding is not an option. We have to go

out and meet this thing head on. We have to find Marcy and seek the answers, for the answers will not just come to us.

The icy sensation within me is fortitude. That I must be equally as ruthless as the infection but retain the essence of humanity or else there is no point defeating it, for we would be the same.

To be human is to laugh, cry, feel, and react. Without that, we are the hive mind pack of the infected. We are allowed to be angry and righteous, for it's those emotions that will see us through the worst times yet to come.

Fuck me, Blowers is immune. Cookey. Lani. Me and, of course, Meredith. Too many thoughts, too many strands of thoughts all pushing off into different directions, and my tired mind slowly sinks into the blissful state of oblivion.

CHAPTER THIRTY

The devil sits on one shoulder, the angel on the other. In the middle rests the common sense of a mind that feels the equal pull of both. By the presence of both, we have a balance of thought. The desire to achieve and get more is coupled with the conscience to do so decently. To act within the boundaries of the acceptable behaviours of our species.

We see evil. We feel evil. We see good. We are good.

One race.

One race to be born without the concepts of good or evil. With no devil. No angel. Just the purity of existence.

One race that can see the folly of humankind. A free mind is never truly free. The species is wrapped up in a plethora of differing rules that sculpt each mind, depending on the factors around it.

False gods. False prophets. False ideals and beliefs. A society of lies spun so deep within us, we cannot now, nor ever will be truly free.

One race.

Machines bleep in the quiet of the hospital bay. Run by diesel that powers the generators that give life to the machines that watch life.

The heartbeat is steady. The blood pressure recovers. The wounds were deep and life threatening, but they healed, clotted, congealed, and the body did what was needed to stem the loss of the vital fluids needed to function.

She lies still. Her chest rises with the breath taken in and lowers by the breath exhaled. Lisa Franklin stares down at the body and watches with a focus only a mind trained from years of study can bring to bear.

The wounds are bad. No. They *were* bad. The patient exhibits injuries that are days old, but they only just happened. The area round the wounds should be bruising, but they aren't. The body should be weak from fighting infection of the open wounds, but it isn't weak.

The antibiotics administered through the drip were stopped. An act done without the knowledge of the other doctors. Lisa Franklin simply twisted the valve on the tube and switched it off.

Nothing happened.

Nothing.

No change to heartbeat, pulse, temperature, or breathing.

. . .

That was hours ago.

Once again, she pulls the cover back to reveal the golden skin on the Thai girl's shapely legs, and once again, she shakes her head at the laceration on the inner thigh. A deep laceration. A laceration that would require stitches. A laceration that would cause swelling in the surrounding soft tissue as the body reacted to protect the injury. A laceration that would see bruising in the skin.

Nothing.

A clean wound that does not require stitches and is not swollen and that is surrounded by normal-coloured flesh of a golden hue without a trace of bruising.

She leans closer and uses an old-fashioned magnifying glass to inspect the wound. The scabs are thick but different. They seem to be fusing with the living skin surrounding the wound. The scab is the protective layer that serves to guard the tender injury. In time, and as the wound heals, the scab comes away. This scab is not going to come away. This scab is part of the healing process.

Doctor Franklin checks the other wounds. Albeit they are not as serious as the thigh wound, but still, the same process is underway.

If this were normal times. If this patient were a normal patient in a normal hospital, then by now, that hospital would be packed full of regional and national experts with international experts on route.

She would be isolated and subjected to every test known to modern medicine because what Lani is doing, or rather, what her body is doing, defies everything.

. . .

Outside the hospital, the Fort is alive with sound and motion. A riot of colours from the modern fabric worn by the survivors. Tents erected shelter some from the hot sun. Others stand and chat to new neighbours. Lilly strides through the middle with clipboard held firm in her hands. Lenski, by the police offices, sips from a bottle of water as she watches the ammunition brought over from the shore being carried through to be stacked deep within the walls of the Fort.

Within the old armoury, there is near silence. Clarence snores. Meredith whimpers in her sleep, her back legs twitching as she chases one of the things within her dream. An infected with many arms that all need to be taken and kept.

Blowers murmurs as he scratches at the bite mark on his arm that itches from healing. The scabs of dried blood fuse with the skin surrounding the wound.

Cookey sleeps peacefully. His own wounds healing as the body floods with the exact chemicals in the exact order needed to repair the damaged tissues, ligaments, tendons, and muscles.

Doctor Franklin purses her lips and stands up with a low groan at the dull ache in her lower back from being bent over the patient for too long.

She lacks the knowledge to deal with this. All of the doctors do. They need blood specialists, scientists versed in tropical diseases, and virologists to even begin to understand what could be happening.

Yes, she can take a blood sample and study it and possibly even work out a way of identifying something within the blood that is different to people who are not infected. But the variables are too great, and the risks of getting it wrong are too much.

With a sigh, she accepts she does not know what she is looking at. She can fix the limbs and injuries. She and the other doctors can do basic operations and administer medicines, but that's it.

But.

But she can sense something. A gut instinct that Lani is different to normal people, but she is not infected in the way they have seen. The infection has changed her. Changed her ability to heal.

That would be the same for all the members of that team that have proven to be immune. Howie. Blowers and Cookey.

Are they carriers? Can their blood infect someone else? The only way to tell for sure would be to take Lani's blood and physically put it into someone else's body and monitor the results.

She turns slowly to face the bed opposite from Lani. An old man with a weak heart lies dying. Too many days without his medication coupled with the constant fear and strenuous action of running have placed too great a burden on the already diseased organ within his chest.

She looks at his bare arms lying exposed at the sides of his body and takes a breath. What she is thinking is incomprehensible to a modern doctor within the western world of medicine. It goes against everything she has ever sworn to do.

But that one act will give a huge amount of information. To take Lani's blood and put it in the old man, then wait to see if he becomes infected.

He's out of it. Sedated by strong drugs that do their work to rid his body of pain until he expires.

He wouldn't feel a thing. He would have no knowledge.

Barbaric? Yes. Essential? Also yes.

'Lisa, please tell me you are not being serious?' Doctor Carlton asks slowly. Twenty minutes since Lisa had the idea, and around her stand the other three doctors with Maddox and Lenski.

'You can see Lani's rate of healing with your own eyes,' Lisa says. She knew this would be a hard sell and rightly so, but she also knows it makes sense.

'I agree,' Andrew says with a nod, 'the old chap is sedated and won't feel a thing, and to be honest, I thought he'd already be dead by now.'

'Andrew!' Anne stares at him with shock, 'think about what you're saying. All of you, think about this.' She glares round at the group.

'Anne,' Lisa says softly, 'we're all four of us pissing in the wind on this.'

'Lisa ...'

'No, Anne. We're blind. We're worse than medical students, trying to understand our first biology lesson. Lani could be infected with this virus ... It's certainly doing something to her physiology.'

'But sacrificing a human life?'

'Anne, he's dead anyway,' Lisa says. 'The second those meds wear off, and the pain hits him, he dies ... At least this way, he's giving something back before he dies.'

'Okay,' Anne lifts her eyebrows and pauses, 'so to be clear. You are suggesting we use a human test subject without the patients consent or knowledge?'

'And we have hundreds of people living here,' Maddox interrupts her. 'If Lani is a carrier, then it means Howie and the rest are carriers. We need to know that information. Do the test.'

'Listen, Maddox,' Anne holds a hand as though to gain his attention, 'you are not a doctor and ...'

'But I am responsible for the welfare of every person within this fort.'

'If we, er ...' Andrew turns to look at the old man sleeping so peacefully. 'I mean ... do we need to restrain him? In case he turns or ...'

'Not here,' Maddox states. 'We'll take him outside, to the beach.'

'Oh no ... not happening,' Anne says firmly. 'This patient is under my care, and there is no way you are dragging him outside to sacrifice him for some butchered bloody test that won't tell us anything anyway.'

'It'll tell us if Lani is a carrier,' Maddox replies.

'Will it?' Anne asks archly. 'Is that right? We take blood from Lani without knowing anything about her medical history and put it into that man without knowing anything about his medical history. Have you any concept of the variables at play here? He could die from a heart attack simply by moving him ... He could have other pre-existing conditions that we have no knowledge of, which could affect the result of this so-called test. We have no idea what effects this virus has on people and–'

'Not true,' Heathcliff Stone speaks for the first time, having watched the conversation in silence, 'we do know what effects it has.'

'Heathcliff, we know nothing about this virus or the physiological results on the human body.'

'We do,' Heathcliff offers a wry smile. 'We know that an infected person craves the flesh of people. That is a crude symptom, but one we are familiar with. We know it makes the eyes go red and fill with blood. We know the patient will lose cognitive function. We know there will be an inability to communicate or feel pain. Modern medicine is all about what tests we can run or undertake, but sometimes good old-fashioned doctoring has to suffice. We know what a zombie bloody looks like because we have seen them. If the old chap turns into one, we know Lani is infected *with* the virus.'

'They don't bleed like normal,' Maddox says quietly. 'They heal faster too,' he motions towards Lani. 'There are signs.'

'And if the male patient doesn't become infected?' Anne asks. 'What then? We take it as fact that Lani is not infected?'

'My dear,' Heathcliff rocks on his heels, 'we work with what we have. Young man,' he fixes Maddox with a glare, 'I am the senior physician here, and I give you consent to run the test ... That man,' he points to the old patient, 'would not be here, receiving this care, if it was not for Howie and his team. He would not be receiving pain medication nor lying peacefully in a clean hospital bed. It is because of the actions of those few that we are able to have this discussion at all. Therefore, we owe it to those few to determine what we can, and I would stake my professional reputation on the fact that, if this old chap were to wake up and be told the facts that he *is* going to die within the next few hours, *but* we will sedate him and let him go peacefully, and by doing so, he may further our understanding of this event, which may assist the saving of many more lives ... well, I dare say he would agree himself.'

Heathcliff trails off as he casts a pained look at the old man before glancing over to Lani. 'We must do what we can,' he says so quietly as though almost to himself. 'But,' he looks at the faces watching him, 'it will be done with what dignity we can muster. A stretcher will be used, and we will increase his dose of Morphine, just in case. He will not be restrained or tied down. Can your chaps handle that?' He looks to Maddox, 'In the event he does turn?'

'I can handle it,' Maddox says quietly.

'Anne,' Heathcliff turns to the younger woman, 'I note your objections. I want you present so you can see what happens.'

'I will,' Anne says with a small nod. An overwhelming instinct that what they propose is wrong, but then everything Heathcliff just said makes it seem okay. An older man with a deep voice that gives gravitas to his words. Bearded and refined, and somehow, he makes it sound like they are doing the right thing.

Lisa checks the charts at the end of the old man's bed, nodding to herself as she works out the last administration of morphine given and quickly calculating what can be given safely.

While a stretcher is brought in and the muttered orders given, the old man is lifted gently from his bed and placed on the board. He doesn't murmur or flinch; not a reaction is given from his heavily drug-induced comatose state.

Wearing gloves, a face mask and taking the greatest of care, Lisa draws a few CCs of blood from Lani's arm. The thick, red liquid filling the bottom half of the syringe. She caps the needle and points it down, then rethinks, and wraps it in tissue before placing it inside a cardboard box.

A procession of four doctors is led by Maddox and Lenski as the cortege heads out of the rooms and into the Fort. Survivors glance over with interest but say nothing. Death is common now, and the man on the stretcher is clearly old and frail.

Through the inner gate, across the gap, and out onto the beach. Just the guard crew present, and they form a loose half circle round the stretcher that is gently laid out on the ground.

Anne watches with a heavy heart but does lift her gaze enough to see the glittering surface of the sea and the deep blue sky above their heads. Gentle waves lap at the shore, and in the sky, a gull gives voice as it soars on the thermals.

She exhales a slow breath and realises with a jolt that billions of lives have probably been lost in the last few days, and to go like this, sedated and watched by genuinely caring people, on a pretty little beach, under the gorgeous sun, is better than many could have wished for.

She drops down and takes the old man's hand gently in her own. She knows the level of morphine in his system means he couldn't possibly feel it, so the action is done for her own conscience.

Lisa looks at Maddox who draws his pistol and nods while stepping closer to the old man's head. She opens the box, unwraps the syringe, and for a second, stares at the red liquid held within.

Silence as she lifts his right arm and runs the tip of her thumb over a thick vein protruding through the thin skin.

'Ready?' she doesn't look up but holds the needle close.

Maddox checks round and motions with his head for everyone else to move back.

'Anne,' Heathcliff says gently, 'come back now.'

'I will,' she says, then looks at Lisa. 'Go on.'

'Okay ... the vein is clear. The needle is inserting now, going straight into the vein. Drawing back. The syringe draws blood, and I am now administering the blood taken from Lani into this patient ... Syringe empty ... Withdrawing and applying pressure to the...'

'Move back now,' Maddox says.

Anne and Lisa lower the limbs they hold, and both swiftly move back as Maddox stands over the old man with the pistol held ready and looks down at the small dribble of blood coming from the pinprick in the crook of the old man's arm.

One race that is unbound by the restraints of the human desire for the individual to be worthy.

An infection that deepens an understanding of the human brain with every passing day. An infection that takes mere seconds to infiltrate every cell within the human body to stop the heart and restart it in the true way of being.

An infection that entered Lani but found itself pushed back as her own immunity rallied and took back what was taken.

Lani's body defeated but did not eradicate the infection. It pushed it back far enough so the infection was hidden and harmless, contained by healthy DNA that refused the spread it was designed to undertake.

Lani is torn. Damage was wrought to her body. Blood was lost. Too much blood, and it weakened her already exhausted body. Hours of running and fighting, and she had nothing left to fight with. That tiniest remnant of the virus was suddenly unbidden to release once again, but in the time it was held, it changed.

It was not the thing it was when it entered her system. It got into the blood and went through the heart. It made changes to her blood and made it clot faster. It changed her DNA and bolstered the immunity made weaker by the damage to the system.

As it detected death and a loss of ability to live, so it

rushed hither and thither throughout the body, driving oxygen into the brain and working hard to keep the heart pumping.

As Roy worked Lani's chest. So the infection worked inside to keep the host alive. As Lani strengthened, so her own immunity and natural antibodies came back into production.

The Lani on the bed in the hospital is not the Lani the infection entered, and nor is it the Lani that was torn.

As Lani got stronger. So the infection withdrew.

As Lisa pulled Lani's blood into the syringe, so the infection was once again contained.

The old man lies under the sun as two minutes go by. Sweat beads down Maddox's face and runs down his cheeks. His hand remains still. His eyes watchful. Someone shifts position. Someone else exhales audibly.

Tension high. Eyes staring. Everyone focused.

'Three minutes,' Andrew looks up from his watch, 'we should look at the eyes.'

Maddox drops in a fluid movement that has the barrel of the gun resting but an inch from the side of the old man's head. He reaches down and uses the tip of his thumb to gently lift the right eyelid.

'White,' he says clearly.

'Let me see,' Lisa moves forward cautiously. Leaning over Maddox as though using him as a shield. 'Check the other one.'

Maddox lifts the left eyelid and shows the perfectly normal eye to the doctor, who swallows and steps back, blowing air out through puffed cheeks. 'Looks normal,' he twists round to first stare up at Lisa, then beyond her to the waiting crowd.

'Lani isn't a carrier, then?' Maddox asks.

'At this stage,' Heathcliff steps in closer to peer down at the form of the patient, 'it appears not.'

1900 hours. Lani snaps awake with a start. Comatose one second and bolt upright the next. Breathing hard with wide eyes, she looks down at her own body, then slowly at her surroundings. Machines bleep softly, and the air smells clean. In the bed opposite, an old man lies deeply asleep while one of the doctors holds his wrist with a look of worried concentration.

Lani goes to, speak but her throat is dry, and she makes sound with no discernible sense. The doctor turns quickly as she clears her throat and tries again.

'Fort?'

'Yes!' Lisa Franklin crosses the short distance, hardly able to contain the surprise at seeing Lani wake so quickly. 'Lie back. You need to rest.'

'Thirsty,' Lani coughs again.

'Here,' Lisa heads to a side table and takes a bottle of water, 'sip it first.'

'Sod that,' Lani gulps greedily as the cool liquid soaks into her dry mouth and tumbles soothingly down her throat. She downs the bottle and burps without shame before offering a wry smile, 'Sorry.'

'What for?'

'Been around the lads too long;. No manners ... Er ... why am I in here?'

'You were injured,' Lisa rests on the edge of the makeshift hospital bed. 'Deep wound to your thigh, more to your stomach, arms, shoulders ... pretty much everywhere.'

'Oh,' Lani blanches, 'yeah, I remember getting overwhelmed ... Wow, the painkillers are good.'

'Painkillers?'

'Can't feel a thing,' Lani grins. 'What have you given me?'

'Funny that,' Lisa says softly. 'We haven't given you anything.'

'Pardon?'

'Nothing. You're not on *any* pain relief. No morphine, no codeine, no anything ... not even paracetamol.'

'Seriously?'

'Seriously.'

'How long have I been out of it? Where's everyone else? Did they go for Marcy?'

'They're sleeping too.'

'Sleeping? Why?' Lani casts round as though trying to work out how long she's been unconscious.

'You've been here about seven hours.'

'Seven hours?'

Lisa nods once and watches the Thai girl closely, taking in the rosy, golden complexion of her skin and the lustre of her silky black hair, which is the opposite of what someone waking up from a coma should look like.

'Excuse me,' Lani pulls her knees to her chest with a motion that would have a normal person with those injuries screaming in agony. With Lisa off the bed, she pushes the covers back and stares at the injury on her thigh and the puckered skin of an old wound fused and healing.

'It's itchy ... Can I scratch it?'

'Guess so. Just do it gently.'

'Ah, that's so nice,' Lani gently scrapes the tips of her fingernails over the wound.

'Nice nails,' Lisa leans in to stare at the fingertips and the perfect, white tips edging the healthy, pink plate.

'Yeah, they're a bitch to keep clean.'

'Don't they break with all the fighting?'

'Lucky, I guess,' Lani shrugs. 'Has someone washed me?'

'Of course, we did. You weren't stepping foot in here in the state you were in.'

'Thanks, I guess,' Lani thinks for a second. 'Oh god.'

'What?' Lisa snaps to attention.

'I actually crave coffee ... actual coffee ... I hate coffee. Bloody Howie and the others always drinking it.'

'Coffee?'

'Oh, they go on about how they don't get enough coffee but really, the amount of time we spend messing about making coffee, getting coffee, or breaking into places just to find coffee is ridiculous.'

'Lani.'

Lani looks up sharply at the tone in the doctor's voice and waits for the inevitable questions.

'I don't know.'

'Don't know what?' Lisa asks with a gentle tone.

'Why I healed so fast. Why my nails don't break. Why my hair is in such good condition, or any of it. I don't know. I was infected. I turned. I got better. End of,' she shrugs defensively. 'Can I go, please?'

'Of course, you can go but ...'

'Thanks.' She stands up, expecting a wave of dizziness to sweep over her but finds her legs feel stronger than ever. 'Where are my clothes?'

'Incinerated. Listen, why don't you stay a while and rest ...'

'Got work to do.'

'What work?'

'Howie will be off to find Marcy, and if you think for one second I'll let him do that alone, you can think again.'

'We need to examine you.'

'You have examined me ... Er ... what can I wear? I'm in my underwear right now.'

'Just lie back and let us find some clothes for you. Tell me–how do you feel?'

'I feel great,' Lani says with no intention of lying back down.

'No pain?'

'No.'

'Anything unusual?'

'No.'

'Lani, was your hair and nails always in such good condition?'

'Yes. No. I ... no, they weren't.'

'Did you ever get hurt before this? Like, say, cut your hand or something?'

'Of course, I did, and no, I did not heal like I do now. I healed like a normal person and put plasters on and everything.'

'So you are changing, or rather, you have changed.'

'Listen,' Lani fixes the doctor with the eyes of a killer, dark and brooding, and the intensity has Lisa's stomach flipping, 'I appreciate your help, but I'm going.'

Lisa swallows and rallies as she forces her gaze away from Lani eyes, 'We need to know what's going on.'

'Help him,' Lani points across the room to the bed opposite. 'He looks like he needs it more than me.'

'Him?' Lisa follows her gaze. 'He was dying a few hours ago.'

'Was?'

'Well, I should say he was expected to die a few hours ago.'

'That's good then, isn't it?'

'Heart,' Lisa sighs. 'He was in a bad way. We had him dosed up to high heaven on morphine.'

'And?'

'Then we took him outside and injected him with your blood.'

'You did what?' Lani's voice drops to a low tone.

Ignoring the warning, the doctor continues, 'We took blood from your arm and put it into him. We wanted to know if you were carrying the infection. He didn't turn. He didn't die. He didn't die then, and he hasn't died since.'

'Doctor, you cannot ...'

'And we haven't given him any morphine since the injection was administered either.'

Lani freezes mid-sentence as she takes in the sleeping form of the old man. Flicking her gaze back to the Lisa, she steps slowly across the aisle and closer to the man.

'His colour is returning,' Lisa says flatly from behind her. 'By now ... by rights ... he should be suffering the pain of his heart condition that should have killed him ...'

'He looks alright,' Lani whispers the words as she stares at the ruddy cheeks of the patient.

'He does. And you know what else?' Lisa steps silently next to Lani and gently lifts the wrist of the man. She goes quiet, focussed, then looks at Lani, 'Feel this.'

'The pulse?'

'Feel it ... put your fingertip here. Can you feel it?'

'Yes.'

'Dum, dum, dum, dum, dum,' Lisa nods with each beat of the pulse. 'That tells us his heart is beating normally ...'

'Normally?'

'Yes,' Lisa holds the eye contact, 'normally for a person with a healthy heart ... not for an old man dying of a heart condition.'

'My blood did this?' Lani asks quietly.

'In truth, we don't know,' Lisa says with sad shake of her head.

'But in our combined medical experience,' the deep male voice makes Lani turn quickly as Heathcliff walks further into the room, 'old men with heart conditions do not suddenly get better.'

Lani blinks quickly as she looks off to the side, 'Can I go now?'

'We want you to stay,' Lisa says in a tone too gentle.

'I'm going,' Lani says.

'Lani, we really want you to stay so we can find out what's happening ... happened to you ...'

She looks at the older, bearded doctor as the hairs on the back of her neck prickle, 'I want to go.'

'Lani.'

She spins again to see Maddox walking into the room from the main entrance.

'Maddox! How's everyone? They okay? Did anyone else get hurt?'

'No, just you,' he replies. 'They told you, then?'

'About him?' Lani asks, nodding at the old man. 'Yes, but ... where's Howie and the ...?'

'Asleep in their rooms. We need to run tests on you all and find out how–'

'I'm going to the rooms,' Lani interrupts him. 'I'll wait with the others.'

'They're asleep, Lani,' Maddox watches her closely, his own voice gentle and unchallenging.

Lani takes him in, the easy stance he holds, with his

arms resting at his sides. The atmosphere in the room charged and heavy. 'What's going on?' she finally gives voice to the creeping sensation plucking at her insides. 'I'm going now ... right now ...'

'Easy,' Maddox smiles as he takes a step forward. 'Nothing bad happening here, Lani,' his tone is soft and relaxed, 'you cured an old man about to die ... They put your blood in him and–'

'Awesome,' Lani drops her head an inch to widen her peripheral vision, 'come tell me about it in the rooms with the others ...'

'Lani, whatever got inside you has changed you,' Maddox says quickly. 'Look at how you healed. Look at *you!*'

'What about me?'

'You look radiant,' Lisa says from behind.

'I'm freaking out right now,' Lani says. 'I'm getting the feeling you don't want me to go.'

'Lani, what if the thing inside you can heal others,' Maddox says. 'What if you can stop other people dying too?'

'That's great,' Lani swallows, 'but please, I'd really rather talk about this with the others.'

'We'll let them come over when they've woken up,' Heathcliff says with what he hoped would be a paternal tone, but instead his words cause an inward wince from Maddox.

'Let them?' Lani picks up on the choice of words instantly. 'Let them? This is our fort ... I'm going ...'

'Lani, you've only got bra and knickers on,' Lisa says quickly. 'We'll get you some clothes.'

'Fuck the clothes,' she heads down the aisle, towards Maddox. Her threat perception picking up that he is the only viable threat in the room and knowing full well he carries a pistol on the back of his belt. The whole thing is creeping her out, and the claxon in her head screams to get out, go now, run, danger close.

'Lani,' Maddox spreads palms towards her, 'you got to stay here, okay?'

'Not okay, Maddox.'

'Sorry, Lani ...'

'Maddox!' she snaps. 'Do not pull a gun on me,' she watches as his right hand reaches behind his back.

'You're staying ...' he says firmly. 'Listen ... please just listen ...'

'You pull that gun, and you know what will happen,' she stands her ground and points at him.

'You've changed. Your physiology has changed. Lani, you saved that man from dying. What you have ... whatever is inside you can help people, can help us ...'

'I get it,' she says without blinking, 'and I said we could talk in the rooms with the others ... Do not stop me, Maddox.'

'Lani, I'm sorry ... but ...'

'You force me to stay, and all hell will break lose, you fool,' she says quickly. 'You've got ten heavily armed and *very* experienced people across the way that will *not*–'

'You're staying.'

'Dave,' Lani says with a shake of her head, 'you have no idea what that man can do.'

'Then don't let that happen.'

Lani stares at Maddox, then turns to look back at Lisa and Heathcliff further back. Movement at the back of the room as Darius steps into view, holding an assault rifle gripped and ready.

'You idiots,' Lani sighs. 'We would have stayed ... We would have done anything to sort this out ...'

'Cool,' Maddox shrugs with his right hand still behind his back, 'do that then. Stay and let us sort this out.'

'Like this?'

'What? Shit, Lani,' Maddox grins, 'you can't blame us for wanting to protect you.'

'Protect me?'

'Protect what you are.'

'What we'll do,' Lani says slowly, 'is let me go and talk to the others, and we'll discuss it round the table like we normally do.'

'You'll go and find Marcy.'

'What?'

'You'll go find Marcy,' Maddox repeats, 'and we can't let that happen. We can't let you go back out there, knowing what you are and what you can do. There's no way you'll split your team, and you stay here while the others go ...'

'I'm going,' Lani rolls her eyes disdainfully as she steps towards Maddox.

'Wait!'

'Or what? You'll shoot me? Shoot the girl with the cure for old men with bad hearts?'

'No,' Maddox holds her gaze levelly, 'but we will sedate you if we have to.'

'Good luck with that,' Lani smiles slowly and drops her hands to her sides as she slides her left foot back a fraction.

Maddox notices the stance and brings his right hand round to the front, showing Lani the open palm. 'No need for this.'

'Let me go, then.'

'You have to stay here.'

'Maddox, when Howie and the rest wake up, they'll ...'

'That has been planned for,' Maddox cuts across her words as a sinking sensation hits Lani in the stomach.

'What?' she asks softly.

'You are the same as Howie ... and Cookey and now Blowers so ...'

'Blowers?'

'Blowers was bitten on the arm during the fight. He's immune too.'

Lani reels from the news, her heart ramping up with the sudden turn of events and the situation rapidly getting out of control.

'There's no need for this,' she says quickly. 'If ... my god, if I knew my blood could do that,' she waves a hand towards the old man, 'or ... I mean, if any of us thought for a second we could do that, we'd do exactly what you wanted.'

'You wouldn't,' Maddox says with a shake of his head. 'Howie is an amazing leader but ...'

'But what?'

'But he's on a mission and,' Maddox pauses to think. 'If we ...' he stops again.

'If we what?' Lani prompts. 'What?'

'You wouldn't stay in here. You know you wouldn't,' Maddox replies heavily. 'Howie's driven to ... to do whatever he thinks he needs to do ...'

'Saving everyone!' Lani says. 'Doing exactly what he's being doing the whole time ... If he suspected his blood or my blood or any of us could help people, he'd do exactly the right thing.'

'There's another consideration to this, Lani.' Lisa says quietly from behind. Lani doesn't turn but drops her head an inch to acknowledge the comment.

'I get it,' she says, 'but it won't happen.'

'Something in you made you heal. That something is

making this man heal from a condition that *was* killing him …'

'I said I get it.'

'But what if you turn? What if you have a delayed reaction? What if this man has a delayed reaction? What if the virus is mutating?'

'Like I said. It won't.'

'Viruses mutate all the time. The common cold. Ebola. HIV … they–'

'I heard you, and I said it won't happen.'

'How do you know, Lani?'

'Stop saying my bloody name,' she spins to stare angrily at the doctor. 'It's a form of manipulation that I do not find acceptable.'

'I'm sorry. I wasn't trying to manipulate you.'

'If we were going to have turned, we would have done it days ago. We've killed thousands of them … Don't you think we would have been stopped by now? It sends more and more against us, and we still kill them.'

'Mutation,' Lisa says simply, 'you're suggesting the current virus has a hive mind or a conscious awareness of self. If that is the case, then the strain you have may be different … The hive mind in the others is not the same as in you.'

'Conjecture.'

'We have to work with what we have,' Heathcliff says.

'What? Wild guesses?'

'Lani, they're–'

'Stop … saying … my …'

'Sorry! Look, Lani. We're doing the best we can with what limited information we have. You *might* be infected … You *might* be a carrier … You *might* have saved that man,' Lisa says imploringly.

'See sense,' Heathcliff says. 'This is the best for everyone.'

'We brought you here,' Lani says. 'We risked our lives again and again to find you and bring you back.'

'And everyone is grateful,' Maddox says carefully, 'but situations change, and things happen, and we've got to adapt as we go. You are staying here, Lani. Howie and the others will be confined to their rooms, but they'll be safe. If I honestly thought you would all stay here and stay safe, I'd have done it that way ... but I know Howie won't relinquish his weapons, and Dave is too dangerous even without weapons ... I've thought this through, and this is my decision for it to happen like this.'

'Against our will?'

'There's no need for–'

'Say it,' Lani demands, 'admit you are doing this against our will. Say it out loud.'

'Shoe fits,' Maddox shrugs. 'Yeah, against your will, but know this,' he takes a step forward as his voice drops in tone, 'I will do whatever it takes to protect the people of this fort and everyone who turns up here and ...'

'Like we did.'

'Yes, but the situation has changed, and your team is now at the crux of the issue. Either you are infected and therefore a danger to everyone here, or you are not ... but with what happened when we put your blood into that man, we must ... *must* take whatever steps are necessary, and if that means ...'

'Fuck off,' Lani spits, 'I'm leaving right now.'

'Don't do it,' Maddox warns as his right arm once more goes behind his back.

'Better shoot me then,' she walks at him, confident in the knowledge after everything said that Maddox won't risk her life. That he would have calculated that a gunshot will carry in the fort, which will wake the others and bring them running.

'On you,' Maddox brings the hand round to the front and grips the handle of the weapon held pointed at Lani.

She looks down and feels her heart sink as he fires. 'You prick,' she utters the words as the barbs of the Taser shoot from the bright yellow device and sink into the flesh of her exposed stomach.

CHAPTER THIRTY-ONE

'What happen?'

'They sedated her.'

'You said this,' Lenski remains poker faced but watches Maddox closely. 'You say this happen.'

'I tried talking to her but ...'

'Oh, she never to listen,' Lenski cuts him off. 'I not listen if you do this to me. What now? You wake Howie?'

'We're ready,' Maddox stares down the fort at the crews positioned directly outside the old armoury rooms. All of them now equipped with assault rifles and fresh ammunition. The fort occupants have been pushed back to create a sterile area immediately beyond the crews and told it's for their own safety as one of the group inside could be infected.

The mere mention of the infection being in the fort swept like wildfire, and within minutes, the survivors were gathering as far away as possible with haunted and frightened looks etched on their weathered faces.

'Committed now,' Maddox says before breathing out noisily through his nose.

'You doubt this?'

'No, but ...'

'The man, he living now. Lani and the others they must understand this. We have many here ... Many more they come here. We do this for the many.'

'Lilly,' Maddox nods at the young woman striding across the fort towards them. 'Does she know?'

'I tell her,' Lenski admits. 'She had to know.'

'Sure.'

'What the hell?!'

'Lilly, just wait ...'

'You cannot do this, Maddox.'

'It's done.'

'What's done?' she demands and comes to a stop directly in front of him, hands on hips, and a look of defiance clear on her face.

'Lani, she's been told.'

'Told what? What's going on?'

'I tell you,' Lenski says. 'I tell you this.'

'You are holding Lani in the hospital and the others in their rooms. Is that right? And you're doing it because they ...'

'Lani's blood was given to a man dying from a heart condition,' Maddox keeps his tone soft but firm. 'We thought he'd turn. He didn't turn. He didn't die of the heart problem either. He got better. He's still getting better.'

Lilly listens and forces the initial fury from her tone and manner. The crews facing the armoury armed to the teeth, and every single one of them looking serious. The wheels are in motion, and the situation is evolving rapidly. She knows they didn't tell her straight away because they knew what her reaction would be.

'That is amazing,' Lilly makes herself nod and appear impressed. 'I mean ... and the doctors have verified this?'

'He's unconscious,' Maddox admits, 'but his heart rate, blood pressure, and other visible signs all indicate he's recovering. They expect him to wake up any time now.'

'Gosh,' Lilly lifts her eyebrows, then nods, 'and it was Lani's blood that was given to him?'

'That's right,' Maddox tilts his head a fraction of an inch as he picks up the minute details of her posture and tone, and in those few seconds his respect for the girl rises significantly.

'I understand,' Lilly says, 'and I assume you are considering that the disease that got into Lani has somehow changed her? Lenski told me she has healed far quicker than she should. So again, I assume you or the doctors think Lani's immunity has somehow coupled with the disease to give her a greater ability to heal herself and that it was passed to the heart patient.'

Maddox nods as she talks, 'Correct. That is the assumption we are working from. We don't know anything for fact, but if Lani is infected or a carrier, then we cannot take the risk of her exposing others. On the flip side, if she has the ability to recover in ways far beyond the normal human body, then again, we cannot risk her doing anything that could jeopardise her own safety.'

'I agree,' Lilly takes her turn to nod while Maddox speaks, 'but forgive me speaking out of turn, Maddox. It does not feel right that you have forced her to remain in the hospital against her will.'

'Okay, I understand your concern but ...'

'And I spent time with Nick,' she continues with a diplomatic look, 'and know first-hand the honourable intentions of his team, especially Mr Howie. Surely if he was told what had happened, he would stay here and allow the tests to be done without the need for force.'

'And I factored that in my considerations. Howie is driven to find out where this infection came from and how it can be stopped ... but not in the same way we are.'

'How so?'

'He knows he is immune. That gives him an element of recklessness. Same with Lani, and now, of course, with Cookey and Blowers. They are more likely to place themselves in harm's way *because* they are immune.'

'I see, but again, I would respectfully point out that if you simply spoke to them, they would most likely concede to your request to remain within the fort for a period of time.'

'Which would last about a day. They've been fighting non-stop. They couldn't stop now for anything.'

'Oh, I don't think so,' Lilly allows a tactical smile to form on her face, 'I think given the chance to lounge about the fort getting in everyone's way and eating us out of house and home would be the blessing they are craving. Plus, of course, Nick would get to spend some time with me–'

'They want Marcy,' Maddox interrupts her with his own strategically deployed smile. 'They will go for Marcy.'

'Do they even know where she is?'

'She'll be close.'

'Yes. I see your point, but no, I do not agree. I think a simple conversation outlining what you had established, and they would stay here and do as bid.'

'What if they didn't? Lilly, if they step outside those rooms with weapons, we would never stop them. Not with Dave and Clarence on their side ... They're all highly skilled fighters now and would wipe this place out in seconds ...'

'Why would they ever do that?'

'They are infected, Lilly,' Maddox says seriously. 'The experiment with Lani proves that. Yes, it's helping the old man now, but the doctors have all said it could be a delayed reaction. He could still turn. Mr Howie and his group could still turn, and with their skills and knowledge, they'd kill everyone ... Not just in here but everyone they came into contact with. They would be unstoppable. They alone could wipe out what few survivors are left. Have you heard them joke about being thankful Dave is on their side?'

'Of course, Nick told me they talk about it sometimes.'

'Imagine Dave turned. Imagine Dave as one of them.'

'Howie ... I mean Mr Howie would never let it happen.'

'How would he stop it? None of them could stop Dave.'

'Meredith would,' she lets the smile show again but knows she's lost the argument.

'She'd try,' Maddox allows the point, 'but we can't base our sole chance of survival on a dog. It has to be this way. I'm sorry, Lilly.'

CHAPTER THIRTY-TWO

'Fucking hell!'

The voice has me on my feet before my eyes have opened and already moving towards the door that Dave has reached. Sounds of movement from within the armoury as everyone wakes up to rush into the middle room.

It hits me within a few steps and causes instant stinging in my eyes, and I'm bend double, almost gagging.

'What the fuck?' Nick exclaims and turns away.

'What?' Clarence lumbers into the room, wearing just underpants and holding a broom with a double-handed grip like an axe with the bristly end inches above his head. 'Holy shit ... Oh my god ...' he drops the broom and staggers backwards.

'We're so fucked,' Cookey drops to his knees. 'This is it ... the end ...'

'We're done for, Cookey,' Nick sags against the wall with his hands clutching his head.

'I know, Nick,' Cookey wails. 'Been nice knowing you.'

'You too, buddy.'

'Buddy? Did you just call me buddy?' Cookey looks up with a confused look.

'Can't hear you,' Nick grunts. 'My senses are shutting down ... I'm fading ... I can't take it ...'

'Hold in there ... buddy,' Cookey says. 'Mr Howie ... make it go away!'

'Fuck that ... Every man for himself.'

'What about me?' Paula asks from the doorway of the room she shared with Roy.

'Who said that?' Cookey cries out. 'Can't see you ... can't hear ...'

'Oh, grow up,' she says with a sigh. 'It's just dog shit.'

'It's not dog shit,' Nick wails. 'It's toxic waste ...'

'Infected toxic waste,' Cookey adds. 'Blowers ... come out and smell this.'

'Fuck off,' Blowers muffled voice rings out.

'Blowers, really ... it's really bad ... Come and smell it.'

'I don't want to smell it. Fuck off.'

'Mr Howie, make Blowers come and smell it,' Cookey half-laughs as he gags and moves quickly away from the nearest dollop of liquid shit plastered across the floor.

'Who ...' Clarence coughs and takes a breath from the safety of his hand plastered over his own mouth, 'who shut the bloody dog in?'

'Door was open,' I turn away and let the tears drip from my eyes.

'Someone closed it,' Clarence says needlessly, 'and that person will be in here cleaning this shit up ... How has she done so much?'

'She ate a lot,' Nick replies. 'We were feeding her beans and canned meat.'

'And tuna,' Cookey adds.

'And canned sausages, and she was drinking tea from a bowl,' Blowers calls out.

'You can't be part of this conversation,' Cookey yells. 'Only the truest people who have experienced the smell can be part of this conversation.'

'Fuck off.'

'She needs proper dog food,' Paula states and retreats a few steps as her initial bravery wears off.

'Fuck! That is bad,' Blowers gets to the doorway and starts chuckling at the sight of the ground covered in thick puddles of shit. 'She looks happy, though,' he nods to the far corner and the sight of Meredith flat on her back with her four legs in the air and her tongue hanging out the side of her mouth. She senses the attention and gently wags her tail as her back legs twitch.

'You can be part of the conversation now,' Cookey nods solemnly.

'Mr Howie, I saw Cookey close the door before he went to sleep,' Blowers says.

'I did not! I didn't ... Really, I didn't ...'

'I saw it too,' Nick holds a hand up.

'Liars! You're all liars ...'

'Fuck this,' I can't help but laugh at the sight and absurdity of it all, 'I'm getting out ... Last one in here cleans it up.'

The stupid words spark an all-out run for the door as we hop and jump the patches of shit as the three lads descend into the inevitable scrap. Clarence uses the broom end to hook Blowers and yank him back with a yelp. Roy is out of the room and rushing ahead. Dave walks calmly, safe in the knowledge no one would dare touch him. In underpants, and Paula in shorts and a t-shirt, we fight, push, pull, and gag our way towards the door, and as one we burst out into the warm but clean air of the fort.

'Fresh air!' Cookey sinks to his knees in a dramatic gesture with his arms held up to the sky.

'Cookey was the last one out,' Blowers laughs.

'Confirmed,' Nick says.

'Was not ... It was ... er ...'

'Yeah, go on,' Blowers laughs as Dave strolls out last.

'Um ... Dave ...' Cookey mutters.

'Mr Howie ...'

'You telling Dave to clean the shit up, then?' Nick laughs.

'Like fuck am I,' Cookey says.

'Mr Howie ...'

'Dave, you got to clear the shit up,' I say with tears falling down my face half from the putrid smell and half from laughing so much.

'Mr Howie!'

Roy's voice snaps my glance up and out. I go quiet. We all go quiet. Silence amongst us as Cookey gets slowly to his feet.

Without a word uttered, we range out into a line with hands at our sides and a total lack of humour.

Weapons pointed at us. Assault rifles. Shotguns. Pistols. Rifles. Maddox's crews all holding weapons in steady hands, and not a smile or a smirk amongst them. Dead silence in the fort, and my eyes sweep across the long line as I take in the double ranks. The front rank kneeling, and the second rank stood over them.

It hits me in the blink of an eye. Images and thoughts surge through my brain as I take in the sight.

'Easy now,' I say calmly, 'lower the weapons.' Not a flicker of movement from them.

'LOWER YOUR WEAPONS,' Dave's voice booms

with such ferocity it makes nearly every single one of them twitch, and I'm surprised they didn't start firing.

'Dave, not now ... stand down,' I drop my head and speak the words softly. 'And don't attack them, for fuck's sake,' I add hastily at the thought of Dave attacking a double rank of armed people wearing just his underpants. He'd probably still win.

A low growl signals the arrival of Meredith, and I turn to see Nick grabbing her quickly.

'Maddox?'

'Here,' he walks into view from the left side but stops short of moving into the way of the pointed guns.

'Lani turned?'

'No. She's fine.'

'So she healed, then?'

'She has, Mr Howie,' that he uses my formal name gives me some hope out of this.

'And what?'

'We took her blood and put it into an old man dying of a heart condition. He didn't turn, and he is getting better from–'

'Do what?'

He takes a step forward, 'A patient in the hospital. He was dying. He was dosed high on morphine. The doctors said he was ready to go any minute. We injected him to see if Lani was a carrier. His heart is getting better now.'

'So ...' I look towards the weapons, 'that calls for this, does it?'

'I don't like having guns pointed at me,' Clarence says clearly, 'brings back bad memories. Get them to lower their weapons.'

'No,' Maddox says the word respectfully, but the firmness of his tone is unmistakable. 'I'll explain why we're–'

'Lani's blood saved the old man,' I cut him off, 'but you don't know if he will turn or get better ... Either way you're figuring that she ... and possible me, Cookey, and Blowers have something in us that is either dangerous or a cure for old men with bad hearts. That it?'

'Pretty much, Mr Howie,' he nods.

'So you figured we were a risk to the fort and everyone in here.'

'Yes.'

'You're a prick,' the words come out a snarl, 'a fucking prick. We wouldn't ever do anything to harm this fort ... Cookey ... what do we do if one of us turns?'

'Shoot them in the head, Mr Howie,' his reply is instant.

'Nick, what would you do if I turned?'

'I'd shoot you in the head, Mr Howie.'

'Dave wouldn't,' Maddox replies. 'Dave would never hurt you.'

'Dave. What would you do if I turned and got shot in the head? Actually, don't fucking answer that!'

'Okay, Mr Howie.'

'You're too dangerous,' Maddox says in an almost apologetic tone of voice, 'all of you.'

'Where's Mo Mo and Jagger?' I realise the two lads aren't with us as I spin round to look.

'With us. We got them out,' Maddox says. 'They didn't want to go but ...'

'Where are they?'

'Safe.'

'Who closed the door?' I ask. 'The dog has shit all over the bloody floor.'

'We saw that,' Maddox says.

'And you didn't clear it up?' I ask him reproachfully. 'That's cold, mate.'

'Sorry,' he shrugs.

'No need for all this,' I motion my head towards the unwavering weapons. 'We would have just stayed here and done tests and stuff.'

'I'm sorry. But when I realised Lani was infected, we couldn't take the risk of any of you turning. And you wouldn't stay here either. You'd find a reason to go and find Marcy.'

'Yeah,' I nod glumly, 'probably.'

'Maddox,' Paula steps to my side, 'is Lani okay?'

'She's fine. She's awake and still in the hospital.'

'And she knows what's going on?' Paula asks.

'She does.'

'And she accepted it?' Paula casts a quick, confused look at me before looking back to Maddox.

'No. She tried to leave.'

'How did you stop her?' I ask quickly.

'She's not hurt.'

'How? How did you stop her?'

'She was sedated by the doctors.'

'They wouldn't get close to her,' I reply in a quiet voice that should be setting alarms off. 'Lani would destroy everyone in that place if they tried to touch her.'

'She was tasered,' he says honestly, 'and then sedated.'

'STAND DOWN,' I turn and shout the order as the team behind me make motion forward. Guns bristle with motion as Maddox waves them to stay still.

'You tasered Lani?' I ask him. 'She's gonna go fucking nuts, mate.'

'Probably.'

'And me,' I add without taking my eyes from him, 'know that.'

'Hence all this,' Maddox holds a hand out to the ranks of weapons. 'We need your guns, please.'

'Come and get them,' Blowers says.

'Pass them out ... disassembled.'

'What's that, then?' Cookey asks quietly.

'Taken apart, you thick twat,' Blowers whispers back.

'Oh, right ... nah, you can fuck off,' Cookey says.

'If you turn,' Maddox raises his voice but without any inflection of anger, 'you will kill everyone here ...'

'We won't turn,' I say simply.

'That's not a chance I am willing to take.'

'Okay,' I hold my hands up, 'me, Cookey, and Blowers will stay here. The rest haven't been cut or bitten so ...'

Maddox smiles broadly with a slow shake of his head, 'Yeah, and I'm going to let Clarence, Dave, and Roy walk about here?'

'What about me?' Paula says quickly. 'I'm dangerous too.'

'He didn't say you, Nick,' Cookey points out. 'Maddox thinks you're a pussy.'

'I do not think that,' Maddox says.

'He does,' Cookey whispers. 'He told me earlier.'

'Weapons. Taken apart and thrown outside, part by part.'

'After we get Lani back,' I say.

'Lani is staying in the hospital.'

'Good luck getting the weapons then, mate ...' I look up at the sky. 'It's evening, right? Be getting dark soon.' I look over at the youths holding the weapons. 'Those guns will be getting heavy about now ... How many can you keep watching us?'

'I like the dark,' Dave says, and his voice, so devoid of expression, is chilling in delivery.

'You've got one door,' Maddox says. 'We've got lots of weapons and lots of people to hold them. Listen, this doesn't have to be this way. Let us get some tests done and work out where we go from here ...'

'I know where you're going, dickhead,' Cookey says.

'Where's that, then?' Nick asks. 'Where's he going?'

'I dunno, just sounded cool,' Cookey says. 'What was that word again?'

'What word?' Nick asks.

'The taken apart word.'

'Disassembled,' Nick replies.

'Dis-a-what?'

'Disassembled.'

'How do you spell it?'

'Fuck knows, I can't spell.'

'Paula ...'

'Not now, Cookey.'

'Paula, how do you spell dissatakenapart word that Nick just said?'

'Really?' she turns to face him. 'Now? You want to know right now?'

I have to suppress the smile as the lads do what they do best and show utter disdain for the threat by making jokes and pissing about.

'Maddox,' Cookey calls out, 'how do you spell that word?'

'Weapons,' Maddox refuses to take the bait.

'Ooh, he's a smart one,' Nick chuckles.

'He's a clever bugger, that one,' Blowers says.

'Too sharp for toffee,' Cookey says with a nod.

'Toffee?' Blowers asks. 'What the fuck has it got to do with toffee?'

'I like toffee,' Roy says. 'Gets stuck in my teeth, though.'

'All old people like toffee,' Cookey says.

'I'm not old,' Roy points out.

'Are you over thirty?' Cookey asks.

'Thirty-nine.'

'Ancient, then.'

'Weapons ... pass them out dissa– ... take them apart and ...'

'AH,' Blowers laughs, 'almost had him.'

'Say it,' Cookey urges, 'say the word.'

'Don't piss him off,' Nick says. 'He'll get his mates to shoot us.'

Maddox bursts out with laughter that is genuine and warm. He trails off, shaking his head. 'Okay ... but Lani stays with us until they get passed out.'

'How do you know how many we had?' I ask.

'Dave always has two,' Clarence says.

'And you do,' I look at Clarence.

'Ssshhh,' the big man replies with a mock wink.

'I had two,' Blowers says.

'Did you?' Cookey says. 'Fucking hell, Blowers. I only had one.'

'I had three,' Nick says.

'We need mops, buckets, and a hose,' Paula says. 'I am not going back into that room until it's been cleaned.'

'And coffee,' I add. 'We need coffee and some food.'

'And cigarettes,' Nick says.

'And a ladder ... What?' Cookey asks innocently. 'Might have worked.'

'You'll get everything you need,' Maddox says. 'I want you to know I am doing this for the safety of everyone, and this is my decision to do it this way.'

'Fair enough,' I turn away. 'Everyone back in the room with the stinky dog shit ... Um ... just one thing, Maddox,' I turn back as my team stop, knowing exactly what I'm going to say, 'if Lani is hurt or injured in any way, I will–'

'You'll get what you need,' Maddox repeats and suddenly the fury is in my eyes, and I know he feels it. He doesn't show it, but the look in my eyes silences the fort, and I sweep that gaze across every child holding a weapon pointing at me.

'Boss,' Clarence whispers.

'On you,' I cast a final look at Maddox as I turn away.

'On me,' he says as we file back into the room.

CHAPTER THIRTY-THREE

'Close the door,' I hold my hand up to silence everyone as we file back into the main room of the old armoury.

'Good god, it stinks to high heaven,' Paula screws her face up at the piles of dog shit rapidly drying out on the ground.

'We got anything to clean this mess up?' I ask while scanning round. 'Find a plastic bag and some toilet roll.'

'That's just going to smear it everywhere,' Paula says. 'We need mops and buckets of soapy water.'

'They won't give it to us,' I walk over to the table and grab one of the unused yellow bin liners that Lilly brought in earlier.

'Toilet roll,' Blowers holds one up and drops down to start cleaning the closest pile of dog mess.

'Maddox is switched on,' I drop down next to the mess and take the toilet roll from Blowers and start unwinding a long section. 'They came in to get Mo Mo and Jagger out, so they saw the mess in here. He'll use it as a bargaining tool to get the weapons.'

'Are we handing them over?' Nick asks.

'Not a chance,' Clarence shakes his head.

'Jesus,' I twist my head away while grabbing handfuls of liquid shit through the thin toilet roll, 'how many rolls have we got?'

'One more after that,' Blowers replies.

'Rags? Anything else we can use?'

'Fuckers!' Cookey exclaims. 'They've taken our clean clothes ... They were piled up in the corner.'

'Someone do an inventory of what we do have,' I mutter the words out while getting most of the first pile splodged into the yellow bin liner. We work from pile to pile, smearing the shit over the rough concrete floor but getting dollops at a time into the bag.

'Right,' I stand up and look round at the smeared patches, 'what have we got?'

'Case of water,' Paula replies. 'Clothes and boots have been taken. We've got no food, no toilet roll left ...'

'No cigarettes,' Nick continues. 'We've all got our assault rifles and the magazines that were in them. Pistols but no hand weapons ... They were left in the main room.'

'Cunts,' Blowers seethes, 'cleaned us out while we fucking slept ...'

'We've got water, and we've got weapons,' I nod quickly. 'The rest will have to be bargained for.'

'He's a cunt,' Blowers says again. 'I can't believe they've done this.'

'They think we're infected,' Roy states. 'You can't really blame them for taking precautions.'

'Roy,' Paula says gently, 'this might not be the time to take their side.' She looks round at the thunderous looks being sent towards Roy.

'He's right,' I say quickly. 'Maddox has thought this through. If he had come to us and said, we still would have gone out to find Marcy.'

'Why didn't they let us leave then?' Cookey asks. 'We'd have been out there and away from everyone.'

'Because, mate,' I say slowly, 'if we turned out there, we'd still pose a risk to the Fort. We know the layout, how to get inside ... and he's right, the skills we've picked up make us too dangerous to be trusted anywhere but in sight and under armed guard.'

'You're taking this very well,' Clarence says to me while looking ridiculous in his underpants.

I snort with dry laughter. 'I had my hissy fit earlier. That's enough for me for a while. Right,' I say decidedly, 'we need options, but before we have options, we need information. I want every inch of this place examined for a possible exit point or something we can use to our advantage. Look at the walls, the floor, and the ceilings. Look for anything broken or eroding. Blowers and Cookey, you two first in that room,' I point to the room behind them, 'then Nick and Clarence will check the same room, followed by Paula and Roy, and then me and Dave. We'll all check every room so there is no doubt of anything being missed. Go.' I nod at them to start.

'I see your point,' Paula says, 'but why don't we divide the rooms up, and all make a start and then cross check each as we–'

I hold my hands out. 'You sort it out then, but I want every room checked by each pair. Keep it simple and check properly ... You two,' I point at Blowers and Cookey, 'make a start now and no fucking about.'

'On it,' Blowers says as they head off into the first room.

'I'm going outside. Everyone else, stay here.' I head to

the door, feeling utterly stupid in just my underwear. Once outside, I close the door behind me and watch as the crews suddenly notice me and start lifting weapons up to aim in my direction. 'Lads,' I tut and shake my head, 'who is meant to be watching?'

The teenagers glance guiltily at each other, but I notice most of them are aimed towards the middle.

'You?' I point to an older-looking girl. 'You're the crew chief, right? You should be watching us and not chatting. If we'd have burst out, we'd have been on you by the time you got those guns up.'

'Sorry,' she huffs and looks quickly away.

'Sorry is not good enough,' I say firmly. 'If Maddox tells you to keep watch, then you keep watch, and the rest of you can stop gawping too,' I look at the rest and the confused but slightly guilty expressions they offer back.

'You heard, Mr Howie,' Maddox's voice booms out as he walks through the ranks towards me. 'I said I wanted a close watch, and that means you keep watch ...'

'I'm coming over,' I call out and start strolling as Maddox walks free from the first rank to meet me halfway.

'What's up?' he asks, stopping a few feet away.

I peer round him at the crews and lower my voice so just he can hear. 'Don't be a dick, Maddox. We need a mop and bucket. It fucking stinks in there.'

'Weapons.'

'Be decent, mate,' I say quietly but with an imploring tone. 'Fuck me, Maddox. We've been non-stop for sixteen fucking days now. Snatched sleeps, shit food, and constant fighting. Downtime will do us good, but leaving us in underwear, without food, smokes, or coffee will drive them nuts ...'

'Weapons.'

'Look around you. Look at what we gained and what we took. We got this, Maddox, and we took you in ...'

'It's simple. Weapons.'

'I get it, mate,' I keep my tone level despite the rising anger within me, 'keep the crews watching us. Keep us under observations, and we'll do whatever tests you want with the doctors, but for fuck's sake, don't treat us like this ... mate, be decent.'

'Pass the weapons out disassembled, and you will be provided with everything you need.'

'Ah, you see,' I screw my face up and shake my head, 'it's when you talk to me like, that it starts niggling. Do you understand? Don't talk at me, Maddox. Don't tell me what we'll be provided with. You got the power now, mate. But what if the docs do tests and find out none of us are infected? What then? You wanna go back to be best mates after treating us like this?'

He holds still and shows no visible reaction to his thoughts.

'Whatever you think we are,' I rush on hoping he's taking it in, 'just remember what we've done. We got the doctors. We got the ammunition. We got the food you are eating and the weapons you're pointing at us. Send Lilly over with a mop and bucket.'

'Howie,' he says as I go to turn away, 'we're gonna be needing those weapons. You're too dangerous to be left with them.'

'And you don't get to dominate this entire situation,' I reply. 'You don't treat us like twats and expect we'll do exactly as you say. Behaviour breeds behaviour, mate. Yeah, you're switched on, and you run this place brilliantly, and yeah, I can see why you're doing what you're doing ... but you're still young, and despite the confidence you portray, you don't know everything. Your idea is excellent, the execution of the idea is poor as shit. Now get a fucking grip and do things properly!'

Now I walk off and head back in to find the main room empty and everyone off in the side rooms, examining them inch by inch.

'Anything?' Paula steps out, leaving Roy running his fingertips over the wall behind her.

'I tried reasoning with him.'

'And?'

'He's young,' I sigh and rest my backside against the edge of the table. 'He's fucking good at what he does, but ... you know, I think he realises he's done this wrong but doesn't know how to fix it or be seen as weak by relenting or changing his mind.'

'You asked for clothes?'

'And coffee, food, and cigarettes. He just kept saying he wants the weapons.'

'Can we give them over?'

'Bad idea,' Clarence says from the doorway of his room. 'We've got something to bargain with, and he won't come in while we're still armed.'

'Makes sense,' she says. 'I don't think there will be a way out of here.'

'Probably not. It was the armoury,' I say glumly and fold my arms.

'We can always think of a distraction to get one out when it's dark,' Clarence suggests.

'Yeah,' I nod and glance up sharply at a soft knock at the main door. 'Who is it?'

'Lilly,' a female voice says, muffled by the thick door. 'Maddox sent me down with a mop and–'

'Hi,' I pull the door open and smile as Lilly gives me an

embarrassed look while holding two mop buckets each with a mop wedged into the soapy water. 'Thank fuck for that. Are you allowed in?'

'I think so,' she shrugs.

'Hang on, don't make things worse,' I step round her and see Maddox stood amongst the ranks of his armed youths. 'Can she come in?'

He nods but doesn't reply.

'Lilly!' Nick comes rushing to the door and takes the buckets from her hands. 'You okay?'

'Fine,' she says and steps into the room with a grimace. 'Nice pants, by the way.'

'Sorry,' he smiles sheepishly.

'Nice pants, Nicholas,' Cookey says as he grabs one of the buckets. 'Hi, Lilly.'

'Oh my,' Lilly blushes furiously as the room fills with the team all dressed in various forms of underwear.

'You get used to it,' Paula tuts. 'They're nice lads really.'

'No, we're not,' Blowers laughs. 'We're contagious animals that need locking up.'

'Is Lilly safe?' Cookey asks with a mock sideways glance at her. 'We might eat her!'

'Gobble her all up,' Blowers says, then notices the look on Nick's face. 'Or, we won't do that at all,' he adds quickly. 'Will we, Cookey?'

'Eh, oh ... oh no ... not at all ...'

'Alex, Simon. Clean, please.'

'Yes, Dave.'

'Sorry, Dave.'

'I tried talking Maddox out of it,' Lilly says quickly, 'but I didn't know until after they'd told Lani ...'

'Not your fault,' I reply. 'Have you seen Lani?'

'No,' she shakes her head. 'I can try after this. Maddox

hasn't lost it or anything ... He seems really calm and ... like normal?'

'Yeah, I know,' I say. 'I spoke to him.'

'What about Lenski?' Paula asks.

'She agrees with Maddox,' Lilly replies with another apologetic frown. 'Sorry.'

'Lilly, you don't have to apologise.'

'Thanks, Mr Howie ... Er, I got these ... for Nick,' she pulls a packet of cigarettes from her pocket. 'Not just for Nick, er ... for everyone.'

'Shit,' Nick takes the packet and blinks, 'bollocks. I mean ... er ... cheers.'

'Awkward!'

'Alex.'

'Sorry, Dave.'

'Not that I agree with smoking, but I heard you ask for them outside.'

'Do not light up in here until that stench has gone,' Paula says firmly.

'And Maddox said I could bring some coffee over next.'

'Did he?' I smile at the thought that maybe our chat had some effect after all, which also means he isn't so stubborn as being unable to back down.

'Interesting,' Paula shoots a quick nod at me, 'might be a way out then.'

'Gently,' I reply.

'Not that it's my place to ask, but what will happen now?' Lilly asks. 'Not that Maddox asked me to ask ...' she adds quickly, 'I mean I'm not a spy or anything ... I was just asking!'

'Lilly, it's okay,' Paula smiles warmly at her. 'We'll work it out somehow.'

'I'll get the coffee and come straight back? Is that okay?' She looks to me first, then Paula.

'Sure,' I say, 'that would be lovely ... Our door is always open.'

'Okay, I'll, er ... I'll be right back, then,' she smiles awkwardly at Nick and blushes again before heading out.

'Nick, close the door,' I say quickly and wait while he crosses the room and pushes it shut. 'Listen up, keep doing what we're doing. No aggression, no anger, no nothing like that. Whatever we do now will be fed back to Maddox.'

'She said she's not a spy,' Nick says.

'And I believe her, but she's also very intelligent and will read our dynamics like an open book. She already said she tried stopping him, and right now, she's about the only friend we've got.'

'We should get her to pass a message to Lani,' Paula says quietly.

'That's not fair. Don't involve her,' Nick says.

'We've got to do what we can,' Paula explains. 'Just a message.'

'Like what?' Nick asks. 'What can Lani do?'

'Create a distraction,' Dave says.

'Then what?' I ask him. 'We get out of the armoury, but then what? We've still got the whole of the fort to cross.'

'Not unless we go out the back,' Clarence says.

'Up and over the wall?' Roy suggests. 'I could get up the side of the fort here and onto the top ... maybe pull a rope up behind me the rest of you can use.'

'We need to be clear on what we're escaping from,' I say to everyone. 'There is always the option of simply handing our weapons over and staying here. Shit, we've earned the downtime and ...'

'Sorry to interrupt,' Paula says with a glance at the door, 'but no chance. I don't know about everyone else, but I'm not staying here as a prisoner under armed guard. Not after what we've done for them ... no.'

'I'm with Paula,' Clarence says. 'I'm not risking being a summary execution at the hands of a nineteen-year-old tyrant who wants to control this place for himself.'

'I don't think it's like that,' I say with a shake of my head.

'What if that old man turns?' Clarence says. 'They'll be gunning us down within seconds. Throwing bloody grenades through the door. Christ, it's hardly a scientific study, is it? Taking Lani's blood and stuffing it in some other poor sod. We could have done that days ago.'

'Fair one. Right, escape it is then, and right now the "up and over" plan sounds the best. We get Lani to create a distraction; then, we get Roy out and up the wall. Then we try and get as many out as possible ... Those that get free sort something out to get the rest of us.'

'Ssshhh,' Nick rushes to the door.

'Coffee,' Lilly announces brightly. She comes in, carrying a big tray full of steaming mugs. A smaller cup is filled with sugar, and she's even put packets of biscuits and milk portions on there for us.

'Lovely,' Clarence claps his hands together and starts rubbing them as he heads for the central table. 'Everyone okay out there?'

'Tense,' she says quietly. 'What do you want me to do?'

'Do?' I ask while grabbing a mug of coffee.

'To help,' she says quietly. 'What can I do?'

'What do you mean? We've agreed to stay here and do the tests.'

'Hmmm,' she looks at me, then straight at Nick who tries staring back but blushes and quickly looks away, 'no, no I don't think so.'

'Lilly, look, we're grateful for the coffee, but we'd never ask you to do anything that ...'

'Nick saved my life,' she fixes me with a level look, 'and he went to rescue my brother. Then you rescued Nick, and all of you got my brother out. I like Maddox and can see why he's doing this, but my loyalties are with you. What can I do?'

'We need to get a message to Lani,' Nick steps closer to Lilly. 'If that old man turns, they'll probably try and kill us. So we can't stay here.'

'I understand,' she nods and stares only at Nick. 'What shall I tell her?'

'We need a distraction,' Nick explains, 'something big enough to draw attention from us so we can get over the wall.'

'You can't,' she says. 'The wall is too smooth here. I looked when I was coming in. No footholds, no handholds ...'

'I can boost Dave up,' Clarence steps closer to the conversation.

'Dave?' I look at him.

'Yes, Mr Howie.'

'Right,' I take a breath, 'is that 'yes, Mr Howie, I can do it' or 'yes, Mr Howie, what do you want'?'

'Yes,' he nods and stares at me, 'I can do it.'

'Good. Distraction. Get Dave up, and we try and get out. The distraction will need to be big. Something that goes bang ...'

'Lani won't be free to get out,' Nick looks at me. 'They'll either have her sedated or restrained.'

'I can do the distraction,' Lilly says.

'No,' Nick says firmly.

'Nick, I'm not feeble,' she says gently. 'You saved me and my brother. Let me help.'

'A distraction has to be something visual and something audible,' Dave says, 'and it must be enough to overcome the training of the soldiers to stay watchful on their posts.'

'Did they bring the ammunition in yet?' Blowers asks Lilly.

She nods before replying, 'They've stored them at the back.'

'The back? Which rooms?'

'Er, they've got double doors.'

'The workshops,' I nod. 'Where they made the foot traps before Darren got here?'

'Can you get in there?' Blowers asks. 'Get a grenade or something?'

'Fuck's sake, Blowers,' Nick says with a hard glare, 'that's asking a bit much.'

'Sorry, mate,' Blowers says instantly, 'forget it.'

'They've got a couple of the guards up there,' Lilly replies. 'If I can get in ... what am I looking for?'

'Grenades,' Blowers ignores the look from Nick. 'You know what they look like?'

'Are they the same as on television?'

'Exactly the same,' Blowers nods. 'Get a few and head into the gap between the walls and find all the old vehicles that got mangled in the storm ... chuck the grenades in that lot.'

'Blowers,' Clarence snaps, 'that's a bloody good idea ... especially if they've still got fuel left in them.'

'Are you right-handed?' Blowers asks. 'Good, hold the grenade in your right hand with your fingers holding the little metal bar in place. There's a metal loop at the top. You twist and pull firmly. The grenade will not be armed until you release the metal bar, which is only done when you throw it. You with me?'

'Go on,' Lilly nods and watches his hands as he pretends to hold a grenade and loop the forefinger of his left hand through the imaginary hoop, twist, and pull it clear.

'Big throw,' he says, 'but not like as hard as you can ... That's when mistakes happen, and you drop it or fumble ... Throw it overhand like this.' He mocks a throw with a smooth overhead motion, 'It will detonate after about three or four seconds.'

'Three or four seconds, got it.'

'They won't see it,' Dave says. 'It has to be both visual and audible.'

'What do you suggest?' I ask him.

'Throw the grenades in the fort.'

'Dave, are you being serious?'

'Yes, Mr Howie. A distraction has to be both visual and–'

'Audible, yeah, got it. Lilly, don't throw the grenades in the fort.'

'But Dave is right, Mr Howie,' she says with a purposeful look at me. 'If I heard a big bang outside the walls, I would just hide. I wouldn't try and see it.'

'Back gate,' Cookey offers. 'If we get that open, we stand a better chance of getting out.'

'The risk of injury is too great,' I say while thinking.

'What's the, er ...' Lilly stops to think for a second. 'I mean, when the grenade goes off ... How far can it cause damage?'

'The blast radius?' I ask, and we all look at Dave.

'I was in the army too,' Clarence points out.

'How far is it, then?' I ask him.

'I don't know,' he shrugs. 'Dave?'

'Five metres to cause fatality, fifteen metres to cause casualties, but if the fragments are unhindered, they will go much further.'

'What would happen if I threw one into the ammunition store?' Lilly asks to a stunned silence.

'Yeah, don't do that,' Clarence says softly.

'Good distraction,' Dave nods.

'And everyone is dead, and we can just stroll out,' Clarence beams. 'Do not throw the grenade in the ammunition room.'

'If I can get on top of the walls, I can drop them up there,' she says thoughtfully. 'There's dips and little areas of concrete ... Would that be okay?'

'Very good,' Dave says. 'Get near the front, drop them into the vehicles as Simon suggested and wherever they will be both seen and heard as a distraction works best when it is both–'

'Visual and audible. Got it,' Lilly beams at Dave, which makes us all hold our breath for a second as I'm normally the only person that would dare to cut Dave off mid-sentence. Her smile seems to win him over, and he nods almost happily, which for Dave means he doesn't try and kill her.

'When do I do it?' she asks with enthusiasm. 'Do we synchronise watches?'

'Er, I wouldn't know how to,' I admit. 'Actually, how do they do that on the movies? They do it in like two seconds. Why don't they all have to take them off and press the buttons to select the time change and ...'

'Countdown timer,' Clarence says, 'but I've never actually done it. Have you?' he asks Dave.

'Never,' Dave says.

'It gets dark about ten,' I say. 'We'll need to leave it a few hours … Let the crews get relaxed … We can make some noise in here so they think we're pissing about …'

'Lilly,' Maddox calls from just outside the door, 'everything okay?'

'Coming,' she calls back quickly.

'Everyone sod off,' I whisper urgently. 'Leave Nick and Lilly in here.'

We all depart the room as I whisper, 'Aim for two in the morning and tell Lani to get out.'

We get into the side rooms, and I peer through the crack in the door as Lilly suddenly flings herself into Nick's arms.

'Oh,' Maddox's voice is closer, he must be at the door.

She plants her lips to his, and he freezes for a second before visibly softening into the kiss, and I can't help the warm smile on my face as I look away.

'I'd better go,' she says to Nick. 'Say thanks to the others for giving us some space.'

'Will do,' he beams and rocks back on his feet.

'Nick, you alright,' Maddox says.

'Eh?' Nick turns slowly to the door. 'Er … eh?'

The door closes, and we give it a few seconds before heading back into the main room, and I watch as Paula rushes to Nick with a bed blanket which she quickly wraps round his waist. 'Go and sit down for a minute,' she urges gently.

'Eh?' he asks again.

'Nick, go and sit down in a quiet room for a minute,' she leads him by the elbow towards one of the rooms as Cookey and Blowers start pissing themselves with laughter.

'Why?' Nick asks slowly.

'Cos you got a stiffy in your underpants, mate,' Cookey lets rip with an evil cackle.

'Leave him alone,' Paula says with a stare of daggers at the two lads.

'She kissed me,' Nick says dreamily.

'We saw,' Paula replies softly.

'I think everyone saw,' Cookey laughs.

CHAPTER THIRTY-FOUR

She looks round the table in the old police offices and takes in the faces of Maddox, Lenski, Darius, and three of the four doctors, noticing that once again Doctor Carlton has chosen not to take part in the group discussion.

'How were they?' Andrew asks, leaning forward in his seat, and the worry lines on his face appear that little bit deeper.

'Completely normal,' Lilly replies. 'The lads were messing about. Dave was as quiet as normal ... Mr Howie and the rest,' she shrugs, 'just like before.'

'Did they say anything?' Andrew leans forward again.

'They said lots of things,' Lilly smiles with a snap decision to dumb down her intelligence. 'They wanted to know if I'd seen Lani, if she was okay ... if everyone else was okay ... if the fort was okay, if Lenski was okay,' a gentle tilt of the head side to side as she reels the list off. 'Mo Mo and Jagger ... if they were okay ... Like I said, they were the same as before. Except they were all in underpants.'

'Lilly,' Maddox watches her with just the faintest hint

of amusement behind his eyes, 'they asked you to pass a message to Lani.'

'Is that a question or a fact?' she asks flatly, completely forgetting to dumb the intelligence down.

'Did they ask you to pass a message to Lani?'

'They did,' she says, fighting an urge to stare at him, knowing that would appear confrontational.

'What was it?' he asks softly as the atmosphere in the room charges.

'They want me to tell her not to worry, that they are all okay and everything will be alright and to do as you say.'

She senses the shift and knows she delivered the line with perfect execution. Everyone was ready to hear a plot or a plan to escape or fight back, but the words strike a chord, and she notices a fleeting look of guilt on Andrew Stone's face as he sinks back into his chair.

'Is that it?' Maddox asks.

'Am I a spy?' she asks. 'Is this why you told me to go in there? Am I an agent working for you? I watched my father get beaten to death and my friend raped *while* she got beaten to death, and I watched my brother get kidnapped. Nick saved my life and risked himself to find my brother. Howie and the rest then risked their own lives getting Nick *and* my brother *and* all of the children out there ...'

'You are not a spy,' Maddox says.

She pushes on, mindful of the looks being cast between the doctors and the uncomfortable shift in position from Lenski, 'Are you a tyrant?'

'What is this word?' Lenski asks.

'A tyrant is someone who rules from fear and force,' Lilly looks round the room, 'and you're scaring me with this interrogation.'

'You are not being interrogated,' Maddox says simply,

'but we need to know what they are planning or doing. We have the welfare of ...'

'I am being interrogated,' Lilly looks round and holds Lisa Franklin's gaze for a long second. 'I was told to come in here. I was told to deliver the cleaning supplies and coffee to them. What choice do I have? I rely on this fort for the safety of my brother. I have to do as you bid.'

'It's really not like that,' Maddox says.

'Can I go then? Leave the fort?'

'Pardon?' Andrew asks.

'This is no longer a safe place for my brother. You have teenagers armed with machine guns and a girl tied up in a hospital bed after being tasered. This is the first step towards a tyrannical rule, and I do not want to stay here. If those *children* out there start firing, then anyone could get caught with a stray bullet. I want to leave.'

'Lilly,' Maddox sighs with the first show of stress, 'you are perfectly safe, and everything is under control.'

'Control is exactly what it is,' she says. 'Control of the people who have given us this place to live ... and those people kept saying it was a free place where people could come and go as they saw fit. I believe that you have tasered a person who opposed your view and then injected her with sedatives against her will. Not just you,' she looks at Maddox, 'but the ordinary and decent people in this room have chosen a course of conduct that by any standards would be abhorrent. I am a fifteen-year-old girl with the care of a young child, and right now, I would rather take my chances out there than risk being in here, being controlled by this round table of despots.'

A stunned silence by the eloquent words given by an earnest, young lady. Her chair scrapes the ground as she stands up. 'You've told the people that one of Mr Howie's team might be infected.'

Maddox looks up sharply, realising the error of judgement he made.

'That is not true. You have purposefully left out important facts to gain support for your actions. Is that not the work of a tyrant? I'll be leaving first thing in the morning, and *I will* be telling the other survivors the truth of what is happening.'

'Stop,' Maddox gets to his feet in a fluid motion.

'Maddox,' Andrew says quickly, alarmed at the expression on the young man's face.

'Will you taser me too?' Lilly asks as she locks eyes across the table, 'and then tell everyone I might be infected?'

She steps into the open air and walks steadily across the fort without thought to her direction or purpose but just to walk and ease the trouble within her soul. A gentle hum of noise from the survivors easing down into quietness as the day draws to an end.

Two crews remain watching the door of the old armoury. Weapons held ready, eyes alert, and she notices the lack of banter between them. They look mean now, young and feral, but now guided and armed and under the supervision of a crew chief who stands as easy and relaxed as Maddox would. The sight sends a chill running through, and she looks to see the other crews are all nearby. Sitting and talking quietly with more weapons within reach.

A sudden vision of the future, dark and bleak, as the power is held by those who take up the guns. The older survivors cling to the values they held dear of a society fallen and gone. They see the youths as the rightful authority now.

They even look different, something has changed. She

notices the clothing they wear is dark, like a uniform of sorts. Black tops, vests, and t-shirts. Like a paramilitary force. Something done amongst them as they seek to look the same and be a part of the gang.

The words she spoke in the meeting spilled from her mouth as fast as they entered her head, but the truth in them sinks low within her gut. This is the way of things now. Tyranny doesn't start with a maniac doing bad things. It starts with someone doing an action they believe in and having the ability to convince others of their vision.

Maddox is charming. He has a presence that makes you want to listen to him, to watch the way he speaks, and the so subtle inflections of his tone and manner. He is inspiring and very capable and all the more dangerous because of it.

What he is doing now he is doing for the right reasons. But the road to hell is paved with good intentions. He thinks clearly and maps his own actions and the reactions it will garner. A game of chess in his mind where all the pieces are laid out.

That he feels the sense of wrongness is palpable. He is not an evil man, Lilly knows this. She senses the kindness within him and the desire to do right. But the life he comes from is not the same as hers. The values he holds dear are not the same, and these youths worship the words that fall from his mouth the way the team worship Howie.

A tight ball of fear knots in her stomach, and suddenly she sees things very differently to just a few hours ago.

The survivors clustering at the back in a self-imposed suppression of views, opinions, and thoughts simply for the fear of being cast out or killed.

The journey Lilly took to get here is scarred in her memory, and the mere thought brings the emotions flooding back, but what she endured has been endured by every man, woman, and child here.

That's not our way.

Those were the words Nick kept saying. Like a code of ethics born between them. A way of doing the right things *for* the right reasons. Not the wrong thing for the right reasons. Howie's way is clear. The right thing at the right time. You do good because that is expected. You help those that cannot help themselves. You take the fight to the bad guys and never give in. You never leave a man or woman behind. You always fight for them. You do the right thing for the right reasons.

You carve a path through the misery and abject terror, and you bring a ray of sunshine and hope. You show others that ordinary people can do extraordinary things. They sacrificed everything to gain this place and never gave up, and she knows, with an instinct stronger than anything she has ever felt, that every member of Mr Howie's team would have run into death in that house to save Nick and the children.

That's our way.

Choose a side. Pick a team. Gain that commitment and strive to be the best you can.

That's our way.

She threads through the fort with a knowledge that the decision she has just made will end her life, but it will free those that gave her that life back, and those people will ensure everyone else remains free.

'Billy,' she spots her brother near the vehicle ramp.

'Lilly!' On his feet, and he rushes forward to fling his arms around her neck.

'What are you doing?' she asks gently as the tears start to prick the back of her eyes.

'We're gonna have a story.'

'Going to have a story, not gonna,' she rebukes mildly.

'Going to, then,' he smiles a toothy grin. 'Will you stay for the story?'

'I'd love to,' she pulls him back in for another cuddle, 'but I've got work to do.'

'Please,' he says, muffled, with his head pressed tight against her shoulder.

'You know I love you, Billy.'

'Love you too,' he stays pressed against her, feeling the maternal love given by his big sister.

'I always will,' she whispers into his ear. 'I will always love you.'

'I know.'

'Be good. Grow strong and be good, always be good.'

'I will Lilly.'

'I have to go now.'

'Will you come back for the story?'

'I'll try,' she bites the sob down, gritting her teeth and forcing a smile. She kisses his head tenderly and smooths his hair down. 'I will try.'

'Okay.'

'Everyone ready?' a woman walks past, holding a big picture book.

'Enjoy your story,' Lilly lets him go as his attention switches instantly to the gathering group of children.

She stands with a heart fracturing into a thousand pieces as she watches the last surviving member of her family take his seat in the half circle of children, and for a second, she falters, hesitant, unwilling to move away. She could sit down and listen. Be here with the children and listen to the story, then tuck Billy in, and help with the others.

She turns to see the dark figures of the youths across the open ground of the fort, the long barrels of the weapons they hold, and the vision floods back as her top lip threatens to curl up with the coldness of the decision made.

Lilly heads away from the children and scoops to pick up a clipboard left at the bottom of the ramp. She plucks the pen free from the metal clasp, and while walking, she taps the end against the hard edge of the board. Her face is set, determined, and she feels calm now, safe in the knowledge that Nick will always be there for her brother, and that's what Billy needs. He needs Nick and people like him. He needs Mr Howie to be here and watching. Clarence and Paula. All of these people need them.

'Lilly,' the youth nods in greeting as she walks steadily up to the three sentries. She stops and rolls her eyes, blows air out through her cheeks as she makes a senseless note on the clipboard.

'I'm so tired,' she grins and shakes her head. 'Can't wait to just sit down.'

'Yeah right,' the youth grins, a pale boy with bags under his eyes and wearing a black t-shirt at least four size too big for him, and it accentuates his thin frame, which, in turn, makes the shotgun look that much bigger.

'Right, one last duty, and that's me,' she sighs again. 'Maddox wants me to take a box of grenades down to the crew watching the armoury, but,' she casts a quick look round and steps closer to the three kids, 'I don't actually know what a grenade is, and I didn't want to ask and look stupid ... You won't tell Maddox will you?'

'Nah, course not,' the boy giggles. 'They gonna use 'em?'

'I have no idea,' Lilly states, 'and I do not care ... I want to take the box over, hand them over, smile sweetly; then, I am off duty and will sleep forever.'

'Here'ya,' a boy steps out holding a green wooden crate by two rope handles at the ends.'

'Is that it?' she asks hopefully.

'Yeah,' the lad nods.

'What do they look like? Can I see one?'

'They're fuckin' awesome,' he puts the crate down and lifts the already unlocked lid to reveal rows of small, round metal objects each with the metal hoop as described by Blowers.

'Oh wow,' she says, 'I think I've seen them on that game ... er ... Call of Duty, is it?'

'COD? Yeah,' the lads stare in wonder at the beautiful girl. 'You play, do ya?'

'Me?' Lilly laughs. 'No, but it looks good. Right, I'd better get this over to Maddox.'

'It's heavy,' one of the lads says quickly. 'Want me to carry it?'

'I'd love that,' Lilly beams, 'and thank you for being a gentleman, but Maddox said you had to remain here.'

'Ah, yeah, course ...' the lad nods quickly with a blush spreading up his pale cheeks.

'Well, I'll see you later,' she rests the clipboard on the closed lid and grasps the rope handles before hefting the box up.

'See ya, Lilly.'

So easy. Too easy, and that ease cements her belief that these are the wrong people to be in control here. A pretty smile, and she walks away with enough bombs to kill everyone in here. No orders, no check on the radio, nothing.

She sticks to the inner wall and walks steadily along with an expression of tiredness forced on her face. Carrying a heavy box and running errands like she's done all day. Following the curvature of the wall, she takes a sharp turn and walks towards the rear of the crews on guard watching the armoury.

A distraction has to be both visual and audible.

One of the youths turns quickly as she approaches. She smiles and nods. He smiles, nods back, and turns away.

Five metres is the killing zone. Fifteen to cause casualties. She stops five metres away from the back of the crews and places the heavy box on the ground. Twilight now, and the clear light of the day is dwindling. She flips the lid and pulls one of the small, round objects out and takes a breath.

In her right hand, and she curls her fingers tight over the metal bar. Her left forefinger fits into the hoop easily. She twists, pulls it free, and pauses as she casts a quick look back to the vehicle ramp and the children hidden from view in the shadows of the wall. Torches are lit, lamps and lanterns. Orange, glowing lights that bathe the fort in a beautiful, soft glow.

A solitary tear falls to roll down her cheek, and the sadness she feels mingles with the hope for the future and the complete belief that these people cannot be in charge for the future is as bleak and dark as the night that comes across them now.

CHAPTER THIRTY-FIVE

'Holy fuck,' Cookey says as we gather round to peer down into the black hole.

'How did you find it?' I ask.

'Brilliant engineers back then,' Roy says. 'It's almost seamless, and I doubt it's been opened in years.'

'Echo?' Nick asks.

Roy nods. 'I was tapping and thought it sounded different. It's darker in here, so finding the edge was done by fingertips. It's a trapdoor, though,' he says as we look down into the black abyss below the levered-up hatch.

'Have we got a torch? I ask around. 'Candle? Anything? A mobile phone?'

'Nothing,' Cookey says in a low voice. 'That fucking prick has taken everything.'

'Oh,' I stare down, 'how deep is it?'

'Don't know,' Roy replies. 'Hang on,' he rushes off and comes back, holding a teaspoon. 'Ready?'

He drops it down, and we listen at the brief pause and the clatter when it hits the bottom. 'Not far,' he says. 'Six ... maybe ten feet.'

'Roy, you had night-vision goggles,' Paula says.

'Yes, I *had* night vision goggles along with lots of other things in my van, which I abandoned ... along with the peaceful life I was living too.'

'Ah, you love it,' I say while staring down the hole.

'Idea,' Roy drops down and shoves his head deep into the hole. 'The air is fresh.'

'That's nice. Did they hoover too?' Cookey asks.

'It means there is ventilation, you twat,' Nick says, 'otherwise the air would smell stale.'

'I knew that,' Cookey shakes his head and tuts. 'I didn't know that,' he adds with a shrug.

'Nick, pass me your lighter,' Roy says with his head down the hole and his hand hovering up into the air.

'My what?'

'Your lighter,' I nod at Roy's hand.

'My lighter?'

'Yes, Nick. Your lighter.'

'It's the only one we have,' he says with a look of panic. 'What if he drops it.'

'I won't drop it,' Roy's muffled voice says.

'Oh, fucking hell,' Nick huffs and reluctantly passes the lighter into Roy's outstretched fingers. 'Don't use all the fuel.'

'I think our safety is more important than you having a cigarette,' Paula says.

'Humph,' Nick says.

'Tunnel,' Roy shouts up, 'well, a door that leads off anyway ... and there's a ladder built into the side.'

'Great, just don't drop the lighter,' Blowers looks as nervous as Nick.

Roy shuffles back to sit up. 'Fresh air and what looks to

be a room or a tunnel. I'll go down first. Have we got anything we can use a torch?'

'We don't have any torches,' Paula says. 'Maddox took them. We just had this conversation.'

'No, I mean like an old-fashioned torch,' Roy says, 'on fire?'

'Oh, right,' I look about and head quickly into the main room. 'We've got a table and some chairs we can break up, but that's it, no clothes to– ... Hang on, we've got the bedding.'

We all dart about, dragging rough woollen blankets and sheets into the room. Clarence grabs a wooden chair, turns it upside down, and grabs the two front legs before yanking the whole thing apart with barely a grunt.

With a strip of blanket wrapped round the end of the chair leg held by Roy, Nick holds his lighter to the material, and we watch as the material smoulders and burns but refuses to ignite.

'We need an accelerant,' Roy says with a look at Nick.

'No.'

'Nick, we need to douse it in something flammable.'

'Oh, come on,' Nick whines, 'really?'

'What?' Cookey asks.

'The lighter,' Blowers says, 'we need the fuel from the lighter to douse the blanket so it catches alight.'

'Oh,' Cookey says, 'that's alright.'

'No, it's not alright,' Nick says. 'Then we won't be able to smoke, you dickhead.'

'Er,' Cookey says slowly, 'what about the fucking big match you're gonna be holding, dickhead ... The big match you're setting on fire?'

Nick stares at the chair leg for a second before snorting a dry chuckle, 'Fuck it.'

'Clarence, can you snap the lighter in half but hold it over the end so the–'

'Thank you, Roy,' Clarence says, 'I get it.'

With the torch on the ground, Clarence drops down and holds one end of the plastic tube in each hand while holding it a fraction above the blanket material. An audible snap, and the room fills with the pungent aroma of liquid gas.

'Light it before it soaks in,' Roy mutters.

Clarence fumbles with the end of the lighter holding the rough wheel and flint. Three times he thumbs the wheel, and we hold our breath until the spark ignites the material, and a second later, the blanket flames bright.

'We'll have to move quick. Get some more strips ready,' Roy heads towards the opening and eases his legs down onto the now visible first rung embedded into the side.

We gather at the top and wait as he reaches the bottom, pauses, and heads out of sight, into the shadows of a doorway.

'Room,' he calls out, 'really big room ... Hang on ... Yes, there's another tunnel leading off ...'

'Right, everyone, get weapons and, er ... shit, I was about to say get dressed. Fuck it, just get the weapons.'

I lower myself down the hatch, onto the ladder and scrabble down to the bottom. The ground is hard concrete underfoot, and Roy was right, the air doesn't smell that stale. A bit musty, but no hint of damp, and there must be fresh air coming from somewhere.

'Roy?'

'Through here.'

I head into what must have been the room he said was there, but pitch black greets my eyes. I hold my hand out, feeling for a trip hazards as the orange glow of the torch bobs back into sight.

'Tunnel,' he says quietly as though speaking loud down here isn't right, 'more rooms too ... This place is huge.'

'Does it go anywhere?'

'No idea, it feels flat for a bit, then a slight gradient downhill. That's when I came back.'

'What direction is it? I mean in relation to the fort?'

'Er, so the hatch is there, and the main door is ... So that means the front of the fort is over there ... So yes, yes, I think it heads towards the land.'

'Bollocks.'

'Pardon? Isn't that good news?'

'It is, but we told Lilly to wait until two in the morning before making a distraction, but if we're going to go, then we need to do it now, before the torch dies.'

'What do you want to do?' he asks me quietly. 'I doubt we'll get the torch ignited again.'

'Back to the ladder,' I head back and climb up into the room to find everyone gathered and looking even more stupid, holding pistols and assault rifles while in underwear.

'Tunnel looks like it leads towards the land, but ...' I heave myself free from the top and stand up. 'If we're gonna go, then we need to do it now, before the torch dies out.'

'What about Lilly?' Nick asks, his voice as hushed as mine now the darkness of the night is upon us.

'Roy,' Clarence leans over hole, 'will I fit?'

'Yes, tight, but you'll get through.'

'I say we go now,' Clarence says. 'We get free, get supplies, and come back for Lani.'

'How the hell are we going to get back in for Lani?' Paula asks in a rushed whisper.

'We'll have time to plan and do something,' I say, 'but it's better than waiting here.'

'What if we get trapped?' Cookey asks.

'I don't think we will,' Roy calls up. 'There's definitely a flow of air coming from somewhere ...'

'Shush,' Blowers whispers, closest to the door, and we all fall silent.

'What?' I ask.

'... Nothing. Thought I heard some shouting outside.'

'Decision made. We're going while we got the chance ... Everyone ready?'

CHAPTER THIRTY-SIX

The tear falls to drop through the air as she stands straight and takes a deep breath.

'Excuse me,' she speaks clearly into the gloom. 'I said excuse me ...'

'What's up?' someone asks her, one of the crew chiefs or a youth. A young voice, and a few heads turn to look at her.

'I am holding a grenade. The pin is pulled out. I am holding it above a box of grenades. If you run or shout, I will drop the grenade. If you shoot me, I will drop the grenade ...'

'Are you fucking nuts?' a voice asks as a torch beam is switched on. The illuminated beam sweeps over the ground and up her body until picking out the grenade held clearly in her right hand. The torch holds steady for a second before sweeping back to the open crate of grenades at her feet. Murmurs of panic sweep across the guards, shuffling feet, and the clunks of guns being knocked into each other.

'Do not run or move away,' Lilly forces power into her voice. 'You have until the count of three, and if you do not put the weapons down, I will drop this grenade, and we will all die.'

'Everyone, put the guns down,' a voice says.

'ONE,' she shouts now, a clear voice that carries easily through the fort.

'Okay, okay ...' guns start getting lowered to the ground, but some of the youths remain unresponsive.

'TWO ... I am prepared to die ... Are you?'

'Down ... put 'em down, for fuck's sake,' the crew chief barks the order, 'MADDOX ... DARIUS ... .YOU BETTER GET OUT HERE ...'

The clatter of weapons sounds clear as Lilly's eyes adjust to the gloom. The crews stay close, too afraid to run or do anything, and the torch remains focussed on the grenade in her hand.

'What's up?' Maddox walks quickly from the offices.

'Crazy fuckin' bitch has a grenade,' the crew chief yells back.

'Maddox?'

'Lilly? That you?'

'I have a grenade. The pin is pulled out, and I am holding the metal bar down. If I let go, the grenade will arm as it drops into the box of grenades by my feet ...'

'Okay,' Maddox stops a few feet away, 'I can see,' he says softly.

Lilly clears her throat and draws breath, 'EVERYONE NEEDS TO LISTEN ... PEOPLE IN THE FORT NEED TO LISTEN ...'

'Lilly, please stop this,' Maddox holds a steady hand out, 'one grenade will not set the other grenades off. The pin has to be pulled ...'

'That is not true,' she replies, 'and by all means, take

that chance if you so wish ... Please let Mr Howie know he can come out now.'

'Lilly, they might be infected ... That is not a chance we can take.'

'I will not live under tyrannical rule ...'

'Grow up,' Maddox snaps, 'you'll kill everyone in here if you drop that grenade ... Your own brother included.'

'Please tell Mr Howie they can come out ... and if you move, Maddox, I will drop this grenade, and we will all die ... and then Mr Howie can come ...'

'Lilly ... what you do? Put that thing down!'

'No,' Maddox shouts, 'do not put it down.'

'What?' Lenski asks. 'Put it down and–'

'It's a bomb,' Maddox says. 'She lets go, and it explodes.'

'Oh,' Lenski frowns with a hard glare at Lilly. 'Why you do this?'

'You know why, Lenski.'

'We help you. We give you safe place, yes? We do this. We give Billy the safe place.'

'You have boys with guns dressed in black clothes,' Lilly replies. 'You have people cowering at the back because they're too afraid to do or say anything ... You have the people that gave us this safe place locked in a room with nothing to eat or drink ...'

'Okay, we can talk about this,' Maddox says soothingly. 'Let's just keep our voices down yeah.'

'No, I will not. Please someone inform Mr Howie that they can come out now.'

'Lilly, this is too dangerous. What if they're infected?'

'Then I am also infected,' she says clearly. 'Nick has been with them the whole time, and I have kissed him, and if I am infected, then perhaps it is best to drop this grenade and–'

'No, no,' Maddox interrupts, forcing his tone to remain calm. 'We can do some tests and ...'

'What tests?' she asks. 'What tests can be done?'

'I don't know ...'

'No, Maddox. You don't know. You are four years older than me. Even the doctors don't know what tests they can do. We have no idea of anything, yet you choose to lock away the very people that have given us this freedom. Let Mr Howie know he can come out.'

'Lilly.'

'Let Mr Howie know they can come out!'

'We will, but can I just say ...'

'ONE ...'

'Okay, take it easy ...'

'TWO ... I will drop this grenade on three and kill us all.'

'HOWIE ... COME OUT HERE ... Easy now, Lilly.'

She clutches the grenade and waits. Her eyes flicking from Maddox to the youths watching and the armoury door beyond them.

'MR HOWIE,' she yells, 'COME OUT PLEASE ...'

'Darius?'

'Right here.'

'Go get Howie.'

Lilly scans the area, tracking Darius as he crosses the open ground to the armoury door, which he knocks soundly. Once. Twice. He waits and knocks again. Lilly feels her heart rate going up and her arm trembling from squeezing the grenade so tightly but not daring to loosen her grip even a little.

Darius pushes the door open and calls out. He waits and calls again.

'No one there,' he shouts across to Maddox. 'Someone get me a torch.'

One is found and taken over, and the youth flicks the beam on and into the armoury where he sweeps it over the central room, the table, and the broken chair on the ground. He takes a tentative step inside. 'Mr Howie ... it's Darius ... Lilly is holding a grenade ... Mr Howie? Clarence? I'm not armed.'

He creeps forward step by step and points the torch to all corners. Room to room he goes with his own heart hammering in his chest as the first beads of sweat roll down his forehead.

On the last room, he stops and spins round, mouth hanging open and a creeping sensation crawling up his spine. He checks again, more thoroughly this time. Checking, looking, staring.

Finally, he exits and stops dead a few feet from the door. 'They've gone,' he says simply.

Lilly twitches at the news. She checked the door every few seconds, and there was no way they could have got out in that time.

Maddox stays quiet and watchful, his mind spinning with the variables at play. That Lilly was creating a distraction, but like her, he kept a watch on the door of the armoury and knows they couldn't have got out.

'Check again, take more in with you,' Maddox orders to buy time. 'Where are they, Lilly?'

She doesn't reply but grips the grenade and thinks furiously, 'Get Lani out here, please.'

'She is sedated,' Maddox says quietly.

'Then bring her out sedated.'

'Lilly, where did Mr Howie go?'

'I am still holding this grenade, and I will still drop it.'

'They've gone,' Maddox shrugs. 'What now? Kill everyone for the hell of it?'

'They have not gone,' Lilly says. 'This is a trick.'

'Darius? Are they in there?'

'Nothing, Mads,' Darius walks free from the armoury. 'Seriously, spooky as fuck in there, I swear down ...'

'Where, Lilly?'

'You tell me, Maddox.'

'Where, Lilly?'

'Bring Lani out here, please.'

'No.'

'Bring Lani out here, or I will drop this grenade.'

'Do it,' Maddox says in a dangerously low tone, 'drop the grenade.' His intelligent mind swarms with the confidence that the power play is back with him. Too many questions but you deal with what you got right in front of you, and right now, he stares across at a frightened fifteen-year-old girl who's holding a grenade in a trembling arm.

She listens intently. Eyes closed. Breathing normally. The muscles of her stomach were sore from the Taser barbs, but the pain, like the pain elsewhere in her body, faded quickly. Did they sedate her? Probably. She woke up, so that must mean they injected her with something. Whatever it was wore off quickly, and she had the sense to remain conscious but inert. Listening to the sounds around her and daring only to peek through her eyelids when the voices of the doctors had receded.

Something going on outside. Raised voices, a girl shouting. Lilly? It must be something to do with Howie.

She wants to look but fights the urge and remains still, knowing she'll only have one chance if she makes a move.

'What's going on?' a male voice demands, deep and refined, the voice of Heathcliff Stone.

'Lilly's got a grenade,' young voice pants from the exertion of running. 'She's pulled the pin and is saying she wants Howie to be let out, but he's gone, and now she's saying she wants Lani and–'

'Slow down,' Heathcliff snaps impatiently. 'Howie has gone? Gone where?'

'Dunno, Darius was checking his rooms, and he's gone, you get me?'

'Just him or everyone?'

'Like everyone, all of 'em ... gone, innit? Maddox is telling Lilly to drop the grenade.'

'Can't they just put the pin back in?'

'No, like ... he's telling her to drop it and let it explode. Calling her out, you get me?'

'Stop saying that. Good god, he'll blow us all to smithereens.'

'She's got the whole box of grenades.'

'Jesus fucking Christ!' Heathcliff roars. 'What a complete shower of shit. I knew we should never have listened to that ...'

Lani dares a peek, a fluttering of eyelids and enough of a glance to see Heathcliff and Lisa Franklin stood talking to a young boy.

'Maddox told her Lani is dosed up and, like, she can't come out.'

Lani knows they'll be turning to look, and she breathes easily, normally, not twitching, not moving. The air comes in, and the air goes out.

'She'll be out for hours on that bloody dose,' Heathcliff

groans, 'and I'm not going out there if some little shit is running about with grenades.'

She darts another look and spots them once again focussed on the boy, and in that split second, the decision is made.

She groans and fidgets, then lies still, but makes her breathing louder than it was. She groans again and twitches her legs, then her arms.

'What the ...?'

'Is she fitting?' Lisa crosses the floor quickly, her voice getting closer. 'Lani? Lani, can you hear me?'

Fingers press into Lani's wrist with well-practised movements, and Lani senses from the pressure applied that it's Lisa Franklin checking her pulse.

A fluid motion and an explosion of energy. Eyes snap open as she twists her arm and snaps a rigid grip on Lisa's wrist, yanking her forward as she drives the heel of her palm hard into the centre of her face. The nose breaks, blood spurts thick and fast as the doctor goes to yell, but Lani is already moving up and out of the bed. A hard fist smashes into the back of the doctor's skull, and she twists round to see Heathcliff standing shocked to the core with his mouth hanging open.

The infected kill if you don't keep motion. They lunge and snap; they rake and bite. They press ever forwards with a desire to tear you apart, and so Lani doesn't stay still. As Lisa bends double on the still warm bed, so Lani spins and closes the gap between her and the big, bearded doctor. Judged to perfection, and her knee lifts to drive deep into the older man's groin. An explosion of air from his lungs as the pain hits, and she batters his face with a barrage of blows as he drops down. As he goes down, she grabs the thick hair on his scalp and pulls him at the same time as ramming the hard point of her knee into his temple.

Two seconds, maybe three, and both doctors are down. She spins and spots the youth turning to run and grabs the metal bed pan from the side table next to her. It gets launched hard, spinning and glinting through the air and into the back of his head with a dull thunk.

He goes down, sprawled on the ground, and squeals like the child he is, high-pitched and frightened. She charges down the aisle, slamming the heel of her foot into the side of his head. He goes quiet, and she moves fast towards the entrance. No remorse, no time to stop and worry.

Out the door, and she meets the two guards ploughing towards her in response to the clatter of the bed pan and the scream of the boy. Two youths, bigger than the one she just knocked out, hard faced and grim with determination. Both of them carrying assault rifles, but they move awkwardly and unused to the weight and bulk of the weapons.

She seizes the advantage and lunges into the gap between them. They yell and turn but slam into each other. She grabs one barrel and slams a fist into the nose of the other boy. He reels back with a nose as cleanly broken as Lisa Franklin's. Her arm jerks back, and the elbow drives hard into the eye socket of the one she holds in place by the barrel of the weapon. She hits him once, twice and feels the bone of his eye socket fracture from her hard elbow.

She goes low and grabs his right ankle, wrenching him up as she grabs a handful of his privates to give them a vicious twist. He crumples on the spot, and she catches the assault rifle before it hits the ground.

She spins it right way up, pausing only to check the magazine, slam it back home, and rack the bolt back as the first youth writhes on the ground with his hands clutching at his face.

The single shot rings clear through the fort, and the boy writhes no more as his brain is scattered over the hard ground of the fort. On autopilot, and she brings the assault rifle up and into her shoulder, aimed, locked, loaded, and ready.

She strides towards the middle and the silhouetted figure of Lilly standing with her arm held out and Maddox stood but feet from her.

Motion to the right, she twitches, aims, locks and fires. A body goes down. She senses movement ahead and spots someone bending over. Not knowing if the person is ducking or going for a weapon, she fires the single shot and watches as the body is blown back.

'STAND DOWN,' Lani bellows, 'STAND DOWN NOW ...'

'Lani!'

'Lilly, where is Howie?'

'Gone ... Darius said the rooms are empty.'

'Maddox, you fucking move, and I will put a bullet through you.'

'I'm not moving.'

'You tasered me, you fucking piece of shit. You tasered me!'

'Lani ...'

She twitches, fires, and another body goes down. Movement on the top of the wall, and she fires again. The body slumps and falls down with a blood-curdling scream before landing with a sickening splat that silences the cry.

'DO NOT MOVE,' She watches Maddox twitch. 'You fucking tasered me!'

'You are killing children,' Maddox says quickly.

'I WILL KILL EVERYONE IN HERE,' Lani screams, 'AND DRINK THEIR FUCKING BLOOD.' She adopts the methods learnt from Dave with an overwhelming assault of the senses and a display of utter intent to kill. '... Where is it?'

'What?'

'The Taser ... Where is it?'

'On me.'

'Take it out with your left hand and put it on the ground, then your pistol, and if ANYONE MOVES, I WILL SHOOT MADDOX ... Lilly, are you holding a grenade?'

'Yes.'

'If I shoot Maddox, drop the grenade in the box and blow them all to hell.'

'I will.'

'Taser ... pistol ... NOW!'

Using his left hand, Maddox reaches round and draws first the yellow Taser from his belt and drops it quietly to the ground. The pistol follows.

'Step back ...'

'Lani, just ...'

She fires into the crowd behind him, blowing someone off their feet, and the screams rip through the fort.

'JESUS! Stop,' Maddox cries out.

'Stop? You want me to fucking stop? We risked our lives again and again for you, and you ... you tasered me ... Lilly, get that Taser. Move back ... further ...' she motions with the assault rifle, forcing Maddox to take back steps as Lilly quickly scoops the Taser up.

'Give it to me,' she holds the rifle steady in her right

hand and reaches for the Taser with her left. 'This is going to hurt, you prick,' she aims and fires the barbs dead centre into his chest. One second, he stands watching; the next, he's on the ground, convulsing as thousands of volts pulse through his body.

'Did it hurt?' She waits for him to come round and groan before pressing the trigger again, and the *tickticktick* of the Taser clicks audibly as it powers the juice through the wires and into the barbs embedded in his chest. 'How about now? Does it hurt, you prick?'

She presses it again and again, waiting for seconds each time before once again squeezing her finger.

The smell of shit hits her as the muscle contractions void Maddox's bowels. Unconscious, he lies on the ground in his own shit and piss.

'Bitch,' she spits and discards the Taser to the side. 'Lilly, drag that box of grenades into the armoury ... You ...' she motions to an older youth stood shaking nearby, 'get those weapons off the ground and into the armoury now ...'

She backs through the group, sweeping the assault rifle left to right as everyone stays rock still. A child cries at the rear of the fort, but not another sound other than the boy running back and forth as he carries the weapons into the armoury.

'Kneel down, hands on your heads ... do it slowly,' Lani barks the orders and watches the crews drop one by one.

'I want every single one of the crews in here doing the same ... If they are not here in ten seconds, I will start executing people ...'

'But–' someone speaks and is shot through the chest without hesitation, regardless of gender or age.

'ONE, TWO, THREE, FOUR, FIVE, SIX ...' she

counts fast and clear and listens as people run towards the centre.

'WEAPONS DOWN. ON YOUR KNEES. HANDS ON YOUR HEADS.'

They come. Scared. Terrified and having witnessed Maddox tasered again and again. Brave boys and girls who rely on a feral pack instinct surge to drop in front of Lani, and the power play shifts once more to a young Thai woman holding an assault rifle after showing what true battle experience is.

They come running. They come whimpering in fear, and the illuminated ground in front of her fills with the young, black-clad bodies, who only moments before felt invincible in the glory of their weapons.

Dressed in bra and knickers, she holds the assault rifle rock steady and with deadly purpose in her mind. She just killed people. Not infected. Not those that were turned, but people–young people, children. But the warning was given clear, and the choices they made were their own. These days are not the days of before.

'Darius?' she looks round. 'Where is Darius?'

Young heads turn to look, low mutterings break out between the youths.

'DARIUS,' Lani shouts, 'I want you hear now ... Lenski too ...'

Still no response.

'Lilly, throw that grenade into the middle ...'

'WAIT!' Darius's voice sounds out in the night. 'Don't do that ... don't ...'

'Get on your fucking knees now,' Lani snarls the words. 'Who the fuck do you think you are? You think you're above this lot? You think you're in charge here? Get down now ...'

'I'm down ...' Darius drops with his hands clamped to the top of his head.

'Lenski ...'

'Here, I'm here.'

'You let this happen,' Lani shouts across the distance to the Polish woman standing still in the shadows.

'Yes, you are not trusted. You kill children. You shoot them ...'

'Get over here and get down.'

'You shoot me?'

'Without hesitation.'

The Polish woman walks towards the centre and slowly drops down onto her knees as she lifts her hands onto her head. Begrudging and disdainful, but the act is done.

'Lilly, are any of the people back there police or military?'

'I don't know ... er ... We've got lists but ...'

'I NEED EX-SERVICES DOWN HERE,' Lani shouts. 'POLICE OR SERVICES ...'

'You think they ...'

'You speak to me again, Darius, and I'll put a bullet through your head ... MY NAME IS LANI. I'M WITH MR HOWIE ... I NEED ASSISTANCE FROM ANYONE WITH SERVICE EXPERIENCE ...'

'They ain't gonna help you, Lani ...'

Screams erupt from the single retort booming into the quiet of the fort as Darius is killed instantly from the single shot fired into his head from short range. The back of skull explodes out to shower those behind in grey matter.

The screams ease into soft whimpers at the terrible sight of the woman holding the assault rifle bathed in the flickering, orange light of torches.

'This was a mistake bringing you lot in here,' she speaks

slowly through gritted teeth. 'A mistake to think we could trust you ... Children who steal and hurt others ... .drug dealers and feral little shits ... I NEED ANYONE WITH SERVICE EXPERIENCE DOWN HERE!' She roars into the stillness of the night and waits for a response that doesn't come.

CHAPTER THIRTY-SEVEN

'That was interesting,' Clarence sags against the wall after putting Meredith down onto her feet. The sight of the big man holding the big dog while trying to lower himself down a ladder was a unique experience and one I shall never forget. She took it calmly at first, then decided she didn't like being held and started squirming. The squirms turned into a scrabble as she bucked and writhed until displacing his hand on the rung and letting them both fall to a heap at the bottom, where she bounded free and happy with a new place to sniff. 'She isn't going back up. That's for sure.'

'Roy, you take point with the torch. Clarence at the back?'

'Do I have a choice?'

'Of course, you have a choice. Do you not want to take the back?'

'It's not that I don't want to take the back ... but ...'

'But what?'

'Nothing, the back is fine.'

'Eh? What's wrong with the back? Dave, can you take the back?'

'I'm better at the front, Mr Howie.'

'I'll take the back,' Clarence says in a strange tone of voice.

'Dave, you take the back and let Clarence up front.'

'I always go up front,' Dave says.

'I don't want the front,' Clarence mutters.

'What? Why not?'

'Nothing, just ...' he peers round into the gloom and shudders.

'Holy shit,' Cookey mutters, 'Clarence doesn't like the dark.'

'Not the dark, you little shit,' Clarence growls. 'Big people and confined spaces do not mix well.'

'Middle then. Blowers, you're at the back and ...'

'Why me?'

'Fuck's sake ... Don't you like confined spaces either?'

'Er ...'

'Right, who is not bothered by the dark or confined spaces?'

'I don't mind either, Mr Howie.'

'Thanks, Dave. You take the back then.'

'I always take the front.'

'Fuck me! Paula?'

'Not a chance.'

'Cookey?'

'I'm not bothered,' he laughs with delight. 'I'll be the hero at the back who gets eaten by the monsters.'

'Shut up,' Paula says in a strained voice.

'Oh my good god,' I sigh. 'You are shitting me ... How many have we killed now?'

'Yeah, but it's dark and scary as fuck down here,' Blowers says.

'We are the scariest thing down here,' I say. 'We are. We have a big dog and guns ... and a Dave.'

'I always take the front.'

'Yes, Dave. You are at the front. I'm just saying we have a Dave.'

'Okay.'

'And a Clarence,' Clarence mutters.

'And we have a Clarence,' I add with a groan, 'and a Nick and a Blowers, and fucking hell! Can we go now?'

'So,' Roy asks slowly, 'I'm at the front still?'

'Oh, for the love of Pete ... yes ... yes, you take the front, and Cookey will take the rear ...'

'I always go–'

'Dave! Roy is taking point as he has the torch.'

'I can take the torch.'

'I made the torch,' Roy says dully. 'It's my torch.'

'Our torch,' Nick says. 'I made it too.'

'I broke the lighter.'

'Paula ... do something before I shoot everyone.'

'Right,' she says firmly, 'Roy takes the front with Dave behind him ... Everyone else behind them with Clarence at the, sorry, Cookey at the rear ... Let's go! NO! No arguing. We are moving off right now.'

'Cheers,' I nod into the gloom.

'Welcome,' she smiles. 'How the hell have you managed this lot so far?'

'No idea ... You wouldn't believe how hard it is.'

'I can imagine.'

'We're right here,' Clarence points out.

'Paula is now the resource manager for our team,' I announce.

'Ah, thanks,' she says sarcastically. 'Do I get a pay rise?'

'Yep, and a company car.'

'I want to be a manager,' Cookey says from the back. 'I'd be a good manager.'

We head slowly off, following the flickering light of the flaming torch that spews foul smelling fumes in our faces. It lights the way for Roy, but that's it. We go through the cavernous room, with no idea of size or dimensions, and then into the tunnel.

Cooler down here, and Roy was right–the air is relatively fresh, which indicates there must be an air flow from somewhere.

'I hope they don't block that hatch,' Cookey says after a few moments of silence.

'Why did you say that?' Clarence asks. 'Why would they?'

'So we don't get back up and kill everyone,' he replies. 'I'd block it.'

'Cookey, maybe not the right time to talk about getting trapped, mate.'

'Sorry, Mr Howie. I was just saying that I would block it.'

'Shut the fuck up, Cookey.'

'Get bent, Blowers.'

'They probably won't find it,' I say to stop the bad thoughts encroaching into our minds.

'I found it,' Roy says from the front, 'and they'll know there's a way out, so they'll look for it.'

'Can we talk about something else?' Paula asks.

A few more minutes of unhealthy silence. The dark doesn't bother me, and confined spaces have never really worried me either, but they've planted a seed, and even my nerves start to fray. Like everyone else, I keep my eyes fixed on the bobbing orange glow ahead.

The tunnel is smooth brick with a curved roof and a

concrete floor. No handrails or marking but solid, smooth walls. Not a drip or broken piece of mortar anywhere–the engineering back then was outstanding in achievement.

'Nick, why is the roof curved?' I ask simply to break the silence.

'Stronger,' he replies quietly, 'like bridges–the structure supports the mass.'

'These don't have those keystone things, though.'

'Downward gradient,' Roy announces. 'Watch your footing.'

I feel it within a few strides, a gentle shift of gradient under my feet. Gradual, but it goes on with amazing precision as we head further beneath the surface of the land.

'Er, Nick?' Blowers says almost whispering. 'You know that storm.'

'Yeah.'

'And that it took away the land ... so the sea is there now ...'

'Yeah, and no, don't worry ...'

'You sure?'

'I think so. Roy?' Nick calls ahead.

'We're deep underground now,' Roy calls back. 'The storm only shifted the top few feet of the land mass on the spit of land. We'd have seen signs by now if this tunnel was breached ... Water, damp ... It doesn't even smell damp, so we can assume the structure is sound.'

'Cool,' Blowers says.

'Imagine if it caved in now,' Cookey can't help himself, the daft idiot, and gets a solid chorus of abuse thrown back at him.

'What?' Cookey laughs. 'I was only saying.'

'Where will it come out?' Blowers asks again, showing

his nerves with a steady flow of questions from the normally quiet lad.

'I was thinking about that,' Roy answers. 'Probably not the housing estate as that was there after the fort, and it's also the most likely place an opposing army would set camp if they were to lay siege to the fort.'

'Further back then?' I ask.

'Most likely. There's an industrial complex there now. Is that right?'

'In there?' I ask.

'More than likely. It will be an old building or ... something that was present or built at the same time as the fort. Did you see anything like that?'

'Never really looked,' I reply.

'After we've got through this,' he says without preamble. 'I want to go my own way.'

'Roy!' Paula blurts. 'Not now.'

'What? We talked about it last night.'

'This morning. We talked about it this morning, and I don't think now is the time to bring it up.'

'Why not?'

'Because we're trapped in an old tunnel!'

'Hang on,' I say. 'You want to go off?'

'We're not trapped,' Roy says, 'and yes, I'm not good round people and ...'

'No shit,' Cookey mutters from the back.

'Where?'

'Don't know, Mr Howie ... but all this stuff just causes me more anxiety and–'

'Is Paula going with you?' Cookey asks.

'You should ask me, not Roy.'

'Sorry, you going with him, Paula?'

'We sort of discussed it earlier, but I didn't realise we'd actually made a decision.'

'Oh. I thought we had.'

'No. We did not.'

'Right after we had sex ... we agreed then ...'

'Roy!'

Splutters of laughter from Cookey, and even a smirk from Blowers shaking his head.

'You had sex?' Clarence asks wistfully. 'Where the hell did you get the energy from?'

'It releases all sorts of calming hormones,' Roy replies.

'Can we not talk about this now, please?'

'Moving on,' I say quickly. 'So you're getting anxiety from all this?'

'Yes.'

'What does that mean? What sort of anxiety?'

'I get anxious.'

'What, from the constant threat of death? The fact we've probably got the entire population of zombies coming after us or just general anxiety?'

'I get health anxiety.'

'What's that then?'

'It's when I keep thinking I am dying, like I imagine I have tumours and diseases.'

'Right ... and ... okay, but we've got doctors now and ...'

'Oh, I don't get the anxiety now,' he says brightly. 'It stopped because of everything we're doing.'

'Okay ... so ... isn't that a good thing?'

'No. If I stop worrying about it, that's when it will get me.'

'What will?'

'The diseases and tumours.'

'Do you have diseases and tumours?'

'I hope not.'

'So ... fuck me, I'm confused ... So you worry about it when you're not doing anything, but because we've been doing stuff, you don't worry, and that worries you because you're not worrying about it? Is that it?'

'That's it.'

'That makes no sense, Roy.'

'It doesn't have to make sense.'

'But wouldn't you rather be busy and doing stuff so you don't have to worry about it?'

'That's when it gets you.'

'Roy, er ... I'm not a doctor or anything but ... I don't think things like that get you when you're busy.'

'Magical thinking,' Roy says.

'What is?'

'My thought processes are called magical thinking. Like I protect myself by worrying about it ... but if I stop worrying about it, then I know ... like *I know* the diseases will get me.'

'Like a shield?' I scratch the side of my head as everyone else walks quietly, listening to the conversation.

'Exactly like a shield.'

'Fuck,' I say quietly, 'but ... but then you'll be just worrying all the time, and doesn't worry and stress make shit like that worse anyway?'

'That's what I said,' Paula says.

'Plus, we kind of rely on you now, mate. You're part of the team.'

'I only came here with Paula to find a doctor.'

'We've got doctors. We've got four of them.'

'Doctors are no good for me.'

'Eh?'

'If I'm near doctors, it makes me worse ... I want to keep asking them about things, and they get fed up; then, I get worried and start imagining things are worse.'

'Well,' I say with a snort through my nose, 'Lani has probably killed them all by now anyway.'

'We need more rags,' he says.' These are starting to burn out.'

Silence. Worrying silence that grows heavier as the flames grow smaller.

'Er ... who has the rags?' I ask. 'Nick?'

'Nope, I thought Roy had them.'

'I thought you had them,' Roy says.

'I don't have them,' Nick says quickly.

'Does anyone have them?' Paula asks.

'We need something,' Roy says. The light dims quickly as the flames devour through the material and start dwindling.

'Someone needs to surrender their pants,' Roy says.

'Blowers will,' Cookey says from the back. 'He likes being naked.'

'Not a chance with Cookey down here,' Blowers says.

'Someone then,' Roy says, 'or we're walking in the dark.'

'Roy, you do it,' Cookey says. 'Paula has seen your willy anyway.'

'Alex!'

'What? It's true,' he says to Paula. 'Roy said you had a shag ...'

'We did not shag. We had sex.'

'I'd rather not,' Roy says in a rare polite tone.

'Someone has to,' I say, 'and Cookey's right, Paula has seen your, er ... um ...'

'Penis,' Paula sighs, 'it is a penis.'

'Ha! Paula said penis,' Cookey laughs.

'Can't we tear a strip from Paula's t-shirt?' Nick asks.

'Good idea,' I say. 'Paula?'

'What? Why me?'

'You're the only one wearing a top.'

'That's because I have boobs, and we've already seen the reaction these boys get from the mere presence of a woman.'

'Eh?' I ask.

'Nick, earlier.'

'What? Oh yeah ... he had an erection.'

'Boss,' Nick groans, 'that was Lilly anyway ...'

'So Paula wouldn't give you an erection?'

'Alex!'

'Alex!'

'Cookey!'

'Sorry, Dave. Sorry, Paula. Sorry, Mr Howie.'

'We don't the need the entire top, just a few inches from the bottom,' I say. 'Can you tear a bit off?'

'Bloody hell,' she says with a huff and starts feeling for the seam of her top. 'I'm not wearing a bra.'

'Interesting fact,' I reply carefully.

'I can't ... I'm not strong enough to rip it ... Clarence, would you mind?'

'Here,' he bends forward, and a second later, the sound of tearing is clear in the tunnel.

'Not up,' she says quickly, 'don't tear it upwards ... It needs to be torn along ...'

'Okay ... bugger ... it won't tear straight ...'

'It's not paper ...'

'Oh, Christ, sorry, Paula.'

'What? Cookey asks from the back.

'It's okay,' she sighs, 'you can't see the nipple.'

'...'

'Yes, I said nipple ...' Paula groans, 'and no, you can't see the nipple ...'

'Eyes front,' Clarence says, 'and if I see any of you trying to peek ...'

'Here,' she pulls the last bit free and passes it forward.

'Quickly,' Roy says as the tunnel plunges into darkness as the last flame dies out.

A frantic bustle takes place as the thin rag is passed hand to hand, fumbling in the dark as we all watch the soft, glowing embers on the head of the torch. Roy wraps the rag on and starts blowing the embers gently, which grow brighter but don't produce a flame.

We all wait, staring intently and listening as he exhales to make them glow, but they start dimming faster and faster. He blows harder, they rally and spark but then extinguish, and we're in the absolute pitch dark, with not a flicker or glimmer of light from anywhere.

'At least we can't see Paula's nipple now,' Cookey breaks the silence.

'Should I keep going?' Roy's voice comes from the front.

'No, mate. I thought we'd stay here for a bit.'

'Er ... was that sarcasm?'

'Yes, Roy. It was sarcasm. Keep going.'

We head off but slower, much slower. All of us walking with bare feet, shuffling along the ground and arms outstretched to the sides to feel the tunnel walls. Assault rifles strapped to our backs, and pistols held in hands. The breathing noises become louder as the fear factor starts working on our minds.

I've never known such blackness before. A complete

absence of light, like a void. So dark I can't tell if my eyes are open or closed.

'Water,' Roy says from ahead, 'on the ground ... Don't be alarmed.'

'Fucking alarmed,' Blowers mutters.

My spine ripples with fear as my feet slide into the cold, unseen puddle, and my right hand traces over a damp patch on the wall.

'We're under the sea then,' Nick says.

'Another one,' Roy calls back.

This one is bigger and takes two steps to get through, and my hand comes away wet from the feel of the trickle on the wall.

The ground has levelled out now and just keeps going straight. Without light, there is no sense of time. I try counting in my head, but it only serves to increase the knot of tension in my gut. None of us speak as we strain to listen and stare into the pure blackness around us.

It feels like the tunnel is getting smaller, that we're walking into an ever-decreasing tomb. The sensation of being trapped becomes palpable and threatens to take over. My own breathing becomes faster, and I can tell the others are the same.

A noise ahead. A steady noise. Dripping. Water or fluid dripping to land in a pool. Still none of us speak until Roy shudders audibly from the drip on his head. Dave remains completely quiet; then, I feel it.

An icy sensation as the water hits the back of my neck, and my feet slide into the much deeper puddle that is deeper than the size of my toes.

'Salt water,' Nick says. 'Just tasted it.'

'So that means sea water,' Blowers says in a hoarse whisper.

'Yeah,' Nick says in a heavy breath.

'Stop,' Roy comes to a sudden stop, which brings us all up sharp. 'On the right ... the bricks are fractured ... Water is coming through. Do not touch them.'

'Oh fuck,' Clarence says with a whimper.

'Just walk through,' Nick says. 'It hasn't breached yet, so it'll hold.'

We move on, and the puddle this time is long until we're all walking through inches of standing water that sloshes noisily. I want to touch the wall, to feel or know how bad the bricks are, but the image in my head of them falling apart at the gentlest touch has my arms held firmly at my sides.

'Brick in the puddle ... Watch your toes,' Roy announces.

'Fucking brick ...' Clarence's voice is far higher in pitch as his breathing gets faster. 'Where from?'

'Does it matter?' Nick asks. 'It'll hold ... Just keep going.'

Still in the puddle, but it's deeper now, deep enough to wade through. Up to my ankles and getting higher as we go forward. Icy cold, and it sends shivers through my body. Clarence gasps with increasing concern.

'You okay?' Paula asks him gently.

He swallows but doesn't answer.

'Put your hand on my shoulder,' she says. 'I'm right here ... That's it. Just keep going forward.'

'It's getting deeper,' he says.

It is. The water is halfway up my shins now, and I gently stretch my hand up until my fingers brush against the roof, and the water runs down my hand.

'Okay,' Roy says, 'we're getting deeper now, and I can feel bricks in the water ...'

'Oh Christ ... oh Christ ...'

'Easy now,' Paula says to the big man as he starts panicking.

'Fresh air,' Nick says. 'There has to be an airflow in here ... which means a way out.'

'We should go back,' Clarence says, 'just go back.'

'We can't, mate, you know what will happen.'

'I'll go back ... You lot keep going.'

'No!' We all stop as Paula fumbles in the dark to grab him.

'Cookey, move,' Clarence orders.

'Um ... no?' Cookey stands his ground, blocking Clarence from moving past.

'Clarence, keep going.'

'I can't, Boss. The fucking thing will collapse.'

'It won't,' Nick says calmly. 'It's just a leak.'

'You're alright,' Paula says gently. 'You are alright ... Come on ... We've got to keep moving.'

The water gets to my knees, then my thighs, and starts lapping at my groin, which makes my teeth chatter–the icy feeling ten times worse. The sounds from the others all signal when the water hits their bits too from the gasps and foul utterances that go down the line.

The panic in me is building. Wading through freezing salt water in the complete blackness of a tunnel that hasn't been checked or used for over a hundred years. I swallow and focus on what we need to do. Knowing that by now we must be near to the land.

Up to my stomach and still rising. Water trickles from many points, like a tap left on that is steadily filling the tunnel. We plough on and keep moving forward as every instinct in our bodies tells us to turn back. But we can't. To go back is simply not an option.

'Rifles up,' Dave orders, and I lift mine up to hold clumsily above the water while trying to grip my pistol at the same time.

Sternum now, and it gets deeper still. A steady flow sounds from nearby, then a dull crack and a plop as a brick falls from the wall or ceiling to splash into the water.

Clarence is near on hyper-ventilating, and he's not the only one. Blowers, Paula, and even Dave in front of me; then, I remember how much Dave hates the water and realise the utter terror he must be going through too.

Nothing to say, and I urge myself to speak, to make noise and somehow distract our minds, but the very act of speaking seems too dangerous, as though our voices alone could rupture the walls of the giant coffin around us.

The thought of drowning here in the pure darkness and no one ever knowing we are here is more terrifying than anything I have ever done. For it all to just end now, and we die, alone and scrabbling in abject fear.

Another brick gives, then another. Gasps of fear, and we wade through the deepening water. Roy keeps us at a steady pace, neither rushing ahead and causing waves or going so slow we feel even more trapped.

My chest now, and moving forward is getting harder. The waves created by Roy and Dave ahead ripple out to the walls and back at me. The others behind feel the same, and we hear crack after crack as the bricks fall randomly into the freezing sea water.

My rifle is held above my head but to one side because of the curvature of the roof, and my sides start to cramp. The weapon grows heavier until my arms are aching and shake. I want to lower them, if only for a second to relieve the burning pain building in my shoulders.

An inch or so below my neck, and I'm blinking the

tears of pain and fear away. Clarence sobs behind me. His deep voice broken by terrified yelps as though made by a child.

'We will not die here,' I say without realising the words are coming from my mouth, 'We will not die here.'

'What the ...?'

'What?' we all snap the words from the exclamation from Roy at the front.

'Meredith,' he gasps. 'She's swimming back.'

'Shit, I forgot about the dog. Is she okay?'

'She must be tired,' Nick says. 'She would have been swimming for ages now.'

I track her panting as it gets closer and feel her body swim past me.

'Clarence, see if she needs help,' I call back softly.

'We're all holding weapons,' Nick says.

'Clarence can hold his one handed all day long,' I whisper back. 'Clarence ... make sure Meredith is okay.'

'Got her,' he pants. 'She's under my arm.'

'Is she letting you carry her?'

'Sort of ...' he says, but the panic in his voice is less than it was a few seconds ago.

'I bet she was aiming for you,' I say, 'like she knows who the strongest is to carry her.'

'Maybe.'

'We're not going to die here ...'

'Mr Howie ...'

'Dave? You alright?'

'I can't swim ... I'm on the tips of my toes.'

'Ditch the rifle and pistol and come back to me.'

'We should not discard our weapons.'

'Okay, keep hold of them then but come back ... Hang on, let me turn round and get on my back.'

'Mr Howie,' Nick says, 'I'm taller than you. I can take Dave.'

'He's here,' I feel as Dave pushes up and onto my back and holds his assault rifle and pistol one-handed with the other one wrapped round my shoulders.

'We get into some fucked-up shit,' Cookey laughs suddenly. 'I mean ... fucking hell!'

Ripples of nervous laughter along the line.

'Clarence is carrying a dog. Mr Howie is carrying a Dave ... We're all carrying guns, and Paula has a nipple poking out. Meanwhile Roy wants to be somewhere he can worry so he doesn't have to worry about not worrying.'

Giggles that threaten to spill over into hysteria, but it helps the nerves frayed almost to breaking point.

'I mean ... shit,' Cookey yells first as the wave lifts him from his feet. It sweeps along from behind, and the swell takes us all up and under water for a second before easing us back down.

Panicked gasps cry out, spluttering and coughs as we gag on the salt water in our mouths.

'What the fuck?' I heave the words out between breaths.

'Tunnel's collapsed behind us,' Nick says. 'Roy ... we've got to move ...'

'Brace–' Roy's voice is cut off by the wave coming back towards us, and again we're lifted up and submerged as the wave sweeps back the other way.

The weapons are ditched, and it becomes a desperate fight to stay alive. Water stings my redundant eyes and the sounds around me make the whole thing much worse. Crying and sobs, pants of fear, and gasps as the waves lift us to scrape our head on the roof, then ease away. They come from behind, then a few seconds later from the front.

'It's good,' Nick splutters, 'waves coming back means...' he splutters and gags for a second before vomiting into the sea, 'means we're near the end ... Go ...'

'It's getting deeper,' Cookey says in a voice I don't recognise for the level of panic in his tone.

Up now and off my feet; arms spread out to feel the crumbling walls, and I drop down to bounce forward and surge up to take breath. Dave is heavy, almost too heavy, but I can tell, from the strength with which he clamps on, just how scared he is.

Gagging and puking, gasps of air, and the finality hits me. We've got inches of space left above our heads now and no hope to sustain this any longer.

'Keep going,' Nick sputters. 'Got to be close.'

'Paula!' Clarence heaves the gagging woman up one-handed while holding the dog afloat. 'Kick,' he says, 'kick your legs and move ...' The strain in his voice, and the strength of the man being able to hold Meredith *and* Paula is staggering.

'Not going to die ... not going to die ...' My head impacts on the ceiling as I surge up and off my feet, stars flash in my eyes, which seem so bright from the illusion created by my mind.

The strength in me saps, draining with every second, and I take what breaths I can when the waves go down, but the constant motion is sickening, and my senses start shutting down.

'Wall!' the words from someone ahead sound out. Only Roy ahead of me. A wall. A hand thrashes in front of me, and suddenly Dave is gone, his weight removed.

'Dave ... Dave's gone ...' I thrash about, trying to feel for his body as I sink back under the waves.

'Got him,' Roy gags and spits, 'here ... HERE ...' A hand

finds my arm and drags me forward until I feel a solid wall. Somehow, in my panicked state, I find a metal rung embedded in the wall and cling on.

'Take Paula,' Clarence gurgles, and I reach out to grab the woman and pull her in towards the ladder.

'Up,' single words are all any of us can manage. The space above me is free, and I climb on shaking hands and legs, shivering from head to toe as the puke falls from my mouth.

'Stuck,' Roy heaves against the hatch that must be above his head. 'Jammed ...' grunts of exertion and bangs as he slams himself against it.

'Me,' Clarence pushes forward with his big frame and finds a rung.

'Let me down,' Roy says.

'Together,' Clarence squeezes up alongside the archer.

'Here, it's here.'

In the darkness, I listen as the lads reach the ladder, and we all grab a rung, grab each other and help hold Meredith above the water. The waves slosh harder and faster, but with Clarence and Roy above us, there is no space to climb.

'On three ...' Clarence grunts. 'One ... two ... THREE.' An almighty explosion of energy, and the rung under Roy's feet screeches and buckles. A grinding noise, and the sustained roar of Clarence heaving with every ounce of his strength as he pushes the hatch open.

Light spills in, silvery and dull, but after the pitch dark, it's a beauty to behold. I don't know who gets out first, but I feel a hand gripping me and helping me up. I turn and grasp Paula, who holds the dog by her neck as the lads push Meredith from underneath.

We disgorge dripping, panting, and puking onto a rough concrete floor and crawl away from the hatch as though scared we'll get sucked back down. Meredith runs to each of us, stopping to shake every few seconds. Rough licks from her tongue, and she gives low whines before flopping down to rest.

'Everyone alive?' I lift my head and count the bodies lying flat out before I flop back down and stare up through the high windows to the beautiful moon and stars high in the sky.

CHAPTER THIRTY-EIGHT

The pure fury coursing through her veins eases back as the true facts of the situation present unravel. Howie gone from a set of rooms with only one entrance that was being watched the entire time.

Lani wants to look for herself but can't risk leaving the crews without constant observation, and not one of the terrified survivors moved forward when she called for assistance.

She has control but what now?

'I can't see anything in there,' Lilly steps close to Lani and whispers with a low voice. 'I'll need a torch and two hands, but this grenade ...'

'Throw it over the wall.'

'I might miss. What if it bounces back down?'

'Go out the front, then throw it into the sea.'

'You'll be okay here?'

Lani nods and thinks. The sullen expression etched on her face is masked by the dim light and deep shadows.

How many did she kill? One outside the hospital, another was running. Wasn't there someone on top of the walls? And Darius. She bites her bottom lip at the thought of the death brought by her hands. Control was needed, though. Instant compliance to gain control and ensure the safety of Howie and the rest.

She thinks and watches the crews, using a torch found on the ground to sweep over the young, petrified, and sulky-looking faces. Some look down with wet cheeks; others stare back with utter hatred in their eyes

A dull thud booms into the night as the grenade detonates safely in the sea. Thrown by Lilly without any thought of the tunnel running under her feet and the percussion effect of the energy displacement on the old bricks and mortar.

She walks back inside, flexing her right hand open and closed with relief from finally being rid of the heavy object.

'Done,' she looks to Lani, then back at the supplicated youths crammed together. 'What now?'

'We need to search the inside of the rooms and find out how they got out ... Wait,' she says quickly as Lilly goes to head inside. Holding the torch, she once again sweeps the beam from face to face. 'Where's Jagger and Mo Mo?'

'I haven't seen them,' Lilly steps towards the kneeling children to scan the faces.

'Lenski, where's Jagger and Mo Mo?' Lani holds the beam on the Polish woman.

'Offices.'

'Lilly, go check ... take a weapon with you. Do you know how to fire one?'

'Nick showed me how to shoot a pistol.'

'Take one with you, make sure the safety is off, and don't hesitate to shoot if they turn on you.'

'Okay,' Lilly darts into the opening of the armoury and the pile of weapons dropped there, coming back out with a pistol held in both hands like Nick showed her.

She runs down the inside of the wall and pauses at the doorway. Feeling stupid and somewhat self-conscious, she peers through and into the lantern-illuminated interior; pistol held low.

'Mo Mo?' she half -whispers, half-shouts, then steps inside. 'Mo Mo? Jagger?'

Nothing here. She creeps through the room, checking under the table, and heads to the doorway at the back, which she cracks open and stops again. 'Mo Mo?' she calls out louder this time and hears a muffled voice shouting, then a solid bang against the door at the far end.

She checks each side room going down. The pistol held ready until she reaches the bottom door. 'Mo Mo? Are you in there?'

'Who's that? Tell Maddox I'm gonna fuckin' kill him,' Mo Mo's voice seethes through the door. 'Has he hurt Mr Howie?'

'Stand back from the door. I'll open it.'

'Who is that?'

'Lilly, it's Lilly ... Are you armed?'

'Armed? Fuckin' wouldn't be stuffed in here if we was armed. What the fuck is going on? Where's Maddox?'

'Please stand back from the door,' Lilly asks politely. 'I have a gun, and I need to see you before you can come out.'

'Lilly, it's Jagger ... You on your own?'

'You have to stand back from the door,' Lilly says urgently.

'Okay, okay, we're back,' she frowns, unable to tell the voices apart but picking up the greater distance.

The key in the lock, and she flicks it over before stepping back with the pistol up and aimed, 'Okay ... open the door ... but do not do anything ...'

'Take it easy,' one of the voices says. The handle creaks

down, the door cracks and swings in as Mo Mo and Jagger show themselves with arms raised.

'Are you alone?' Mo Mo mouths the words to Lilly. 'Where's Maddox?'

'What happened to you earlier?' Lilly asks.

'Maddox got us out at gunpoint ... The fuckin' prick held a pistol to my head.'

'Darius did me,' Jagger says angrily. 'What the fuck is going on? We've been in here for hours.'

'Come out,' Lilly says, 'but move slowly.'

'No way,' Mo Mo shakes his head as he places a hand on Jaggers arm to prevent him moving. 'You tell that cunt he can come in here if he wants to kill us.'

'Who?'

'Maddox ... fucking coward ... MADDOX? YOU THERE?' Mo Mo's voice booms loud and frighteningly sudden.

'He said Lani was infected,' Jagger says, 'but she ain't ... We saw her on the way back, and she ain't infected. He said Howie and thems are infected, but they ain't.'

'I know,' Lilly says quietly.

'What's Maddox doing, Lilly?' Mo Mo asks. 'Why's he doing it then?'

'Come out,' Lilly beckons them forward, 'but please go slowly.'

'We ain't coming out,' Mo Mo says firmly.

'Things have happened,' Lilly says.

'What things?' Mo Mo asks quickly. 'Lilly ... what things? Is Howie and that lot okay? What about Lani? She okay?'

'I, er ...' Lilly hesitates, knowing Mo Mo and Jagger were working with Howie, but they were originally with Maddox. How can she tell where their loyalties lie?

'Please,' she pleads, 'just come out and speak to Lani.'

'Lani?' Mo Mo and Jagger spare a glance at each other. 'Where is she?' That gets them moving as they head down the corridor and into the main room.

'Where is everyone?' Mo Mo looks round at the vacated room. 'Where's Lani?'

'Outside,' Lilly says.

'Is this a trap?' Jagger asks.

'Which side are you on?' Lilly asks the question outright.

'Side? What side?' Mo Mo asks. 'What you on about?'

'Howie and Maddox?' Jagger nods. 'We're with Howie. Maddox is a dirty cunt ...'

'Mo Mo?'

'Howie,' he nods, 'and fuck you if you shoot us for it ... and you tell that coward we died calling him out.'

'Come outside, but please, please move slowly and don't shout or do anything.'

They both stare in confusion but follow the plaintive pleads as Lilly backs up through the room to the main door and out into the fort.

'Fuck,' Mo Mo gasps at the sight before them. 'Lani? That you?'

'Here,' she says. 'What happened to you?'

'Maddox forced us out at gunpoint,' Mo Mo says as they head towards Lani, 'had a hand over our mouths and pistol shoved in my fuckin' ear ... Darius did the same to Jagger.'

Lani hesitates for a second as the two lads walk over. They were there, in the munitions factory, and they fought like demons to protect Howie. They were part of the team, and sometimes a chance has to be taken.

'You with me?' Lani asks quickly, 'or with them?'

'Mr Howie,' Mo Mo says without hesitation, 'we're with him ... Where is he?'

'Grab a weapon from the armoury,' she nods to the doorway, knowing this is the point of risk. The two lads run inside, and she listens to the all-familiar sounds of magazines being taken out, checked, and put back in before bolts are pulled back and the guns made ready.

'Did you know you got your bra and pants on?' Mo Mo asks as he steps beside her and holds his weapon at the ready, pointed towards the crews.

'Yep.'

'Awesome,' Jagger joins her other side, and suddenly the one is a three, and the lines are drawn.

'Is that Darius?' Mo Mo asks with a nod to the mangled remains a few metres away.

'Yep. Shot him.'

'You missed out, Jagger.'

'Fuck him, dead is dead,' Jagger spits to the side. 'Where's Mads?'

'Over there somewhere,' Lani nods towards the middle. 'I tasered him ... like eight or nine times.'

'Fuck,' Jagger lifts his eyebrows. 'You alright then?'

'I am now,' she says and allows a brief smile at the two lads. 'Thank fuck you're on our side.'

'Always,' Mo Mo says. 'Now, what the fuck is going on?'

Lilly blinks in awe at the sight. Lani taking utter control of the fort in seconds. No hesitation, no pause, no bargaining. Pure ruthless action that displayed a readiness to do what was needed. The risk she took, and the calmness in doing it by trusting Mo Mo and Jagger. But the bond is clear, an almost tangible thing between them. The way they stand with legs planted. The way they hold their weapons, and the way they watch, always observing, always scanning.

Jagger and Mo Mo must be the same age as her, and a day or two ago, they were just kids, but now–now they've grown and have the manner of men. That's Mr Howie's team, right there. The bond and the manner of unspoken loyalty between them, and in those few seconds, she knows she did the right thing.

Lani brings them up to speed with clipped sentences that convey the bare facts. The lads nod and listen but watch the crews ranged out in front of them.

'Got to be a way out, innit?' Mo Mo says. 'Jagger, you go with Lilly and check ... I'll stay here with Lani.'

'On it,' Jagger emulates the affirmative response given by Blowers, Cookey, and Nick as he heads inside with a nod to Lilly to follow him.

'I can't believe he did it,' Mo Mo shakes his head, 'not like that ... Fuckin' bang out of order, you get me?'

'I do.'

'I don't wanna be part of anything they were,' Mo Mo says with hard glares at his former friends. 'You lot disgust me ... Mr Howie gave us this place ... Yous got no idea what he's done for you.'

'What's gonna happen, Mo Mo?' a girl asks quietly.

'Tasha? That you? What the fuck? I mean ... what the fuck? Maddox said yous got to tell him if he does the wrong thing. He said that ... We all heard it ... All the crew chiefs ...'

'He no do the wrong thing,' Lenski speaks out in furious voice. 'She shoot Darius ... She shoot children.'

'Not children.' Mo Mo shakes his head. 'Armed guards ... You get me? You threatened them first ... They just brought the fight back to you and showed you up for the fools you are. Yous lot are trying to be like the feds, all dressed in black ... You waited till they were asleep and got me and Jagger out at gunpoint! Fucking gunpoint …'

'Mo Mo, you gotta see this,' Jagger rushes from the armoury.

'Go on,' Lani nods for him to go. 'Everyone, stay quiet now.'

'What?' Mo Mo asks, following Jagger through the main room and into a side room.

'Trap door, innit?' Jagger says excitedly. Mo Mo stares down at the now clear lines in the hatch back in place in the concrete floor.

'Try and open it,' Lilly says, holding the torch while the two lads get their fingertips into the edge and start prising it up.

'Flooded,' Mo Mo stares down at the sloshing water still animated from pouring into the breached roof further in the tunnel, 'but they went that way.'

'So they's gone then,' Jagger says. 'You reckon they got out?'

'Fuckin' hope so,' Mo Mo says standing up.

A minute later, and while Jagger and Mo Mo keep watch, Lani is shown the trapdoor and the still rising water within by Lilly holding the torch.

'Oh my,' Lani shakes her head, 'that water's rising … See the sides?'

'I saw,' Lilly says. 'It's gone up inches in the last minute.'

Lani exhales and stares down at the inky water. 'Just got to wait now,' she shakes her head with a slight smile.

'Wait? What for?' Lilly asks softly.

'For them to come back,' Lani says with a shrug, then notices the pained look on Lilly's face. 'Oh, you think they'd get stuck down there? No. You've not worked with them. They'll be somewhere, bickering and arguing like normal …'

'Do they bicker?'

'All the time,' Lani laughs, 'like non-stop.'

'I thought you were all really professional,' Lilly says with another look down into the dark access hatch.

'Ha! Us? Are you joking?' Lani chuckles again. 'We get the job done, but ... no, professional is not a word I would use ... Wait till I tell 'em everyone thinks they're professional. Come on, I need some clean clothes.'

CHAPTER THIRTY-NINE

'I really don't think that getting cigarettes and a new lighter is at the top of the list,' Paula says for the third time.

'That's cos you don't smoke, Paula,' Nick explains. 'If you did smoke, you'd understand.'

'So let me get this right. We've just almost drowned in a horrible, horrible tunnel. We are in our underwear, with no weapons, no clothes, in the middle of the night, and you want to get cigarettes and a lighter first?'

'Yes,' Nick nods firmly.

Paula pulls the sodden material of her top down to cover the exposed boob that everyone is actively avoiding looking at. 'Do we even know where we are?' she asks round the group.

'We're here,' Clarence groans, still laid flat out on the ground, 'and not down there ... That's all that matters.'

'That was nasty,' I say quietly. 'Got to be the nastiest thing yet.'

'I had a spider,' Paula says.

'Eh?' I look up, then quickly drop my head as she tugs the t-shirt back down.

'Spider,' she says again. 'I was trapped in a toilet in a garage ... Two of them were outside the door, and a spider was crawling along the ground, towards my foot.'

'Nasty,' Cookey winces. 'What did you do?'

She smiles with a low chuckle, 'I thought it went up my leg, so I ran out and attacked the zombies while trying to get rid of it.'

'Not worse than that,' Clarence says. 'Nothing could be worse than that.'

'Ah, well, we're here now. Best get on with it.' I sit up and think for a second. Lani is in the hospital, and we've got until two o'clock before Lilly sets the distraction off. If we move quickly, we could time it to break in when the distraction goes off. Grab some weapons and get Lani out.

'There'll be a crew on the beach,' I say quickly, 'Maddox said he's leaving one there all the time.'

'They'll be armed,' Paula says, 'and near the Saxon ... which is armoured.'

'And has a GPMG on the top,' Clarence adds.

'Maddox would have radioed them by now,' I say. 'They'll shoot us on sight.'

'Moon's up,' Clarence says, glancing up at the windows. 'No chance of sneaking up on them.'

'Roy could take them out with a bow,' Nick suggests.

'They're children,' Roy says. 'I'm not killing children.'

'Shoot them in the legs,' Cookey says.

'How's that going to stop them shooting at us?' Blowers asks.

'Shoot them in the hands, then? Roy could do it.'

'I could, but I won't.'

'Listen,' I gain the attention of the group, 'they are children, but they're also armed and in control of the fort ... If we're going to get Lani out, we might have to accept the fact they will sustain losses.'

'Fair enough,' Roy says. 'I'll return fire if I am fired upon, but I won't do it first.'

'You can't argue with that,' Clarence says. 'I agree.'

'Dave, can you get in and get Lani out?'

'Yes, Mr Howie.'

'Could you do it without killing everybody?'

'Everybody? Yes, Mr Howie.'

'Could you do it without killing anybody?'

'No.'

'So a distraction has to be both visual and audible. Is that right?'

'Yes, Mr Howie.'

'Will visual work on its own, without audible?'

'If it's strong enough, it will.'

'Excellent, we're moving out. Everybody ready?'

'What now?' Clarence groans.

'Yes, you need more of a rest?'

'No, I'm fine,' he says, levering himself up.'

'Good, because we ain't getting one.'

'I think I preferred the grumpy Mr Howie.'

'Right,' I stand up with the idea charging through my mind. 'Where the hell are we, and how do we get out?'

Roy was right. We're in an old warehouse that must have been built at the same time as the fort and now turned over to boat repairs. We get from the back room into storerooms and through to offices and finally break down a door before getting into the open. A quick scout round, and we find our bearings, slap bang in the middle of the industrial units, behind where the housing estate once was.

'Where are we going?' Paula asks as I peer up at the moon, then round at the team gathered in a circle.

'It is bright tonight,' I say quietly, 'really bright ... You don't even need a torch. I can see everything really clearly.'

'Boss?' Clarence casts me a slightly worried look.

'This way. Oh no ... is that way east?'

'Yes,' Roy replies, 'did you want east?'

'I did ... Come on.' I take the lead in my underpants and let everyone fall in behind me, in their underpants, and Paula tugging her top down constantly.

'Are you sharing this idea,' Paula asks, 'and does it involve getting clothes?'

'Yes, and yes,' I stare ahead and work out the way to the housing estate and then head away from it. 'Fuck it, I'm hopeless at finding my way. We need to find the houses across the bay ...'

'Marcy,' Clarence nods knowingly.

'Yep. Roy, can you find the way?'

'I can,' he takes the lead, and we fall in behind him. Walking in silence and feeling only slightly vulnerable being out in the open mostly naked and without weapons. Bare feet pad on the road until we hit the hedge. We head down, find a gate and go across fields but stick to the perimeter.

'Why are we going to Marcy?' Clarence asks.

'Ssshhh,' I whisper back, and for once, I want to keep my plan quiet.

'Bay is right there,' Roy points towards a thick hedge. 'Stay quiet.'

I pass the message down, and we creep along as quiet as possible until we reach a five-bar gate at the end. Roy goes first, then motions me forward.

Peering through the bars, I can make out the bulk of the Saxon and the figures on the beach standing about. The red embers of cigarettes glow, and muted snatches of conversation drift back.

'They look relaxed,' Roy says in a low whisper.

'Maybe Maddox hasn't noticed we're gone yet. Keep going.' We get past the gate, one at a time, and through into the next field that borders the access lane into the seafront houses.

Safely out of view of the beach, and we scurry along the lane, moving silently on the tarmacked road as we strain to keep watch on all sides. I take the lead and head us further down past the backs of the houses and through an alley running between two big detached, wooden-built chalet-style houses. With the moon so bright, we navigate easily without the worry of trip hazards.

The main road through the middle of the big, expensive houses is directly ahead, and we stop in a huddle, staring along to the darkened windows and the silence of the area.

'Stay here,' I whisper.

'Where are you going?' Clarence asks.

'Find Marcy,' I dart out, then stand straight, and walk with purpose to the middle of the road, where I stop dead and slowly turn. I can almost feel that she'll be watching. One of these windows will have her hidden behind, watching, waiting. That I'm only wearing pants makes me feel utterly ridiculous. I move a few metres to one side so the houses further down can see me, then back the other way to do the same thing the other end. Up and down the road. Pacing in my pants.

'Doesn't appear to be working,' Paula strolls out, 'and I need a bra.'

'Okay,' I nod as the rest come walking out, with the silvery moon glinting off their naked torsos.

'Did you think she would just walk out?' Paula asks me quietly.

'Pretty much,' I shrug. 'Had to be worth a go.'

'Eyes up,' Dave nods across the road to the seaward side and the front door opening.

Marcy walks out with her head held high and dressed immaculately in jeans and a simple white top. The sight of her takes my breath away, and I have to steel myself not to react. She stops at the end of the short garden path and stands easy for a second before folding her arms.

'What on earth?' she shakes her head slowly as Reginald comes bustling out behind her. 'What do you look like?'

I shrug and look round at the group all standing still.

'Hi, Marcy,' Cookey waves without shame.

'Hi, Cookey,' Marcy smiles a huge grin. 'Blowers, Nick.'

'Marcy,' Blowers nods.

'Hey,' Nick tilts his head back, 'how are you?'

'Fine,' she says with a nod, 'better than you by the look of it. Hello, Clarence.'

'Hullo,' he says in his deep voice. 'Er ... thanks for saving us in the fort that day.'

She nods, then shakes her head with a confused look.

'Dave,' she nods formally.

'Marcy,' he replies but watches her and Reginald with the same deadpan expression as ever.

'I'm Paula. Er ... this is Roy,' Paula says, tugging her top down again.

'Hi, er ... would you like to come in?'

'Do you have a spare bra?'

'Yes, yes, I do, and I have clothes too ... You're welcome to take what you need.'

'Thanks,' Paula goes to move off, then stops when I don't move. 'Oh, er ...' she falls silent and steps back.

'Marcy,' I nod across the distance and feel the same as I did when I met on the flatlands for the first time. Like the world is spinning and time ceases to be. Something here, a connection, a bond. Something intrinsic and organic, yet too fleeting to grasp or understand.

'Howie,' her tone changes when she says my name; perhaps it drops a little, or maybe it's higher. I can't tell but it's different.

'We got your message.'

'Good.'

'So ...?'

'So you thought you'd visit me in the middle of the night, wearing your pants?'

'Had some trouble.'

'You wouldn't be you without trouble. I mean that collectively.'

'Right ... so ... do you have any zombies in there?' I point stupidly at the house behind her.

'No, no zombies. Just me and Reggie, and he prefers the term–'

'Living challenged, I remember.'

'Reginald,' Reginald mutters.

'Are we safe?'

'Probably more safe in here than out there, unarmed and naked.'

'Sod this, I need a bra. Can I come in, please?'

'Sure. We've got a gas bottle, running water, and coffee too.'

'Wait for it,' Clarence rumbles as the group sets off as one. 'Mr Howie hasn't said we can go yet.'

'We can go.' I'm halfway across the road and feeling oh so very self-conscious as Marcy appraises me up and down with a perfectly sculpted raised eyebrow before turning to lead the way with a wry smile on her face.

CHAPTER FORTY

The eight of us stand clustered in the huge shaker-style kitchen, all of us watching Meredith as she tracks Reginald with a look that suggests she may pounce at any second. Ears pricked, and she hardly blinks.

Marcy walks in, holding a bundle of clothes for Paula. 'I think these will fit. You look about my size. They're clean.' Without thinking, she heads straight to Meredith, who simply leans over to peer round her and keep watch on Reginald.

'Thanks,' Paula takes the bundle. 'Through there?' She nods at a door behind us.'

'Sure, or upstairs. There's hairbrushes in the bathroom.'

'Any hairbands?'

'Loads,' Marcy smiles. 'I can't walk past one now without picking it up.'

'Oh, I'm the same,' Paula groans. 'They break so easily.'

'Tell me about it,' Marcy says with a roll of her red, bloodshot eyes as her hand drops in an absent-minded way to stroke the soft fur on top of Meredith's head. The dog shows no reaction, a flicker of movement as she looks briefly up at Marcy. A twitch of her tail, but she remains locked on Reginald.

'You don't look infected,' Paula stares with interest at the other woman. 'Your eyes obviously, but ... your hair is in amazing condition ... Can I touch it?'

'Sure,' Marcy steps forward so Paula can reach out.

'Wow, so soft. And your skin ... You look better than me!'

'Oh, I don't know,' Marcy smiles coyly. 'You look great, considering what you've been through.'

'Thanks,' Paula smiles back. 'I mean, you're not pale, or ... your skin looks incredible ... Are you infected?'

'I am,' Marcy nods, 'definitely.'

'Why is it different in you?'

'Me and Blowers are immune now,' Cookey announces, quite clearly wanting Marcy's attention. Can't blame him. I can't take my eyes off her.

Marcy looks at Cookey, then at me with a sharp gaze. 'Is that true?'

'Yep,' Cookey says wistfully, 'me and April could have got married and had babies after all ...'

'Oh, fucking hell,' Blowers gives voice as the rest of us groan in dismay.

'Until Dave chopped her head off.'

'I did not cut her head off.'

'Okay.' Cookey shrugs, then stage-whispers to Marcy, 'He did.'

'Are all of you immune?' Marcy asks with a look round.

'We don't know. Me, Lani, Cookey and Blowers and Meredith, of course ...'

'And I'm not infected to the level of everyone else ... Neither is Reggie ...' she frowns in a gesture which just makes my stomach flip.

'Clothes,' I suddenly feel too naked and exposed, 'we need clothes.'

'Yes,' she says quickly as though snapping free from the same thoughts as me. 'Er ... Reggie, what have we got here?'

'Oh, I do apologise,' he says after a pause. 'Are you addressing me?'

'Yes,' she sighs with the same exasperation I have with Dave sometimes.

'I only ask because my name is Reginald and, of course, not Reggie. Surely, with the influx of people, I assumed there was someone called Reggie standing nearby, wearing only his undergarments.'

'It's painful sometimes. It really is.'

'Try working with this lot,' Paula says.

'In answer to your question,' he says huffily, 'yes, there are some clothes, but none that will be suitable, and none that will fit Clarence. However,' he adds with a flourish, 'during my forages, I have identified a house further down the road that appears to have had a larger built occupant.'

'Clarence, you take the others and find clothes ... Perhaps Reginald can show you where that house is.'

'The house in question is two down on the same ... Oh ...' he trails off with an arched look from Marcy. 'Of course,' he smiles briefly, 'I would be delighted to be your tour guide.'

'Sure?' Clarence asks me quietly as the rest start bustling out.

I nod back. 'Yeah, Paula is here.'

'You keeping Meredith with you?'

'Up to her,' I shrug as the dog sets off to keep her two soft brown eyes fixed on Reginald.

'Mr Howie will be fine,' Marcy says softly.

'Good,' Clarence smiles without humour, 'because I will kill you if he isn't ... Won't be long.'

We remain in the kitchen. Marcy and I. Paula in another room, getting dressed.

'You can't blame him,' I say after a while.

'Oh, not at all,' she replies quickly. 'No offence taken.'

'I mean, you did try and kill me before.'

'Really? From my memory I saved you ... and then saved you again.'

'Yeah, what about the bit in the middle?' We lock eyes with only a few feet between us, and right now, I don't see the red in them. Just her. Just Marcy. Marcy.

'Oh that,' she says sheepishly. 'Yeah,' she bites her bottom lip gently and motions as if to say '*oops*'.

'From my recollection,' she says slowly, 'I wasn't so much trying to kill you as ...'

'As what?'

'Stop it,' she says softly.

'My god, you are actually blushing,' I lean forward to stare at the crimson flush spreading across the golden skin of her cheeks.

'I'm still a woman,' she mutters.

'Are you?'

'Yes, Howie. I am,' she says defiantly, 'very much a woman.'

'I need your help,' I realise with a start that I have been here only minutes, and I'm flirting. 'Maddox turned against us.'

'Maddox?' She shakes her head. 'Who is Maddox?'

'Oh, right, bloody hell ... Didn't we tell you about him?'

'The name rings a bell, but ... er ... council estate? Wasn't he the man in the council estate?'

'That's him. He turned up after we killed all your zombies, and you know about Lani?'

'Lani? You said a minute ago that you are immune ... and Lani ... So from that I gathered she was okay.'

'We found her locked in the toilets ... Where you left her.'

'I see,' she says carefully.

'And she wasn't infected. No red eyes, no nothing ... She's fine. More than fine, in fact. She heals incredibly fast.'

'Heals?'

'We all do. I mean me, Blowers, Cookey, and Lani. Even Meredith. We get busted up in every scrap, bitten, punched, hit, kicked, raked ... You name it. But we heal.'

'The others?'

I nod slowly. 'We don't know for sure, and to be honest, we haven't even had time to discuss it ... but I've noticed Nick is the same, but then he's a good fighter and doesn't get hurt that much. Clarence is Clarence, and as for Dave ...'

'Nothing touches Dave,' she finishes my sentence.

'Exactly. Maddox turned up, and we sort of joined forces. He took over the fort while we went out and got what we needed.'

'Can I come in?'

I twist round to see Paula in the doorway, brushing her still damp hair.

'Course.'

'You look better,' Marcy says with a smile.

She walks in, wearing jeans and a black t-shirt but still barefoot. 'I feel human again,' she smiles, 'and I have two hairbands ... Two hairbands! A bloody luxury. And I hate not wearing a bra,' she scowls.

'Oh, I know,' Marcy says with a shake of her head, 'bloody things bouncing about.'

'Just feels better,' Paula says earnestly, 'you know? Like all back together ...'

'No fun being busty sometimes,' Marcy says.

'Poor lads,' Paula chuckles softly. 'One of my nipples kept poking out ... They didn't know where to look, bless 'em.'

'I saw,' Marcy laughs, 'and them all looking everywhere else ... Still, that's nice that they were decent about it.'

'Oh, they're lovely,' Paula replies. 'I am gagging for a cuppa. Mind if I make one?'

'Sorry,' Marcy turns towards the sideboard and the camping grill attached to a gas bottle.

'I'm getting split ends,' Paula sighs while holding a few strands of hair in front of her face.

'Conditioner upstairs,' Marcy says. 'Help yourself.'

'Sod it, I'd rather have the cuppa.'

I shake my head slowly and marvel at the way of the woman. They chat like women chat. About hair and bras and split ends. They roll eyes and make tutting sounds while moving deftly round each other to get cups and teaspoons. I guess they must be the same age, and I can't help my eyes drifting back to Marcy.

'I'll go find clothes,' I head towards the door. They both mutter goodbyes and resume the conversation about the difference of washing your hair in hot water compared to cold.

Feeling somewhat dejected, I head outside to see the lads walking back, carrying bundles in their arms and shoes hanging from laces.

'Everything okay?' Clarence asks at the sight of me standing outside.

'Talking about split ends,' I motion towards the house with a tilt of my head, 'and hairbands and bras and ...'

'Oh,' Clarence stops and nods slowly, 'so we getting changed here or inside?'

'Here will do,' I shrug and watch as they unceremoniously dump the clothes on the ground for a free-for-all dive into the piles. Jeans are pulled free; tops are held up to see if they will fit. Odd socks, and we press shoes against the soles of our feet. Five minutes, and we're all dressed in a range of dark clothes.

'Nice shirt,' I nod at Clarence tugging on a smart, black dress shirt.

'All I could find,' he says and rolls the sleeves up. 'It'll do.'

'Any smokes?'

'Oh yes,' Nick nods and produces a sealed packet. 'They got a light in there?'

'Gas stove. They're brewing up now.'

'Blowers, you don't wear socks with deck shoes,' Cookey says, staring down at Blowers' ankles.

'Who gives a fuck?'

'You look like a twat.'

'So?'

'They're odd socks ... in jeans ... with deck shoes.'

'And I say it again, so?'

'Fine,' Cookey holds his hand up, showing the palm to Blowers, 'but when the other children laugh at you, don't say you weren't told.'

'Dick,' Blowers says but stares down at his feet.

We head back into the house and the pleasant aroma of coffee filling the room and the sight of Paula and Marcy deep in discussion with much nodding of heads, rolling of eyes, and tutting. Lots of tutting.

'Can I use the stove to light up?' Nick asks with a cigarette already hanging from his mouth.

'Carry on,' Marcy says. 'Coffees on the side. Help yourself. None of them are sugared, and we don't have any milk.'

'Cheers,' Nick bends and holds the end close to the blue flame. Once lit, he hands it over to Blowers and repeats the action with Cookey, then me.

'Christ,' Paula tuts again and opens the back door, 'stand over here, you lot.'

This is too normal. Far too normal. The way the lads interact with Marcy is like she's one of us. Even Reginald bustles about, chatting amiably with Clarence, and I remember how well they got on when we got drunk that night. She smiles warmly at them, passing mugs over and teaspoons so they can put sugar in. She and Paula comment on the clothes now being worn, and both remark how smart Clarence looks in a proper button-up shirt.

'Seen Blowers' shoes?' Cookey says as Blowers rolls his eyes with a groan.

'Why?' Marcy leans round to look down. 'Oh ... oh right ...'

'What?' Blowers says defensively. 'Does it matter?'

'Socks and deck shoes don't go,' she says apologetically.

'Ha! Told you,' Cookey nods in victory.

'Really? I mean fucking really? They'll rub my feet without socks.'

'Couldn't you find normal shoes?' Paula asks.

'No, I bloody couldn't,' Blowers exclaims. 'Fuck off, Cookey.'

'Funny as fuck, mate.'

'And you can fuck off too, Nick.'

'What? You're the one wearing socks with deck shoes.'

'Oh, for ...' Blowers puts his mug and lifts a leg to pull the shoe off. 'Fine ...'

'No, keep them on,' Paula says. 'They're fine, really.'

'No ... too late now. God forbid we don't look right,' he tugs the sock off, which gets launched at Cookey pissing himself against the kitchen side. 'Better?' he asks with both naked feet shoved back in the deck shoes.

'Right,' I announce, 'where were we?'

'Paula has got me up to speed,' Marcy replies.

'Oh,' I say and blink quickly, 'right ... so ...'

'Sorry,' Paula says quickly, 'did you want to tell her?'

'No, no, no, it ... er...doesn't matter. As long as you're up to speed on everything ... I mean ... so you know about the doctors?'

'Yes.'

'Great ... and the, er ... the munitions factory?'

'Yes.'

'Okay, and er ... did Paula mention anything about my, er ...?'

'Yes. She said you flipped out.'

'Right, yes, well, I can see you're fully briefed on the, er ... the current situation at, er ... at hand and ... What the bloody hell are you lot looking at?'

'Nothing, Boss.'

'Sorry, Mr Howie.'

'So we've got to get Lani out?' Marcy asks.

'We?' Clarence asks.

'I say, I am sorry to interrupt the slightly awkward proceedings and the obvious piqued annoyance of Mr Howie, but is this dog okay?'

'She's fine,' Nick says.

'She keeps staring at me.'

'She's probably hungry,' Nick says.

'Hungry?'

'They're teasing you,' Marcy says. 'Just ignore her.'

'Ignore her? Have you seen how big she is?'

'I wasn't annoyed,' I say quickly to another awkward silence in the room. 'Fuck's sake,' I sigh, 'right ... anyway ... Lani, yes, we've got to get her out.'

'Paula said you had a plan.'

'Yes,' I feel a sense of pleasure that at least Paula couldn't tell her *what* the plan was, 'er ...' I freeze and remember what the plan was, which suddenly doesn't seem such a good plan.

'Well, what is it?' Paula asks.

'Um ... Dave said a distraction has to be both visual and audible, but ... if the visual is strong enough, then it will work on its own.'

'Okay,' Marcy prompts me, 'what is it?'

Hesitantly and feeling like an idiot, I outline the plan to a stunned silence and a smirk plastered across the face of Cookey, who I knew would love it.

'You are joking, right?' Paula glares at me.

'Um ... not really?'

'Great plan,' Cookey nods admiringly.

'Fucking awesome plan,' Nick says.

'Best one yet,' Blowers says.

'You are joking, right?' Paula glares round the room. 'Roy? Did you hear this?'

'I did,' he says from the back, 'and er ... yes, yes, it sounds good.'

CHAPTER FORTY-ONE

Voices of teenage boys drift on the warm thermals of air. Voices of boys in the full throws of puberty. Voices that are trying to sound deeper than they really are. The scratchy tones of inner-city accents, clipped, curt, and constantly bordering from passive aggressive to confrontational.

I glance and watch the others all staring through the bottom of the five-bar gate and through gaps in the hedge. The beach is just across the road. Close enough for them to hear if one of us so much as farts or coughs.

Nick keeps Meredith close to him, and she seems to sense there is action afoot as she stays quietly by his side, but her ears are pricked, and her eyes are constantly flicking side to side as the snatches of conversation come at us.

The idea suddenly seems full of folly. Ridiculous and doomed to fail. My initial instinct was strong, but it's waning fast, and a part of me wants to rush back to stop them proceeding.

Too late, and we all tense as the sound of laughter drifts over from the far side of the bay.

'You hear that?' a teenage voice asks the others, and I

watch as first boy gets to his feet and stares about. He turns to look and scans the area within which we lie waiting, but he completes the turn. 'Wassat?' He takes a step away from the others at the next sound of laughing.

'Dunno, someone pissin' about, innit?' another boy says, lumbering to his feet with the oversized weapon hanging from a strap across his back.

'You look ... so ... so ... silly!' Paula's voice, shrill and excited, yet slurred. She bursts out laughing with a sound that has every youth on the beach getting to his feet. 'It's nighttime!'

'I know,' Marcy says back, slurred and full of righteous dignity, 'but I wanna look good.'

'For who?' Paula laughs. 'They've ...' she hiccups, and they both laugh, 'oops ... I mean for who? No ... no men now.'

It sounds too fake, too forced. Contrived and weird. Paula acting drunk and giggly. Marcy being drunk and mock serious. The lads on the beach glance at each other but remain silent as they bring weapons up and make ready. The crew chief, a bigger boy, waves his hand at them to stay still and quiet.

'GONE!' Marcy shouts so loud it makes everyone jump–not just me, but the others with me, and every lad on the beach too. 'ALL GONE.'

'Sssshhhhh,' Paula giggles.

'Don't care,' Marcy says petulantly, 'fuck 'em ...'

'You wish!'

They both cackle, and I cringe at the awful noise. I cast a glance at Clarence, who shakes his head in resignation. It won't work.

'Too much,' he whispers softly. 'They'll never buy it.'

I shrug and tense my body, ready to leap up.

'Nice idea,' Roy says from the other side.

Fuck it. Stupid. Bloody stupid, and I've ruined any element of surprise.

'Call it off,' Clarence urges.

'No.'

We all twist to stare at Dave who doesn't turn or take his eyes from the lads on the beach. 'Wait.'

Dave is, without doubt, the most amazing human being I have ever met. But to rely on his inability to hear a contrived and obviously forced, pretend drunken play-act is too great a risk.

I go to speak as everyone makes ready to lift and run forward, but he simply holds one hand up and looks down the line at me. 'Wait,' he says, 'wait for the visual.'

Jaws clenched, eyes wide, and hearts hammering, we force ourselves to hold position despite every instinct urging us to react.

The drunken laughter gets closer. Slurred female voices and suddenly the visual element of the surprise comes into view. Executed to perfection, and a perfect spot chosen as they both stumble into a patch of beach bathed in the bright light of the moon.

'Holy fuck,' someone says. I don't know who. It might have been me. The sight renders my ability to focus on anything else completely redundant.

Paula and Marcy. Both of them holding a wine bottle that they keep lifting to their mouths. Both of them dressed in skintight, flimsy dresses. Hair immaculate. Make up perfect. Toned, fresh. Heaving cleavages, legs, and thighs that seem to go on for ever and ever. Clearly drunk as they stagger and collide into each other. Giggling, stopping to swig, laughing, and spraying the wine out when they do.

Not girls but women. Real women with figures to make

a sculptor weep. Marcy in apt black, and Paula in white. The contrast between them is incredible, and with the moonlight just so and the setting of the beach just so, they capture every eye and hold every head transfixed.

'Where is it?' Marcy spins round dramatically.

'What?' Paula slurs.

'Fort ... the bloody fort,' Marcy turns round in a slow circle. 'This famous fort full of men ... Where ... I mean ... can't see it ... oops,' she crashes into Paula, and they go down in a heap of bare legs and tight dresses.

We crane our heads up, completely disregarding the lads on the beach but desperate to see the two women sprawling out.

Cackling, laughing, and giggling, they paw and shove playfully at each other and end up both crashing backwards with legs in the air.

'Ah ... comfy,' Paula says as she wriggles into the soft sand.

'Come on.' Marcy gets onto her hands and knees and grabs the neck of the wine bottle, 'Get up.' She crawls towards Paula, knowing full well her cleavage is presented perfectly to the crew staring with open mouths. 'Come on, you ...' she tugs playfully at Paula's arm, 'Gotta get up ... fort the find ... I mean ...'

'Fort the find?' Paula bursts out laughing. 'You're soooo drunk.'

'So are you.'

'Am not.'

'Are so.'

'Did you call me an arsehole?'

'What? I said are so ... Get up.'

'Staying here,' Paula sighs. 'It's soft and warm.' She

pulls Marcy down with another giggle as Marcy sprawls out in a tangle of limbs.

'S'warm,' Marcy shuffles over until her head rests on Paula's chest. 'Men are right.'

'About what?'

'Boobs,' Marcy sighs, 'they are like cushions.' She wriggles her head into Paula's chest. 'I'm so drunk!'

'Me too,' Paula giggles again. 'I ... I don't think the fort place is here ...'

'No,' Marcy sighs drunkenly. 'I might sleep now.'

'No, no, no,' Paula bucks her off. 'I'm staying here to get eaten.'

'You wish,' Marcy laughs and flops over before starting to clamber unsteadily to her feet. 'Oh shit,' she says as her sunglasses drop onto the sand, 'my glasses.'

'Daft cow,' Paula reels back as she gets to her feet. 'It's night ...'

'They're Prada!' Marcy wails. Plucking them off the sand, she makes a meal of getting them back onto her face.

Paula turns and goes to move off, then stops, and sways on the spot. She blinks and shakes her head before staring again in a perfect act of trying to focus.

'Here,' she says suspiciously.

'What?' Marcy gets to her feet and starts tugging her dress as though to get it back in order.

'Look,' Paula says dreamily, 's'men ...'

'S'what?'

'S'men.'

'S'what's men?'

'Here.'

Marcy frowns, tugging her dress down too much as her cleavage threatens to spill out. She looks up and over at the crew. 'Oh ...'

'S'men.'

'Is,' Marcy sways, 'men.'

'Are you men?' Paula asks with a swaying arm pointing at the crew. 'Are they men?' She looks over at Marcy.

'What the fuck?' the crew chief says dumbly.

'Oh ... my ... god ...' Marcy claps her hands excitedly.

'Hello,' Paula makes an effort to stand up straight and walks falteringly towards the crew chief. 'Hello, man? I'm woman ...'

Marcy bursts out laughing and staggers forward. 'You can't say that!'

'Sorry,' Paula slurs, 'we had ... we had a glass of wine.'

'Ooh ...' Marcy sashays past the chief staring at Paula and heads deeper into the gaggle of youths. 'You've all got such big guns ... ' Hips swinging and cleavage bulging.

'We,' Paula tries to say politely, 'are trying to find the fort. May you know where this place may be, young sir? Do you? Do you know?'

'S'here, innit?' the older lad stammers.

'But where?' Paula exclaims. 'Where is this fort?'

'Oh ... like ... over there. Gotta get a boat, you get me?'

'I'd like to get you,' Paula giggles. 'Is there a fee for crossing?'

'Fee?'

'Do you ... say ... need payment to get over there?'

'I know' Marcy says quickly, 'we can swim there.'

'Swim?' Paula goes to walk past the lad but bumps into him slowly. 'Oh, I'm so sorry,' she beams. 'Oh, you're big,' she blinks and stays close for a second.

'I know,' Marcy repeats, 'we can swim there.'

'You just said that,' Paula turns and heads down the beach, towards Marcy.

'Did I?' Marcy frowns and locks eyes on a young lad. 'Did I really?'

The lad nods quickly and goes to say something high-pitched and inaudible. He clears his throat as Marcy reaches out to stroke his face. 'You're a cutie.'

'Can't,' Paula announces, 'got no swim suit.'

'Pah!' Marcy says. 'Don't need our costumes ... Is the water warm?' she asks the boy closest to her.

'Think so,' he nods quickly, 'like, really warm.'

'S'really warm,' another boy says.

'Oh,' Marcy turns slowly, 'in that case ... would you mind?' She presents her back to the same boy. 'Undo me.'

'Eh?'

'My zip ... I can't reach it.'

The boy blinks and looks at his mates, who all nod, urging him on. He swings the gun round onto his back and reaches up to pull the zip down.

'Why thank you,' Marcy purrs and shifts just enough for the dress to slip down to her ankles. In bra and knickers, she reaches down, picks the garment up, and hands it to the boy. 'Would you hold it for me? It's Versace.'

Leaving the boy holding the dress, she steps towards the sea. 'Hmmm.' She stops and looks back. 'Are you coming now?' she asks Paula.

'Looks that way,' Paula says in a tone slightly less drunk now. She slips her own dress off and tugs it down to reveal a slender body dressed in bra and knickers.

'How about now?' Marcy asks with a grin round at the boys. 'Look at you ...' She laughs. 'Catching flies.'

Her eyes fleetingly look past the boys and straight to us, and I realise not one of us has moved or made any effort to do anything other than stare in wonder.

A huge hand clamps on my wrist. 'Just a second,' Clarence whispers but doesn't look at me.

'You lucky bastard, Roy,' Cookey groans softly.

'Yeah,' Roy sighs dreamily.

'How about now?' Marcy asks again. 'I think we're being stared at,' she says to Paula.

'Enjoy the show, boys,' Paula smiles.

'Oh fuck, they mean us,' I realise guiltily. 'Come on.'

'Now?' Cookey whispers. 'Really?'

'Five more minutes,' Blowers says.

'Now,' I nod frantically.

'Let them get in the water,' Cookey pleads.

'Now, Cookey.'

We start snaking forward, pushing through whatever gaps we can find. The blood thunders through my ears, blotting out the soft conversations on the beach ahead of us. From my position, I can see Marcy glancing at the figures moving across the road. She suddenly grins and says something to keep the attention on her and Paula.

Paula rallies, and they both start inviting the lads to join them for a swim. Beckoning and teasing and the whole lot of teenage boys take a step towards the women.

On the tarmac, on our bellies, and it takes forever to close that gap down. No weapons. No guns, nothing. Dave has more than likely pilfered a knife or two from the kitchen.

Halfway across, and I hear a sudden commotion and look down to see Nick struggling to stay low while stopping the dog from bounding ahead. She knows Paula is there and is clearly desperate to break free. She wriggles and writhes, yanking her head back from Nick's grip on the thick fur of her neck.

I shoot a glance down and lock eyes briefly with Marcy.

She gives an almost imperceptible nod and suddenly reaches behind, towards the clasp on her bra.

'It's stuck!' She laughs.

'Topless?' Paula asks with a laugh. 'Are we going topless?'

'I think so.' Marcy grins at Paula. 'Give these nice young men a treat.'

Meredith whines, Nick grips her harder, but she's too big and too strong. She knows Paula. She knows Marcy, and she doesn't understand why she can't go to them, and staying quiet and hiding is clearly not her way of doing things.

We start to rise, all of us. Meredith is giving us away, and we need to close that gap. Paula glances to the boys staring at her, then quickly beyond to us and what must be the clear view of Nick and now Blowers struggling to contain Meredith.

'A treat.' Paula nods. 'Why not?' She reaches behind, unclasps her bra, and pulls it free in an act of sacrifice to keep all eyes on her and Marcy.

None of us notice, and if we do, we don't pay any attention as we do our best to get across the road and onto the sand. Meredith whines again, agitated and getting annoyed at being restrained.

Marcy unclasps her bra and suddenly throws it into the air with a whoop. Both of them topless, and I notice the young lads all take another step forward. The sight of naked bodies and boobs is too much for them. A hungry lust and a pack desire to take what they want.

'Take your knickers off,' one youth, bolder than the others, breaks the silence with the sudden order.

'Boys!' Marcy says as though shocked.

'Off!' The lad moves towards them. 'Get 'em off ...'

'Now, now,' Paula says jokingly.

'Shut your mouth, bitch,' the boy speaks without humour and lunges towards Paula as all hell breaks loose.

I nod at Nick and Blowers, and they release their grip on Meredith who bursts away and streaks towards Paula.

We start running silently onto the soft sand as the teenage boy grabs Paula by the arm and reaches out with his other hand at her boobs. She reacts from instinct and slams a fist into his nose. He reels back as the others all surge forward, shouting loudly.

Both the women move back towards the sea as the crew chief runs ahead towards Paula as he brings his weapon round to the front.

'Fuckin' stay there,' he shouts and lifts the weapon to take aim a split second before being ripped from his feet as Meredith slams into him from behind.

Full speed sprinting, and we push as fast as we can. Dave and Roy faster than us as, they soar ahead.

The crew chief is killed instantly as Meredith rips his throat out. A tearing sound, and she bounds away, twisting to identify the next target.

Guns are pulled forward and fumbled as panic sweeps the lads. Shouts and chaos as Meredith sinks her teeth into the already bleeding face of the one Paula hit. He goes crashing down from the weight of the animal, and her gnashing teeth savaging his head.

Dave is there. Into the first one at the back, and he simply grabs the first head, snaps the neck, and moves off. Roy plunders through them. Punching and shoving in desperation to keep them wild and unfocussed.

A shot goes off, and the rest of us sweep into the fray. Punching, kicking, and moving fast. Clarence hits hard, knocking teenage boys out cold. The crew panic, screaming with shouts and yells of pain. Some try and fight back, but we've already won. Marcy and Paula don't hesitate but dive in.

'**STOP OR YOU WILL DIE,'** Dave's voice roars into the night and brings the fight to a sudden end. An assault rifle in his hands, and he holds it straight and true.

'GUNS DOWN,' I give the order to the crew and watch as those still standing drop their weapons.

'Get dressed,' I call over to Marcy and Paula while snatching an assault rifle up off the ground. 'If any of you move, we will kill you.'

Several are dead. Either from Meredith shredding them or having their necks snapped by Dave. One lies with his head over at an unnatural angle from the single almighty punch delivered by Clarence. I step in front of the body to shield it from the big man and the inevitable attack of remorse he'll suffer.

'Did you have a nice time?' Paula seethes with anger while she holds the dress in front of her naked body.

'Nice time?' I ask, confused at her meaning.

'How bloody long does it take to cross a road?'

'Sorry.' I shrug with a pang of guilt, knowing we all got caught up in the view.

'Where's Reggie?' Marcy asks with a pained look round at the dead bodies and the mangled remains of the ones Meredith killed.

'Back there probably.' I motion back across the road. 'Was he the crew chief?' I ask the group of lads staring dumbstruck at me. 'Him?' I nod towards the body seeping dark blood onto the sand. 'Was he the crew chief?'

A few nods and murmurs of affirmation as they take in their situation.

'Radio?' I ask and watch as they look to the dead crew chief and the radio fixed to his belt. I head over and pick it up. A squat, black thing with a stubby antenna. 'I'm going to ask a question now, and if anyone lies to me, I will set that bloody dog on the lot of you. Are we clear? Good. Does Maddox know we got out?'

Head shakes, too many at once for them to be lying.

'What was the last transmission from him?' They stay quiet, too afraid to speak.

'You.' I point to the closest one. 'What was the last transmission?'

'The what?'

'Transmission. What was the last thing Maddox said on the radio?'

'Nuffin, just ... just said we had to stay awake, innit? Swear down, that's wot he said.'

'How long ago was that?'

'Er ...'

'Few hours,' another one answers.

I glance at Clarence, who shrugs and shakes his head as though saying he doesn't know.

'What we doing with this lot?' he asks. 'Can't leave them here.'

'I'm thinking,' I reply slowly.

'There's a boat yard back there.' Marcy walks over, doing the same as Paula and holding her dress to cover her body. 'It's secure.'

'Secure enough for this lot?'

'Boat yards have rope,' Nick calls out. 'We can tie them up.'

'Blowers, you, Nick, and Cookey take this lot ... take the dog with you in case any of them try and run.'

'Reggie,' Marcy calls out, 'you can come down now.'

'Are you decent?' his voice replies immediately. 'My eyes have been closed since you ...'

'Yes ... ' Marcy sighs. 'Bring the clothes.'

He pops up from behind the hedge and carefully opens the gate before walking down with a bundle of clothes under each arm. 'Is it safe?'

'Yes,' I call over.

'I say that was a nerve-shredding display of ... well, I don't know what to call it.' He blusters pointedly. 'Really, I was terrified you'd be caught out, but I must say I have not seen a performance quite like it before.'

'Never been to a strip club, then?' Nick asks politely.

'I have not!' Reginald says with a huff. 'Never in my life, and nor would I. Demeaning and thoroughly inappropriate places of ...'

'Yes, yes,' Marcy cuts him off. 'Where can we get changed?'

'Saxon?' I reply. Paula shoots a look of thunder at each and every one of us before storming off with Marcy in her wake.

'Worked, though.' Marcy smiles wryly at me as she draws level. 'Shame.' She stops and glances back at the dead bodies.

'No way round it,' I reply quietly.

'I know, but they're so young.' She winces. 'Just boys.'

The remaining crew members are shepherded past, with the three lads keeping a close eye on them.

'Where is it?' Blowers asks.

'Just before the houses,' Marcy replies. 'You can't miss it. The door is only pushed closed.'

'Cheers, Marcy.' He nods as they walk past, and the simple interaction isn't lost on me. So normal, like he's talking to any member of our team.

'Boys, yes,' I say once they're out of earshot, 'but they were coming after you and Paula.'

'You know,' she lowers her voice and slips the sunglasses off, 'for a second I was actually scared ...'

'I'm not surprised.'

'The looks on their faces ...' She shudders. 'You couldn't see, but they just changed, in an instant.'

We lapse into silence while I feel like a complete prick for watching the way I did. The way we all did. Men watching women. Men watching women get undressed.

'Sorry.'

'What for?'

'I was watching,' I admit darkly.

She snorts humourlessly. 'You're a man.'

'Yeah, but ...'

'No buts, Howie. And anyway ...' She flashes me a quick smile. 'I would have watched you.'

'Yeah.' I feel the blush creeping up my face as I smile. 'You better get dressed.'

'Hmm, suppose so.' And she's off, walking towards the Saxon, and I have to use every ounce of strength not to turn round and look. Control. Have control. I am not an animal. I am an adult with control. I will not look. She is only wearing knickers and walking away. I will not look.

'You alright?' Clarence asks me with a strange look.

'Fine.' I cough. 'You got a smoke?'

'I don't smoke, Boss. Nick smokes. I'm Clarence.'

CHAPTER FORTY-TWO

'Mo Mo.'

Mohammed looks across the crowd, trying to identify the speaker.

'Mo Mo.'

Directional now. The sound uttered by a mouth, and his ears pinpoint the area while his eyes scan the sullen faces until he finds one looking up expectantly.

'What?' He inclines his head with a sharp gesture at Carl.

'My knees hurt,' Carl says. 'Can I move, bro?'

'On your arse but keep your hands on your head.'

'Cheers, bro.'

'Mine hurt too.'

'And mine. Can I move?'

'Mo Mo, what's gonna happen?'

'You number one now, Mo Mo?'

Mo Mo stares dispassionately at the sea of faces as the verbal flood gates open. Hours of silence with not a sound uttered, but the feeling of instant danger has waned, and they know Mo Mo and Jagger. The two lads are part of their group, their crews. They were from the compound run by the Bossman, and yeah, they're up there now, holding weapons, but it's still Mo Mo and Jagger.

The older crew chiefs and Lenski can see the difference in the two lads. The way they move and watch, always watching, always scanning. The way they stand with legs planted apart, and the way they hold their weapons, emulating Blowers, Nick, Cookey, Clarence, and their new team.

They can detect the subtle changes in the way they speak too. The dropping of the slang expressions as they subconsciously adapt to fit in with the new team–and more, they see the battle-hardened expressions from two lads who have fought overwhelming odds, given death, yet have walked away. Hard expressions on their faces, but different from the hard expressions of the youths from the compound. Less sullen. Less resentful. Older.

'Be quiet,' Jagger says from a few metres away.

'Why you on their side?'

'Yous not with us now, Jagger?'

'No,' the reply is given instantly and in a hard tone that stops the youths in their tracks. Silence follows. Drawn out and only broken by the nightmare-driven wail of someone crying out in their sleep.

'Can I be on your crew?' a small voice speaks out, and again the floodgates open as the voices sweep across the fort with pledges of loyalty to the new gang.

'Enough!' Lani strides from the armoury, bare foot and dressed in simple jeans and a t-shirt. 'They might not kill you, but I will ... I don't want to hear another sound.'

In truth, Lani knows she couldn't shoot anyone in cold blood now. The anger has subsided enough for rational thought to seep back in. Regret, guilt, and the cold hand of remorse grips her stomach at the death she has already inflicted. It was necessary at the time, but that time has passed, and now she can see them for what they are–children. Young children as frightened and desperate as everyone else but without the knowledge and experience of life to guide them.

What the hell do they do with them? She glances down to the main gate and the hopeful prospect that Howie will come bursting through and be able to sort this out. He'll know what to do. He always knows what to do.

A frown crosses her face, a scowl at the thought that he'll have gone to Marcy. The idea that the team would have got caught in the tunnel doesn't cross her mind. The energy between them, the power they radiate, the effervescence of keeping each other alive.

They will have to deal with the crew on the beach, get the boats, then get across. But they'll also be thinking that Maddox is still in control, so they'll be doing everything covertly, whereas they could just stroll right in now.

'Radio,' she says quickly. 'Who has a radio?'

'Radio?' Mo Mo asks. 'What for?'

'Howie will go through the crew on the beach ... If we can contact him ... Actually, no, bad idea. If we tip the crew off, they'll be even more alert.'

'Nice idea, though,' Jagger says, 'but they'd get suspicious as fuck if it weren't Maddox or Darius talking.'

'Yeah.' Lani nods and slips back into thoughtful silence and the problem of what to do with a big bunch of kids that know how to use guns.

'Lani? Maddox?'

'Who's that?' Mo Mo turns towards the far end of the fort, rifle raised as Lani peers into the darkness and the figure tentatively moving towards them.

'Don't know,' she says quietly. 'WHO IS THAT?'

'Doctor Carlton ... Is that Lani?'

'It is ... Come forward but keep your hands in sight and away from your body.'

'You won't shoot me, will you?'

'I have no intention of shooting anyone if they follow the instructions given,' Lani states with a glare at the youths and Lenski.

Anne Carlton walks slowly, hands held out from her sides, dressed in a white lab coat that serves as a visual aid as to her position of medical doctor and non-combatant.

'Christ.' She stares at the youths all seated with hands interlocked on their heads and the bodies lying still within the pools of blood. 'What happened?'

'You know what happened,' Lani replies in a tone that doesn't encourage stupid questions. 'I was tasered and sedated against my will while Howie and the others were locked in their rooms after–'

'I was against it,' Anne says quickly, 'firmly against it.'

'Done now.' Lani shrugs and scans the crowd. 'I hurt the other two doctors. They okay?'

'Two broken noses, and the young lad is a bit concussed ... They'll live.'

'I'm sorry,' Lani says without a hint of apology in her voice.

'So am I.' Anne looks round again and sighs deeply. 'Where's Howie now?'

'Gone.'

'Gone? Gone where?'

'They got out,' Lani says simply, not wanting to reveal the exact details in front of everyone else. 'They'll be back.'

'Maddox? Darius? Where are they?'

'I killed Darius,' Lani says with a defiant look at the

doctor. 'Maddox is lying over there somewhere in his own shit and piss.'

'What?' Anne says, hardly believing the turn of events.

'I shot Darius,' Lani replies, 'and some others ... Maddox was tasered ... about eight times until he shit himself and passed out.'

'Jesus, Lani.'

'Jesus my backside,' Lani snaps. 'I didn't see that reaction when he tasered me or when you stuck the needle in–'

'I did not sedate you. I refused to have a part in it. Where is he?'

'Maddox? Over there, towards the back.'

'Can I check him, please?'

'Go for your life but do nothing without saying so first ...'

'I understand.' Anne nods quickly while threading through the young people. She spots the prone form of Maddox and, seconds later, detects the smell of faeces. She drops down, pressing a hand gently to the side of his neck. 'He's alive,' she calls out.

'He was only tasered,' Lani replies.

'Enough times to kill him.'

'He tasered me first, and be thankful I didn't shoot him ... which is still an option.'

'An option? To execute someone?'

'The same options he was discussing with us.'

'Which makes you as bad as he ... When does it end?'

'It ends when bad people stop being pricks ... If I hadn't of taken action, he would have killed Howie. Or, he would have considered killing them.'

'They're gone,' Anne says hotly. 'Howie is gone and therefore the risk.'

'Maddox didn't know he'd gone, or if he did, then he

only just found out. Either way, I'm not risking the lives of the people who gained this fort for anyone.'

'You know,' Anne says firmly, 'there is always the existing possibility that you *are* infected.'

'I probably am,' Lani replies quickly, 'and I turned, but I came back. Cookey was bitten right in front of us, and he didn't turn. Do you know how Howie found out he was immune?' She doesn't wait for the reply but pushes on, 'He had a human heart pushed in his mouth. A still beating, infected human heart ... during a fight that we went back to in order to save all of these people.'

'There has been too much death here.' Anne shakes her head sadly. 'It has to end.'

'What do we do now, then?' Lani asks. 'Give me the solution.'

'Now?'

'With this lot?' Lani motions at the youths with the point of her rifle. 'What do we do with them? We can't just let them go, but they can't stay where they are.'

'Let them go,' Anne says with a shrug. 'You've got their weapons ...'

'Three of us against a group this size? Still loyal to Maddox and Lenski? No way.'

Voices break out pledging loyalty to Howie, Mo Mo, and everyone else besides Maddox. Other voices argue defiantly, telling the turncoats to shut up.

'ENOUGH,' Lani shouts. 'See what I mean? We let them in and now look ... We've got a shit load of bloody kids to worry about, and what's more–they're kids that know how to use guns and kill people.'

Anne falters and looks round with desperation as the realisation of the situation unfolds in front of her eyes. She can see the dire consequences of what could happen if these children were just let go. Their propensity for violence will provoke them into an act of retribution, which will result in more deaths, more bloodshed. But to leave them here, sitting quietly, with their thin arms raised up like prisoners of war. That isn't right either.

'They need food and water,' Anne says. 'Leaving them like this is unacceptable.'

'That's fine, but they eat and drink where they are until Howie comes back.'

'Will he come back?' Anne asks. 'How can you be so sure?'

'Because there is no way on the face of this planet that Howie–or any of my team, for that matter–would leave someone behind. More than that,' Lani speaks low but clear as she takes a step towards Anne as though to emphasise her point, 'even if Howie died ... if they all died, bar one ... that one remaining would come back or die trying ... I'd do it. Nick would do it. Cookey and the rest ... and that,' she snaps the word out with a glare at the children around her, 'is loyalty. You know your mates will come back because that's what you'd do for them. You fight for them. You'd die for them. You give everything you are and know they give it back. It isn't about wearing black clothes and looking hard holding a gun. You do it without guns. Without weapons, and you do it until your hands are bloody and your legs can't take another step. All of you look at Mo Mo and Jagger. Go on ... look.' She paces through the crowd as they turn from looking at her to take in the solid forms holding steady at the front. 'See them? See the way they stand? Without doubt. Without question. You do the right thing for the right reasons, and you know what? If I started shooting you all now, one by one, what do you think they would do?'

She pauses, letting the words sink in. 'Mo Mo, what would you do?'

'If you started shooting this lot, one by one, without a reason?'

'Yep.'

'I'd shoot you ... and if I did it, Jagger would shoot me, you get me?' He looks down at the faces.

'You do the right thing for the right reasons,' Lani repeats. 'Mo Mo and Jagger didn't take up their guns because I was in control, and they wanted to pick the winning side. They could have both shot me by now and taken over. They do it because we have a way of doing things.'

'The right thing for the right reasons,' a young girl speaks out, no more than thirteen, and the braces on her teeth glint in the orange light of the lanterns. For a second, Lani stops and stares down, wondering who will know when to take the braces off and having a vision of the girl wearing them for the rest of her life.

'Yes,' Lani says with a tone made softer by the sadness of life and the knowledge that everything there was before is rapidly disappearing, 'the right thing ... for the right reasons.'

She trails off with a lingering look at the main gates and wishing the team were here right now.

CHAPTER FORTY-THREE

'That's a bit shit, then,' I say heavily as we stare out at the almost perfectly flat water between us and the fort.

'A flaw in an otherwise cunningly-perfect plan,' Cookey says. 'We subdued the bad guys, got the guns, and saved the girls, and now ...'

'Pardon?' Paula turns to fix a steady on him.

'Saved the girls,' Cookey repeats, 'you and Marcy.'

'Saved us? You were gawping at us, more like.'

'Gawping? It's gawking, isn't it?' Nick asks.

'Definitely gawping,' Cookey replies.

'Sure? I always thought it was gawking.'

'Gawking isn't even a word,' Blowers says.

'Yeah, it is. It's ... like ... when you gawk.'

'Gawk? You mean gawp ... with a P.'

'I don't need a pee.' Cookey laughs.

'Paula,' Nick says, 'is it gawp or gawk?'

'Both.'

We all turn to stare down the long line at the edge of the sea at the dapper little man, who turns and smiles happily.

'Eh?' Cookey asks.

'The words mean the same thing, which is to stare rudely. Gawp *and* gawk.'

'So I was right.' Nick nods firmly.

'And I was,' Cookey says.

'We are gawping now, *and* we are gawking ...' Reginald turns back to the sea. 'We are gawping and gawking at the wide expanse of water that is devoid of a suitable vessel.'

'What did he say?' Cookey asks.

'He said we don't have any boats,' Marcy says and looks at me, 'which, as you say, is a bit shit.'

'Bit shit,' I nod.

'Big shit,' Clarence mutters.

'Nah, just a bit shit,' I say.

'No boats.' He motions ahead. 'That's more than a bit shit.'

'Shall we radio Maddox and ask to send some over?' I ask lightly. 'Who can do the best street voice?'

'Swear down, brother,' Roy suddenly says in a perfect clipped tone of a BBC newsreader, 'gis us some boats, innit? Do you get me?'

Chuckles of laughter more at the unexpected outburst than the awful accent.

'Roy can do it,' Cookey says.

'Yo, Mads,' Nick says, 'wes got some people here ... You get me? Like ... you know? Like ... boats, innit?'

'Nah,' Cookey says, 'Mads, word up, mofo. Send thems boats over so's we can get some schnizzle on our nizzles.'

'What the fuck?' Blowers snorts.

'Ere, Mads,' Marcy goes next with near perfect execution of a teenage boy, 'wassup? We needs the boats, innit?'

'Oh perfect.' Cookey laughs in delight. 'Do it ... Oh, you gotta do it.'

'No,' she smiles coyly, 'he'd recognise the voice … or rather not recognise the voice.'

'Oh, do it,' Cookey urges, 'go on … Oh, you got to.'

'Was bloody good,' Blowers nods.

'Where on earth did you learn that?' Paula asks.

'God knows,' Marcy laughs.

'Might work,' I say and turn round to stare at the Saxon, 'if we had some background noise …'

'What if he asks who it is?' Marcy asks with a laugh.

'Bollocks, did we get any names?' I ask the group who all shake heads and shrug.

'Pretend it's breaking up,' Nick suggests. 'We'll make some radio cackling noises.'

'No way!' Marcy shakes her head. 'You're seriously thinking of asking them to send the boats over?'

'Easiest way.' I shrug. 'No other boats round here, and we ain't swimming that far.'

'Probably get sucked down into that tunnel too,' Cookey says. 'What?' he asks when everyone looks at him. 'Might happen.'

'Well,' Paula says with a grim smile, 'the last plan was utterly shit, but it worked, so why not?'

'Try it again,' I urge Marcy with a smile.

'I can't.' She laughs. 'I'm on the spot now.'

'Go Marcy … Go Marcy,' Cookey chants.

'Ere, Mads,' she squawks, 'gis the boats, innit? Got survivors 'ere.'

'Perfect,' I say with a grin, 'we'll give it a go.'

'Howie!' Marcy shakes her head, laughing. 'No … seriously, no …'

'Decision made. Who's got the radio?'

'You have, Mr Howie.'

'Thanks, Dave ... Right ... Nick, get the Saxon fired up, and we'll get Marcy next to the engine so it's noisy.'

'What if he looks over?' Roy asks. 'We'll have to make it look like we've got them sat in the back.'

'We'll do it,' Cookey says. 'We'll stand at the back, facing in. He'll never see details from that far.'

'Clarence will have to go out of sight,' Paula says, 'and give Reginald a gun.'

'Me? A firearm? Good heavens, no.'

'You're small,' she says apologetically. 'No offence, but you'll look right from a distance.'

'Here,' Clarence pops his magazine out before handing the weapon to Reginald.

'Oh my, really? Gosh, that's heavy. I really don't think I match the type to be holding a firearm.'

The scene is set quickly. Reginald, Dave, and the lads at the back of the Saxon, with the lads giving a nice slouch to reduce their height. Roy and Clarence, both taller and larger built, get into the Saxon while I tuck myself up next to Marcy holding the radio like it's a bomb about to go off.

'This won't work.'

'It will,' I urge her. 'Just keep your head close to the engine so the noise carries. You ready?'

'Now?' she asks, aghast at the rush.

'Yes, now ... go on ... press the button on the side and ...'

'I know how to use it.'

'... Go on then.'

'Oh, this is ...' she shoots me a dark look, which makes me notice her red eyes for the first time in ages. Clearing her throat, she leans forward towards the radio, then stops, shakes her head, grins, and sighs audibly. '*Ere, Mads, you there, bro?*'

'Bruv, they call each other bruv, not bro.'

'Cookey said bro,' she hisses at me. '*Mads, bruv ... You there ...? Wes need a boat, innit?*'

'Oh, perfect, fucking perfect,' I say with a nod of admiration. We wait, staring at the handset as the seconds tick by.

'Try again.'

'*Ere, Mads, bruv. You 'earing me? Wes need boats, innit.*'

Another pause while we wait, but the radio remains silent.

'Is it working?' she asks me.

'Should be. Yeah, the green light is on ...'

'*Mads, Darius ... Wes need boats 'ere ... You 'earing me or wot?*'

I suppress a snigger at the awful accent, but the constant thudding of the big diesel engine blots the worst of it out. Still no response.

'*... Up ... who ...*' The radio crackles to life, but the words are distorted and broken.

'*Mads, it's me, innit? Wes need boats, bruv,*' Marcy drops her voice out every few syllables to intentionally break the transmission.

'*...S'up? Innit ... in ...*'

'*Mads, I ain't getting ya. Boats! Wes need boats, Mads.*'

'*... Now ... ues ... wait ...*'

'What's he saying?' I lean closer to the crackling come-back on the handset.

'Can't tell.' She moves an inch or so closer. 'Something about wait? Waiting?'

'*... On ... Darius ... down ... busy ...*'

'Darius? Something down? I heard busy, though,' she whispers.

'Me too,' I glance up into her face, which is about two inches from mine, the moon casting a glow on her skin that catches the breath in my throat. She blinks sudden and widens her eyes as though just as surprised at the close proximity. She speaks, says something, and her lips move, and sounds come out, but I can't tell what they are. Transfixed by her mouth and the flash of white teeth, the plump lips and the way they move to form the words.

'Fuck,' I shake my head to clear the fog.

'Focus, Howie.' She tuts with a smile. 'Your girlfriend, remember?'

'Yes!' I snap more to myself than at her. 'What the fuck is going on?'

'We're trying to get a boat to get to the fort so ...'

'No, between us,' I whisper quickly.

She stares back with an almost imperceptible shrug. 'I don't know.'

'I passed out,' the words tumble from my mouth without control. 'I had these dreams ...'

She locks eyes, like Meredith staring at Reginald, unblinking and focussed. 'Go on.'

'Some old man in a tube station, and ... then I saw all of them ... in the munitions factory, and ... then I was in this street with a horde all stood in perfect rows ...'

'And you attacked them,' she blurts, 'to get to me.'

I nod, the breath trapped in my throat.

'And we spoke,' she continues in a rush of warm air against my cheek. 'You didn't want to go back but ...'

'You told me ...' I swallow and blink hard. 'You said ...'

'One would be bitten, and I said Lani was at the rear, holding them back. She was on her own ... Howie, how did I know that?'

'You said something else. Do you remember?'

She nods, too pained or scared to speak, too worried about the consequences of admitting we shared a vision.

'About Lani, you said ...'

'Lani was torn.'

'Fuck, Marcy.'

'And we kissed,' she says suddenly, 'right before I woke up.'

'Did you slap me?'

'Slap you? No, I did not.'

'Oh, must have been Dave. then.'

'Dave slapped you?'

'Someone slapped me. I thought it was you, but apparently not.'

'I don't think I slapped you.' She thinks for a second. 'I kissed you, but no ... no, I don't remember slapping you.'

'Bloody hurt,' I say earnestly.

'Aw, did the bad man slap you?'

'Don't take the piss. It really hurt.'

'Be thankful it wasn't me.'

'I can't imagine you'd slap harder than Dave, Marcy.'

'Want to test it?'

'You want to slap me?'

'Actually, yes. Yes, I do.'

'Why?'

'For being such an annoying prick.'

'Eh? That's a bit harsh.'

'Like my life hasn't been turned upside down since meeting you.'

'Do what? Darren did that. Darren? Remember him? He was your boyfriend who tried to kill us ...'

'That was then.' She shrugs it off. 'Before.'

'Before what?'

'Before I met you.'

'And then you tried to kill me again!'

'I did not. I bloody saved you.'

'Yeah, you saved me, then got me drunk, and tried to seduce me!'

'No, oh no ... I was upset, and you were the one pawing at me.'

'Pawing? I did not paw a bloody thing.'

'You so did,' she hisses, 'and I came to you for help.'

'Fucking what? That wasn't help. That was luring, Marcy. You lured us. Your infected, rancid girls tried to ... to do luring to the lads.'

'Lure, you idiot. You don't *do* luring–you lure.'

'Whatever. You sound like Reggie now. You tried to infect me with your sex! Then we had to kill everyone again, and then we found Lani tied up in the toilets, and then–'

'And then and then,' she mocks me spitefully. 'You think you're the only one suffering here?'

'No, and–'

'And I didn't exactly see you trying to stop it.'

'Stop what?'

'The sex, the bloody sex. You weren't exactly trying to stop it.'

'You were pumping out pheromones!'

'Was I?'

'Yes. Bloody yes. The lads succumbed to it. Even Clarence and ...'

'Well, yes,' she admits reluctantly, 'there *may* have been things happening beyond my control ...'

'May? Just a tad.'

She leans in with a furious look. 'You and I both know it would have happened with or without the bloody pheromones.'

'Get off.'

'Really? Where were your pheromones, then? Was the infection making you pump stuff out too?'

'Eh?'

'I was attracted to you just as much as you were to me.'

'Yes, because of the bloody pheromones or the bloody chemicals making you turned on.'

'Oh, like when we first met? And then in the fort after and then in the bloody street a little while ago ... and of course, it was the pheromones making you dream of me, and it was the pheromones that had me waiting at the bloody window, hoping you'd come, for days on end ...'

'... Really? You did that?'

'Yes,' she snaps and glares, but the harshness fades as quickly as it came. 'Yes,' she says softer, 'yes, I did.'

'I was coming,' I say quickly. 'I was coming to you. Nothing would have kept me away from you ...'

'Why?' She shifts position, easing the pressure from her right hand holding the radio that was wedged between her and the vehicle.

'I don't know. I figured you'd have some answers.'

'No.' She shakes her head sadly. 'Just more questions.'

'There's something between us, between all of us ... Between me and you and all of us ... This, Lani, me ... all of us ... Something we're all in together.'

'Fix it, then.'

'Oh, fuck off, you sound like Dave saying that.'

'You,' she says, prodding me in the chest, 'are the key around which everything else is built. You know that. Your team knows that.'

'I worked in Tesco,' I say wildly, 'and I do not have a fucking clue what I am doing.'

'And you think anyone else does?'

'No, but–'

'Whatever it is driving you, you have to go with it. If your instinct tells you to do something, then do it. Lead, Howie. You lead, and we all follow.'

'We?'

'Yes, we. I'm part of this now as much as you. The ... infection, disease ... virus ... whatever it is has drawn back. I don't feel it ... I get hungry and thirsty for normal food and water. I sleep and wake up. I sweat and make body odour. I had my period, for god's sake.'

'Drawn back?'

'Gone, receded, faded ...'

'But your eyes?'

She shrugs and gestures as though knowing as much as I do.

'Did you feel it draw back?'

'No, no, I didn't,' she says. 'After the fort, I got away with Reggie, and ... I don't remember that much. I was so tired ... exhausted to the bone, and I think I slept forever ... When I woke up, I wasn't like I was before.'

'S'fucked up,' I incline my head.

'Telling me,' she says with a sad smile. 'Lani ... we've got to get Lani.'

'Yeah, yeah, we have to.'

We hold position, static, non-moving. Neither willing to pull away from the cocoon of being nestled comfortingly by the thrumming engine of the Saxon and the sudden privacy gifted to us. A moment in time, a shared bond, and a desire that we felt before. Both of us longing to do it, to lean in, to let our lips touch for just one fleeting, brushing sensation of intimacy. My heart beats hard, and a small piece of it breaks off at the sadness within the smile she gives me.

'We can't,' she says so quietly the words are gone before they form. 'Lani ... We have to get Lani.'

I nod, and with every will in my body, I pull back and break the magic of the second we seized for ourselves.

'It worked then?' Cookey calls down.

'What did?' I turn to look out and see the boats drifting across the sea towards us.'

'Oh.' I look down at the radio, tucked in Marcy's hand and held in place while we talked and edged ever closer. 'At least something is going right for once.'

CHAPTER FORTY-FOUR

Silence. Utter and complete. Nobody speaks. Nobody dares speak. The atmosphere thick and charged. Mo Mo and Jagger cast worried glances at each other, then back at the frozen figure of Lani.

'Lilly,' Mo Mo calls to the girl without taking his eyes off the woman, 'can you take the boats over?'

'I, er ...' Lilly hesitates, wanting to say she doesn't know how, but senses the need to move quickly. 'Of course.' She rushes off towards the front–walking, then jogging, then all-out sprinting–as the urgency lifts the rising panic.

Through the gate, across the middle section, and out onto the beach she goes. The lead boat is nose-in towards the beach, with a long rope attached to a metal shaft hammered into the soil. A simple action of untying the rope and wading out into the shallows before clambering over the side.

At the back, she stares down at the small outboard engine. She's seen this done many times, on television, movies, and in real life too. You pull the rope, and the engine starts. No, wait. Isn't there always a switch or button to press before you pull the rope? Using just the moonlight, she feels the top of the engine and down the sides until she fingers a broad dial with two preset positions: On and Off. She can't see the words, but it makes sense to have an on and an off. She moves the dial, grasps the spoke fitted to the end of the pull cord, and yanks it back.

The engine starts first time–a cough, splutter, and it thrums down into a steady beat, and the immediate air fills with the stench of fuel. How do you drive it? Where's the accelerator? The person always stands at the back, with their hand on the handle. She copies the action, standing with her back to the engine and one hand gripping the end that turns, and when it turns, the engine changes beat, and the water behind the boat churns. Motion is generated, and the boat goes forward. She pulls the handle towards her and shakes her head. Shouldn't the boat turn?

It does turn, but the slow speed makes the directional change just as slow. Okay, she nods, and while keeping the rudder hard over, she gently twists the grip and waits as the propeller increases in pitch and tone as it bites into the water. The turn comes faster, and she watches as the front end turns slowly round to face away from the beach in front of the fort.

She turns, checking the rear view and noticing the rope pulling taut as it flexes to take the strain of pulling the boat behind her, then the next and the next after that. If she changes the direction now, those boats might impact on the beach. She keeps the rudder pulled over and moves gently out to sea until the last boat is clear of the shore before manoeuvring to aim towards the curvature of the bay and the solid form of the Saxon.

Intelligence and a clear head sees Lilly undertake an

action previously unknown to her. Rational thought and a process of understanding and being able to recall the memories and stored knowledge that will assist with the situation at hand.

Gut-punching emotion fogs a clear head, and Lani reels from that gut punch. A sinking sensation of the ground opening up. Of her heart shattering into a thousand tiny pieces and her world crashing to an end. A desperation to reach out and take it back. A burning desire to take back the words she heard. Not an escalation of events that starts with a suspicion and unfolds with tentative caution but sudden and jarring. Cheated. Sordid. Filth and disgust.

Her hands grip the assault rifle. Still nobody dares speak. No movement. Not a cough or a shift of position. Not a head moves, but the eyes remain fixed for the words that, blurted out from the radio held in Mo Mo's hands, were clear to all.

Like my life hasn't been turned upside down since meeting you.

Her eyes narrow, then widen. Nostrils flare wide, and the vein in her head throbs with pressure.

No, oh no ... I was upset, and you were the one pawing at me.

Words that sang clear in the night air of the fort. The street accent given by Marcy matched by an intentionally broken transmission returned by Mo Mo as neither side wished the other to know what was going on.

The sex, the bloody sex. You weren't exactly trying to stop it.

Howie said they never had sex. He said it. He promised

it. He swore and looked her right in the eyes when he made that promise. Here, in this fort. In this place that she fought and died for. She died and was turned and came back only to die again now as her heart breaks and the blood in her veins turns cold as ice.

... You and I both know it would have happened with or without the bloody pheromones.

Tears form in the back of her eyes, but they don't fall. They stay glistening in the whites that reflect the orange glow of the lanterns. A connection is made, and those glistening eyes flick to the lanterns with the knowledge they are the same lights that Howie and Marcy made love under. Here, in this fort. In this place that she fought and died for.

I was attracted to you just as much as you were to me.

The crackle of the radio and the steady beat of the Saxon only made it worse. Like an old record, scratchy and worn out, but the music remains the same. She could feel the heat between them as the words were spoken. She could see in her mind how close they were standing, inches apart, lingering with eye contact and energy that sparked and fizzed.

She turns slowly, not realising she moves. Her eyes scan the crowd from a habit ingrained after spending days of her life defending her team by always watching, always scanning. A team that cheated her. A team that knew Howie was in love with Marcy. A team that knew Howie and Marcy had made love.

The thought of it only multiplies the level of deceit, and with it, the hurt inside ramps up until her throat constricts with physical pain. She wants to weep. Break down here and weep, but there's still a job to do, and you do the right thing for the right reasons. You stand by your mates because

... because they stand by you ... But they didn't stand by her. They left her to die.

In the toilets–taped, bound, and gagged–while Howie fucked Marcy. They left her then. But no. It was pheromones. The infection manipulating the chemicals within the body.

... *You and I both know it would have happened with or without the bloody pheromones.*

The gut punch comes again. Rational thought is attempted and tried yet thwarted at every turn by words uttered and broadcast for all to hear.

They left her to die in the munitions factory. They held the side door as a team while she took the rear alone. They left her. Abandoned. They knew. They all knew Howie fucked Marcy and Howie was in love with Marcy. Lani had become a problem, and the solution was for her to be killed, taken, turned, and destroyed.

'Do not look at me,' she explodes with an eruption of violence at the young face staring up. The tone and temper of her voice snaps the heads down as sudden tears of fear start to roll down the young cheeks.

A reject. Worthless and cheated. She should have stayed on the Isle of Wight. Stayed in the shadows of the place she was hiding.

'LOOK DOWN,' she roars at the heads below her.

Howie fucked Marcy. Howie is in love with Marcy.

... *And of course it was the pheromones making you dream of me, and it was the pheromones that had me waiting at the bloody window, hoping you'd come for days on end ...*

Marcy is stunning beyond compare. A rare and radiant beauty with a figure to bring men to their knees. Pledging her love for Howie. Telling him she was waiting. Telling him she dreamt of him. No man could deny that. What am I? Who am I? The words burn and sear into her mind.

'DO NOT LOOK AT ME!' She stabs the end of the rifle into the back of a young head, driving it into the ground.

'Lani,' Mo Mo steps forward.

'STAND DOWN.' Her rifle is up and aimed, locked on Mo Mo.

This filthy place, full of death and deceit. Tasered and injected with drugs. Taken from her home. Following a man around the country who she loves. Loved. But he never loved her back. They never had sex. Howie was tired, exhausted from battles, but he fucked Marcy on the night she died.

I was coming to you. Nothing would have kept me away from you ...

Her breath quavers, slow and unsteady, as her mind fractures as quickly as her heart. Vision closing in, yet everything is suddenly so much clearer now. Everything is perfectly clear.

Howie loves Marcy. This was always about Howie and Marcy. Not Howie and Lani. Marcy. The rancid infected whore that killed and took lives as quickly as she took the love of the man she adores. A thieving, stealing, cheating, filthy bitch who looks like a million dollars. A woman who sways with sexuality. Her lips are full and plump, her eyes heavy with naturally thick lashes, her skin a golden hue of perfection. Lani is lithe and fast. Athletic and flexible, but she can never hope to match the raw sexuality of Marcy. Marcy wants, and Marcy gets. Marcy takes, and Howie gives.

I was coming to you. Nothing would have kept me away from you ...

She followed Howie through thick and thin. When he was taken in the car park, she fought through them and would have given her life for him to live. In the munitions factory, she held the line while all was lost. She knew she would never walk away, and as her gun clicked empty and her blade was taken up, she did it for the man that lay unconscious in the far end, dreaming of Marcy.

The whole of them. All of them. The team turned against her. The team don't want her. They love Marcy. They want Marcy.

'Lani.' She fires without thinking and sends the round slamming through Jagger's heart, killing him instantly. Blown back off his feet to slump down in a crumpled, bleeding heap. Mo Mo turns to see his friend shot down. His own reactions too slow, like wading through mud, and it's that reaction that saves his life. The complete stunning of his senses that prevents him from bringing his assault rifle up to bear.

'Jagger,' he mumbles the word, frozen, rooted to the spot, 'mate.' He steps drunkenly towards the body. 'Mate,' his voice catches with raw emotion, 'Jagger ... mate ...' The assault rifle falls from his grasp as he drops down to lift the head of his best friend. 'Jag, mate ... Fuck's sake ... wake up, bro ...'

Lani's head drops, and she stares up and out at the sight of the pain given. A sickening sense of righteous deliverance that someone else should suffer now.

I was coming to you. Nothing would have kept me away from you ...

She turns back to the crowd that stare in horror at the sight of Mo Mo down and cradling Jagger's dead body as he weeps tears onto the face of the person he loved most of all.

'He was going to her,' Lani mumbles. 'Going to her ...

going to her ... GOING TO HER,' she screams the words into the air and drops with lightning speed to stare deep into the eyes of a child that whimpers with a jet of piss released by the fear gripping his stomach.

'He was going to her,' Lani whispers to the child, 'he was going to her.' She smiles warmly with kindness that shines from the depths of her soul. 'Are you okay?' she asks so gently, like a mother. 'I'm not okay,' she says. 'He was going to her.' She nods urgently at the little boy. 'Funny, isn't it?'

On her feet, and she sways as the shock reduces the flow of oxygen to her brain. Blood pressure plummeting, blood sugar dropping just as fast. Rational thought gone. The ability to think clearly disappeared.

Nothing matters. Nothing matters now. It's all a pile of shit. Infected, filthy shit that is tainted by the blackness of Marcy's soul and the love Howie has for her.

'... Jag ... bro ...' Mo Mo grips his friend's body as the tears fall freely from his eyes. The prodding in the back of his head gets progressively harder until he freezes, with the sobs ending suddenly in his throat.

'Get up,' Lani says in a dangerously soft tone. Mo Mo sucks air in through his nose as the cold fury starts to rise. 'Get up,' Lani kicks his weapon away and prods him harder in the back of his head. 'Did you know?'

'Know what?' Mo Mo rasps the words out.

'About Howie and Marcy? You knew. You all knew.'

'I will ...' His words are cut off as the butt of the rifle slams into the side of his head. Stars behind his eyes, and a wave of nausea passes over him as he lies stunned on the ground.

Mo Mo forgotten, and Lani strolls off. She kicks Jagger's assault rifle deep into the shadows at the base of the wall, then looks down to Mo Mo's a few feet away. Idly she strolls towards it and starts shunting it towards the first of the children still on their knees.

'Want it?' she asks the closest. 'Go on! Pick it up.'

The child looks away in the only response possible that might avoid being shot dead. She kicks it again, scuttling it across the hard, compacted earth deeper into the ranks of children.

'Anyone?' she asks lightly.

I was coming to you. Nothing would have kept me away from you ...

'SOMEONE PICK IT UP!' Spittle flies from her mouth.

I was coming to you. Nothing would have kept me away from you ...

They left her to die at the rear door. All of them at the side while she took the rear.

I was coming to you. Nothing would have kept me away from you ...

It hurts. It hurts more than any physical pain she has endured so far. The only reason she doesn't put the rifle into her mouth and pull the trigger is that she doesn't think to do it—because the pain swells and grows with every passing second.

Howie and Marcy fucked while she was bound and gagged in the toilets. They fucked, then lied about it. They fucked and blamed it on the pheromones.

The assault rifle slams into small bodies, kicked harder and harder, but not one hand is even tempted to reach for it.

Lenski stares with wide eyes, desperate to do something, but like everyone else–she knows the consequences that any action will take.

Anne Carlton fled when Jagger was shot. Running back

to the perceived safety of the hospital bay. Children remain on their knees while Mo Mo lies vomiting on the ground.

Lani boots the gun, screaming for someone to pick it up as the last tendrils of sense in her mind tell her there must be an action for her to have a reaction. She wants death now, and the pain to be felt by everyone, but no one will lift the gun up.

She freezes, head cocked to one side as the steady chugging of the boats comes into earshot. They're coming back. She nods and smiles slowly with a grin that spreads across her face without any trace of humour.

I was coming to you. Nothing would have kept me away from you ...

Lani stands still, the rifle held at waist height, while she listens to the engines getting closer. The boats will beach. The team will get out, and they will come home through those doors. Marcy and Howie coming home to the place they fucked in.

She cocks her head, still smiling as the first engine cuts out, followed by the next. The rifle is brought up, pushed back into her shoulder, and the index finger of her right hand touches the trigger. Aimed, steady, and waiting.

Mo Mo rolls and blinks through the blurred vision to see Lani aimed and waiting. The noise of the boats ends, but to shout a warning will mean Lani killing people here. His eyes flick to the assault rifle in the shadows over by the wall. To move in that direction will put him into her peripheral vision. The armoury. It's the only chance. Crawl slowly and get close enough to grab a weapon from the armoury. On his belly, and he starts shifting, willing Howie to stop and wait before bursting happily through the inner gate.

Maddox blinks. Snapped awake from the gunshot fired at Jagger. His body weak and pained from the multiple electric shocks delivered by the Taser. Lani stands just feet away. Her rifle raised and aimed at the inner gate. He heard the boats coming and knows something is wrong. Lani kicking the gun into the ranks of children, screaming for them to take it up. Jagger shot down. Mo Mo beaten down.

Movement to the side. He turns his head slowly to see one of the kneeling crew chiefs extending a leg to shove the assault rifle towards Maddox, who gives a subtle nod in reply.

Mo Mo shuffles on his stomach, inch by inch, as he imagines the terrible sight of Lani turning to fix that aim on his back. His head spins with waves of nausea that urge him to gag and puke.

Maddox stares at the rifle being nudged, bit by tiny bit, towards him.

Lani stands true and steady as a rock. Waiting.

Voices drift on the clear night air. The deep rumble of Clarence. The tones of Cookey. Female voices talking. Marcy.

I was coming to you. Nothing would have kept me away from you ...

The head injury threatens to pull Mo Mo back under, but he bites it down as the searing pain rolls round the back of his skull. Got to reach the armoury. Got to get there.

Maddox starts leaning, tiny increments of motion as his left hand starts moving out towards the barrel of the rifle. Eyes flicking between Lani and the weapon.

The sound of the outer gate being closed–the voices closer now.

Mo Mo has to stop and draw breath, but the pause is for a second only, and he snakes ever closer towards the doorway and the cache of weapons within.

Mo Mo fingers the tip of the barrel, leaning harder as

the pain in his damaged muscles radiates around his body. Finger that flex to grip to draw the weapon closer.

The crew chief dares another motion to punt the gun that bit closer. Maddox grips as his fingers clamp round the barrel, and his eyes go wide.

The inner gate opens. The voices clear and distinct.

Lani tenses, the finger on the trigger exerting pressure as she readies to fire. She knows Dave will fire back, and his aim never misses, but two shots is all she wants. One for Howie and one for Marcy.

Mo Mo hears the inner gate and knows his movements have been too slow. His head snaps to the gate opening and the doorway of the armoury still feet away.

He sucks in a ragged breath and screams with everything he has left.

'AMBUSH,' the word bellows with a voice that breaks midway through the warning, and with a heave, he lunges for the doorway.

Maddox snaps onto his back with the weapon being pulled fluidly across his body, left hand on the barrel, and his right hand already moving towards the trigger as Lani twitches at the warning given by Mo Mo. She fires into the shadows of the armoury doorway. Maddox roars with the pain of moving but pulls the trigger to fire into the space where Lani was as her quick reactions have her dropping to the ground.

Mo Mo bursts out with a rifle up and ready. Lani fires. One shot, two shots. As one, the gathered children burst to their feet with the chance of escape. Mo Mo paces out with his assault rifle held up and aimed, tracking the chaos of movement with a desperation to see Lani.

Another shot, and a child is sent bowling off to the side.

Maddox screaming for them to run. Lani screaming for Howie.

Movement from the gate as Howie and his team burst through–guns up and aimed. Chaos meets their eyes of a fort exploding with movement and motion. Children running in all directions. Maddox stalking through them with his gun raised. Mo Mo across the way, heading towards Maddox. Lani, glimpsed through the streaming ranks of children running.

Shots fired. Maddox, Mo Mo, Lani. All of them firing.

'HOLD,' Howie gives the order. The account of Lani given by Lilly as they made their way in the boats–that Maddox was down, but Mo Mo and Jagger were on Lani's side.

'AMBUSH ...' Mo Mo's voice carries through the chaos. 'LANI ... SHOOT LANI ...'

The team spread instantly into a line. Weapons up and aimed. No faltering steps, and as one, they pace into the confusing fray. Meredith bounding ahead, but for once, even she has no idea who to attack.

'LANI?' Howie shouts.

'EVERYONE GET DOWN,' Maddox's voice booms the order out, 'DOWN NOW ... DOWN, DOWN, DOWN!'

Children drop where they are, ingrained to instantly obey the voice of their leader. Screaming and wailing, but suddenly there are three within the centre.

'Hold,' I shout the order at the sight of the chaos in front. Children screaming as they run in all directions, tripping, falling, and slamming into each other. Gunshots clear and distinct coming from Maddox, Mo Mo, and Lani, but no discernible notion of who is shooting at who.

'EVERYONE GET DOWN.'

The recognisable boom of Maddox's voice, and he screams the order, which penetrates the minds of the panic-stricken youths. They drop quickly to lie flat, arms covering heads, leaving three figures standing.

Lani aiming at me. Maddox aiming at Lani, and Mo Mo moving with frantic twitches as he tries to aim at them both.

Across the ground, and I see all I need to see. Lani's face is tortured with pain. A grimace that morphs her features into a terrible beauty captured by the soft, ambient light, and the barrel of her weapon held directly towards me.

'Dave ... no ...' I know he'll have Lani in his sights at the perceived threat to me. 'Lani ... Mo Mo ... Maddox ...'

'Mo Mo ... not me,' Maddox grunts the words out as though in pain.

'Drop it,' Mo Mo sounds weak but settles his aim on his former leader.

'Maddox,' I shout, 'put it down! All three of you ... put them down ...'

'NOT ME!'

'Are you going to her?' Lani asks lightly.

'Lani ...'

'Mo Mo ... not me ...'

'Please,' Mo Mo shouts. 'Mads, put it down,' his young voice cracks with emotion, 'please, Mads ...'

'Not me, bro,' Maddox sways, then visibly tenses with the effort of staying upright.

'Hello, Marcy.' Lani grins. 'He was coming to you ...'

'Lani,' Marcy says cautiously.

'DON'T SPEAK TO ME, YOU FILTHY, CHEATING–'

'Easy,' I call out. 'Eyes on me ... Lani, look at me ...'

'That's all I've ever done,' she says dreamily.

'Mo Mo,' Maddox sounds weaker as his voice loses power.

'Mads, please ...' Mo Mo pleads, 'put it down, Mads.'

'Can't, Mo Mo,' Maddox shakes his head against the side of the rifle held aimed at Lani.

'Did you go to her?'

'Lani ...'

'She was waiting for you ...'

'Lani, please ... just listen ...'

She pauses, holding position, and the tension soars sky high, and I know the final few seconds are being played out. Maddox intent on Lani. Mo Mo begging him to stop, and Lani staring at me with a look that will stay with me to my dying days.

We lock eyes. Hers dark and defiant. Mine dark and brooding. The power in her. The power in me. The sparks that erupt across that distance between us, and in those eyes, I see the pain of the world and all the hurt a man ever caused a woman. I see the destruction we have played out and the desperation to be something, to do more, to take more, to have more, to never stop hoping and never stop taking. She flinches, a snarl that curls the top of her lip up, and I see that anger and raise it with my own hand dealt by the devil himself. I stand straight, waiting, knowing, cursing, and praying that this won't happen, but it's preordained and written in the fucking scriptures. We're fucked. All of us. We're dying a slow, painful death of life being drawn out in hours and days instead of months and years, and yet there was hope that life could go on. Hope that was given by the coming of the sun each day and the refusal to lie down and die.

But this. This sickens me. This appals me–that so much life is being taken, wasted, killed, dying. Death. Destruction. Suffering. So much is being taken from our grasp, and yet it comes back to this. Back to the emotions of one and the inability to ask a fucking question and seek a fucking answer but instead to allow the base state of being to take over.

New death surrounds me with the metallic tang of blood hanging in the air. Darius shot dead. Jagger shot dead. Children shot dead. Maddox holding an assault rifle pointed at Lani. Mo Mo aimed at Maddox. More guns. More killing to be done. More death to be given out.

'THIS,' the word blows from my mouth like the thunder in the sky that made this fort an island, 'IS ... NOT ... OUR ... WAY.'

The shame of them shows. The shame of the waste of life given for nothing. For a snatched conversation overheard in the frantic desperation of trying to survive. For what she heard, I am sorry, but for what she has done–cannot be forgiven. Deeds that cannot be taken back, but she knows this. She knows the step across the line is taken, and she cannot ever go back to where she was.

The sanctity of her mind hangs in the balance with a righteous battle displayed for all to see as her eyes narrow, widen, her mouth morphs into a cruel line of pursed lips, yet she smiles sweetly. Too much. We've seen too much. We've done too much. Evil done by our hands in the name of good. The bodies of those we have killed and ripped apart. To know every inch of a human body inside and out and the thousand ways to kill, to inflict injury, and to stop others from hurting you.

Too much. The mind breaks and shatters. It plays tricks and warps the perceptions of those around you.

But not Lani. The distance is closing, and I see something else now. In her eyes, I see the bloom of the crimson blush spreading through the whites of her eyes that comes and goes with every blink of her eyes. I step closer, and she steps back.

'Everyone leave,' I give the order quietly but in a tone that leaves no doubt as to the urgency of my intention.

In the light of the fort, I see her eyes changing. Red to white. White to red. Her body and mind fight the infection pulling to drag her back down, and she knows it. She defies it yet wants it. She senses the power to be gained and the utter control to be given over.

'Go ... go now ...' I turn my head slowly to stare at Maddox. He stares back as strong and defiant as ever. Then, on the spot, he sags before turning away. The children at our feet silently rise. Onto their feet to move away from me as I step closer to Lani. No voices. No speaking. No orders given, but the whispered words uttered from me that clear this space faster than Dave ever could with his drill sergeant voice.

As they stream away from us, as the space around us empties, so the bodies of those killed lay stark in the places they fell.

'I see you,' I step closer.

'See you too,' she says with a smile of pure joy that morphs into anger, into pain, into hurt, into malice.

Closer I step, and back she goes. The assault rifle never lowering. Mine gripped one-handed at my side.

Lani turns to watch the only one I cannot order come closer. Meredith off to the side. Meredith holding position, eyes locked on Lani. Meredith with head held low and tail steady. Meredith with lips pulling up to show the big, white teeth, and our one infallible test shows true.

Lani twitches, and my rifle is up and aimed. She pauses midway towards pointing her weapon at the dog. Eyes rotated to look at me. She smiles and blinks, then turns to look at the dog. She steps back. We go forward. Meredith and I–one pace to keep that distance the same. Lani back one. A game being played. A chase. A taunting, but not one done by the woman but the thing inside her.

'We both see you,' I call out softly.

Her eyes flick side to side with a feral, haunted look. She steps away, pacing out the strides in the way taught to us by Dave so we don't trip or stumble. Wide strides that sweep the foot just above the ground.

Without words, we walk, and she leads us round until I'm facing the front, and I can see what she saw behind me. Guns. Lots of guns being held and aimed by the steady hands of the team: by Mo Mo and Maddox, by the crew chiefs, and by everyone who can hold a weapon. United and together, they form a line against the foe we all oppose for the foe is within our midst now, and Maddox is proved right.

'Big gang,' she says with a quick look at them. 'Mines bigger, though.'

I step after her. After the infection. Unafraid. Relentless. She moves back, and we move forward.

'Let me go.'

I shake my head.

'Let me go, and I will build an army that will wipe you off the face of the planet.'

'Good bargaining skills there, fucktard.'

'Alex!'

'Sorry, Paula.'

Towards the armoury, she moves with those strides that check the ground the way we were taught by Dave. Leading Meredith and me with her. Nothing to be said. Nothing to be gained from speaking, but she stops at the halfway point, and moving slowly, she lowers the assault rifle until it hangs from one finger, hooked through the trigger guard, and with a clatter, it falls to the ground.

Unarmed and yet she steps back again with a challenge given. My own rifle is lowered until it too hangs from one hand. I don't drop it but lower it down in one smooth motion before standing upright.

Back she goes. Back towards the armoury, and with a final glance at the team, she steps through.

'Mr Howie,' Dave calls a warning, clearly worried that I'll head inside and out of his view, but I'm not afraid now. A calm settles within me, and with a nod at them all to stay still, I walk into the near-perfect dark of the old armoury.

'Don't go in,' Mo Mo shouts.

A silhouette of Lani moving within, a metallic noise, then a click, and a battery-powered lantern that lights the massive pile of guns and the big box of grenades resting at her feet comes on.

'Cock it,' I mutter. 'Nicely done.'

The lantern is bright enough to see her eyes clearly–red, bloodshot, and so very terrible, not only in appearance but for what they mean.

'Is it you, Lani?' I peer closer and ask the most stupid question I have possibly ever asked.

'I don't know.'

'How do you feel?'

'Feel?' She pauses with a nonchalant shrug. 'I feel fine.'

'Okay.' That seems to cover it.

'I feel awful.'

'Okay.' Maybe not, then.

'I feel ...' She stares hard at me. 'Everything.'

'That's a lot ... Whoa! What the fuck are you doing?'

'They're small.' She hefts the grenade in her hand. 'But so deadly.'

'Bit like Dave, then,' I reply nervously. 'Put it down.'

'No.'

'Okay, Lani, don't ... What the fuck ...?'

Her finger hooks into the metal hoop but doesn't move. 'It's like a wedding ring.' She rolls the hoop down to the base of her finger. 'But nothing like a wedding ring.' Her eyes dart up to fix on mine.

'You fought it off before,' I blurt the words out while wondering how long they take to go off and if one grenade detonating will set the rest off. Which is possibly the second most stupid question I have ever asked.

'What?'

'The infection ... You made it go before ...'

'Who says I'm infected?'

'Eh? Er ... your er ... your eyes, Lani ... and you know ... shooting people and–'

'I was rescuing you.'

'Right, rescuing me ...'

'All of you, the team. I was rescuing the team. I only killed those that opposed me–Darius and–'

'How did Jagger die?'

'He was shot.'

'Who by?'

'By me.'

'Why?'

'Felt like it.'

'You fucking what? You felt like it?'

'Yep, the same way you felt like fucking Marcy that

night. The same way you felt like lying to me, and the same way you felt like going back to her.'

'I did not have sex with Marcy.'

'You did. I heard you on the radio.'

'No. You heard half a conversation ... and forgive me being blunt, Lani, you know, what with you holding a bomb and all, but ... we all know the reasons for going after Marcy.'

'To, going to ... not after ... You were going *to* Marcy.'

'Lani, this isn't you.'

'It's me.' She nods dumbly. 'All me. Come here.'

'No! No way. You've got a grenade in your hands.'

'Brave Howie,' she mocks, 'super Howie, the leader of the living army ...'

'I'm immune, not fucking bomb-proof.'

'I won't blow us up. Come here.' She motions me forward.

'What for?'

'Howie, come here.'

'What for, Lani?' I take a tentative step forward, trying to calculate my chances of getting to the grenade in her hand.

She beckons me closer with a wry smile twitching at her lips.

'Why, Lani? Put the grenade down so we can talk.'

'No more talking.' She sighs. 'Just come here.'

'Ah, you're gonna blow me up.'

'God's sake, Howie. I am not blowing you up.'

'But you've got a grenade and–'

'Just come here and bloody kiss me!'

'Eh? Oh ... oh, right ... you want a kiss.'

'You really know how to ruin a romantic moment, don't you?'

'Er, thing is ... Kissing a woman holding a grenade isn't that sexy.'

'Well,' she says and takes a step towards me, 'if Howie won't go to the mountain ...' She takes another step, her eyes darting left to right at mine. '... Then the mountain shall go to Howie.'

I should run. Leg it. Billy big legs and be away, but I don't. I stand my ground and wait as she sidles up closer and closer with the grenade held gripped in her right hand.

Funny thing is, the really weird thing is that I get an urge to kiss her. Like a really strong urge. She looks sexy as anything–long, black hair hanging straight down and still just wearing her bra and knickers. Her lithe body reflects the light, showing the fading bruises and healing cuts. The swell of her breasts, and the long expanse of skin on her muscled yet slender legs.

'Oh, this is bad.' I shake my head. 'Are you doing the pheromone thing?'

'No.'

I swallow and suddenly feel the heat from her body that edges closer to mine. The supple motion of her, the graceful manner. Her lips so dusky and perfect. The eyes are red, but ... but I can't stop myself. She's Lani, right there, and my right hand comes up slowly to cup the side of her face, and those red eyes closer at the touch.

She nestles into my hand, pushing her head harder into my hand. I draw her closer and lean in as her lips open to embrace the most erotic kiss I have ever experienced. Slow, tender, and charged beyond anything I have ever known.

The danger of it. Like taunting the devil and getting a kick. The death outside makes the desire to taste life all that stronger. To have lived through all this and not to experience life is the greatest shame of all. I know this is fucked up, and every common-sense bone in my body is screaming for me to get out, to run, and flee, but I won't.

Her lips part. My tongue darts between them. She groans and pushes harder against me, and the kissing grows in passion with an insatiable hunger.

My god. What the fuck am I doing? Grab the grenade. Punch her in the face and knock her out. Grapple her to the floor ... Something ... do something.

We move back as one until her backside hits the edge of the table with a dull thud. Grunting, panting, and so lust-filled, we kiss like we have never kissed before. Hot and fuelled by a desire to have life and feel life.

The smell of gun oil, ammunition, brass, and the stench of the cleaning detergent that was used to mop the floor fills the room. The air is hot and heavy. Lani is holding a grenade and has the red eyes of the infected, but right now, we're tearing clothes off as fast as we possibly can. I reach for the hand holding the grenade, and we entwine fingers round the bulbous body of the weapon. Taunting danger and edging forward as I stick one finger up at the devil himself.

Her top is pulled up and off, her jeans tugged down. My trousers are undone so they fall about my ankles. My top ripped off. Bodies press against one another. Her bra falls to the floor, and my mouth fills with the soft flesh of her breast and the hardening of her nipple.

A hand to the back of my head pulls me closer into her. She arches and groans, wrapping her legs around my backside while forcing me closer still.

Then I am inside her. A pause as the sensation hits us both with a sudden realisation, and our eyes widen at the wonder of it all. At the feeling it gives. At the joining of two that become one.

Stupid. Reckless. Foolish and impulsive but fucking wonderful. I move back and forth with small movements that bangs the table against the wall with an increasing rhythm. Her mouth finds mine with demanding kisses, and I cannot get close enough to her. Even being inside her isn't close enough. Eyes open and staring deep, and I don't see the redness. Just Lani. Lani–the woman who has saved me time and again and given everything for me to live. Shame and failure grip almost as strongly as the lust to complete this carnal act. The weakness of a man, the weakness of my kind to buckle and falter when the mind should be strong.

Is this wrong? Yes. Yes, on every level apart from the one that makes me want to forget everything apart from this moment right now.

The climax builds to the point of no return, and her legs wrap harder, grip harder. Her arms reach round to my back, pulling me in, as I release and shudder, with my thighs pressed into the edge of the table.

Her mouth kisses my shoulder and up my neck that only serves to heighten the pleasure as the climax rolls on and on. She nips at my earlobe and sends quivering ripples down my spine. Her breath exhales into my ear so soft and warm.

'One race ...'

If any other words had been spoken, they would have gone unheard. But those two words whispered at this point sends a surge of energy through my brain. She goes to move, to reach round my back to join her hands so she can pull the pin, but I'm already opposing her, pulling back to keep her hands from joining. Her strong legs dig into my sides. Her teeth dig into my shoulder with pressure that tears through the flesh down to the bone. In pain, and I react, and still inside her, I headbutt with violent force that slams my forehead against hers and burst back with a hard wrench.

As I go back, so an arm wraps around my neck. I drop down but end up offering myself into a headlock, with my face planted into the flesh of her stomach. I grab the backs of her legs and lift before slamming her, and me at the same time, down onto the table that implodes and shatters with the force of the impact.

Stunned, and I scrabble for her right hand while she does the same. Her left hand trying to force a way to grab the hoop of the grenade's safety pin. Grunts of exertion, panting from sex and now fighting to stay alive. Rolling over and over each other in the worst postcoital embrace I imagine anyone has experienced.

She changes tactic and slams the grenade into my face. I yelp in pain and shock, and she does it again. Whacking the hard metal ball into my skull again and again.

'Stop it,' I hiss the words and get another wallop for good measure. 'Fucking hurts.'

The teeth go at me, biting and tearing while the grenade is used to batter me senseless. Her left hand pinned under my body, and I grip the wrist double-handed and try to force myself up so I can trap it beneath my legs. She hits harder and straight into my ear that sends an explosion of pain through my head and flashing lights behind my eyes.

With my focus on keeping the left arm pinned, she changes tack again. The clever sod stops trying to get her left arm free to find her right arm but instead drops her right hand down to her left. I roll and flatten her completely. Her right arm now trapped between us, and her left arm still held pinned.

She bucks and writhes, demented with pure venom to

kill me. Our faces but inches apart, and it isn't Lani I see but something else. Something horrible, twisted, and macabre.

'Die,' she spits fully in my face.

'Lani ...'

'Die,' she says it again and starts fighting as though having a fit. Her head slamming side to side, the body bucking, and I can't hold her down. The access she has to strength is awesome, drawing on more power from her small, lithe frame than I could ever do. The infection pumping her full of chemicals that whips her into a frenzied, all-out assault to get free and kill me, and then the right hand is free, and the grenade is lifted to her mouth. She grips the pin between her teeth, and I'm off, scampering onto my feet, my trousers still wrapped round my ankles. I jump as fast as I can and keep jumping as I hear the pin being pulled and spat out behind me.

'DIE!' On her feet now, and as I reach the door, I glance back to see her naked and terrible and beautiful all together as she holds the grenade out to her front.

Out the door and running naked into the fort, a hard turn, and I'm following the line of the wall away from the armoury.

'BOMB !' the word is shouted, and the line in front of me comes apart as every single person decides it's time to be somewhere else.

Jumping, hopping, and running in tiny strides, I get further down and realise the grenade hasn't gone off.

I stop, pausing to turn slowly back towards the armoury. A dull thud, metal against concrete. My eyes widen, and those three seconds seem to last forever.

The first explosion is an instant boom of detonation. A split second later, and the wall of the armoury blows out from the mass combined explosions, and despite the distance I gained, my feet are lifted from the ground as I sail bodily through the air, and the last thing I see are chunks of masonry and concrete being sent sailing across the fort with huge licks of scorching, orange flames lighting their way and the sound effects of war as the ammunition within the weapons explodes.

My senses assaulted. My body impacts on the ground, and my head slams hard into the earth.

Blackness. Pitch blackness and nothing more.

CHAPTER FORTY-FIVE

DAY FIVE

The house was a lucky find. Old and isolated yet with views of the surrounding countryside. Isolated. Quiet. Perfect.

Big gardens with high, thick walls running the perimeter. One corner was hidden from view by thick bushes that were quickly removed.

A well in the garden with fresh water.

The larder stocked with provisions. Tinned foods and dried goods. Two bedrooms, each with a double bed. One at the front and one at the back with the doors opposite each other.

Two days ago, they found the house. Two days ago the decision to remain here was made. Not to hide. Not to run and flee. Not to seek refuge.

To learn and to train. To educate.

A battered Ford Transit navigates the bumpy, unmade road through the winding fields and pasture lands. Past thickets and copses, it trundles slow and steady, laden down with heavy weight, but there is no rush, so the driver takes his time.

The lane leads to the front of the house, and the battered Ford Transit glides to a halt. The engine is switched off, and the handbrake applied. The driver and passenger doors open at the same time, and the occupants of the cabin drop down to stretch in the beautiful, warm sunshine.

'What do I get?' the one who dropped from the passenger side asks.

'All.'

'Okay.' He jogs off and into the house as the driver stands still to soak up the ambience of the place. Listening for any noises that shouldn't be there. Sniffing for any smells that shouldn't be there, but the air is tainted by the load carried in the back of the van.

The passenger walks backwards from the front door of the isolated cottage, dragging a heavy canvass bag behind him. He tugs it across the ground and off to the side several metres away from the side-opening sliding door of the beaten-up Ford Transit.

He looks up, checking the position is good for the driver, who nods once and firm. The passenger drops down and unzips the canvas bag, exposing the contents to the sky.

'Can I choose?'

'No,' the driver replies, 'wood.'

'We did wood yesterday.'

'Wood.'

'Oh, not fair. We did wood *all day* yesterday ...'

'Wood. No argue. Wood.'

'Gregoreeee, please can I use the knife now?'

'Wood. We use wood.'

'Can I use the knife later?'

'Wood. You make ready. I open now ...'

The sliding door is pushed back on creaking runners, and the infected strain to get at the *ugly man* but are held in place by thick dog collars secured by ropes tied to metal hoops riveted into the frame of the van, and they choke themselves red in the face, with arms that stretch forward with clawed hands.

Gregori checks the boy still dithering with the contents of the bag. With a rueful shake of his head, he whips a knife-wielding hand into the van. The blade slices the rope holding the nearest infected in check. The infected staggers and falls from the side as Gregori steps smartly back.

'I'm not ready!' the boy whines.

Gregori shrugs and leans back against the side of the van with his arms folded–a statement made that he will not help.

'Fine,' the boy huffs and reluctantly hefts the wooden baseball bat from the bag. Taking a two-handed grip so remembered from the hours of training the day before, he walks steadily towards the target.

'Boy?'

The boy pauses, thinks for a second, then grins at Gregori. 'Sorry, I forgot.'

'We forget. We die.'

'Okay.' The boy nods and stares hard at the infected struggling to get upright. 'A man. Er ... he is fat.' The boy frowns with concentration. 'And he is bald and ... and fat and ... He doesn't have his shoes on.'

'What else?'

'Er ... he's fat.'

'You say this. What does fat mean?'

'Heavy!' the boy announces. 'Harder to knock over.'

'Good.' Gregori nods. 'The body is thicker ... so?'

'Head,' the boy says, 'I should go for the head?'

'Good.'

'Come, we go,' the boy mocks the accent of the Albanian as he stalks towards the heavy-limbed infected rising up into a seated position. 'I BOY,' the boy shouts playfully. He aims, pauses, and strikes with a dull thud as the bat impacts on the solid male adult head. The infected slumps down with a gargle, but the boy is ready and whips the bat overhead to slam down with brutal efficiency. As trained by Gregori, he keeps his arms slightly unlocked at the elbows to prevent the jarring effect of striking a solid object.

'What you do?' Gregori asks with a harsh tone.

'Oh,' the boy steps back and remembers he is not meant to hit the head at the front or the back if a side strike is open and the chance of breaking the neck is offered. He goes back to work, thudding the bat again and again into the side of the skull until the bones cave in.

'Brains,' the boy calls out excitedly. 'He's dead.' He steps back, panting from the effort.

'Good.' Gregori nods again. 'Next ... Wait for him to be up ... on feet ...'

'With a knife?' the boy asks hopefully, then shrugs at the dark look given by the Albanian. 'No knife,' the boy sighs.

One by one, the infected are taken from the van and released into the garden area. One by one, Gregori makes the boy wait until they're on their feet and mobile before letting him attack. The boy uses the bat. Striking, hitting, slamming, and learning. Building strength of grip, dexterity, and angles of approach. Learning that different body types take hits in different ways. Learning the reactions of hitting knee joints to make them topple, then being in position to strike them as they go down.

Halfway through, and they stop for a break. Drinking cool water in the shade of the isolated cottage. Only when they finish will the bodies be moved as the boy needs to learn to navigate obstacles during combat.

'Knife now?' The boy burps from the water and looks up hopefully.

Gregori stares down into the blue eyes of the child, so playful, so willing to learn, and utterly without remorse or thought of what it means to take life. The boy doesn't have nightmares but sleeps soundly. He eats whatever he is given. Drinks water and asks questions.

'Okay.' Gregori nods. 'Small knife only.'

'Yes!' The boy laughs with delight. 'Thank you, Gregori!' He rushes forward to wrap his arms around the Albanian's waist before running off across garden, leaping dead bodies, and getting to the weapons bag.

Gregori allows a rare smile and sips his water. The same thing has happened that has happened since he met the boy.

Rounding the infected up was hard work. Getting them into collars was hard. Driving back, then releasing them, one by one, into the garden is hard, but the same pattern happens again and again. Not voiced. Not spoken about.

The infected hunger for flesh. They are driven with an urge to kill and feast. But they don't go for the boy, only for Gregori.

As the realisation sunk in, so Gregori knew to watch for it. Not once has one of them turned towards the boy, lunged for the boy, tried to bite the boy, or even shown a flicker of reaction at the boy.

What it means the ugly man knows not, and with a contented sigh, he pushes off from the wall and heads over to change the grip of the knife held by the boy as the killing training continues under the beautiful warm sun by the isolated cottage, in the wide-open countryside.

ALSO BY RR HAYWOOD

Washington Post, Wall Street Journal, Audible & Amazon Allstar bestselling author, RR Haywood. One of the top ten most downloaded indie authors in the UK with over four million books sold and nearly 40 Kindle bestsellers.

GASLIT

The Instant #1 Amazon Bestseller.

A Twisted Tale Of Manipulation & Murder.

Audio Narrated by Gethin Anthony

A dark, noir, psychological thriller with rave reviews across multiple countries.

A new job awaits. ***Huntington House*** *needs a live-in security guard to prevent access during an inheritance dispute.*

This is exactly what Mike needs: a new start in a new place and a chance to turn things around.

It all seems perfect, especially when he meets Tessa.

But ***Huntington House holds dark secrets****. Bumps in the night. Flickering lights. Music playing from somewhere.*

Mike's mind starts to unravel as he questions his sanity in the dark, claustrophobic corridors and rooms.

Something isn't right.

There is someone else in the house.

The pressure grows as the people around Mike get pulled into a web of lies and manipulation, forcing him to take action before it's too late.

-

<u>DELIO. PHASE ONE</u>

***WINNER OF "*BEST NEW BOOK*" DISCOVER SCI-FI 2023**

#1 Amazon & Audible bestseller

A single bed in a small room.

The centre of Piccadilly Circus.

A street in New York city outside of a 7-Eleven.

A young woman taken from her country.

A drug dealer who paid his debt.

A suicidal, washed-up cop.

The rest of the world now frozen.

Unmoving.

Unblinking.

"Brilliant."

"A gripping story. Harrowing, and often hysterical."

"This book is very different to anything else out there - and brilliantly so."

"You'll fall so hard for these characters, you'll wish the world would freeze just so you could stay with them forever."

*

<u>FICTION LAND</u>

****Nominated for Best Audio Book at the British Book Awards 2023***

***Narrated by Gethin Anthony**

***The #1 Most Requested Audio Book in the UK 2023**

***Now Optioned For A TV Series**

***#1 Amazon bestseller**

#1 Audible bestseller

"Imagine John Wick wakes up in a city full of characters from novels – that's Fiction Land."

Not many men get to start over.

John Croker did and left his old life behind – until crooks stole his delivery van. No van means no pay, which means his niece doesn't get the life-saving operation she needs, and so in desperation, John uses the skills of his former life one last time... That is until he dies and wakes up in Fiction Land. A city occupied by characters from unfinished novels.

But the world around him doesn't feel right, and when he starts asking questions, the authorities soon take extreme measures to stop him finding the truth about Fiction Land.

*

EXTRACTED SERIES

EXTRACTED

EXECUTED

EXTINCT

Blockbuster Time-Travel

#1 Amazon US

#1 Amazon UK

#1 Audible US & UK

Washington Post & Wall Street Journal Bestseller

In 2061, a young scientist invents a time machine to fix a tragedy in his past. But his good intentions turn catastrophic when an early test reveals something unexpected: the end of the world.

A desperate plan is formed. Recruit three heroes, ordinary humans capable of extraordinary things, and change the future.

Safa Patel is an elite police officer, on duty when Downing Street comes under terrorist attack. As armed men storm through the breach, she dispatches them all.

'Mad' Harry Madden is a legend of the Second World War. Not only did he complete an impossible mission—to plant charges on a heavily defended submarine base—but he also escaped with his life.

Ben Ryder is just an insurance investigator. But as a young man he witnessed a gang assaulting a woman and her child. He went to their rescue, and killed all five.

Can these three heroes, extracted from their timelines at the point of death, save the world?

*

"An original and exceptionally entertaining book."

"A beautifully written and humorous adventure."

Sam, an airlock operative, is bored. Living in space should be full of adventure, except it isn't, and he fills his time hacking 3-D movie posters.

Petty thief Yasmine Dufont grew up in the lawless lower levels of the ship, surrounded by violence and squalor, and now she wants out. She wants to escape to the luxury of the Ab-Spa, where they eat real food instead of rats and synth cubes.

Meanwhile, the sleek-hulled, unmanned Gagarin has come back from the ever-continuing search for a new home. Nearly all hope is lost that a new planet will ever be found, until the Gagarin returns with a code of information that suggests a habitable planet has been found. This news should be shared with the whole fleet, but a few rogue captains want to colonise it for themselves.

When Yasmine inadvertently steals the code, she and Sam become caught up in a dangerous game of murder, corruption, political wrangling and...porridge, with sex-addicted Detective Zhang Woo hot on their heels, his own life at risk if he fails to get the code back.

*

<u>THE UNDEAD SERIES</u>

THE UK's #1 Horror Series

Available on Amazon & Audible

"The Best Series Ever..."

The Undead. The First Seven Days

The Undead. The Second Week.

The Undead Day Fifteen.

The Undead Day Sixteen.

The Undead Day Seventeen

The Undead Day Eighteen

The Undead Day Nineteen

The Undead Day Twenty

The Undead Day Twenty-One

The Undead Twenty-Two

The Undead Twenty-Three: The Fort

The Undead Twenty-Four: Equilibrium

The Undead Twenty-Five: The Heat

The Undead Twenty-Six: Rye

The Undead Twenty-Seven: The Garden Centre

The Undead Twenty-Eight: Return To The Fort

The Undead Twenty-Nine: Hindhead Part 1

The Undead Thirty: Hindhead Part 2

The Undead Thirty-One: Winchester

The Undead Thirty-Two: The Battle For Winchester

The Undead Thirty-Three: The One True Race

Blood on the Floor

An Undead novel

Blood at the Premiere

An Undead novel

The Camping Shop

An Undead novella

*

A Town Called Discovery

The #1 Amazon & Audible Time Travel Thriller

A man falls from the sky. He has no memory.

What lies ahead are a series of tests. Each more brutal than the last, and if he gets through them all, he might just reach A Town Called Discovery.

*

THE FOUR WORLDS OF BERTIE CAVENDISH

A rip-roaring multiverse time-travel crossover starring:

The Undead

Extracted.

A Town Called Discovery

and featuring

The Worldship Humility

*

www.rrhaywood.com

Find me on Facebook:

https://www.facebook.com/RRHaywood/

Find me on TikTok (The Writing Class for the Working Class)

https://www.tiktok.com/@rr.haywood

Find me on X:

https://twitter.com/RRHaywood

Printed in Dunstable, United Kingdom

67248899R10302